A Crafty and Devious God

After

Praise for Ted Krever's books:

Mindbenders

"…a storyline that takes hold in the first few pages and doesn't let go…"

"…really fast paced…I found myself unable to put it back down."

"…dialog that left me breathless."

"…[a] global, international conspiracy of corporate and governmental politics, mind control, murder and intrigue."

"OMG!...finally crawled into bed early hours of the next day."

"This is that rare piece of fiction based on fact in such a way as to make the two seem to blur."

"Mindbenders…will make you wonder if your mind really does belong to you."

Mindbenders 2: The Fiery Sky

"…a more than worthy followup to the 1st book, fast paced, well written and exciting!"

"…takes me places that were only in my imagination - I feel like I have been to that island in the South Pacific living on the water, and I've been parched in the Aussie desert - it's all real."

"…A complete thrill ride from beginning to end…great style and substance."

"…intense, memorable scenes…"

"…seamlessly weaves multiple storylines together, delivering a powerful punch of an ending."

GREEN

"…not your typical romance…

"…a unique look into the mindset of men, rather than the typical romance, which is told from the woman's point of view."

"… a smart, witty and wise look at love later in life…"

"I found myself laughing aloud more than once, only to shortly thereafter find myself deeply touched."

"The descriptions…of Ireland are alone worth the price of the book…"

"If you like reading about horses, Ireland, friendship, love in any form…"

"Part a love story, part a political thriller, and part a satiric commentary on life and politics…"

"Green is a charming book."

Howling at Wolves

"This book, simply put…is funny!"

"Keep your tissues handy as you won't stop laughing."

"Nothing is sacred…"

"…like Garp on steroids (or maybe Viagra?)

Mindbenders

A Max Renn thriller

by

Ted Krever

Little David Publications

www.tedkrever.com

To David, who wanted a superhero

One

June 2008

The screams pulled me into the hall and through the open bathroom door, to where Uncle Dave lay in the tub dead; blank-faced, stupid-looking, lights-out-nobody's-home dead.

The tinny screaming poured out of the tube on the counter by the window, where the Prime Minister of India was getting shot on CNN. The anchors scrambled to make sense of the pictures—the frantic crowd stampeding the exits, true believers moaning and pleading behind the podium, bodyguards taking down the gunman in a pile in the corner—everybody screaming, screams in bunches and too late, surely, hopeless, useless, for who, in that insane moment, was listening?

Only those of us across the world, on the far side of the room, where Uncle Dave's head was lolling crazy, like a cup tipped on its side in a saucer, his tongue hanging, eyes open, bits of brain bobbing among the soapscum, the blood rolling down his cheek and fanning out in the water like spider veins. I reached out to touch his cracked forehead and then his eye, just to be sure, to *know*. A little hole nippled the glass of the window, cracks radiating like the blood in the water.

It was right in front of me but then, I wasn't there anymore. I was receding fast, pulling away like a tortoise into its shell. It's not like I could deny what was happening but I did anyway. That's how I did everything in those days. I knew more than I understood, as Renn would tell me later; more than I could bear to understand.

If I'm going to tell this story, you have to know how I was back then, back when I could shut out a bullet through the brain, back before I knew what it was to *know*, back before I even knew him as Renn—back before everything, really.

I turned the TV off and suddenly the place felt too quiet, too empty, echoing-barn empty. Somebody should have been screaming for Uncle Dave, except there was nobody to scream for him but me and I was lost inside myself. The screams rang in my head, same as they had for a long time.

I wandered to the front door, looking away, way away. A little breeze rustled the willows and the long grass, not that it cooled anything off. If you could sell Florida air by the pound, you'd be richer than Gates. Someone was out there, surely not far off, staring back at me—someone with a gun.

Instead, I heard a fluttering and looked up at a pelican gliding overhead, working its heavy wings, pumping air like some wheezing arthritic climbing steps. It circled the house and the marsh full of vines and camellias, sassafrass and begonias, the hoots and hollers of a thousand birds, the hissing of the big snakes and gators and me and Uncle Dave's body.

And then the back door opened and there came Mr. Dulles up off the porch, not real tall but way too skinny and looking like he hadn't slept in a week like usual. He marched in with that clunky walk of his, just stopping off on his way someplace else, someplace maybe he'd forgot already. You live in the Everglades, nobody has someplace else to go, at least not someplace they can't go tomorrow. Mr. Dulles didn't look like tomorrow; he looked like *now*.

"Where's your stuff?" he said.

I pointed to my room. I didn't know him much but enough that he wouldn't have expected more. Dave had guys in the house who stuttered, guys who put their fists through the wall and guys who didn't know the difference between a wall and a window and a door. I was the one who didn't talk.

"Get it together." He didn't even look me in the eye, just slipped by and away.

I didn't really want to go to my room since it meant passing the bathroom, the smell setting in and all, but I went and pulled some clothes together and my toothbrush and a couple books. Not much for living in a man's house for a year but I had nothing when I came and little or nothing left over once I put in for rent and food.

Mr. Dulles was in Uncle Dave's room, tearing apart his bureau. The clothes were on the floor and he was pulling out the drawers when I came in.

I picked a drawer off the pile and shook it in his face. Dave kept them *locked*.

"Not anymore," Mr. Dulles said, pulling out the middle one, inspecting the sides and back and tossing it on top of the others. The man was shifty, slippery; I never trusted him, not that I'd ever had need to.

He seemed to have known Uncle Dave a long time— together, they never had to finish a sentence. Dulles lived farther out in the glades, they said, someplace where he didn't have to pay rent or talk to anybody for days at a time if he didn't want to.

When he came over, he would sit in the corner while we watched TV or rooted for a game or played music. He never seemed to be doing what we were doing; it was more like he had a quota for being with people every once in a while.

He wouldn't play cards. "It wouldn't be fair," he'd say and Uncle Dave would nod like that was obvious and no more about it. Shifty, like I say. Now he looked up and said, "You ready?"

I nodded. Maybe I shrugged. It was about the same thing; I didn't know what I was doing anyhow.

He pulled the bottom drawer out, tilted it backward and upside down and then peered inside the bureau. "Ah!" he said and pulled out a taped-up bundle of cloth. He ripped it open to show me a piece of paper and a small key. "Let's go," he said, heading for the back door.

It threw me, him heading out that way and suddenly I heard my own voice: "You want to go *this* way? Nobody knows this way."

"*You* do," he said, like that was an answer.

The back was the water side. The weeds between the house and the water were like eight feet high and the path jumped around tree trunks and dipped under hanging willows but now Mr. Dulles led me straight down like somebody'd painted a yellow line through the swamp.

I didn't like this. I had no interest in going anyplace with him. Of course, while I'm thinking this, he's not slowing down, so we're practically on the dock already.

"I'll drop you at the VA," he said, stepping into my boat like that was his, too, "on the way through town. Okay?" He held out his hand for my bag but I didn't offer it.

"I live *here*." It was weird hearing my voice—it had been a long time. I couldn't feel my mouth moving but there were the words so I was talking.

"Nobody lives here anymore," he said, pulling the bag off my shoulder and throwing it in the boat. I didn't see his mouth moving either.

What does that—? was as far as I got before the air flashed white-hot all around and blew me off the dock. Mr. Dulles grabbed my shirt in mid-air and dragged me down onto the floor of the boat. I scrambled onto the bow seat as he pulled a couple hard strokes away on the oars—the bow line was gone, burnt from the blast; he didn't even have to cast off. The whole curtain of eight-foot weeds was blazing all around us.

I could see where the house was—where it had been. A fireball curled out of the black smoke, crackling burning itself out as it sucked up into the sky overhead. It looked like the oil blasts outside Fallujah. I think it was Fallujah—I have trouble keeping places straight.

Mr. Dulles rowed up under a stand of low trees, put up the oars and held a finger to his mouth to warn me, not that I needed warning.

The breeze wasn't much but it began to part the smoke and we could make out the men around the house and hear their voices, if not what they were saying. They gave the once-over to the wreckage and started uphill, back toward the road.

Mr. Dulles was hunched on his seat, watching, humming to himself. His hands were on his thighs, palms up, fingers curled inward, meditation-style. Every once in a while, his eyes would flicker with the pupils up under the lids. It was gross, actually.

When I heard their car engines starting up the hill, I got upset—I teared up, to tell the truth. I hadn't heard them coming, when it might've done some good. You never hear what you really need to.

Mr. Dulles opened his eyes and put the oars back in the water. He made a few quick strong pulls and brought us over to the bank on the other side. He grabbed onto a tree and held the boat steady, waiting for me to get out. "C'mon," he said. "We should get moving."

"What just happened?" I burst.

"What do you mean?"

"What do I mean? The house blew up!" Whoa! Now I *felt* the words, my throat vibrating and the rumble in my chest.

He *shrugged*. "Gas main?" he offered.

"In a *swamp*? They blew it up!"

"Who?"

"Who? *Them!!*" I was pointing and yelling. Suddenly I knew I had a larynx because it hurt like hell. If I felt it *now*, why didn't I before? "Shot Uncle Dave! Getting away! *Now!!*"

"Gregor, you don't see things clear sometimes."

"I'm disabled, not stupid," I blurted. Every syllable was an explosion inside. A thought is just a spark; words need muscles flexing, tendons stretching. "And I'm Greg, not Gregor."

"You know Gregor Samsa?" he asked with his cockeyed smile. And somehow I did.

"Cockroach guy?"

"Yeah," he said. "That's you, the cockroach guy." And he stepped off up the hill. "C'mon—I'll drop you at the VA."

"Not going to the VA." I never thought arguing with somebody was the way to make sure they'd follow you around but it seemed to be working for him. "Got to do something!"

"I will."

"When?"

"Soon."

"They're gone."

"I know where they are."

"How?"

"I know." Before I could yell at him some more, he held up his hand. "If I do something about it, will you let me drop you at the VA?"

I nodded. I didn't want to talk; all that came out was bad Tarzan dialogue. *Cheetah—get Boy!* I felt a whole lot smarter when I only heard the voice in my head.

We came up on top of the hill now, where his car was stashed in the weeds off the road—a '67 Camaro. I don't remember lots about my past but I can tell I paid a lot of attention to cars. We gunned it out the back road to the highway.

"Call the cops?" I barked. Literally—the way I was forcing words, I sounded like a dog.

"Not yet," he said. It was unnerving that none of this seemed to be throwing him—people getting shot and houses blown up. Maybe that was why he lived in a swamp and never talked to anybody.

No AC in that old car of his—didn't look like it ever had it, but driving around in Florida with no AC in June, you might as well just stick your head in an oven.

When we got to town, he took the back way off the main drag, past corrugated warehouses, the old frame houses falling apart behind neon gardens of wildflowers ten feet deep off the street. Small town South Florida. Finally he pulled onto a sidestreet half a block from Uncle Dave's store.

Uncle Dave had a gift shop—all of us, all the vets who lived in his house, made crafty things for the store. Once we finished them, he would stomp on them and grind them into the dirt and tell people they were from the Indian digs to the west of town. I don't think anyone really believed him but we made some money out of the place.

"Wait here," Mr. Dulles said. "I'll be a few minutes."

"Not waiting," I said, following him out of the car. First I didn't want to go with him; now I wasn't letting him go without me. Both answers came from the same place, the same doubts in my mind—I just didn't trust the man. If he was going into Dave's store, I was going with him.

"There's something there that Dave left for me," he said.

"Guys that killed him. Take care of them."

"I will."

"Where?"

He pointed up the block.

"Coming here?"

"They're here already," he said, tilting his head back like he could smell them in the air. He wasn't shifty—he was flat-out strange. "I've got to get what Dave left me."

"*Mine*," I yelled now and he groaned. "I'm last guy in Dave's house. Like next of kin." This was like the Gettysburg Address, coming from me but I wasn't done. "Dave said, '*What's mine is yours—what's yours is mine.*'"

This was flat-out weird from the first second I heard it coming out of my mouth. I didn't know what it meant and I didn't really even remember Dave saying it, to tell the truth. But as soon as I finished, Mr. Dulles shot me a look with those hawkeyes of his that burned right through my skull—I mean *really* burned; it felt like somebody had shoved the back of my head against a skillet.

"Okay," he puffed, "you'd better come. But you do what I tell you; don't go improvising on your own. Got me?"

I nodded but I didn't really mean it. He sighed and reached into his shirt pocket and fished out the paper from Uncle Dave's desk. He unfolded it and handed it to me:

```
                      Greg:
     Dulles will get you to safety if anything
happens to me. Don't worry. You worry too much. I
     trust him to get you where you need to be.
                      Dave
```

I was downright shaky on Mr. Dulles but I trusted Dave. "Okay," I said and we went up the block fast. A van was parked in the alley behind the store, shiny black with smoked windows and a couple of stubby cellphone antennas popping out of the roof. Mr. Dulles stepped over to it and knelt at the rear fender, running his hands over the surface without touching, like he was worshiping it or something. When he turned back, he said, "It's them. There's three of them, they have weapons, two of them are decent shots but the third one is the most dangerous because he's out of control. No judgment. Everyone is afraid of him because he goes off for no reason." He shook his head. "Idiots send other idiots into the field."

I leaned over and took a close look at the fender. There was nothing written there. I ran my fingers over the thing, in case it was Braille or something. Of course, there was nothing there and he'd never really touched it anyway. I was feeling a bit dizzy.

"Okay," he said, "when we go inside, the storage room is just off the door. You know it?"

"How do *you*?" I couldn't ever remember him coming to the store.

"Just go inside and stay down. It should be over fast. Okay?"

I nodded but he could stick it. I'd been with him the whole time since the house. The killers left way before us and we never sighted anybody on the way that looked slightly like them. I had more reason to worry about him being nuts than about three or four or twenty guys waiting inside Dave's store with guns.

I wouldn't have been with him at all if I had anyplace else to go. Whether it was the VA or the hospital or another halfway house, with Dave gone, I didn't have a home, I didn't have a friend, I didn't have any reason not to do anything anybody—even Mr. Dulles—wanted me to do.

His expression softened. He looked almost friendly for a moment. "If I tell you I know something, I know it. If you ask me how, I'll have to lie to you—so don't ask. You'll go in the back room and stay down, yes?"

I hadn't said I wouldn't.

"Well, you said you would—but you didn't mean it," he answered, just like that.

"Okay, okay," I said, impatient, busting him for being such a pain in the ass. And then, with my stomach going queasy, I realized he'd replied to something I hadn't said.

"Let's go," he told me, loping to the back door and throwing it open like he knew it was unlocked. He pointed me immediately into the storage room. I nodded and headed that way but lingered, watching him barrel down the hall straight for Uncle Dave's office. As he got there, a bulky man in a dark t-shirt and blue nylon pants came out of the door, reaching for the gun in his belt.

I yelled—at least I did all the instinctive things you do when you mean to yell. I felt my vocal chords tighten up and air pouring out of my mouth but nothing happened—no sound came out at all. Not that it made any difference. Mr. Dulles touched two fingers to the man's temple and he collapsed in a heap, like all his bones had just disconnected from each other.

He came back down the hallway to me now, eyes sharp. He held a finger up in my face. "If you can't stay put, stay quiet," he whispered. "I have to concentrate on *them*, not you. Okay?"

The finger he was wagging in my face had just made the t-shirt guy fall apart like a toy—I stared at it like it was a gun. He turned down the hall again and headed, crouched, into the showroom.

The showroom was as wide-open as the hallway was cramped, display cases and thick-bordered tables heaped with our junk. We moved past the severed alligator's heads with little feet sticking out of them, the arrowhead fossils I used to pound out at the kitchen table and the wind chimes with an Everglades mosquito stuck inside each glass piece. All our little toys.

Dulles motioned me up one aisle while he took the next. A moment later, I heard a sizzling electrical sound and a thud and then he was next to me again, whispering, "Two down—that way," pointing me to the front of the store.

And then a huge man in a Hawaiian shirt stepped out around the edge of a big display case with a dark Glock in his hand—a nine millimeter, a real nasty gun—pointed right at us.

"Stand your ground!" he shouted. "Identify yourself!"

"You first," Mr. Dulles answered, calm as could be. They stood facing each other for a long moment, each waiting for the other to speak.

"I just sensed you coming," Hawaiian Man said. "I'm usually faster than that."

Mr. Dulles shrugged. "Maybe I'm not really here," he said lightly. This seemed like a crazy response to me but the guy holding the gun on us seemed to take it real serious. His eyes narrowed. *Maybe I'm not here?* Everyone tells me I'm addled but I was out of my depth with these guys.

And then, all at once, Hawaiian Man began to sweat. His face started twitching, as though he was under some kind of pressure he didn't want to admit to. He was still the one packing the gun but it didn't feel like it all of a sudden. His arm wavered up and down, as though the gun had suddenly gotten heavy. He kept staring at the arm, then back and forth, first at Mr. Dulles and then at the arm again. He looked like he kept trying to swallow but couldn't. Finally, Mr. Dulles said quietly, "You can scratch if you want."

Hawaiian Man lifted his hand to scratch—you could see how bad he wanted to—but he flinched an inch away and burst, "There's nothing there! It's a trick!" He couldn't stop those quick flicking stares at his arm, though. "It's a trick!" he repeated.

"Your gun's not there either," Mr. Dulles said quietly. The gun *was* there—I was sweating over it bigtime—but, as soon as he said it, Hawaiian Man jerked back in surprise, stared at his hand and held it up in front of him, as if to say, *Where the hell is it?* He opened the hand in disbelief and the Glock fell to the floor with a clang.

Ohhhh, he didn't like that. An evil look crossed Hawaiian Man's face as he leapt for the gun. But, as he got close, it jumped away from him, a little hop and skitter across the floor. He jumped after it again—it was only half a foot from him—but again it slid away, across the floor towards us. He looked up, eyes fiery at Mr. Dulles, who was holding out a finger, moving it lightly back and forth. The gun moved as the finger moved.

One last lunge brought Hawaiian Man just a foot away. Mr. Dulles jumped forward and touched his shoulder for just a second. With a crack and a flash of light, Hawaiian Man flew backwards three feet and slammed hard into the wall. When he settled, limp against the yellow-painted bricks, his body was twitching, his head and arms freelancing, his shoulder, where Mr. Dulles touched it, smoking, the steam rising eerie off the fabric of his shirt. Mr. Dulles' arm was quivering too—he turned to hide it but I could see it took several seconds to get back under control.

He kicked a chair over in front of Hawaiian Man. "Sit," he ordered. It took Hawaiian Man a couple tries to get into the chair and then he just stared resentfully.

"You better call whoever sent you," Hawaiian Man said once he got his mouth working. "We're protected."

"The sheriff loves you?" Mr. Dulles asked. "Personally?"

Hawaiian Man's lips curled. "I don't give a damn about the fucking sheriff," he said.

"Me neither," Mr. Dulles replied, real quiet. "So you're *not* protected." He held a finger up, pointing it at Hawaiian Man's forehead.

Hawaiian Man had six inches and at least a hundred pounds on Mr. Dulles. His gun was on the floor about two feet away but he never looked at it. He shrank, involuntarily, at the sight of the finger.

"Not much point to it," Hawaiian Man shrugged. "We're blank slate—double-blind. They give us coordinates and a suggestion—when we see the target, we know it. But that's all. We got no over-the-horizon at all."

"What's the target?"

"I know it when I see it."

Mr. Dulles stepped forward and slapped his hands to the man's temples, one to each side, and he sat up rigid as a statue. His mouth came open but nothing came out—I knew what *that* felt like. When Mr. Dulles released him, he sank back onto the chair, huffing like a steam locomotive.

"You really *don't* know anything," Mr. Dulles said, frustrated.

"I'm just a foot soldier," the big man answered. "Who the fuck are *you*?"

"A footnote."

Mr. Dulles ran one finger lightly over the bridge of Hawaiian Man's nose. "Sleep now, " he said, almost tenderly and by the time he finished speaking, the man was snoring, a little smile on his lips. He slumped off the stool and hit the floor hard — we both winced at the sight of it.

Mr. Dulles shrugged and headed toward the back of the building. I followed but every step was a struggle.

"You…you touched him and…" I wasn't sure which touch upset me—the one that threw the man, sizzling, against the wall or the one that put him to sleep. Both. Either. I was sweating. Once I realized it, it felt like I'd been sweating for a while.

He went right to the storage room, flipped the light on and the sight of it didn't help my dizziness any. Papers strewn all over the floor, all the drawers ripped out of the cabinets, all the extra store stock pulled off the shelves and smashed. They'd been in a hurry—for what? What was here that was worth searching for, much less killing for? Uncle Dave was dead—dead now, dead forever. I was beginning to absorb that now, just beginning to feel the hurt of it.

Mr. Dulles stalked around, hovering his hands over the surface of the cabinets the way he'd done with the van outside. He caught me staring at him and held up the key he'd gotten out of Dave's drawer. "Dave left me a key. A key has to have a lock."

"Not here," I said. That seemed to get his attention right away.

"*What's mine is yours—what's yours is mine,*" he said in a different voice, a voice that seemed to echo inside my head. "Where's the lock?"

"It's mine," I said—at least the words came out of my mouth. I heard them and felt them. But they didn't come from me—I heard them at a distance, same as he did.

"Okay," he nodded. "If you say so, it's yours. But Dave wants me to see it. Where is it?"

My legs started moving, that's the best I can describe it. I wasn't against whatever I was doing but it wasn't my idea either. I led him down the hall into the boiler room across from Dave's office. Kneeling, I pulled a small toy box out from under the furnace and held it up to him.

He gave me a sharp look and I could see he was trying to figure out how much of this I understood. The simple answer was nothing—I knew nothing at all. I had no control over anything my body was doing. I was sweating and frightened. It wouldn't have shocked me if my head had split open like a walnut—there was more than enough pressure pounding in there to do it.

He held the key up to the lock—it went in without a hitch— threw over the bolt and opened the lid.

"Oh, c'mon," he growled. The box was empty. "Why send us here for an empty box?"

"It's *my* box," I said again, though I'd never seen the thing before that I could remember. His eyes narrowed. The look on his face made me nervous. I'd seen what he *could* do if he had to.

"Where's the next nearest?" he asked.

"What?"

"*What's mine is yours; what's yours is mine,*" he said, enunciating like he was teaching a child a nursery rhyme. "Where is the next nearest?"

"Mark Tauber, Savannah Georgia," I said and nearly fainted.

"Shit!" he said and stomped around the room cursing.

The name came out of my mouth before I knew what I was saying. Actually, I didn't understand it *after* I'd said it, either. I didn't know any Mark Tauber and I didn't know what he had to do with Mr. Dulles' question. Tell the truth, I didn't even understand the question—but I'd just answered it.

My heart was pounding and my shirt soaked through. I couldn't think and I was afraid of what I would think if I could.

"Okay," he sighed, "Let's go."

I stumbled after him but I kept banging into everything, desks and displays and kicking through piles of paper. My whole body was trembling.

"It's not far," he said, leading the way. "You can collapse once we get to the car." But the trembling only got worse when I hit the seat.

"What's happening?" I spurted, the words flying out of me. "Tell me what's going on!"

"Relax, you'll be okay," he said, pulling a map from the glovebox. I reached over and ripped the thing right out of his hands.

"I'll tear this to shreds if you don't tell me—right now!" I screamed and I meant it. I had the pages between my fingers—no power on earth could stop me from doing it if he didn't give me some answers there and then.

He flashed me a sickly smile."They sell them at gas stations, Gregor," he said, taking it back. Then he drove out to Main Street and turned left—away from the VA, away from the police station.

"Where're we going?" I asked.

"Did you know you have a sister in New York?" I didn't have any sister in New York. I mean, there are plenty of things I don't remember but I'd remember if I had a sister. "I'll take you to her—she'll take better care of you than the VA would." But that wasn't enough of an answer, even if I believed it.

"I never *heard* of Mark Tauber," I cried. "I don't get the question but I'm answering it! And you're pretending nothing's wrong. What the fuck is going on?!" I was pitched forward in the seat, choking back tears, I'm not proud to say. It surely wasn't the first time my mind had gone off on its own—but that was a kind of fear I'd thought I'd left behind a while ago.

He pulled over onto a knoll overlooking an inlet where seventeen cranes stood on one leg, waiting for a nice fish to come by. "Sorry," he said, sounding for a change like he meant it. "Dave worked for the government before you knew him. The program was disbanded but Dave kept a list of the members. I thought it was in his office—so did the boys rifling the place. But apparently, he locked it in your head. And my guess is, he wants us to go run around the country warning the others."

"How do you know?"

"Because of the way he did it. He planted the names in your head, and he planted a suggestion in mine so I would recognize your password when you said it: *What's mine is yours; what's yours is mine.*"

I don't know why but, after everything else that had already happened, *this* really upset me. "I don't *want* a password," I whined.

"Well, you've got one and I'll bet—" He stared right through me; the back of my skull went hot again. "*What's mine is yours; what's yours is mine.* Give me a list of all the agents in the program."

I stared back at him, blank as newsprint.

"You see? He rigged it so I can only get one name out of you at a time. I'll bet, once we've found Tauber, you'll give me the next name. Which means, until then, we're Siamese twins."

Two

Whick-whick went the trees along the highway, *whick-whick* like the frames of a movie flashing through the shutter. *Whick-whick* while the fields lazed in sunlight, the grass a little brown from too little rain and too much sun, water spurting from irrigation pipes wrapped in grape vines. *Whick-whick*, marking space, marking time. Marking time, which is all I'd done as long as I could remember, not that that was very long.

I used to be good with words, I remember that. Words and me got along. They tell me I was a writer for Stars & Stripes, till my brains got rattled one time too many. I still play with them but all I get are phrases, flickers—*whick whick*—and each new one just drives out the old. In the end, it's just light through the trees— pretty and whispering all kinds of promises but nothing real and nothing that's a part of anything bigger. And that's not enough.

Mr. Dulles was driving. He was a lousy driver, real intense but never seeming to be where he was. It was like he was keeping real good track of traffic a hundred and forty miles ahead while just barely lurching through the close-up stuff.

"The government?" I asked. "Their program, right?" It didn't *hurt* to talk anymore; it just felt weird. It was so peaceful ignoring everybody once they accepted they weren't getting much out of you.

"They disowned it. Everybody was put out to pasture. Governments are not real interested in re-exploring their failures."

"But if it's a failure—"

"The guys who murdered Dave didn't think it was," Dulles said and it hurt to hear the word 'murder' out in the air. "The guys who hired them didn't either." He was glaring at the driver ahead of him. "Get moving, willya?" he snapped.

"Those guys—part of the program?"

He shook his head. "Too young. The programs ended years ago. But…they must have trained with people from the program. "

"Why?"

"Just procedures they were using, defenses they tried against me."

"Are they dead?" I asked, buying time to think as much as anything else.

"They'll come around by morning," he said. Seeing my reproach, he added, "They don't matter anyway. If you want revenge, you want the guys who sent them."

"Big guns," I said, though I was pretty sure that wasn't what he meant.

"Guns are just their first line of defense. With guys like that, guns always are. They had more dangerous weapons, if they'd been a little more imaginative." He swerved around the car in front of us, cursing a blue streak. "Who teaches them to stack up like this?"

"Who?"

"Look!" he said, gesturing out the windshield. It looked like regular traffic to me. "Three slowpokes, clogging all the lanes. They stack up right next to each other so you can't pass them."

"The guys we're warning—in the program—they dangerous too?" I asked.

"With any luck," he laughed—a nasty, harsh laugh. "Hopefully, they're dangerous too."

I waited a long moment before the next question. "You?"

"Yeah," he said, with a half-smile that actually seemed genuine. "Yeah. You saw. Me too." He banged at the steering wheel. "Okay, that's enough, dammit," he grumbled at the traffic. "*Move!*"

His face turned red and I wouldn't have wanted him looking at me like that. And as soon as he spoke, the car in front of us suddenly swerved out of the way, weaving and pulling to the right. We sped through the empty space and, for the next few miles, anytime anyone was ahead of us, they moved over as soon as we approached. Sometimes they jumped out of the way like something had startled them but Mr. Dulles wasn't leaning on the horn and I didn't see any reflection to suggest he was flashing his headlights or anything. The cars just seemed to be getting out of the way on their own, which didn't seem a bit natural.

"Dave was a spy," I said, straight out. It just seemed like I knew all at once.

"Not the way you're thinking," he answered. "Not James Bond."

I wasn't thinking of James Bond. Well, maybe a little but not seriously. I turned on the radio. It must have been the original radio that came with the car because it had the rotary dial for the stations—you turned the knob to tune in. I hadn't seen one of those before except in pictures.

I didn't like the music they were playing so we ended up with the news, the shooting of the Indian premier. The man who shot him was in custody and being interrogated; a state funeral was scheduled for the next morning. Most of the coverage wondered how the killer got through state security, close enough to fire at close range—and speculated about the next premier.

There was the usual parade of all-male candidates but the headline was the premier's daughter, a woman speaking with an eerie serenity (and Oxford English) to what sounded like a pretty unruly crowd. She proclaimed herself her father's successor and said she would be meeting with party officials that afternoon to claim control. The experts didn't think much of her—Western-educated and an engineer, an attractive face to put on the party, possibly, but untested and not ready for the hurly-burly of Asian politics, they concluded. Probably gone in a week, with the pack of experts and male politicians scrambling to take advantage.

At the end of this, I realized we weren't swerving or speeding any more. We were holding our place in traffic, maintaining a mere 60 miles an hour, Mr. Dulles more focused on the radio than I was. All he said was, "We need the newspapers."

We pulled off at the next exit and he bought every newspaper they had. "Read," he ordered as we pulled back onto the highway.

"Read what?"

"The headlines. Everything. I'll tell you what I'm interested in."

This was a torture. My mouth wasn't used to three words in a row. It wasn't used to *two*. Now he had me reading paragraphs. The muscles just weren't in shape; the sounds were garbled half the time. I couldn't figure out how he could understand what I was saying but he would bark at me to keep going every time I paused.

The headlines were the usual: Gridlock in Washington, each side blaming the other, embargos and sanctions against our favorite enemies, unemployment and gas prices up, sales and real estate booming, some expert says now's the time to buy something or other, if you've got any money. None of that did much for Mr. Dulles though he was paying attention to every line. Then I got to:

POWERPLANT MISHAP 'ONE-TIME GLITCH,' SAYS OPERATOR.

"Read me that," he said immediately. And somehow, with him focusing on me, I could.

"Second Sun Energy, operators of the Biggs Hollow nuclear powerplant, called yesterday's radiation leaks 'minor and harmless' and blamed them on improperly calibrated instruments. State regulators, however, expressed concern at instrument readings that indicated a meltdown, leading to the plant venting radiation and the evacuation of three surrounding towns. After a 'thorough and rigorous' examination of the plant, no actual problems were found. 'Instrument readings,' said a source close to the state regulatory authority, 'have to be foolproof. A false reading can cause as much chaos as a real crisis, as this incident proves.' "

"Tear that out," Dulles said. "Keep reading."

It took a while to find something else that appealed to him:

MAYOR RESIGNS AFTER BIZARRE VIDEO SURFACES was the headline. "Read that," he said.

"Greta Kobel, Mayor of Copenhagen for twenty-four years, resigned today after a bizarre video surfaced on the Internet. The clip, which documented what her spokesperson called 'a momentary breakdown,' shows Mayor Kobel barking, clawing at the podium and spouting gibberish and racial slurs to an audience of Japanese businessmen at a reception yesterday. Among her statements was one characterizing Hindus as 'the dogs of the world,' which sparked riots in several countries last night. A statement from the Mayor's office said she apologized for her behavior and called it 'inexplicable, as the views expressed are not true to my own feelings or views. I take responsibility for my actions without, frankly, understanding them." The Mayor announced that she was resigning, effective Friday, to seek counseling and medical treatment. Longtime friends and critics alike characterized the incident as out-of-character. Mayor Kobel has won numerous prizes throughout her stewardship for open government and human rights."

"Tear that out too," he said. "If there are pictures, keep them."

"What's in common?" I asked, tearing. "The Mayor of Copenhagen and a nuclear plant in Tennessee?"

"There's our turnoff," he said and I saw the sign to merge onto 95. He pulled into the right lane and we waited in traffic for the exit.

~~~

Savannah was hot, hot like they'd set the whole place on fire. The trees sagged under the weight of their own perspiration. Do trees sweat? I don't care; these seemed to. Sweating trees, steaming brick houses from before the Civil War, swans and geese battling for position on a pond in the park as we drove by in slow traffic. Mr. Dulles wasn't much at city driving either, from what I could tell—we would circle the same area several times before lighting out in a different direction.

"You lost?"

"No."

"Why're you circling?"

"Do you have an address? Or just 'Mark Tauber, Savannah Georgia'?"

"That's all I've got."

"Then have a little patience."

Each new direction led to dingier and dingier neighborhoods. In heat like this, most everything looked washed-out but I couldn't miss the missing shingles on the roofs, the cars with missing fenders and the bars over the street-level windows. After about twenty minutes of this, we hit an area where the streets were flat-out empty, scary empty.

And then I looked over and he was driving with his eyes closed.

I grabbed for the wheel but he threw his hand out to block me. "I'm okay," he said.

"Your eyes are closed."

"I know. It's okay."

"No it's not. I'm driving with somebody who thinks they can drive with their eyes closed. That's not okay."

He actually laughed at that but didn't open his eyes. "We have three houses between us and the corner," he said and that was true. "There's a blue pickup parked at the corner but we've got plenty of space to miss it." I checked to see if his eyes were slitted open, if he was peeking. He wasn't. "We'll make the left turn at the corner coming up. I'll wait to see if the red Ford let's us go first." I could see the corner coming up—there was no Ford there. Then, as I watched, it pulled up and waited for us. "There's a silver Nissan SUV parked around the corner with a flat tire on the rear passenger side. There are two garbage cans—black and brown, in that order—lined up on the sidewalk a bit beyond it." He started to hum to himself some odd off-key trance kind of a tune.

We turned past the Ford and onto the street, passing the silver Nissan with the flat on the passenger side and the garbage cans, black and brown in order. And then he swerved around the garbage can lid that blew into the street—still without opening his eyes—and I gave up trying to think. It wasn't that I disbelieved—I couldn't get a handle on what I was disbelieving.

"Okay?" he asked, eyes still shut, as though that settled something.

"No," I answered because I didn't know how to form a question. "Mr. Dulles —"

"Call me Max," he said and that was okay but I still didn't know what to say.

This neighborhood was about a century-and-a-half dingier than the last one. We had started with picturesque dingy and had now descended to watch-your-back, all-the-neighbors-have-guns dingy. Several of the houses looked abandoned; the store on the corner was boarded up solid. A few old people came out to take laundry off the line or walk the dog but they kept a close eye on approaching cars.

When Mr. Dulles pulled to the curb, all at once, there was the tune he'd been humming, tinkling off the wind chimes on the porch. "Your Mr. Tauber lives in the second house from the end," he said. "He's not expecting company." He looked around, like he was surveying the neighborhood, except there was almost no one on the street. "We'll walk directly from the car to his place," he said, as if I needed any prompting. He was planning on leaving me *here*?

He locked the car conspicuously when we got out. The front door of the house was locked the first time he pulled but he ran his finger over the lock a couple times and I heard the bolt throw. As we came into the front foyer, people were scuttering out of sight in the back of the house, like rats running from a light.

Jazz was blaring in the front apartment, honking jazz, Coltrane or Sun Ra or something. Max knocked but it was just pro forma—no one could possibly hear knocking over that racket. So he gave it a moment and then banged. After several attempts, the music went quiet and we heard footsteps. I could sense someone on the other side of the peephole for a moment and then a voice through the thin plywood. "What do you want?" The voice was unwell, full of tremors.

"We're friends of Dave Monaghan," Mr. Dulles—Max—said and waited. After a pause long enough for second thoughts, there was a working of chains and locks and the door cracked open.

"How do you know Dave?" the man asked, looking us up and down. He was tall and creaky, with a stiffness that could have been dignity or arthritis. His hands shook holding his cigarette and his shirt was buttoned wrong, out of synch at the collar, so I bet on arthritis. "Where is he these days?"

"We should talk inside," Max said and flashed him the look that had made my skull hot. Tauber stood up straighter all at once.

"Ah," he said with a wry smile, "*that's* how you know Dave," and he pulled the door open and waved us in.

It was shabby inside, even considering the neighborhood. The furniture was clearly other people's throwaways. The chairs, scattered around the room, needed cushions—they were all stained and torn, bits of stuffing leaking out the seams. A couple of pictures hung at Tauber's eye level, the kind of things they sell at the 99¢ store so you can have something on your wall.

Last night's dishes were in the sink—or maybe they just lived there full-time. A supermarket shopping cart stood in the kitchen, next to heaping plastic bags filled with cans and bottles for recycling. Tauber wandered the room, a proud man in hard times, trying to disguise his frailties. He pushed chairs into a group for us and then pulled up the shades a little, letting in some light.

"Not expecting company," he grumbled. The radio was still playing low; he walked over and switched it off. "Keeps down the voices in my head," he explained—at least he seemed to think that was explaining something. He was slurring a little. I couldn't remember the last time I'd woke up still drunk from the night before—not so long for Tauber, apparently. "So if ya came from Dave," he said, "there's two questions: What'd ya come for and why didn't he come himself?"

"Dave's dead," Mr. Dulles said, no ceremony, just like that, and hearing it made it hurt all over again. "He was shot to death this morning." The words passed through Tauber like a shiver—a couple shivers maybe, replaced finally by a numb stare. I couldn't tell if shock had him or if he was just used to numb most of the time.

"Who did it?"

"The question is who sent them," Max answered. "They were under suggestion and knew what they were doing. They torched the house—expertly—and rifled his store immediately after."

"For what?"

"Dave kept a list of the old team."

"It wouldn't be much of a list," Tauber drawled. "Not many of us left."

"Well, I think they were after the list," Mr. Dulles said. I was having a hard time thinking of him as Max or any other kind of first name. "Whoever they are, they're going after the old team."

"Ha!" Tauber cracked a laugh. "Come after me? If they ignore me, I'll fall apart all on my own."

"You've still got power," Mr. Dulles said. "I felt it at the door."

"Power? For what?" Tauber responded. "I can read the crack dealer upstairs when he pays off the local cop—the cop's got gout and a fixer-upper on the Outer Shoals but he won't make the mortgage if his wife doesn't stop running up the credit cards. The dealer lost some 'merchandise' last month—I found out who lost it for him so he gave me a couple bills but then he put two guys to watchin' my every move for two weeks."

"It's still power."

"Sure—against morons, I'm a master. Against a trained mindbender? Give me a break." Tauber's eyes narrowed. "Who *are* you?"

"A friend of Dave's," Mr. Dulles repeated.

"And him?" Tauber asked, jerking a thumb in my direction.

"He's a vessel," Mr. Dulles answered. "He's Dave's list, actually. It's locked in his head. I can't access it, he can't access it, all he can give me is one name at a time." He watched Tauber closely while explaining, the same way Tauber was watching me.

"Weird," he said.

"I was hoping it was some procedure from the program— something you might know how to break."

"News to me," Tauber shook his head. "Don't remember anything like that."

There was a bang at the door.

"Rent!" came a nasty, snarling, gravelly voice. "Now!"

Tauber clearly didn't want to answer the door, but the banging resumed immediately. "You told me today. Don't think I'm forgetting about it like last month either—I've got it written down!" Tauber cleared his throat and opened the door.

""Now!" she shrieked, bursting into the room. That this was a woman's voice knocked me over—I couldn't imagine what kind of life would have earned her that rasp. It had to have taken hours to paint her face on, not that it was worth the effort. "It was due yesterday. Where is it?" Tauber stood wavering, unsteady.

"He paid you last night," Mr. Dulles said. "Don't you remember?" As soon as he said it, I knew it was a lie but somehow she didn't.

"Last night?" she said, confused. "When?" She was staring at Max now as though trying to place him.

"He gave it to you at the party, remember?" Mr. Dulles answered, speaking slowly and enunciating, his voice deepening as he went, until it sounded like he was in a tunnel. "The party in the back yard?"

Her uncertainty grew. Max was watching her closely, like he was reading the right thing to say off her face. "You were wearing...the green dress?" he offered.

"Uh—I—"

"I *liked* the green dress," Max said. He threw her the smile of a man who's interested. Not that this smile was any more convincing than his regular one but somehow he sold it to her. "I also liked the secret pocket inside," he added, his smile growing. "The check's in the pocket."

"The...pocket...?" she said, flustered. Clearly, she expected that pocket to remain her secret. Her expression changed, a coquettish smile teasing across her kabuki face. "Were you *naughty*?" she snarled. You could see her struggling to remember—she might have forgotten a few things over the years but nothing *good*, dammit!

She stood uncertain for a long moment. I saw her touch the back of her head for a second, the same place mine went hot in the swamp.

"Go check," Mr. Dulles said, in a voice so soft it was like I was just hearing it in my head.

"I'll...go check..." she repeated, her words like half a second behind his, more an echo than a reply and suddenly she was on her way out the door.

I looked around a second later and Tauber had disappeared. "It'll take her maybe three minutes to check that pocket," Max warned firmly in the direction of the bedroom. "And then maybe another two checking drawers and cabinets. She came home drunk so she can't remember where she would have left it."

"If I'd paid her," Tauber's voice came from the bedroom.

"If you'd paid her," Mr. Dulles repeated. "So you've got about three minutes to pack." He turned to me, disappointment on his face. "I guess we're moving on," he said, like he expected me to be sorry too.

Tauber emerged a minute later, zipping his overnight bag. "Not much here I can't replace cheap," he said, cracking the door as quietly as he could. We hustled out the front door. Max unlocked the car, Tauber folded himself into the back seat, the landlady threw open the upstairs window and started screaming and chucking stuff out the window at us but her arm was lacking.

"So where are we going?" Tauber said as we drove away. "Washington surely doesn't give a shit."

"I'll get the list together and you can decide what you want to do."

"What we *can* do is the question," Tauber said. "I can't defend myself against an attack; I'm totally out o' practice."

"That's up to you," Max answered. "Dave wanted me to get you together so I'll do that. Then you're on your own."

"How do you know what he wanted?"

Max turned to me. "What's the next nearest?"

"Miriam Fine, Durham, North Carolina" came out of my mouth like a belch, a reflex. Max reached for the glovebox; I pulled out the map and unfolded it for him.

"Miriam! Oh hell," Tauber said. "Now we're in for it."

Three

We drove for about ten miles and nobody said a thing.

"Okay, tell me what the fuck's going on," I burst finally.

"You don't need to know," Dulles said.

"They would have arrested him too."

"Nobody's getting arrested."

"What the hell—I'm just a vessel anyway." Dulles shot me a look and swiveled in his seat, which would have flipped me out if I hadn't already seen him drive with his eyes closed.

"You're *fortunate* to be a vessel. Everything you know about us can be used to hurt you." He turned to Tauber. "If you're so concerned about his welfare, *you* tell him—am I lying?"

"No," Tauber said, his face reddening. "That's true."

"If they catch us at this point, you can claim you're a hostage. Once you know what's going on, that excuse goes out the window."

"Why? How would they know what you told me if I don't tell them?"

"These people would know."

"How?"

He threw his hand in the air. "If I answer that, I have to answer the rest. It's no good."

"I have to know," I said and I meant it. I'd been stuck away in the Everglades for a year or more and what was the point of knowing anything there? But now, I was loose in the world again and all that was left of the reporter I'd once been was the hunger to know. To know *what*, in this case, I hadn't a clue—hunger's unthinking, whether for food or sex. Or knowledge. Whatever is hidden in my sight must be uncovered. I *had* to know.

"What about the landlady? You weren't at any party with her. You didn't get into her dress."

"That was a lie," Max said, relieved that it was.

"No, it's a lie if you knew there was a party and pretended you were there. How did you even know there was a party?"

I turned to Tauber. "Did she wear a green dress?" He nodded. "Was there a pocket inside?" He shrugged.

I turned back to Mr. Dulles. "If he doesn't know, how do *you*? Is she some kind of enemy agent?"

Tauber burst out laughing. "God help the country that employs her." He turned to Max. "You've got to let him in."

Max scowled. "You know the answer. You got most of it while I was talking to her."

"What do you mean?"

"What were you thinking—back then, while we were talking?"

I tried to take myself back, to recover what was going on in my head at the time. "I knew you were lying."

"Right and that's good," he grinned. Most people don't get all happy when you catch them lying, but I'd gotten over expecting anything sensible out of him. "But, after that? When I told her about the party? When I mentioned the green dress?"

"I got confused then. I couldn't figure out—"

"Don't do that," he jumped. "These are rationalizations you made up after the fact. What did you think *right then*? In the moment?"

I tried to remember. I fished back for the look on the landlady's face right then, her confusion—and for the expectant, offering expression on his face at the same time. "I was thinking...I was thinking you were reading...what to say..."

"How?" he encouraged, like he knew what was coming.

"Like you were reading it off her face." It felt stupid to say it. It didn't make any sense, but it was what I'd been thinking.

"Good! Except I *couldn't* read a green dress off the expression on her face, could I?" Was he making fun of me? It wouldn't have been the first time.

"I'm not making fun," he added a second later and I shivered even before I realized I hadn't said it out loud. "Gregor, you did great. You got as much of it as you could. You just explained it away instead of accepting the strangeness of what you knew." He was giving me the stare but this time, the back of my skull was just tingling, not burning. "I couldn't read a green dress in her expression, could I?"

"No."

"So where's the only place I could have gotten it?" His eyes were as big as the moon over the Gulf, when it's clipping the horizon, shimmering the size of a container ship.

"Just tell him," Tauber interrupted.

"No! It's crucial that he knows what he knows!" Mr. Dulles spit, suddenly fierce. "Don't worry about making sense. Don't worry about sounding foolish. You know the answer. *Know what you know.* Take ownership of what your senses are telling you, even if it flies in the face of everything you believe. Where did I get the information? Where's the only place I *could* have gotten it?"

"Her head." It burped out of me the same as the agent names, the same way I'd known where the box was in Dave's office—autopilot, no thought behind the words, presentation before understanding.

"That's it," he said. "You've got it," as though everything was settled.

"Got what? What have I got?"

"We read minds, son," Tauber answered, with a weary smile. "It's what they paid us for, for a while."

"Oh, come on," I moaned. It was such a comedown, after thinking they were going to explain. Tauber shrugged so I turned back to Mr. Dulles. "Okay, fine—read my mind," I demanded.

"Jesus, give me a break, I'm not a carnival barker." I just stared back. If he could read minds, let him do it or shut up.

"Okay, you're thinking that I can't read your mind, of course. You're thinking you never trusted me, even when I hung around Dave's because I wouldn't play cards and I didn't really take part in things. You're thinking about the Burger King billboard when we got off the highway—you're not really hungry but you want a Double Whopper with Cheese anyhow. There's a part of your mind that's singing 'I Want to be Sedated' and there's a part that's still in Fallujah, in a firefight. The machine guns and rockets are echoing in the background behind everything else."

"I'm not in Fallujah," I said but he turned back to driving without a reply. It took a few seconds to hear them—the guns, the rockets, the shouting and screaming and all the rest, everything he'd described, all there, all at once, once I listened. I realized I didn't really listen a whole lot. Especially to the Fallujah part. I didn't *want* to listen to that.

"Don't be stubborn," Mr. Dulles said. "You saw me do it with the landlady and you knew it for what it was. Your rational mind resists but your instinct knew, right then and there—*he's reading it in her face.* That's what you told yourself and you were 90% right. A minute ago, when I told you I wasn't making fun of you—you hadn't accused me out loud. I've done that several times before, though maybe not so openly." He leaned in and I waited for my head to heat up but he only wanted to talk. "The most important thing is: you *knew.* You not only knew I was reading the landlady, you knew she damned her memory that she couldn't remember me. You knew when Mark was standing at the peephole of his door. You knew he was still drunk from the night before."

"I could hear him slurring," I said. I shrugged, apologetic, in Tauber's direction and he shrugged back. I've known other people over the years who drank from habit—after a while, their dignity gets pretty flexible.

"Some people slur all the time," Max said. "Some people have speech impediments. You weren't guessing—you *knew.*"

"What are you saying—I'm a mindreader?"

"I'm saying *everybody* mindreads," he answered. "Almost everybody. They're just primitive about it. This is scientific fact, not fact published in medical journals, but fact nonetheless, science that's been distributed for years in manila envelopes, hand to hand in code to those with a need to know. And if it's ever published, if the New England *Journal of Medicine* ever provides an acceptable rationale, mindreading will be routine in three years." He tapped the steering wheel as he talked and I realized we were in a moving car, on the highway again. I'd gotten so drawn in I'd lost all sense of the world, of where we were.

"You mean we'd all be doing what you just did?"

"Hell no," Tauber shook his head. "That's like sayin' anyone could paint the Mona Lisa if you give 'em paint and canvas. Some people'll do it better and quicker." He looked at Max. "He's very quick."

"Most of them would justify their wishful thinking and call it mindreading," Max said. He looked over to see if I was satisfied.

I was nowhere near satisfied. This was without a doubt the most ridiculous explanation of anything I'd ever been asked to swallow. There was not one thing about it that felt slightly real — except that it did explain every weird thing that had happened since morning. Once I took the whole thing in wide-angle, I realized I had to either doubt everything that had happened since Dave was shot or this was the best explanation I could think of. It was the only explanation that didn't force me to doubt my own sanity any more than usual.

"When you first told her about the check, she wasn't convinced. She didn't want to check on it. You made her."

"Bravo," Mr. Dulles said. "Good work. Yes, I made her."

"The job was readin' minds and planting thoughts in other people's minds," Tauber explained. "He made her think checkin' was *her* idea."

Mr. Dulles grimaced. "I still think we should stop," he said, talking to Tauber. "Beyond this, he becomes an asset—for whoever's out there."

"He might pick it up himself—he's a bit of a sponge," Tauber said, talking about me(!). He gave Mr. Dulles a moment to protest, then returned my way. "Memory's real sensual. Once you've got that real good mental connection with somebody, you share whatever they're thinkin'. Not just thinkin' really—sights, sounds, smells—you can pull all kinds o' stuff outta their heads. Or you can make 'em see things that aren't there, say things you want 'em to say, things you want 'em to *believe*. It gets pretty comical sometimes."

"That's enough," Mr. Dulles said but Tauber's eyes were bright.

"The thing is, once you make that connection, it's not like you're *in* 'em, it's like you're *them*. You not only know what happened, you know how it *felt*." He was rising up in the back seat now, the power of the thing carrying him, like an addict remembering his first fix, when he felt like he was touching God — hell, when he felt like he *was* God.

"And then ya feed it back to 'em—into their minds—with all those feelings attached and it breezes by every gut check, every guidepost the mind puts up to vet information. It feels like they're *rememberin'*. O'course, you add in some suggestions o' yer own to tip the balance a bit."

He smiled again, amazed at this nasty, awful achievement. He turned to Max. "But I've never known anyone who could do it so damn *fast!*"

We headed out onto the highway. The afternoon was waning—every once in a while, a little breeze actually cut through that hotbox car. I was trying to decide if I was any better off for having the explanation.

"How did Dave die?" Tauber asked.

"I told you—shot by three mindbenders, country unknown."

"When did *you* get there?"

"Right after," I said, which only deepened the lines on Tauber's forehead.

Mr. Dulles reddened. "Dave said he'd been getting probed for a month. He told me something was up but I didn't believe him."

"Why not?"

"Because *I* wasn't getting probed."

"What's probed?" I asked. If they were mindreaders, why didn't they know I had no clue what they were talking about?

"Your mind transmits. Your thoughts have a physical dimension."

"Like molecules?"

"Particles and waves, vibrations, frequencies that can be tuned and amplified. The transmission can also, to some extent, be tracked. I know your base frequency now. If you were arrested, I could follow you from several miles away to the police station."

"So when an agent's nearby and ya don't know his frequency," Tauber said, "ya probe for it. Ya send out a signal that hits a bunch o' frequencies and see if it gets a response."

"And what do you do about it?"

"There are ways to combat it," Dulles said. "You change your frequency or muffle your signal. You move around the time sequence. Or, sometimes, you catch the probe and follow it back to the originator, to locate whoever's searching for you."

Tauber stared at Max. "You're saying ya still get probed?"

"A couple times a year," Max admitted and it was clear they both felt this was significant. "There are people who...want me to work for them. Doing jobs I have no desire to do. When they get annoying, I disappear. Dave was my safe haven. But when he asked me for help, I told him there was nothing to it, because if I wasn't getting probed, nobody was getting probed."

He slumped a bit in his seat. "I'll take you to this Miriam Fine," he continued, "and you can figure out what to do from there."

~~~~

We drove quiet for a long time. We'd had an outburst of talking and now we were ~~done~~ spent — yeah, we were *spent*. I liked the sound of that — it's a better word. Words were beginning to come back to me, at least that one did. After the year I'd had, a trickle felt like a downpour.

A moment later the trickle started, like I had triggered the reality by thinking the word. Raindrops appeared on the windshield. A few moments later, the downpour was pounding the roof, slithering in the slipstream across the windows, a mad river curdling the pebbly ground along the road, a full-fledged sky-dump. *Words have power* — who said that?

It quickly got too much for driving. "We have to stop," Max said and pulled off at the next exit. It was a strip mall of motels — you could see the chain signs buzzing over the treetops miles away. Five sprawling motels in an overlit shiny row, room rates a dollar apart, separated by gas stations with prices varying by three cents a gallon. We pulled into the furthest parking lot, the one with deep woods behind it and took a double room with a cot for the third man. As soon as we'd dropped our stuff inside, Tauber told Max, "Lend me ten bucks out of the stash — I've got some personal maintenance issues."

"Lend?" Max asked.

"Tomorrow, you set me loose with a shopping cart and other people's garbage; you'll see how much money I can make. At the moment, I'm without the tools of the trade." Max gave him some money and he was back in a few minutes with a bottle of cheap bourbon. I hadn't even seen a liquor store but I guess he had radar.

"You could buy *decent* booze," Max said. "We're not broke."

"I don't *want* decent booze," Tauber replied. "Ye'll spoil me."

"So who gets the cot?" I asked. "Should we draw cards?"

"You'd get rooked, son," Tauber laughed. "Reading cards is how they check if you've got the power."

"I don't sleep much anyway," Max said. "I'll take the cot."

Tauber had the bottle drained in fifteen minutes. He started singing after that—not loud but not good either and Max flipped on the TV in self-defense. A few minutes later, Tauber was dead asleep. Max went to wash up. I settled onto the other bed and stared at the tube. I would have stared at anything that moved at that point.

The news stations were running tributes to the Indian Premier, or they would have been tributes if anybody had anything nice to say about him. The people interviewed were stepping carefully, trying to be respectful without outright lying. And then there was the daughter, Aryana Singh, serene and focused, Western makeup and a very stylish white head covering.

"I have been thrust into a situation I could never have foreseen. As head of my father's party, I will be Premier of India until elections are held. In the interim, I am beholden to nothing but my own conscience and my father's memory."

Usually, that was about as much politician as I could stand, but, this time, I kept listening. There was something in her voice, the ring of a real person struggling to handle the curves, the way we all have to. I felt sorry for her, tell the truth. Politician is a bad job if you have any instinct for being real.

"In today's world, danger comes not simply from rival states but from all sorts of enemies in the shadows, organizations that seize power without accepting the responsibility that comes with it. Organizations that use fear to corrupt.

"To break the cycle, we must first stop measuring power by the damage we can visit on others. I have ordered the High Command to prepare to dismantle all of India's nuclear warheads. My father was invited to the G8 Conference on Monday; I shall go in his place and propose that all countries holding nuclear weapons agree to dismantle theirs as well. India will be first if the others agree to follow."

Max came out of the bathroom in time to hear the back end of her statement. "Is this a mindbender thing?" I asked. "It's pretty freaky."

He shook his head immediately. "This gives people hope," he answered. "Governments don't pay for hope." He stared at the TV for a moment. "It *is* odd," he admitted, heading back to the bathroom.

The head of the opposition party called for Singh's immediate resignation, followed by the Russians, English and US State Department spokespersons rejecting her offer and the Pakistanis calling it 'a foul trick', followed by a commercial for leaky bowel syndrome.

Max finished brushing his teeth, pulled down the window shades and placed a glass of water on the floor. Then he sat down lotus-style next to it. "I have a ritual to try to get to sleep. Do you disturb easily?" he asked.

"I don't think so," I said.

Of course, he didn't say he was going to hum. Hum to the point that you could feel it in the walls and floor, hum to where the vibration through the mattress felt like one of those magic fingers things. At one point he started humming two notes at the same time, humming harmony with himself. Just as I was about to say something, he opened his eyes again, fixed on the TV.

"—Illinois officials are scrambling to explain how they executed the wrong man in a state prison on Friday. Marco Velez, serving five years for tax evasion, was executed despite what one guard called his 'hysterical' claims of mistaken identity. Prison officials could not explain how guards removed Velez from the wrong cell after checking his fingerprints, which didn't match the execution order. The attorney general's office is trying to figure out whether executing Jack Slayton, the actual condemned man, would now constitute double jeopardy."

"That's one, isn't it?" I asked.

"They saw fingerprints that weren't on the page," Max nodded. "They saw a different cellblock number." And he closed his eyes and resumed his freaking Ommmm harmonies.

I'd known the man almost a year off and on and this was the first time I knew his name was Max. It wasn't like he was holding out on me—this was just the first time I'd ever relied on him for anything. After about fifteen minutes, he opened his eyes and unfolded himself. He started pacing slowly back and forth in front of the window, like he was looking out even though the shades were down.

"Aren't you tired?" I asked. *I* certainly was—I just couldn't go to sleep while he was pacing like that.

"I'm *always* tired," he said and, all at once, it came to me: this isn't a man who can't sleep *tonight*; this is a man who *never* sleeps. With the greenish light leaking through the blades across the window, he looked like hell. Worn out, dried out, dragged to pieces. His hair was a mess, dark and spiky and sticking out in all directions. His eyes were bloodshot, sunken into deep caves and they didn't shine like eyes should shine. "Too many voices in my head," he muttered, staring out the closed window.

"Ooh I forgot," I needled. "All those hotel rooms. All those tourists *thinking*."

"It's not funny," he muttered limply, like he had zero hope I could ever understand. Which, of course, made me want to.

"What's it like?"

"What?"

"To know *everything*."

"Ha!" he spit. "I have a universe of information and a flyspeck of knowledge. I hear everything they're thinking, everyone around us, all the time. But that's not knowledge. It's excuses and resentment and the lies they tell themselves to avoid whatever they're afraid to think about."

He pointed to our left. "The man over here traveled three hundred miles to a specialist; he's getting the results tomorrow morning. He has cancer—I can feel it in him. I can visualize the tumor, though I don't know the name of the organ that's hosting it." And as he talked, it was like the wall dissolved away and I saw the guy lounging on the bed in the next room, eerie content, leafing through sales brochures like nothing was wrong in the world. "Is he thinking about cancer? No. Living a better life? No. He's thinking: *Plasma or LCD? Plasma can burn-in;* that really concerns him. He's dwelling on it. He won't live long enough to pay the thing off."

"Which isn't a bad reason to buy one," I said. "He's scared."

He turned in the other direction and that wall faded away, leaving a mousy blonde in a negligee and a real unhappy expression, close enough I felt I could reach over and touch her. "On *this* side, Ulna from Orangeburg is waiting for her brother-in-law Rick to get back from the office. She asked Rick for a loan to keep her house out of foreclosure. Rick's doing way better than Ulna and her husband—Early, that's the husband. Ulna and Early—you can't make this stuff up. Rick's always been a little too friendly and now she's waiting for him at the motel, ready to be friendly herself. She'll get the loan—she's a determined girl. Another little everyday tragedy. You know what she's thinking? Over and over?" He began to sing in a weirdly-pitched voice:

I want a girl

Just like the girl

That married dear old Dad…

"That's all she knows," he said.

And then, all at once, *all* the walls dropped away. For a few moments, the whole hotel became visible, stacks of rooms full of people, arguing and ignoring one another, watching TV and fucking, eating McDonalds take-out with the kids, counting money or emptying liquor bottles in glee or misery. And all of them saying one thing and thinking another, or a couple anothers. The first second was overwhelming; after ten seconds, I thought my head would split open. I had my hands over my ears when he realized what was happening and made the voices go away. When he continued a second later, his voice was soft, like he was trying to cut me a break.

"As for the rest? *I'm getting old. This is someone else's fault—* fill in the blank as to who. *Why is my husband/wife/boss/past such a bitch? I want to be happy but I'm afraid to change.* Sometimes you get a bundle of ambiguous regret: *I wish he was dead. Do I really want to take out a mortgage with him? But the rate is really low.*" He laughed his deep, scraping laugh. "Believe me, I'm making it sound better than it is." He sat on the edge of the cot, which sagged like he weighed a whole lot more than he looked. "Other people's thoughts are amazingly banal—what makes them meaningful are the feelings attached."

"But Tauber said you feel things, like you're inside the other person."

"Oh, I feel *everything*," he replied. "So what? Nobody feels one clear, simple feeling at a time. We know what we want to do and twenty reasons it won't work, all at once. The woman's too good for us; if only she was more like Angelina Jolie. *She loves me-she loves me not* isn't doggerel; it's the persistent state of the human mind.

"I spent ten minutes once, standing within three feet of one of the world's billionaires, easy pickings, homed in on him completely. I could have stopped his heart on the spot, given him cancer, shot sparks from his fingers. His conscious mind never let up the whole time: *Build this, talk to so-and-so about that, the deadlines have to be tightened, appease the regulators, after this step, the next step is*...The entire time, without letup, just one level below, a high, sing-song voice kept chanting in his head, *You'll die in the gutter, you'll die screaming in the gutter*, like a schoolyard chant.

This is how *everybody* works. And from this swamp, I'm supposed to pull facts, make life-and-death decisions. So yes, I hear things but it's a very limited gift."

He pushed a couple of vanes apart and stared out into the light. If he could drive with his eyes closed, this had to be a symbolic move. "Meanwhile," he breathed, deep and low, "there are people out there who mean to do us harm."

"You feel them? Are they close?"

"No," he said. "Not yet. But the guys this morning were part of an organization. Whatever country they're from will be scrambling tomorrow." He glanced at Tauber for a moment and then back to me with a look of concern on his face. "Let's not mention the details of this morning to him, okay? Not till we know him better." I nodded. I wasn't sure how I'd explain sparks flying from his fingers anyhow.

He held his hands in front of him, about eight inches apart. "Have you ever meditated?" he asked, sitting on the floor again, his hands about eight inches apart in front of him, palms raised.

"Dave used to ask me to," I admitted. "I wasn't much good at it."

"I need you to practice—it's the first step toward protecting yourself," he counseled. He gestured and I set my hands up in front of me like his. "Okay, just let yourself feel it—good, you're there quickly, that's helpful. You feel the vibration? Right now, it's very limited—you haven't taken control of it. But it's a harmonic, a frequency. Harmonics bind matter together—all matter. If you can learn to feel the frequencies, to distinguish one from another, eventually you'll be able to adjust them. And once you can do that, you'll be able to affect everything around you."

"*Me?*" I screeched. I screech when I'm nervous—it's a bad old habit.

"Better you than someone else," he warned.

"I'm not a mindreader."

"You couldn't *explain* what was happening and you don't like that feeling," he said. "But you *knew* anyway." He smiled his gargoyle smile. "You have had the privilege, thus far, of not knowing what you know. My job will be to deprive you of this privilege."

Four

I hear the crackle in the middle of my head. *Tango Seven—multiple events in your vector, last five minutes. Exercise caution.* Sound is a vibration. This vibration grows, echoes, deeper, shimmying through me. We've been waiting for action since we started staging. We're soldiers, we joined up, no one made us. We want to fight. We want to prove ourselves, to find out who we are when the air bends and the fire fills us. We crossed the border two days ago and we've spent two days driving, swallowing pills, driving some more and sitting out a sandstorm that lasted six hours where nobody could sleep cause we kept saying to each other, *They know this stuff and we don't—when it stops, they'll be on us in a minute* but they weren't and then driving driving some more, past blown-out buildings and blown-out tanks and my headphones screaming.

The waiting is killing. No more waiting. Fight. Fight now. That's what I want because I don't know what else to want. And then, without transition, we're fighting. I hear the CRACK!! over the music and the Humvee right in front of us bounces into the air like a milk carton somebody kicked and we're almost on top of it by the time we stop. It's in the narrowest place, of course, wedged between two cinder block walls set close together, between two neighborhoods that hate each other and both hate us and we're bogged down, nowhere to go, can't get around it.

Man Down! Man Down! Monroe is shrieking into the headset and we see the Vee behind us drive right up and Shumwalt the medic jump out to help but he isn't there more than ten seconds before he's rushing back to his mount, shaking his head like it's detached.

The wait, the wait, the wait, the wait.

I shut off the music, not that it matters much—the gunfire is louder than the headphones all the way up, loud enough to wake the dead. In which case, start with the medic—his head is severed by rounds from three different directions and then blown sky high by a rocket that takes out his Humvee, throwing it six or seven feet in the air and crushing it against one of the cinder block walls. Some guys scramble out—how are they alive?—they get five or six steps before being cut down. There's too much fire from all over. These guys have guns and lots of them.

Half a second later, we're in the crosshairs. The door and windows of our truck are pounded with bullets. It's built for that, we've been told a hundred times but so many are coming at once that I watch the panel buckling right in front of me, puffing like the wrapper around the popcorn in the microwave. I'm embedded, the writer, the carry-along, an extra, an amusement most times, a burden at the moment. I have a gun in my belt but it might as well be a cap pistol.

We've got to move—Ram it! Monroe tells Gunner, the driver. If his name is Gunner, why isn't he the fucking gunner, dammit? Nonetheless, Monroe says *Ram it* so Gunner puts the thing in gear but then all at once, there's a different banging on the doors, banging and screaming—two of the guys from the medic Vee want in. *Get us out of here!* I hear someone screaming and Philips opens his door at the same time Grover opens his. Just in time for the poor son-of-a-bitch on Philips side to get riddled six or seven times in his vest—not dead but knocked over and that saves him and us.

For just a second, everything slows down as the guys on the end lean out to pull the two grunts into the Vee. I'm sitting, staring out the windshield, a dazed drugged-up sedation case and my eyes widen as up the road on the other side of the burning Humvee crawls a *bus*. The local town bus, the rattle-trap skinny-tire flaking-paint Fallujah regular city bus, low-cost rapid transit fucking bus on its rounds, following its route, the driver doing his usual civil service job of looking exactly ten yards ahead of him and no more. And now he's opening his doors at the bus stop — which just happens to be in the middle of a firefight. And as the doors are open on both sides of our Humvee and a thousand rounds are flying at us and Gunner is about to drive right over the flaming fucking Vee in front of us to get out of here, I see a procession of *soldiers in uniform filing neatly off the bus*. Like they paid their fare downtown and waited politely with their guns for twenty stops from there to the war. And now they're lined up, joining the rest of the warring neighborhood factions, shooting at us while the last two start setting up a rocket launcher and aiming it right at *me*.

"Gunner GO!!!" I yell and Gunner puts the thing in gear as they haul the last soldier in through Grover's door. Right then, Philips takes a round right in the neck that spurts all over the cab and he slumps to the floor. The rest of us all lean over to grab him and pull him up. At that instant, I hear a sharp hiss and raise my head a fraction, a millimeter, a milli-millimeter or whatever's smaller than anything—and see a rocket, the one launched by the bus soldiers, hovering right in front of my nose, passing so slow, so slow I can read the serial number on the side, right through the cab of our Humvee, screaming in one door, across the aisle between front seat and back and then out the other door without touching a thing, a person, anyone or anything. It explodes against the cinder block wall, happily about five yards behind us as we jump the other Hummer. My nose is singed black for a week. It's three days before I can hear much of anything, even Metallica. But Gunner hit the pedal at the right time and we will live, at least a little longer.

~~~~

And then I woke in a sweat and Tauber was creaking back and forth with a cup of evil-smelling coffee, singing some classic rock song I knew I'd heard but didn't really recognize. And Max was seated on the edge of my bed, worried face taking me in. And I knew he'd shaken me awake. He was dressed pretty neatly and had even brushed his hair, for all the good it did.

"You'll want a shower after the day you had," he said. "And the night." My dreams were already fading. He probably remembered a whole lot more of them than I did. "You should start getting ready," he urged softly.

When I came out of the shower, they were both staring at the TV, rapt. "...Matthews, the chairman of Mainline Technologies, a security contractor—"

"I know Mainline," I said. "They were everywhere in Iraq," and all at once they were both staring at me like I had pox.

"—had just walked out of merger negotiations with the L Corporation of Herndon, Virginia—"

"Also spooks, I'll bet," Tauber said. "It's the right neighborhood," and Max nodded.

"Authorities at the two companies were unable to explain why the helicopter pilot turned into a water tower instead of following his flight plan."

Video flickered on the screen. "It's bullshit," Max said immediately. "Look at his face," he said. "He's looking where he's going. He went on purpose."

"Which doesn't mean he meant to," Tauber said drily.

Max nodded. "He was 'persuaded'."

"By who?" I asked.

"Let's see," Tauber considered, "what country would want to knock off our security contractors? Name the top six."

"No," Max shook his head. "The question is, who'd be interested in knocking off the head of Mainline, sabotaging the Mayor of Copenhagen and a nuclear powerplant in New York State? When you've figured *that* out, then you've got something."

"Controversy grew today over the proposal for nuclear disarmament raised by Aryana Singh, the new Indian Premier. An attempted no-confidence vote in the Indian Parliament was disrupted by several dozen demonstrators inside the chambers and an estimated group of more than 10,000 outside. Sizeable demonstrations took place in London, Berlin, Frankfurt, Paris and Tokyo."

"What did Mainline do in Iraq?" Max asked.

"Everything," I answered. "Bodyguards for the VIP's, they ran the food concessions at the bases, they brought fuel in from Kuwait."

"Fuel?" Tauber growled. "Iraq's got oil."

"They're not producing it fast enough—at least that's what they told us. What they produced went to paying for the government."

"Paying off the government, more likely," Tauber said.

"We should get going," Max said and I stuffed my things into my bag.

We approached Durham just before 9, joining the morning rush past a skyline that waffled between glass tower and impregnable cliff dwelling. Miriam Fine lived in a suburban town on the outskirts. "I'm unsatisfied with your instructions," Max complained. "Technically, she doesn't even live in Durham."

"Complain to Dave next time you see him," I told him. "I'm just a vessel."

"Why don't *you* find her?" he remarked, looking at Tauber. "This should be perfect for remote viewing."

"I need pen and paper," Tauber said and I knew where it was in the glovebox. He closed his eyes and took several long breaths. His breathing got lighter and lighter after that, to the point that I thought he was either asleep or expiring. But, just at the point that I got concerned, his hand started moving on the page, sketching a very loose oval with a bulge on one side and a couple cross-hatch markings, first towards the top, then leaving a space and continuing the lines below. Beneath the oval, he began sketching a series of small rectangles and then abandoned them, ending with several stacked boxes. His eyes opened and he smiled at what was probably my skeptical expression. "Your subconscious," he said, "is a whole lot more powerful than yer conscious—it's in touch with stuff your conscious mind wouldn't fraternize with to save yer life."

"The conscious mind wants control," Max interjected. "It wants everything in a neat box. If you just let the hand move however it wants to—don't try to control, don't second-guess— you can draw directly from the subconscious."

"You get a bit at a time," Tauber continued, "first a feeling, then a little more detail and a little more and if you're lucky, wham! You get the big picture." He pointed at the glovebox. "Let's see that map," he said and I handed it to him.

"Okay," he said, pointing, "here's the hump in the highway—see it there?" and I did. Where his oval wasn't perfect— where it bulged out in one direction—the highway did the same on the map. He pointed out a spot on the map near the bulge where a bunch of criss-crossing streets were grouped around a long narrow empty space: "Here's all the streets criss-crossing in that neighborhood—well, they aren't quite as straight as I drew 'em. The empty spot's a hilltop." He stared at the stacked boxes as though they were somebody else's work. "She lives at the top of the hill—two-story brick with double-chimneys. It might not be a big hill," he added. "You're boosting the signal, aren't ya?" he asked Max suspiciously. "I wouldn't'a got it this fast on my own. It's been a long time."

"You're still doing the work," Max said.

"But...how does it work?" I stammered. "How do you explain it?"

Tauber shrugged. "That's a conscious mind thing," he said, tapping his forehead. "Having to explain everything. I don't have to know how sex works, son, long as I know how to do it..."

He turned to Max. "But how do you know what *you* know?" He had that same squinty-eyed skeptical look on his face that I'd seen the night before when we started talking about Florida. Smiling, pleasant but there was an edge to it. "I'm not the man I was, but my memory's okay. I don't remember you in the program."

"I was sort of on the edges," Max said, smiling back—two of the worst smiles I'd ever seen.

"What edges? Weren't no edges. You were in or out. Which program? Center Lane? Grill Flame? Stargate?"

"None of them," Max answered. Then he went red, taking both of us by surprise. "I never made it through training. I was drummed out—for insubordination."

After a second, Tauber answered with his own laughter. "That would explain you getting along with Dave."

Max nodded, adding, "Dave was the one who fired me," and that triggered another round of laughter. Throughout it all, though, Tauber's eyes stayed tight on him.

"You're blocking me," he said finally.

"Force of habit," Max answered first and then shrugged. "We all have our secrets. You're blocking me too."

"But you know who I am—Dave sent you to me."

"Uh-huh," Max sighed, "and he sent me to you, didn't he?"

Tauber didn't seem thrilled with this answer, but it silenced him for the moment. And then we were down the offramp into the suburbs. "This is right, isn't it?" Max asked Tauber and he nodded, gruff.

The offramp dumped us into a development, streets of neat well-kept houses on a hilly incline. Max started his driving-with-the-eyes-closed thing and I was stupidly thrilled to see Tauber was just as petrified by this as I was. But this time, we circled the neighborhood several times before Max could get a heading. "Lots of interference," he muttered. He closed his eyes again, made a few quick turns and Tauber pointed at a brick house just where the road curved. "That's it," he said immediately.

Miriam Fine's house stood at the apex, the highest completed point of the development. Streets of blocky brick houses stretched out downhill in several directions. A wide patch of woods filled the crest of the hilltop just behind her, a few construction cranes visible farther back, in a clearing between two developments. This looked like the spot the developer had reached when the construction economy got the hiccups.

We walked up the driveway to the heavy wooden door. Max stood aside and let Tauber knock. The door opened almost immediately.

"Mark?" Miriam Fine said with a sharp gaze. "What's happened?" The look on her face suggested she either wasn't all that pleased to see him or didn't like the way he looked. Neither answer would've been a shock. Tauber definitely wasn't her type—she was a slim, youthful fortyish, dressed in a ruffled white blouse, charcoal just-so suit and pearls. Ridiculously well-put together for 9 in the morning. Where Tauber seemed to have fallen apart without the program, Miriam Fine had obviously thrived. The instant after sizing Tauber up, she turned her attention to me and Max and her expression changed. Her mouth smiled but her eyes didn't—this was a pattern among this whole group and not one that made me real comfortable. "Come inside," she said in a stage whisper. "You don't want to be seen."

The living room was straight out of some decorating magazine, paint by numbers. Everything looked fine and went together, I guess, but the place might as well have been a movie set. There was nothing personal anywhere—no magazines on the table, no trash or cups or loose papers anywhere. Just two matched couches, a TV in an old-style armoire and a neat little computer desk with the CPU in a box attached to the leg. The desktop held her monitor screen and a neat stack of papers—bills, one purple Sticky note and her paycheck stub—a real corporate, computerized stub, not the handwritten job we got whenever Dave made us a little money at the store. The place was so orderly, I was afraid to sit down.

"What's happened, Mark? Why are you here?" Fine asked, but she kept glancing at Max, who was hovering quietly in the background. Before Tauber could answer, she started retreating to the kitchen. "Let me get you some water—I'm sure you're thirsty."

"We're fine," Max said but she was gone for just a few seconds, returning with a pitcher and glasses on a tray. Nobody took any.

"Dave Monaghan's dead," Tauber answered finally. Fine lowered her eyes and took a breath, slow and deep. She daubed at her forehead a couple times.

"How?" she said.

"Shot dead in Florida yesterday."

"How do you know?" she asked, which struck me as an odd question.

"We were there," I said, indicating Max and me. "They shot him through the bathroom window and then they blew up the house."

"Who did?" she asked and I wondered why she was asking questions, with words. She was in the program, wasn't she? Couldn't she just read our minds? Maybe the other two were blocking her, which seemed kind of odd too. Or maybe she felt a need, for some reason, to hear their answers aloud.

"Two mindbenders," Max answered. "Minor league, less than .5 on the Kirlian scale. We met them half an hour later trying to go through Dave's office." Fine's eyes widened.

"What happened to them?" she asked. "Did they—could they tell you anything?"

"They didn't know enough to tell," Max said. "But they came in an expensive SUV under suggestion with after-action forms to fill out and phone numbers to report to."

"Did you get the phone numbers?"

"They're useless," Max shrugged. "You get a recorded message that asks for the extension you wish to dial." He and Fine had a kind of staring contest going. "But they were clearly cogs in a pretty organized wheel."

"Whose?"

"Can't tell. They blocked well—no names or titles. Their thoughts were in English, so no language cues."

"Did you dispose of them?" Miriam Fine said and I squirmed at the directness of the question. I squirmed a little more at being the only one in the room who seemed uncomfortable with it.

"I put them out overnight. They have to be up and around by now—and raising the alarm."

"Which is why you're here," Fine said.

"Dave left a list of agents he felt should be contacted—he must have felt you were in danger."

"That's what you think?" Fine said, settling into a chair by the fireplace, smoothing her skirt under her, her eyes never leaving Max. "What is your plan?"

"My...plan?" Max stammered. "Just to follow Dave's blueprint. Just...just to warn you."

"Against what? Against whom?"

"Whoever killed Dave," he answered, like it was pretty obvious—I thought it was. Fine stood up from her seat like the perfect hostess, like all this life-and-death stuff was getting in the way of her socializing.

"Does anyone want coffee?" she asked quietly.

"Tea?" I asked and Max shot me a look like I'd asked for a handgun.

"I really think we should get going," Max said. "They have to be looking for us."

"Oh?" Fine said, still smiling. "Are they lurking outside, waiting to attack?" She shivered theatrically.

"How can I tell?" Max said, sinking into a chair opposite her. "There's so much static around here—you don't notice it?" Fine just stared at him. "I'm not comfortable when I can't tell what's going on around me."

"Well, I'm not comfortable running away without a good reason," Fine answered, speaking slowly, biting each word off as if

they came *a la carte*. "We don't know why Dave was killed, we
have no real reason—other than your unspecified fears—to feel
endangered ourselves. You say he left you a list, you think you
know what it means, this one here—" she waved her hand at me
"—says he saw Dave die and the house blow up. Even if I grant all
these things on faith, why should we go anywhere?"

"I have no facts to offer," Max said, "but I sensed that these
agents were low-level, low-status. They wanted the list but only to
hand it over to someone well above their pay grade."

"You *sensed*," Fine repeated, the words a hiss. "In what
way? Automatic writing? Ideagrams? Narrating out of a trance?
Which process do you use?"

"I—I have my own approach," Max said.

"I'm sure you do," Fine said and turned, all at once, to me.
"And you? You are?"

"I'm Greg—"

"Greg lived with Dave," Max explained. "Dave had a group
of veterans living with him, making the transition back to civilian
life. Dave helped them ...adjust."

"That sounds like Dave," Fine demeaned politely. Her eyes
were on me. Her eyes glinted at me as though we shared a secret, a
juicy one. She was an attractive, confident, well-organized person,
someone who could help me, who could help us all get ourselves
together. If she was in charge, we wouldn't be running all over the
map. "You saw him dead too, then," she said.

"I saw him first."

To Max: "You weren't there?"

"I arrived late."

Fine's eyes were slitted, like Tauber's had been. "How late?"

"Five, maybe seven minutes—that's right, isn't it?" he asked

me.

"I think so," I said, my cheeks reddening. "I...lost track of

time."

"You were under stress—that happens," Miriam Fine said,

smiling at me. She had a cup of tea for me, the way I liked it. I

didn't remember her leaving the room to get it but there it was.

She was considerate that way, I could tell. She went out of her way

for people. At least, she had for me—neither Max nor Tauber had

anything to drink. She turned back to Max. "If you say you arrived

late, does that mean you were on your way when it happened?"

Now there was something in the air—Max looked

uncomfortable. "Dave warned me they were coming. When I first

sensed them, I didn't realize they were coming after him."

Fine nodded. "You thought they were after *you*," she cooed.

"Because there's always someone coming after you, isn't there?"

With each word, he shrank and she blossomed. His eyes seemed to

shrivel into his head, the hollows under his thick eyebrows darker

and deeper by the second.

"It's not like that," he said but we all knew it was. He'd

already told us it was. Fine might be a bit of a tight-ass but she was the first together person I'd encountered since Dave got shot. She was smart and clean, she lived in a nice house in a respectable neighborhood, she had a regular life and a regular job. She had pictures on the wall and a desk with a big computer monitor and computerized paystubs from a real corporation, not a handwritten chickenscratch job that the bank teller looked at you sideways over. Miriam Fine was a corporation and I was traveling with a freak show. She had every reason to feel good about herself.

"I made a mistake," Max conceded, shoulders slumped. "I left town and got thirty miles away before I realized they were after Dave. By the time I got back, it was too late."

"So your method isn't foolproof, it seems," Fine said. "You aren't Superman."

"He's pretty close," Tauber said and that seemed to break the mood, at least shake it up. "He does things we never did."

"Of course he does," she said. "He can't help himself. So you feel responsible—"

"To an extent, yes. Dave was my friend."

"—and you're going to make amends? By deciding the old team is in danger—based on what, you've no idea—and taking it upon yourself to be noble and save us?" Sarcasm dripped from her voice; the words seemed to hit him like blows.

But something must have struck him funny, too, because his head rose and he was watching Fine now the same way Tauber had been watching him, sizing her up as though he'd never seen her before. "Dave left a trail," he said. "Based on the trail and the way it was presented and the feelings I got from it, I'm here. You know as well as I do that we can't rationalize everything we know. I didn't take *anything* on myself—Dave left me the list."

"It seems to me he left *Greg* the list," Fine said and Max turned immediately to Tauber, accusing.

"She got that out of *your* head," he glared.

Tauber raised his arms in protest. "She's my teammate," he said. "I don't block her."

"So Greg's the list," Fine repeated and suddenly I felt that warm feeling in the back of my head again, though it wasn't as sharp as before, more of a mellow, sympathetic feeling. It would be so nice to have someone looking out for me. She was looking at me in a way that was more than sympathetic. I'd never thought much about older women but she probably had a good TV and really nice sheets. "The list led you to me, is that it?" she continued. "So maybe *I'm* supposed to make some decisions now."

"It's supposed to help us get the old team together, so we can fight the killers," I said.

"That's *his* interpretation," Fine said. "How do you know? Maybe the list needs to be heard by other people. Maybe it needs to be thought about and examined in a peaceful setting, instead of running all over creation like chickens with your heads cut off. Doesn't that make sense?" With the look she was throwing me, it made lots of sense.

"Greg," Max said, "when you gave me the first name, we both knew we had to go find him. I didn't force you—you knew it was the answer. You felt it like I did."

"Based on what?" Fine asked. "What facts do you have for that decision?"

"We don't work on *facts!*" Max spat. "We know what we know! Intuition, embedded emotion and experience."

"He's powerful, Miriam," Tauber told her. "He's not a conscript. He's a natural."

"Oh, no question about it," she said. "He's *the* natural. The greatest there ever was." And now Max looked distinctly uncomfortable again.

"You *know* him?" Tauber said, sitting up in his chair.

"Of course I do. I've seen his picture a thousand times. It's Renn!"

"Renn?!!" Tauber sat up like the name had attacked his spine. The look on his face mixed awe and horror. I felt like Rip Van Winkle, the alien wanderer, the visitor who didn't speak the language anymore.

"Renn," Fine repeated, holding the name on the end of her tongue. "The cream of the crop, the man who knows *everything*. Look at him now—tired, poor, hiding from the world. So paranoid he didn't even realize old Dave Monaghan had enemies of his own. Because everything's about him, *has* to be about him."

Renn—I was just getting used to Max—stared at her, sullen but not denying anything she said. Not even trying.

"Renn—all the stories we heard! And now here you are, not even powerful enough to get whatever Dave left in this one's head." Fine's voice was ringing, commanding, hypnotic. It had been that way, I realized, for several minutes.

"I came in good faith," Renn said after a long moment. "If I had bad intent, I could have dumped them on the front lawn and left them for you to deal with, couldn't I?"

"Why didn't you?" Fine asked.

"I don't know," Renn muttered, looking around the room as though he was lost. "It would have been pretty easy." Then he stopped, staring at me. "Because I had to *know*," he said all at once, his voice gaining strength, gaining its usual power back. "Dave was murdered. I have to know why. And whoever did it has to pay."

"Right," I said immediately. "That's right." It's why I'd come, despite all my doubts about him, about everyone around me, despite all the fucked-up things that had happened. We were going to rally the old team, whoever they were, and go after the bad guys, whoever *they* were. It was as though the sun had just popped through the clouds, as though my head had suddenly cleared.

I'll admit I wasn't expecting *you*," Fine continued. She looked older all of a sudden, her put-together coming slightly apart. "If you'd come from the North, we'd have foreseen...but, no matter."

Suddenly it seemed like Max's head had cleared too. He leapt from his chair to the window. I saw nothing going on outside, but he was ramrod straight with that miles-away expression I'd seen in the car. I knew all at once that, whatever had grabbed his attention, it wasn't miles away.

"The great Max Renn," Fine narrated, "not even powerful enough to see what was right in front of his nose."

Max jumped from the window and grabbed my arm. "They're coming!" he called. "We have to go!"

"Too late," Fine clucked.

"*Now!*" Renn yelled, hurtling toward the back door. I turned—Tauber stood next to Fine, an apologetic look on his face but not moving.

"You don't have to go," Fine told me pointedly. "You're not wanted for anything. We can get that unwanted information out of your head."

I wavered for a moment—all those feelings I'd had a moment earlier flashed through my head. *She had every reason to feel good about herself.* So organized. So put-together. I could see her lying rumpled and naked on those nice thousand-threadcount sheets—boy, I saw that real clear all of a sudden. *What* unwanted information? Get it out of my head *how*?

Fine's face was a look of triumph and that tipped the balance for me. Every time I'd ever seen triumph on somebody's face, it always seemed to involve marching *toward* the machine guns.

I ran for the back of the house. Max threw the door open and we bounced across the short lawn and into the woods, just ahead of the sound of cars screeching to a halt, doors slamming, voices shouting and footsteps coming up fast behind us.

Five

We plunged into the thick brush, the boots pounding out the back door and tearing through Fine's yard, trampling all the neat greenery while voices barked orders from every direction. Max was running really hard—I was puffing just trying to keep up with him. I'd spent a year in the Everglades, where even tree branches get lazy. But the undergrowth was so thick here under the trees that it was dim as dusk at nine in the morning. In such a place, a couple yards might be enough for us to get away.

The footsteps behind were so close, I didn't even dare look back at first. But we started to pull away and I realized that, as Max—Renn—approached bushes and trees, they were actually bending out of his way, like he was projecting some invisible shell ahead of him—and whipped back with a vengeance once we passed, which really helped gain us some space. I heard angry voices cursing and shouting behind my back. And then I was startled by a whooshing sound and turned to see, just a few feet away, a twister sprung right up out of the ground. It was a little one, not one of those Hollywood ones that swallow gymnasiums, but it was enough, sucking up the forest floor and whipping the whole mess—leaves, twigs, bark, branches, pine cones, berries, vines, dust and moss—into a smoky column skittering interference between us and them.

Renn's voice said *Follow me* and he peeled off to the left. I obeyed and then realized he hadn't said anything aloud—I'd heard his voice in my head. The whirlwind continued in our original direction, and I heard what sounded like fifteen sets of footsteps following. "Fan Out!" yelled a deep voice and I peeked through the trees at the leader, a bulky guy in a dark nylon jumpsuit pointing in the wrong direction. "Get around it!" The posse fought through the bracken and uproar into the distance while we sprinted, puffing hard, uphill—I could make out a cluster of houses ahead, somewhere beyond the construction cranes.

And then the hill came to a sudden end, dropping off abruptly to a sunken roadbed cleared to bare earth and huge piles of dirt and stone held back by thick-tied cable netting. Empty bulldozers and earthmovers completed the picture.

The long-finished houses we'd glimpsed over the treetops were just across the roadbed, on the other side of the piles. We slid down the incline and right into two men in dark blue nylon, coming up the other direction between an artificial hill and a high pile of encased stone. They greeted us immediately by pulling out their Glocks. Why did everyone but us have big guns?

"Stand still!" the taller, bearded one ordered Max. "You stay right where you are. You're not touching me." He touched his earpiece. "We've got 'em." He tried it a few times, then turned to the younger man next to him. "Contact them. Let them know."

The younger man touched his earpiece several times. "I'm not getting anything," he said.

"*He's* jamming it," Beardman said. He gestured with his gun. "Okay—cross your hands behind your backs and stand still. G here will wrap your wrists and put on your headpieces. Then we'll go down and meet the others."

The younger man pulled two black plastic bundles from his pocket. When he opened them, they turned out to be wrap-around goggles with prominent earpieces and blinking LCD's at the temples. I had no idea what they were but they didn't look friendly.

"Your bosses won't promote you," Renn told him coolly. "You're too ambitious. They like employees who are grateful."

"Yeah, yeah," Beardman returned. "Try harder."

As G came toward us, Max actually leaned forward and threw a punch. I was shocked—I'd never seen him react in a physical way to anything and, what with the guns and all, it didn't even make sense. He wasn't much good at it either—he completely missed, succeeding only at knocking the goggles out of G's hands.

Beardman kicked Max's legs out from under him and, as soon as he hit the ground, shoved the Glock to his temple. "Okay, if that's how you want it," he said. "Tie him first," he told the younger man, who put the ties around Max's wrists and pulled them really tight. Then he lifted him up again and propped him against me while he turned to get another plastic tie for me off the ground.

I felt the vibrations coming off of Max as soon as he leaned against me. I could feel the hum sweeping from his shoulders and feet into the trunk of his body, intensifying and deepening until he somehow was a tone, a deep bass note that overwhelmed all other sound as long as he was touching me.

"Okay," he called out as the vibration built—I could feel the effort it took for him to talk, "how about this? You've got a spot on your lung. Cancer. You need to have it looked at. It's not big; if they act quickly—"

"Shut up!" Beardman shouted. "I need a diagnosis, I'll call a doctor!" He turned to his companion. "What are *you* waiting for?"

"Are you going to hold his arms?" the kid asked, nervous, looking at me.

"I'm busy pointing a gun at the dangerous one, okay? *That* one should be easy." I guess it was kind of an insult at me, but I'd lost all interest by that point in anything anybody was saying.

Because I could see, all at once, what Renn was up to.

Behind Beardman and G stood the pile of stone—twelve or thirteen feet high, held in place by a web of steel cable. While they were talking, the threads of the cable were unraveling themselves. I could hear Renn humming next to me, his body radiating a tone so powerful, I couldn't believe the Glock boys didn't hear it. The steel threads were separating faster and faster, until all at once, as G grabbed the second plastic tie off the ground, the netting right behind him groaned and split fifty little fissures and then tore open in five or six places, sending twelve or thirteen feet of stone rushing suddenly down the incline at him—at all of us.

Because I saw it coming, I gained a few precious steps head start and that's what saved us. At my first step, I felt Max slump, helpless, behind me—his eyes were open but he was lost in some kind of trance, pumping out his bass note. I grabbed him under the arms and dragged him up the slope in front of us. G was hit by the first couple stones that flew out of the pile—they knocked him down and he was buried in seconds. Beardman yelled after me, pointing his gun at my head but he was two seconds worth of indecisive pulling the trigger and that was one second more than he had. He was hit several times around the legs and feet and then a huge shard hit him full on the side of the head and he went down under the deluge. By the time we reached the rim, the entire trench was a dust-billowing pile of rock. I can't account in any way for how we got out. I heard Max's voice in my head saying *Head for the house on the left* and I dragged him in that direction.

"Are you okay?" I asked.

"Not this one—to the left," he muttered. "I'll be okay." He was starting to use his own legs, still wobbly but beginning to support himself a bit while I steered.

I heard shouting down the hill—some of the stone had improvised its way down the roadbed to where it apparently met some of our other pursuers. As I headed for the house on the left, more blue jumpsuits appeared between the other houses on the block, staring down on the avalanche and calling into their earpieces for instructions. How the hell many people were after us?

We scrambled through the back yard, past a shed, several thick trees, lounge chairs and a portable bar. "Around the house," Max ordered and I obeyed. He was limping and stumbling but at least he was talking normally now—I was ticking off milestones. I needed him full-strength—surely, we had a big fight just ahead. I could see a street just beyond the house but if they had that many guys, how far could we get before they caught us? If this was a movie, we'd hotwire a car but I had no clue how to do that and Max wasn't in shape to do much of anything. Shouts from down below were being answered by others close by—they'd be on us in a minute. What if he needed a doctor?

"You'll drive," he told me. "Not fast, normal speed, don't attract attention."

"Drive *what*?" I asked. *Shit, now he's delirious.* His car was sitting across the woods, in front of Miriam Fine's house, unless it was magical and could find us on its own.

As we reached the front of the house, I felt him lean into my shoulder, pushing me toward the driveway. Where a retirement-aged man stood favoring his paunch, holding open the door of a very pretty Audi coupe. "You drive," Max repeated and detached himself from me. He stumbled to the passenger door and collapsed onto the seat. The car's owner handed me the keys and said apologetically "It's just half a tank." I took the keys and stood staring at him.

"Say 'thank you,'" Renn muttered, pulling on his seat belt.

"Thank you," I mumbled.

"Now get in the car, dammit!"

I dropped into the driver's seat. It was really beautiful, chrome and carbon-fiber and all that stuff they talk about in the car magazines. As I closed my door, a middle-aged woman came out of the house, locking up behind her. She had an overnight bag in hand.

"Time to go, Herb," she called and they climbed into a Winnebago parked outside the garage.

"Don't stare—move!" Renn gasped, smacking me on the shoulder. "That way!" He pointed to a sidestreet a few yards away. I pulled out of the driveway. As we made the turn, I saw the Winnebago head off in the opposite direction.

Max laid way back in his seat now and talked me down the long hill, panting little breaths as though *he'd* just carried someone up a hillside and around a house. We went nowhere and took the most complicated route to get there—right here, left there, his eyes closed the same as when we'd found Tauber and Miriam Fine's house. This time, he was finding a way for us to get lost and stay that way. We kept turning and doubling back on ourselves as we moved progressively through the vast development. More than once I saw a black SUV turning onto a street we'd just turned off of or going down a one-way street we'd just passed.

This cat-and-mouse took more than fifteen minutes but at the end, we were all the way to the other end of the project, having never gotten near a main street. When we finally did turn onto one, we were a hundred yards from the highway entrance.

"There!" he pointed but I didn't need prompting. We were on the ramp before I could ask a single question, before he could fail to answer even one.

~~~~

"Ruben Crowell, Gettysburg Pennsylvania," I said after we'd driven about an hour.

He'd been sitting up properly for a while, his color—never very far from pale—returning. "Ruben who?"

"Ruben Crowell, Gettysburg Pennsylvania. That's the next nearest. You would have asked eventually."

He sat taking me in for a moment. "You're taking ownership of it," he said, nodding. "That's good. And the words are coming back, aren't they?"

It was what I'd been thinking. I certainly wasn't what I'd been—the kid who thought he was going to be Peter Jennings was long gone—but more than words were coming back. I was seeing the story—I was beginning to pull the threads together, to see a bigger picture. It was more than a little creepy, knowing he was inside my head, but at least I believed it now—that uncertainty was gone. Whatever satisfaction I got from that knowledge lasted half a second.

"How the hell many guys are after us?!!" I yelled suddenly.

"What do you mean?"

"What do you mean, what do I mean? There were at least six, seven guys following us out of her house, the two with the serious guns—you sure attract a whole lot of serious guns—by the rockpile and two or three more on the ridge where the houses were. How many fucking guys are after you? How did they get there so fast? Who *are* these people?"

"Good questions. Those are all good questions," he acknowledged with a nod.

"Fuck you! Good questions! You're the mindbender *extraordinaire*—why am *I* asking the good fucking questions?"

He smiled. He seemed to actually find this amusing, which did nothing for me except get me driving 90 instead of 85 miles an hour. Now that we were out of the situation, the fear and anger were all over me. It was amazing my shaking hands could drive straight.

"I don't have answers—not yet," he said. "They're not powerful minds, but the first thing they've been taught is a good blocking scheme. And my stamina isn't what it used to be. Throwing several hundred tons of rock down a hill doesn't suit me anymore." His eyes were miles away again, that look I'd seen a couple of other times on his face.

Was that not a phrase with him? Was he actually *looking* miles away? He started rifling through the glovebox. "We'll need money, a map and to fill the car up," he said. "Then we'll figure out the next step."

"Ruben Crowell, Gettysburg Pennsylvania," I repeated.

"I'm not sure that's it. What if Dave made the same mistake we did—*I* did—assuming the network was under attack? Clearly, at least one part of it—Miriam Fine—is on the other side. I'm not sure what that means. And by the way," he stared at me, "it's not how many fucking guys are after me. *You're* the one with the list in your head."

That stopped conversation for a while. The signs promised a rest stop thirty miles ahead.

"Throwing chunks of a hillside around—that's mindreading?" I asked.

"No, that's my hobby," he laughed. "Electrons are electrons. Matter is bound together by vibration, by harmonic sympathy. So if you can manipulate the vibration, you can manipulate— rearrange—just about *anything* at the subatomic level. Now, it's one thing to know about it—it's another to do it. I've been playing with this for thirty years and all I've got are a couple of childish tricks. Nonetheless, they're good for wreaking havoc." He sighed—I probably looked like a fish, wide-eyed and open-mouthed. "It's exhausting too. If the rest stop has a decent cheeseburger, I want one."

We filled up the Audi and parked it behind a couple of tractor-trailers, out of sight of the highway. On the way to the food court, we bought a map and all the newspapers they had.

"How come they can't read our thoughts to follow us?" I asked as we sat down.

"I'm blocking us."

"You could read the bearded guy—wasn't he a mindbender?"

"Ha! That guy was useless. I broke right through."

"So you can read anybody?"

"No. I couldn't read Dave if he wanted to stop me. But these? Whoever hired these guys, they like people with minimal ability." The waitress brought our food. I had a Caesar Salad; he dug into a cheeseburger with fries.

"That's not good for you, you know," I told him. "Bad for your cholesterol."

"Cholesterol is a myth," he answered like he'd checked it out on the subatomic level, stuffing a few extra fries in around the corners of his mouth. "After a morning of rock-arrangement, we real men want *beef*."

I was wondering if his real name was Max Renn—or was the Max as phony as the Dulles? He could read minds and plant thoughts in your mind and play around with the vibrations that held the world together. The scary part was, I'd seen enough to actually have to take the idea seriously. Knowing he wasn't making up such ridiculous stuff didn't prove any more comforting than the alternative. Thinking about him seemed to lead inevitably to double negatives.

"What about those people? You made them give us their car? And go on vacation? Just like that?" Renn nodded, smiling his chilly smile. If he could read my mind, he knew what was coming, but he was waiting, humoring me, as I edged into my subject.

"They got away," he answered. "So they won't be able to give information about their car for at least a couple of days. And now, since they haven't found us, the bad guys will have to track *them*, just in case we were hiding in the Winnebago." He stared at the parking lot with a look I didn't like. "We'll have to ditch the car."

"It's a nice car," I started. Way nicer than his, though I didn't say so. Air conditioning, for one thing.

"Don't get attached," he warned. "Everything is temporary."

I got back to my subject. "If you could make those people do what they did—are you making me go with you?"

He smiled the best he knew how, which wasn't much. "No," he answered and his eyes softened. "You're here on your own. For which I'm grateful, by the way."

"But you have a reason—for not forcing me," I said. Like the names of the agents and the location of the box under the furnace in Dave's store, it was just something I suddenly *knew*.

"Yes," he smiled and now his eyes were burning. "That's very good. Yes, there's a reason why. Dave was a subtle man, unlike either of us. He left you a suggestion to tell me your password. And he left me a suggestion—I thought I wasn't suggestible—to recognize it when you did. But I had no idea, when I first asked, what information was inside you. It might have been a person or a place or a concept or a plan or...who knows what? So the question that I ask you—*what is the next nearest?*— that didn't come from Dave. It's intentionally ambiguous because I really didn't know what I was asking. So far, it's gotten us some information and allowed us to meet this really interesting class of people," he laughed. "But a better question might have got us a whole lot farther faster. So I'm hoping you'll get stronger and take control of what he left you, of the information inside you. So, I can't force you—to take this trip, or much else. I don't want to get in the way of the work you're doing...inside your own head."

I must have shown a pretty strong reaction because he laughed again. "C'mon Gregor," he said. "You were thinking it earlier. The words are coming back. That's the start. You're beginning to communicate with yourself." He took another bite of his cheeseburger. "The sooner, the better." Then he stopped chewing and his eyebrows shot up. "What is it?"

He'd made me nervous so I'd started shuffling the paper—when I get nervous and there's no TV to stare at, I move things around, and all I had to play with at the moment was the newspaper. On the front page of the national section was an article about yesterday's helicopter crash. The picture alongside it was taken at a press conference in front of L Corp Headquarters.

I was staring at the picture—I couldn't help it, though I didn't know why at first. And then I recognized what had grabbed me—the logo, the logo on the front of the building. I was staring at it in the newspaper but in my head, I was seeing the logo on a different background—greenish stiff paper, a rectangular strip of paper with computer cutouts stamped into the bottom edge—the green stiff paper of Miriam Fine's paystub, on her perfect neat desk, where I'd seen it just an hour earlier.

And then my head went hot again and Renn leaned back in his seat and exhaled hard. "She works for L Corp," he whistled. "Does that mean they *all* work for L Corp? The whole blue-nylon brigade?" He stared out the window now, a long way out the window, considering, gathering himself.

"Okay," he said finally, "we've got to disappear for a while. Until we can figure out the next couple of steps."

He pulled out the map and studied it for a few minutes. "C'mon," he said and we headed out toward the parking lot.

Right outside the door, a dumpy-looking guy in a hardhat got out of his Cherokee and walked away, leaving the thing idling behind him.

"What happens when he remembers?" I asked as we pulled onto the highway.

"He won't," Max answered. "He'll remember going into the men's room and coming out to find the car gone." He put his foot down and we pulled away from traffic, heading North. "I need what I need," he said, "but I'm not sloppy with people. He'll be okay. Now let's take care of money."

"They have ATM's at the rest stop."

He shook his head. "We need a bank. They can track your location from an ATM withdrawal."

"Taking it out of a bank is different?"

"It is if you take it from someone else's account."

A few blocks later, we walked into an old-fashioned bank, with marble floors, dark wood booths and cathedral-type windows, a bank being just a church for money anyway. Teller windows filled the back wall but all but two of them were empty.

Max went immediately to the far side of the lobby, where the senior offices stood behind etched-glass doors. The first opened as we approached, and a slim, balding, depressed-looking man appeared, carefully neatening the creases around the shoulders of his blue suit and wearing a face that said he was expecting someone.

"Mr. Guernsey—" Max began while Guernsey's expression wavering somewhere between polite tolerance and *Do I know you*? Max laid his hand on the man's shoulder and Guernsey immediately stood four inches taller and smiled like Max was the long-lost cousin who hit Lotto.

"Can we talk privately?"

Guernsey ushered us into his office, bubbling over with *good to see you* and all that fizz.

The office dated to when a bank officer was a big man, having built half the town or at least paid for the building. A mahogany desk hovered on shiny brass feet in front of a brand-new untouched-by-man puffy black leather couch, four guest chairs, three large file cabinets and a safe. No cubicles for Mr. Guernsey, nossir—he was landed gentry. He settled behind the desk and affected a look that suggested he was actually interested.

"So how can I help you gentlemen?"

"Your trust in Ms. Rand is misplaced," Max told him brusquely.

"Ms. Rand is in the back at the moment," Guernsey replied and it was obvious that he wasn't interested in hearing what Max had said. "I asked if I could help you?"

Max leaned forward in his chair; Guernsey did the same in response.

"Ms. Rand has been holding back several commercial deposits half a day and investing the money on her own behalf," Max announced in a stage whisper. "She's chosen to loot accounts with heavy activity, where it'll take time for anyone to notice. She's also been skimming currency transactions in several —"

"Who the hell do you think you are?" Guernsey demanded, standing up like someone had goosed him.

"Here are the accounts she's set up for herself and her balances in each," Max said, pulling a piece of scratch paper from Guernsey's desk blotter, scribbling some numbers and handing it back to him. "She's been at it for eight months. If you check, you'll see she's into you for almost a quarter-million."

"This is absurd," Guernsey flushed. "I trust Ms. Rand with—"

"Your job?" Max asked and that shut the fat goose up for a moment. He threw Guernsey his heat-your-skull look and all the sharpness in Guernsey's expression disappeared. "Check the accounts."

"Check the accounts," Guernsey mumbled a half-second behind. We waited while he tapped away at his computer, his eyes widening and collar getting tighter by the minute.

"This started when you two got back from Atlanta," Max said quietly while Guernsey seemed to be calculating the odds of killing himself jumping off a three-story building. "You'll have to explain that weekend trip to your superiors, but it'll play a whole lot better if you catch her *before* the auditors do."

"Before the auditors..." Guernsey mumbled on a one-second lag. He'd turned the color of the diploma on the wall. "George—get me a bank check for 'Cash', would you? No, no, discretionary expenses—just bring it for my signature."

About halfway through, I realized I heard another voice echoing behind Guernsey's; I looked over and Max was mouthing the words, again a half-second ahead of him. I would have sworn no sound was coming out of his mouth, it was just in the air somehow.

George came through in a minute, very green and obsequious, bearing the check. Guernsey filled in the figure and signed it. "Cash this for Mr. Granville here, will you?" Guernsey ordered.

George just stood there, staring. I got the feeling maybe this was a little irregular.

"ID?" George squeezed through tightly pursed lips.

"Obviously, he's provided me with adequate ID. Get going!" Guernsey said heavily and George rushed off, returned with the money neatly folded into two envelopes and disappeared just as fast.

Guernsey sat staring at his desk blotter, the morose look deepening on his face. "I trusted her," he said helplessly, to no one in particular.

"Remember that when you confront her," Max answered. "Our fee is half the interest on her bogus investments—not unreasonable."

Guernsey mumbled 'not unreasonable' behind him but he was slurring now.

"If you only tell them about her first two accounts, the money you recover should cover our finder's fee," Max said, touching Guernsey on the forehead again. "This way, we'll stay anonymous."

"Mr. Anonymous," Guernsey mumbled, "and his brother, Mr. and Mr. Anonymous." He checked to see if we were smiling at his little joke.

It was all I could do to keep from running to the car. Once we got inside, I collapsed in the passenger's seat, puffing like a tugboat. He started talking to me about the route, and I thought, *he's trying to keep my mind off*—off what? Off something. Of course, once that occurs to you, the next thought is to try to figure out what.

"We'll want to turn West just past Richmond—once we get closer, keep your eye out for signs."

My mind was working as fast as it was able, not that that's saying much.

"So now we're bank robbers?"

"We prevented major embezzlement by a bank officer."

"And extorted money for it."

"We got a finder's fee—a modest one, under the circumstances."

"Which you forced him to pay."

"He would have lost his job and found out about the woman at the same time, and probably after she'd pulled him a whole lot deeper into it than he is now. I did him a favor."

Which might really have been true, but it didn't make look any less sneaky. Those old feelings were creeping back around the edges. I liked it better when I thought he was nuts.

"Why didn't they trust you?" I asked. "Fine said you were the greatest of them all but she wanted you captured. And Tauber stayed with her. When she called you...?"

"Renn," he smiled again. "I've had lots of names over the years. It's just a label."

"When she called you that, Mark acted like you were...I don't know what."

"Spies are not notoriously trusting people."

"They trust each other—"

"They know each other a long time, since Stargate."

"Stargate?"

"That was the last name for the program—Fine joined up near the end. There were other names before that—Center Lane, Grill Flame. But Stargate was the last."

"Dave was part of it?"

"He was a high-ranking officer. But he quit—he caused a bit of a stir."

"Why?"

"After Stargate, the program was getting serious—it was moving past research, the tactics were going to become more...direct, let's say. Dave didn't agree with it and he said so. He realized how destructive psychotronic war could be. And," he frowned, "he knew the price we pay who practice it."

He went quiet but he still hadn't answered my question. At least, he hadn't answered the one I hadn't asked yet.

"But you were in the program, until you got kicked out," I continued. "Is that why they didn't trust you? Because you got kicked out?"

He didn't reply for a while. He was driving fast, passing cars left and right and we both saw the sign for Richmond Beltway. We merged into the westbound lanes and he took a quick look at the map as the dark clouds followed us, squeezing the sun from the sky.

"That," he said finally, "that was a lie."

"What was? You weren't in the program? Or you didn't get kicked out?"

"Neither."

"But you're the mindbender *extraordinaire*. She said so." He nodded. I was baffled. "You said Stargate was the mindbender program."

"It was the *American* mindbender program," he said, without taking his eyes off the road. "I never said I worked for America."

Six

By the time we got where we were going, I was driving. At least I was behind the wheel. The road wound around the longest string of mountains I'd ever seen. Every time I thought we were about to start descending, another hill opened up in front of us and we'd climb a little higher. Streetlights twinkled in the valley a long way down. Lightning flickered out of clouds that seemed about ten feet above our heads, hammering trees right in front of us more than once. It was only late afternoon, but the clouds made it feel like midnight.

"Safest place, in a car," I muttered to myself as another bolt hit another tree.

"Actually, that's not true," Renn said, looking like he was about to explain it.

"*Don't,*" I warned him and sent the rest, the *I don't want to know* part, thinking it as hard as I could, wondering if I could make the back of his head burn. Not likely, but he shut up at least.

The road never laid out in front of you, it kept moving and jumping and finding unexpected places to go. There was always that nice low solid rock wall that promised to keep us from driving over the edge of the cliff which was good since the whole damn thing was cliffs but I couldn't help but wondering why the son-of-a-bitch had to put us on a cliff in a thunderstorm at the end of two days of running.

When we neared the driveway, he had to point it out to me three times—I would have gone right by. The roadbed was below the street and overhung on all sides with trees. It was a long driveway, winding past expansive fenced-in grass fields—I thought of horses right away, though there weren't any in sight—and eventually to a surprisingly compact house perched right on the cliffside. The nearest houselight was a mile downvalley, the road visible for at least a mile in either direction. I had to give him credit—nobody was sneaking up on us here.

Once we pulled up in front of the house, he opened his door and I found I could open mine too. I was able to stand up, stand on my own two feet. After twenty minutes in the driver's seat, watching my body drive without any input from me, this was a serious relief. "Thanks for giving me my limbs back," I cracked.

"You threatened to drive off the side of a cliff," he reminded me.

"I didn't *mean* it!"

His eyebrow went up. "Just because I can read your mind doesn't mean I know when you're full of shit." He tapped his finger against my forehead. "Remember that when *you* start doing it," he said and went to work checking inside the planters and the mailbox in the rain.

I followed, rubbing my wrists—they felt like they'd had iron bars inserted. My ankles felt like they *still* did. I wondered about how long it would take me to scramble downhill to town. But with no traffic on the road, a mile drop to those glimmering lights and a raging thunderstorm overhead, the odds didn't add up in my favor.

"For the moment, if you wish, it's kidnapping," he answered, though I hadn't asked the question. "We'll go inside and I'll explain things to you. After that, hopefully, you won't want to run away."

"And if I do? What'll you do? Paralyze me again?"

"As I said, let's hope you won't," he said with the same voice he'd used to threaten Hawaiian Man with his finger. "You know me—I don't offer lots of explanations. Just hear me out." He walked through the trees to the kitchen door and searched all over around it for the key—under the planters, atop the lintel, beneath the windowsill. Finally he picked up a rock, smashed the window and unlocked the door from inside.

"There isn't some sophisticated mindbender way to do this?" I asked.

"I'm tired," he said, "and it's raining."

The kitchen had a nightlight burning and a radio playing in the dark—I'd never realized what a dead giveaway that combination was. The kitchen was the end of the north wing of the house. One wing held the kitchen and garage, the other, three bedrooms and two baths. The wings extended over the cliff, joined by the most incredible double-wide living room I'd ever seen. Huge slabs of local stone covered the walls above a multi-level dark wood floor, every parquet line pointing up the mountain-and-valley panorama through the wall of windows. A simple dining room table and chairs stood on a high shelf floor near the kitchen; couches, bookshelves, a monster TV and computer table filled the other end of the room.

"They'll be gone for two more days," Renn said, coming out of the bathroom with towels. "The people that own the place. The computer has a high-speed hookup. We can research—"

"I'm not researching shit," I told him. "I wouldn't have come this far if you'd told me who you were."

"I'm not an enemy agent," he said, sitting on the couch.

"You said you didn't work for America."

"I've never actually worked for *anybody*," he answered. "The country that trained me no longer exists. I am here by choice, like millions of other illegal immigrants. Sit—I'll explain." I wasn't sitting. Standing up, I figured I was three steps closer to the door than him. "You can ask questions, if you want—I'll answer. At that point, you can run if you want."

I sat.

"Where are you from?"

"I was born a citizen of the Union of Soviet Socialist Republics. I was born in Leningr...uh, St. Petersburg, excuse me, and grew up in a city called Novosibirsk, in Siberia."

"What is your real name?"

"I have no 'real' name, like most people do," he said. "I have no family identity. I was a child of the state."

"You're an orphan?"

"I'm the product of a genetic experiment. The Soviet government began experimenting with mind control in the '20's. Once Stalin pushed out Trotsky, the program began forcibly mating individuals with strong powers. The program was never really successful—there were some physical and genetic problems. Early mortality and a high rate of suicide, for example."

He laughed here a little, his dark laughter. I didn't remember knowing many Russians but this struck me nonetheless as a very Russian type of humor. "They continued to breed the few remaining specimens until the 70's. I am the end result of four generations of 'psychics' bred like farm animals for their desirable characteristics, without love or choice."

"That's why Fine said you were the greatest of them all— most powerful, cream of the crop."

"I was a misfit, a disaster. When I was a child, there were ten of us, mixed into a population of forty or fifty others who showed promise but came from normal families. Most of us died off before completing training and the Soviet became disenchanted with the program as time went on, so the numbers dwindled."

"They got disenchanted…they didn't get results?"

He laughed again. "Oh no, they got results—*everyone* got results, though ours were better than the Americans. But there were problems—political problems."

"Political problems? With spies?"

"With bureaucrats," he answered. "Ideological problems, I should say. Communism likes—liked—to think of itself as a scientific approach to history and the world. The problem that no one likes to face is that science is a moving target. What we know now is not all we will know someday. The idea of thoughts being part of an accessible stream that can be tapped and affected at a distance, the idea that the mind—as opposed to the brain—can be separate from the body, can travel and take action on its own, this struck the ideologues as metaphysics. It strongly suggested the possibility of a soul, separate from the physical body, some remnant that has its own life beyond a single physical identity. To them, this smacked of magic. It was not explainable and repeatable—it was not *scientific*. This didn't play well at the Politburo oversight committee.

"And Renn," he continued, " was the biggest risk of all. I was dangerous, out of control. I responded badly to training. Our training was designed for the average person with some psychotronic ability."

"Psychotronic? Is that like psychic?"

"I don't like that term, psychic. It puts me in a lineup with Nostradamus and Madame Marie the fortuneteller." He shrugged. "Although, otherwise, the words probably mean the same thing.

"Anyway, the problem for most mindbenders is that the mental signal they receive is weak. Any sort of distraction or embedded or suggested thought will disturb it or color it and your whole purpose as a spy is to bring back useful, accurate, actionable information. So they had to desensitize us, to beat down our reliance on logic, on what we thought things *should* mean, anything that might get in the way of our reporting what we found, as we found it. Desensitizing involved a series of beatings—"

"Excuse me?"

"They beat us. They sent good decent men with big families and charitable intentions—and strong arms. They would put us in a small room and send in the strong men to hit us, with absolutely no evil intent. This started when we were around eleven or twelve, in addition to our classroom training. You would show up for geometry to find that the rest of the class had been moved elsewhere and here was Boris to rearrange your attitude—and your bones.

"They were under some sort of deep suggestion, surely, for while they were beating us, they would be thinking about taking their own children to the park or making love to their wives or some movie they saw last weekend. Either they were under suggestion or they searched the Republics for oafs who could be that disassociated from reality."

"This was on purpose?"

"It was crucial to the process that it make no sense. No matter how we tried to rationalize, the reality would defeat us. They beat us viciously while having nothing whatever against us and, being mindreaders, we would know this for a fact. After enough of this—each person has their own definition of 'enough'—you were expected to lay down your need for answers, your expectation that things would make any sort of sense. You were expected to accept what you found, so you could report 'as is.' And you were expected to obey."

He was biting his fingernails as he spoke. He didn't seem aware of it but, by the time he reached this point in the story, he'd worked past the white nail rim on several fingers and into the colored part. As he bit pieces off, he placed them neatly without thinking in his shirt pocket.

"I'm not good," he said after a pause, "at obeying. The first time a man hit me hard, I killed him. We were in a laboratory setting, so of course the place was floor to ceiling sensor arrays. They measured 5000 amps straight to the heart." His eyes were locked onto the desk in front of him but he was rubbing his earlobe red. "It took three seconds for him to die and in that time, I saw what he saw, I felt what he felt, everything that was in him as he knew he was done—his parents, his wife and children, the first three women he made love to, the guard outside he'd made love to earlier that day, his best friends in grammar school, his grandparents…and his anger at the idiots who sent him to beat up the boy who shoots sparks out of his fingers." He looked up at me momentarily but the eyes were blank. He'd killed this memory long before, to the extent he could.

"I continued this way until I was twenty—it took me that long to learn how to only kill intentionally. I spent years in tutoring with teachers on the other side of a glass wall and watching other children play games outside. Occasionally I was allowed outings to the home of one or another of the scientists, for a meal or sitting with the family watching television. I was told it might be dangerous for me to swim—I might electrocute somebody. Ha!

"I can't blame them for being cautious—I killed three other men in that time. They kept trying to find some way to adapt the system or adapt me to the system. I was too valuable to waste—a mindreader who could read the enemy's secrets and memories and then fry him with a touch! A perfect assassin, if only I could be made fit for the task.

"In the meantime, they left me to my waveform experiments, my little hobby, in the classroom by myself day after day, setting off Bunsen burners across the room or making my hand merge with the desk."

"What?"

He looked at me quizzically and then laughed. "Oh! Yeah, it's—" And he placed his hand onto the card table between us and closed his eyes until the hand sank into the desk, until his arm just led to the desk and stopped there. I was gaping at it when he opened his eyes. "You have any change? A dime or a quarter or something?"

I had a two-dollar bill in my pocket. I always have it there. I know they still print them but I told myself it was lucky when I got it so it is. "Something," I answered.

"My fingers are under the table—give me what you've got."

I had to look under the table. There were fingers there, wiggling down out of the surface. I couldn't help it—I reached out and grabbed at the fingers.

"Ow!" he yelped and I jumped back. He huffed at me. "They're real, yes. If you pull on them, it hurts."

He held his other hand up in the air, pointed at me. "Remember what I do to people that hurt me, okay?" He looked serious for a split-second and then flashed the best smile he could.

"Just kidding—I don't do that anymore. Okay?" He looked at my hand—I had the two dollar bill scrunched down inside it. "So give me the change—I'll give it back."

I put my hand under the table and held the bill up against his fingers. He grabbed it away from me and slowly pulled the hand back up out of the glossy wood, the bill in his fingers. The corner was torn-off, just like it was when I first got it.

"Pretty good, eh?" he gloated and suddenly I could see that twelve-year-old boy alone in the lab who'd figured out a nifty magic trick to show off with. Except that, seeing that boy in his face, I knew finally that it wasn't a trick, that he did no tricks, that he could do what he said he could do, that he was what he said he was. The trick made him happy.

All the powers I'd seen—the things a greedy, ambitious man would have coveted—those didn't do anything for him. They seemed to depress him. Putting his hand through a desk and pulling out my two-dollar bill, that made him happy. It was a stupid, real moment. It was what I needed to know about him. I felt something inside me relax.

"It's amazing," I said. "What good is it?"

He laughed again—a sharp crack of a laugh, an exclamation, the laugh of someone who never expects to laugh. "Good? Nothing. If I lock my keys in the car, I don't have to worry. Otherwise, it's just a party trick."

"So you finished your training," I returned to the subject. "You were only twenty. What happened?"

"I was only twenty but I'm not history. History has its own timetable. By the time I learned to control myself, I was the dregs of a dying program in a dying country. The other experiments were long gone to embassies or assignments abroad—or asylums, if they didn't handle the training. The funding dried up, our handlers were bringing the remaining two or three of us meals from their own kitchens.

"Understand," he said, holding up his ring finger—it had a high school graduation ring on it, one of those silly rings nobody wears anymore, "I was raised to be an American. Maybe it was the Russian idea of America but generally, KGB was pretty good at it. Inside the facility, we watched Sesame Street and Beverly Hills 90210. I listened to the Police and Springsteen and Talking Heads—one of my teachers was big on Talking Heads. I read Thomas Paine and Jefferson, Twain and Bellow and Hunter Thompson. Like most immigrants, I know far more about America than most Americans.

"Of course, we were also taught about dialectical materialism and the inevitable march toward a communitarian world. But the training misfired in me. I was excited by the chaos of America, not the super-efficient Soviet state they told me about. If they'd let me out onto the street once in a while, maybe I wouldn't have looked so far away for my chaos.

"But I fell in love with the idea of America, the crazy quilt of too many races and too many ideas all fighting for breath. Communism was an ideology—it had the right answer for every question and I didn't believe in that. America sounded like Indiana Jones: 'I'm making this up as I go.' For a rebellious teenager, what could be better?

"So when they came—my babysitters—when they came one day and said 'It's time for you to go', I said 'Where? To do what?' I'd gotten a little training and I was no longer a danger to anyone, but it was clear to me and to most of the handlers that I was just no use as a spy." He laughed. "I'm just not the type. So I said 'What's my mission?' and they said, 'There's no mission. There's no one to spy for. The Soviet Union is over.'

"Viktor, the head man, gave me a winter coat—I think it was his, it was about three sizes too big for me—and ten thousand rubles, whose value was precisely nothing and less than nothing the next day. And set me out onto the street all alone. I'd never wandered anywhere on my own before, not once in my whole life.

"Novosibirsk was a city—not Miami, not New York, but a big city, big enough for me to see what was happening. The money wasn't worth anything. People continued to show up for work out of habit. There wasn't even food on the black market. The police were up for hire—if you could pay them, in hard currency, they would protect you. Everything was for sale—everything. The fear and the despair in everyone's heads—it was real ice-water for me, a cold shower, that this was the first real world I was let loose in." He stopped, awkwardly. It was like he'd never really talked about this before.

"In the lab, I heard people's thoughts but it was a controlled environment. We all had work to do. I knew from traces I'd picked up that things were getting difficult outside—everyone brings home to work and vice versa. But this was the first time I'd heard all those voices all at once and everyone in panic. It was…it was like being a child again, scared and alone and not really understanding anything that was happening. I wasn't ready for real life, for how ugly it could be."

He got up now and opened one of the sliding doors, hurriedly, like he had to get outside. A balcony stood under a retractable awning, hanging out over the edge of the cliff, a table with a few chairs standing against it and two potted plants going brown. The rain had let up and the streetlights were winking through the settling fog, showing off the contours of the canyon below. The hillside seemed to drop in tiers, first a shelf with trees, then a drop to another shelf, on and on unto infinity or at least unto town.

"I was out on the street overnight. That was all I could take. I have a little shame now for what I did—I could have stayed and tried to help my homeland—but I really doubt I could have done any good there. In truth, it didn't feel like home. They brought me up to be an American. Freedom of speech, press, religion, the sexual revolution, mind-expanding drugs, Pearl Jam, Harrison Ford and Gwyneth Paltrow.

"I found a woman who would take me in that first night. The next morning, I broke back into the program. No one resisted—no one cared. If I'd asked politely, they probably would have given me what I took—my birthrights as a spy; several passports, social security numbers, drivers licenses, the records for my bank accounts at Chase Manhattan, the ones containing dollars that had been set up for me years earlier. The Soviet Union had collapsed and I felt like an American—where should I go?"

He sat back, waiting for me to supply a judgment, a conclusion.

"So now you're an American," I said.

"For almost twenty years," he replied.

"Loyal to America," I said but it was a question. "It's what you were hoping it would be?"

"Hoping? This country? Hell, no. Who reads Jefferson—or Twain—here? Who *reads* in this country anymore? Russians read and debate all the time—they have fanatical debates about philosophical nothing. What is the price of a soul? Ask that on a street corner in Russia and take a seat for four hours—all you do is listen. Here, everything's about money and celebrity, for its own sake, shallowness for shallowness sake, to no purpose. Real estate goes up and up and up even though everyone knows it's overvalued—here, take a mortgage, no money down, no credit, no problem—and eventually it'll crash, down and down even though everyone knows it's land, it will never be worthless. The speculators make loads of money both ways and everyone else is miserable. It's a gold rush—what could be more American?

"No, this country is nothing like I hoped but I'm a true American now. I love what we stand for and hate what we do. I don't file my taxes, I'm hung up on sex but I never get any and I don't think much about freedom of speech, press or religion. And Harrison Ford hasn't made a decent movie in years." He looked down into the narrow infinity below and laughed.

"I'm not answering your question," he said quietly. "This is a beautiful country but there's lots of beautiful countries. There are good people and scumbags everywhere. Generally speaking, governments stink and religions stink and anything that tries to organize people into obedient groups stinks.

"My loyalty now is to Dave. He was a radical—he argued that this time, for the first time in history, human beings should *not* use a power they were given. That was a provocative thought but not one someone should die for. If America stands for anything good, it's that guys like Dave can be their benign crackpot selves without being punished for it."

"Maybe," I said, feeling profound, "he meant you should use the power for a good purpose." If it had been a movie, that would have been a key line. I could see Harrison Ford saying it.

Renn sighed and then coughed up a laugh. "I have a gift," he replied, "that has no positive use. I can root out things people want hidden and force people to do things they don't want to do. Where does positive fit in?" He went back into the living room and slid the door closed after I followed him in.

"And so, now I've told you my story. I've led you to a dangerous place and I'm not sure what the next step is. I don't know who these people are who are after us now; I don't know why they killed Dave. I know they aren't going to give up—we've gone a long distance away and I can still feel them probing for us every few minutes, even here. I won't keep you against your will and I wouldn't blame you for bailing. If you want to, I'll drop you in town in the morning."

"They'll torture me to get what I know about you."

"They wouldn't have to torture you in any case," he said. "But if I drop you off, you won't know anything about me—and they will be able to read that pretty quickly." He shrugged. "It's your decision. I'm not very pleasant but I'm not a jailer."

"What about the stuff in my head? The other names that might be there? Don't you need them?"

"I don't know. Maybe it doesn't matter. It won't bring Dave back, will it?"

"It *does* matter," I said as a reflex and knew in that instant it was everything to me. "We've got to get the guys that did it and find out why."

"Why?" he asked and I could see he was really listening, that for some reason he really needed an answer.

"Because we know they're out there, whoever they are. And because we—you—can do something about it."

"That simple?"

"He was my friend. And yours." He nodded. "That's pretty simple, I guess." Looking at his face, I thought, *He envies the fact that it's that simple for me.* And then I had another thought. "Of course," I said, "you knew I was going to say that."

He shrugged and laughed his grating laugh. "I don't have a choice," he said. "Thoughts like this don't mean much until you say them out loud. Or, really, until you *do* something about them."

"Okay," I said. "So now what do we do?"

"Now," he concluded, "we play cards."

Seven

"Seven."

"Wrong."

"Three," I said, straining to pluck an answer out of the air, trying to imagine the far side of the card he held in front of me.

"No."

"Nine. Two. Six Hundred and Fifteen."

"Funny," he said. "Okay, just stop what you're doing. Stop imagining. Stop trying to figure things out. You can't *learn* this; you just have to know it."

"That's stupid! How can you know something without learning it?"

He reached across the table and pinched my hand, hard. "Yeow!" I recoiled.

"There," he said calmly. "No learning involved. You don't *make* this happen. Stop trying to explain. Your conscious mind demands control; your subconscious just *knows*. Look at the card and say whatever comes into your head. Say it before your mind gets a chance to corrupt it."

"Like the Force," I said. "In Star Wars."

"No!" he said sharply, holding up that admonishing, dangerous finger. "Don't do that. The American mind control program fell apart from that kind of association—'New Age'; crystals, Vulcan mind melds, the love that overcomes all obstacles. *Good Vibrations*. Unless you're getting royalties from the song, there are no good vibrations. What's good in life vanishes in a breath; pain lingers forever."

He went through the deck, sorting the cards into two piles and then shuffling one pile. "Okay. I've narrowed it down—hearts, spades and diamonds, nothing else. Just tell me which. No thinking allowed. No questioning. Just say what you think as soon as you think it. Okay?"

"Okay."

He held up a card.

"Diamonds."

"Good." He made a mark on one side of a sheet of paper on the table.

"That was right?"

"Tell you later. This one." He held up another.

"Diamonds again," I said, sure I was doing it wrong.

"Very good," he said. "Next."

"Spades."

"Good. Next."

And so on. This went on for fifteen minutes. When we were done, the paper had scribbles on both sides. He tore it up immediately without looking at it and tossed it in the trash.

"How'd I do?" I asked, puzzled.

"Don't worry about it," he said.

"I want to know."

"It doesn't matter."

Now I got upset. "What do you mean, it doesn't matter? Why'd I do it then?"

He sighed. "I told you—what matters is that you have the feeling of knowing. Once you get that, you'll get better."

He could see on my face that I didn't find this a very satisfying answer.

"I told my teacher once," he said, "that I didn't think I could develop the skills we were working on. He told me, 'Don't worry about the skills; develop your confidence.' I said, 'How am I supposed to have confidence when I don't have the skill?' His answer was, 'Once you have the confidence, you'll find out you already had the skill.'"

"That's stupid," I told him.

He shrugged. "Maybe it is," he acknowledged. "A lot of life is stupid." He smiled and started putting the cards back in the box. "Once you loosened up," he said, "once you got bored and stopped trying to guess, you got around 65% correct. Way beyond mathematical probability. You have potential." The pleasure leaked out of the smile now. "Nothing kills more people than potential," he mused. For a moment, which was about as long as he ever mused about anything. Then he added, "Start concentrating on some really vivid moment in your life— something that really comes alive when you remember it. Probably something bad."

"Why bad?"

"I said already—pain lingers. Happiness becomes elusive as soon as it's over."

"Why?"

"At some point, things are going to get intense. You're going to have to block for yourself. If you can put your mind in some other place, into some other reality that isn't about *now*, you become hard to read. It's the simplest way to block." If this was the simple way, there didn't seem to be much point asking about the more complicated ones. I was totally lost. "Just try to remember something vivid," he said. "Like I said, it'll probably be bad and you'll have to be able to choose it—to choose to go back into it, really get inside it, at a moment's notice." Why would anyone want that, I thought, but he was already announcing, "I'm taking a shower. Then we should think about food."

I sat in the living room for a few minutes. I could have turned on the TV or caught up on my reading but I got up and opened the sliding door and went out onto the balcony instead. It felt like I'd been enclosed for months.

The view carried all the way on down the valley. The rain clouds were breaking up, the last glints of sun winking over the mountains and slinking through the streets of the town. A breeze was swirling at the base of the cliff, carrying leaves and twigs up off the rock shelves towards the house. The birds were out in packs, swirling around, twittering and making tight turns in loose formation. Together yet separate, like Max's world, bits of matter bound together by Good Vibrations. Or Bad Vibrations maybe, if you listened to him. If you believed he meant everything he said. I didn't believe *anybody* meant everything they said.

Dave used to take me fishing. We'd sit for hours without anything happening, line in the water, staring, barely talking. I'd get lost in the line in the water, in the little ring, the nipple that formed around the spot where the line fell into the water. I could just stare into the dark pool and drift for a long time and when I'd look up Dave would be smiling at me. We'd go for long walks along the boundaries of the marsh nearby, checking the fencing and repairing where it was breached or crooked or the wood frame was rotting. It annoyed me to be doing it; I knew nobody was paying him for the work and I didn't see why you needed a fence around a national park but Dave wanted to and that made it okay. He would point out the joint that needed a few nails and then point it out again, even though I was already looking at it.

Look at that knothole, he'd say, *is that the biggest knothole you ever saw in your life?* and I thought to myself, this guy's the fucking dweeb of the world, who cares about knotholes? But it would be the same thing with the trees and the birds and even the clouds. *Look how the edges change. Constantly shifting.* It took me a while to realize he was doing it with a purpose—he was bringing me back into the world, on a level I could handle. My door was shut tight; there wasn't a whole lot I was willing to let in but Dave just doggedly went at every little crack I'd left open, pushing till it opened a bit wider. I loved him like you love your dotty old aunt who doesn't know anything about the world but would sell her house for you in two minutes if you needed it. That's what I thought he was, dotty. But I also knew he was taking care of me and I knew I needed taking care of.

He convinced Mr. Dulles—Renn—Max—shit, how'd he keep all the names straight?—to come fishing with us once. There was never a man who couldn't fish like Max. He stared at the rod like it was a snake or something and he wouldn't drink beer even, which didn't put a damper on anybody but him. But they started arguing one time about something—something I didn't really get—and I told him to be more respectful of Dave. I yelled, I guess. It was probably about the first words I'd said in months around him or anybody at that point. And the back of my head went hot and I yelped and it stopped right away. And I can remember their faces when it happened—Renn looking sheepish and Dave intrigued.

I looked over the balcony at the birds darting and flickering in their dance and realized that was why I was with Renn, with Max. Dave didn't put me here for the protection of the program. He placed me here for *my* sake, because somehow being around Max was opening me up, helping to bring me back. I couldn't really be grateful to Max for this—it wasn't his plan; I wasn't at all sure he was even aware of it. And it really didn't make me any more grateful to Dave either—I couldn't be any more grateful to Dave than I already was. But it made everything feel a little more sensible, made it fit together. There was a flow to it. A harmonic. A good, positive vibration, haha.

A moment later, I heard his voice and turned to see him coming back into the living room, hair still damp, staring at his wristwatch and talking on a cellphone I hadn't seen before.

"...well, I'm glad I could amuse you. It isn't funny, Nick. Dave didn't just die; he was shot dead in the bathtub. If you guys aren't interested, *somebody* is. Alan Hammond was a visionary. He just hasn't been dead long enough to be proved right yet." He clicked off the phone. "Remember I told you I didn't work for America?"

"Let me guess—you lied."

"I didn't lie—to me, it just feels like it never happened. The job only lasted about three months, just a few months before 9/11.

A friend, an acquaintance really, put me in contact with Alan Hammond, the Senator. He wanted me to work with the Senate Intelligence Committee, to keep an eye on American spooks, keep them in line. That was back when this country still *wanted* to keep their own spooks in line. Of course, as soon as they debriefed me and convinced themselves I was on the level, they started pushing me to do other things for them, the kind of things I wouldn't have done for the Soviet either. Things that sent me running to the Everglades."

"Dave knew you'd run?"

"Dave was one of the guys who debriefed me. There was Dave, Scott Cornwell and Alan Hammond's aide Jim Avery. Cornwell was my runner and it turns out he still has the same phone number. I just called and asked him if they'd restarted the old program—or anything like it."

That's where I stopped him, as you'd imagine. You probably wonder what took me *that* long but, for a moment, I'd thought he had to be kidding.

"Jim *Avery*?" I asked.

"Yeah," he said, giving me the eye again but my head didn't burn. "Cornwell laughed when I asked where Avery was. He said he's got his own business."

I laughed—I didn't want to make him feel dumb but I couldn't help myself. "No kidding," I said. "You don't watch TV?"

"Avery's on TV?"

"*Jim* Avery? This is *Your World*?" He stared at me like I was talking riddles. "He's on 24 hours a day, seven days a week. He's got his own *channel!*" Renn went wide-eyed. My pilot light was on dim the whole time at Dave's but you had to be completely off to miss Jim Avery.

It took a little while to find the channel on the set in the living room—it was channel 152 or something—but then we basked in the glow of Jim Avery's greatest hits: *Be Everything You Are* and *Why Settle for Less than your Whole Self?* and the inevitable *It's Your World*, chanted by Avery and huge crowds in LA, New York, Seoul, London, Rome, Frankfurt, New Delhi, Hong Kong, Moscow, Vancouver and Prague, among others. They had ads for *Your World* vacations and 24-hour video-on-demand.

"Wow," Max said and I had to nod.

"You should ask *him* for a job," I said. "He's the biggest thing going."

Max kept staring at the tube. "It's him," he said haltingly. "But that's not his hair—it has to be a toup, or implants maybe." He started pacing around the room, looking deflated. "I see why they laughed at me—whatever became of poor Jim Avery. Wow!"

"What did Cornwell say about the program?"

"There's no program—hasn't been in years. He said the only reason he could answer me at all was that there was nothing to it."

"You believe him?"

"I'm not big on belief. I listened to the *sound* of his voice more than what he was saying, listened to the vibrations like a stress detector. If he was lying, I would know. And," he added, "he was one of the people who debriefed me several years ago. So he knew I would know, which means there's no point lying." He tapped a finger on the table—the first two times it tapped; the next two it went right into the wood, disappeared right through. He was apparently doing it without being aware of it. This would get real confusing if somebody unaware saw him. Did he do it all time without being noticed? That was a scary thought all on its own.

"I asked him about L Corp," he continued. "He said security was a sideline, they were mostly political consulting and lobbying, media management and such." He shook his head. "Not the place you'd expect a Miriam Fine. Or platoons of thugs with feeble mindbender power." He came back to the couch now. "We can research it later. First, I think we should go out to dinner."

"Out? Isn't that dangerous?"

He shrugged again. "Everything's dangerous—it's just a question of more or less. I don't think they've found us yet."

That sure didn't sound very conclusive. I was hoping for something a whole lot stronger, but he didn't seem to be offering. "Could they have traced the phone call?" I asked.

"I doubt it," he said casually. "Fischel's just a committee staffer—he's not high on the food chain. If they were tapping him for some reason, it would take a minute to recognize this conversation as worth tracing. I bounced the call off two Soviet satellites that are still up there and I timed it—believe me, they're not as fast as the movies."

"That's it? That's all the reassurance the world's best mindbender can offer?"

"If I wait for better than that," he shrugged, "I never get to go out to dinner."

The town downvalley was bigger than it looked—it had the remnants of a low-rent amusement park along with a reptile zoo, several hotels and restaurants clustered along the main roads leading out to the highway—there was also a *Your World* Center, which I gleefully pointed out to Max as we passed. We ended up in a shed-like place off the beaten track, with an electric sign bigger than the restaurant and a round dance floor in the middle of a raised circle of dinner tables. The signs hanging by the side of the door promised Kansas steak, local lake trout and 800 different beers from around the World. They had internet access—you could order dinner from Singapore, though it didn't mention delivery. There were a crowd of customers, but mostly at the bar and dance floor. Max shook the maitre d's hand and he stiffened and led us immediately to a table with a clear view of the entrance and easy access to the emergency exit.

The bar was filled with several clusters, milling and circulating and laughing a little too loudly, the general crowd trying a little too hard to have a good time, as opposed to the hard-core drunks at the small tables near the far end of the bar.

It's funny how you can find the person you're looking for in a crowd, even if you didn't know you were looking. A bright-eyed dark-haired girl standing with her blonde friend right at the center of everything, for example, watching faces and sharing confidences and trying to look carefree. At first I thought, maybe they're more than friends—they were hanging close and you can't tell these days. But when she turned around, her eyes said she was looking and not finding. And it just hit me hard, as soon as I saw those eyes full-on: I just knew who she was. I knew what she was feeling all too well. It wasn't a memory, it was like I was *inside* that feeling, inside her, the hope and bitterness flashing through me all at once. There are other feelings I'd have chosen to revisit before that one.

Max nudged me. "Ask her to dance," he said. "Go on."

"Go away," I said. "We're incognito."

"You're a man out for dinner with his business partner. We're on a business trip—we leave in the morning. A convenient cover story. Get used to having one." He leaned into my ear. "She'll like you," he said.

"You know that for a fact?" I asked but he just sat back, staring at the ceiling, all innocent eyes. When the waiter brought us our two out of the 800 beers of the World, I asked him to bring her and her friend whatever they were drinking. Max said, "No—

ask her to dance," but this was how I knew to do it. And, as soon as they got the drinks, she smiled at me and I smiled back and three seconds later, the two of them were sitting down in the booth next to us.

"I'm Tess," she said, holding out her hand. "This is Cindy. Thanks for the drinks."

"I'm Greg," I said "and this is Max." I hadn't thought twice about it but when I looked over at him now, he looked petrified, frozen in place. He sat straight as a ramrod with his eyes flashing, sharp, like he was surrounded by a vile of snakes. The girls somehow didn't seem to notice, which was kind of amazing.

Cindy offered her hand. Max shook it, jerky, out-of-synch. She didn't seem to notice this either. Tess, meanwhile, was staring at me with eyes the size of flying saucers.

"You guys aren't from around here," she said.

"You know *everybody* around here?" I said and they both laughed, which was charitable—it wasn't much of a joke.

"Actually, I do," she answered. "I'm the county registrar. If you have a last name, I can tell you what you paid in taxes last year." She nestled up next to me, our arms and legs touching—her skin was warm, nice muscle tone. She was actually pretty buff. "Assuming you filed."

"Don't tell her anything," Cindy said and we laughed some more.

"We pay no taxes in this area," Max said, forcing himself to speak. "We're just here overnight—our businesses are upriver. We have inspections to do tomorrow." I kicked him under the table—*lighten up, dude.* He was treating them like the Board of Directors.

"I didn't think there was anyplace around here people wanted to go," Cindy said; I laughed at this too before realizing she was serious.

Every time I looked at Tess, the world calmed down. I didn't feel like I had to do anything in particular to get her to like me. At the same time, Cindy was listening to Max go over the details of our profit projections, all moon-eyes, like it was the most romantic thing anyone had ever said to her. Max kept smiling really hard, which only made his face more frightening-looking.

"What do you do?" I asked Cindy, trying to keep the train from going completely off the tracks.

"I'm a trainer," she said, with a little hesitation.

"Cindy's a *Worldie*," Tess said in a vague combination of envy and disdain.

"I'm a *third-level*," Cindy burst now, with the zest of the true believer. "I train graduates and other trainers. We've got people who come back ten and fifteen times, to make sure they get it, to keep their hope level up. We've only been open a year here but we've already got a base of almost 200 just in this area."

"If she keeps doing what she'd doing," Tess added, "she'll move up to state level."

"It's so *spiritual!*" Cindy exhaled. I saw Max shrinking into the corner of the booth but it was too late to stop myself—the words were already halfway out of my mouth.

"*Your World?* Y'know, Max actually used to know Jim Avery."

If a look could strangle you across a table, I'd have been dead in a dumpster one second later.

"Omigod, you *know* him?" Cindy turned with a beatific look. "He changed my life—he taught me to *believe* in my dreams. Isn't it—?"

"*Knew* him," Max interrupted roughly. "*Knew. Years* ago. For a *very* short period of time."

"When? What was he like?" Cindy sputtered. "What happened? Have you kept in contact? Would he know you if he saw you again?"

"You want to dance?" I asked Tess and we both jumped out of the booth. I felt the back of my head burning hot but I'd seen that one coming and just kept putting one foot in front of the other.

It was a slow song and I got to hold her pretty much beginning to end. I hadn't held a woman in a long time. It was terrifyingly wonderful, though I don't know why terrifying. I'd had women in my arms before. We talked all the way through the song but the words got less and less important as we went on.

'You really aren't staying around?" she said.

"Business," I shrugged, genuinely unhappy about my fictional life, whose consequences were the same as my real one. Which is the merger, I guess, that makes a good cover story work.

"I never thought I'd meet someone like you in a place like this," she said and that turned me around all of a sudden. We'd had one dance and I was a little light-headed too but I couldn't get three words out of my mouth two or three days earlier, so I had an excuse. What was hers? Then she said, "You want to go to the car and fool around a little?" which put me over the limit. I dragged her off the floor and back to the table.

Renn was wedged into a corner of the booth, bending spoons without touching them while Cindy explained the world according to Jim Avery to him. He wasn't even trying to hide his discomfort. Was he gay? I wondered and then rejected the thought. If he was gay, they'd be best friends and discussing window treatments. Maybe he was in the closet? Whatever the reason, he was ignoring her and she just kept yammering, oblivious, like she was getting paid by the word.

"Excuse us a second," I interrupted and grabbed Renn by the shoulder. I might have pulled him out of his chair; I was kind of running on instinct. I'm not sure if he was shocked or relieved but he let me drag him a few feet away.

"What are *you* mad about?" he protested, shouting over the music.

"You're making us wonderful," I said, shouting back. "You're forcing them to like us."

"You're getting lucky and I'm learning how believing in myself—and paying Jim Avery a monthly stipend—will make all my problems seem insignificant. I'm six minutes into a fifteen minute monologue, all of which I've already heard her rehearse twice in her head—so, again, what are *you* mad about?"

"Hey, most people pay $450 for the 2-hour *Your World* evening session. You're getting it for free."

"Free is too expensive," he said. "Anyway, I'm not forcing them. I'm just making them receptive."

I could feel my eyes narrow. "And the difference is—?"

"The difference is, I have some scruples. If she doesn't like you, she doesn't. If she sees something she likes in you, she doesn't fight it."

"That's scruples? You're still coercing her."

"It's easy to be black-and-white," he shrugged, "when you have no power. I could easily force her to sleep with you and everyone in the room. The fact that I don't doesn't make me pure, but it *is* a form of scruples."

"Well, knock it off," I said. "Let me get there on my own."

He sighed okay. We returned to the table, where the ladies were waiting, and I could see immediately that the light in their faces had faded. We weren't so fascinating anymore. Now they seemed to be sizing us up a bit, checking to see if we were worth the effort. More like what I was used to.

"We're working on this new thing—paraskiing," Max stammered, taking furtive, nervous looks at both women. He'd been nervous when he had them firmly under control. Now he was a wreck. "You ski down a hill wearing a parasail...no...I mean, you ski down the hill and...deploy...the sail just after you go...over the edge—there has to be a cliff, of course...and you drift down...to wherever you land. Of course, you need a lot of cleared space down there...down below...for landing...because the sail tends to drift and...you don't...want to come down in the trees. You could break something."

He was dissolving quickly, like a standup comic who knows he's bombing. I realized what must have happened—he'd searched (the room? The state?) for a mind with an edgy entrepreneurial idea and he'd found one—a really *stupid* idea, dangerous on every count. "But you wouldn't believe the numbers," he continued now, trying to cover himself, throwing good money after bad. "Parasails really don't cost much and...the people who pay to take risks pay big money for it. In fact, if you don't charge them *enough*, they get—" I grabbed him, held a hand up in front of the girls and dragged him away again.

"What the hell is this about?" I demanded.

"I'm no good at this," he answered. He was sweating like a pig.

"How good do you have to be? Idiots manage it every day."

"Idiots have instinct," he said without self-pity, as though this was something I should have known about him. "All I know is what's in their minds. They want a man who does something extreme-ish though not too much and Cindy likes money, too."

"That doesn't mean you just start babbling every detail, dammit."

"Well, how else is she going to know?"

"Let her figure it out! It's a mystery—*you're* a mystery. She'd rather guess you have money than be sure." I couldn't believe it. "You're *naturally* mysterious when you're not trying."

"I'm—she's pretty," he stammered. "When the girl's pretty, I'm just not natural," he said unnecessarily and we retreated back to the table.

Tess was flashing looks at me now, with a sort of desperate hope in her eyes. Cindy was eyeing both entrances with an equally desperate hunger. I suddenly remembered what dating was like and understood how alluring it would be to just be able to control things.

"We have several businesses," Renn segued, trying to get himself under control. "Rafting, skydiving, extreme skiing, gliders—Greg's big on gliders."

All eyes were suddenly on me and I realized—shockingly—that I actually knew something about gliders. "Gliders are amazing," I started and suddenly there were pictures in my head and a tingle in my voice because the memories were coming back to me in waves. "They tow you down the runway and it doesn't feel fast enough and then the plane in front of you starts to lift off and you realize you're already floating behind it and you didn't even feel the takeoff. And they pull you higher and higher and it's noisy and buffety and then they release the cable and, all of a sudden, you're just there, all alone, rock steady over everything. There's this amazing moment when you realize it really is going to work, you're not just going to plummet to the ground. You're just a hiss through the air and everything gets slow and easy, like you're suspended in time and space. You're not going anywhere and you have all the time in the world to do it. And then you're on the ground again, way too soon."

I had no idea if this was a memory or a dream. But it felt real inside me. At some point, I'd had a moment of nutty daring and taken that risk, for no reason at all.

The girls were staring at me, eyes wide and bright. I'd put it over. I looked at Max and he was smiling and the look on his face said *You did it on your own, pal*. Except I hadn't—he'd found my best memory to spark, for me to build on.

"C'mon," Tess said, grabbing me by the hand and pulling hard, "we're going for a *drive*."

We didn't drive very far, ending up behind a hardware store nearby. It looked closed for the night but she said 'They're bankrupt' in a tone of voice that said *Don't question the county registrar* and that was enough for me. We parked out near the dumpster in back and pawed each other for an hour or so. It just tore me up to have her—nothing was what I expected. We laughed and got off really nice at first and I was just gassed being there, my hands on her, my mouth on her, giving and getting pleasure. But after a while, my feelings got gummed-up, a bit more complicated. When I kissed her, I tasted other kisses; when I touched her breast, I remembered other breasts. Good feelings here and there, good moments but bad ones too, fights and jealousy and lies. It occurred to me that I was remembering the feelings without being able to remember the women and that felt kind of shameful. I'd lived a while without a memory and that was beginning to feel like a blessing. It took a big effort to try and shove those feelings back into the murk and just be with her. I never completely succeeded at it, to tell the truth.

When we got back to the restaurant with the huge electric sign, she kissed me goodbye like she meant it and said "If you ever get back around here, I'll be at Town Hall." And that really shredded me—it had been a long time since anybody wanted me, much less wanted me *again*. I knew I'd never be back and if I was, it wouldn't be the same anyway. I was pretty sure she knew that too. Which left me tingling with feeling as I got out of the car, feeling in all directions, sensitive to everything everywhere—the breeze and the damp in the air, the sound of the cars on the highway six blocks away, the smell of her on my fingers. I felt *alive.* I wanted to bottle that feeling, hold onto it as long as it would linger. It was already fading by the time she turned out of the lot.

Max was in a Subaru with the flared fenders and big tires, the turbo and the wing on the back, the whole tuner thing. I knew a guy in Iraq who had the same model. He kept buying parts for it off the Web, week by week; his brother would install them and send him the pictures and little videos of it racing in the neighborhood. They lived in Cincinnati. He came home with no arms or legs. I remembered that all at once, looking at the car. It was another thing I'd forgotten—at least, that was my first thought. But you can't be aware of forgetting something, can you?

I got in the passenger seat and Max started driving back up into the hills, toward the house. Neither of us spoke for a while and then finally I said, "This self-awareness stuff is for shit."

"It's a mixed bag," he said. "Like most things."

"It's for shit," I repeated.

He waited a moment—I could almost see him biting his tongue—and then he couldn't seem to stop himself from going on. I wondered if he had some kind of impulse control problem. "You still have a choice. I can let you off and you can go back to the life you had."

"We have to get the guys who got Dave," I said. That wasn't changing.

"It only gets worse," he warned. "There are a lot of things you're getting by ignoring, that are going to be dragged up, that you're going to have to deal with. And eventually, you'll see through everyone and everything."

"But you're in control then, right?"

"Ha! When the girl says 'yes,' instead of feeling your own happiness, you feel her doubts about you—or how inflated her hopes are. When your friends say you told a funny joke, you'll know different. You'll know when you bore them. You'll know when the salesperson is cheating you—you'll know when the doctor asks for tests but knows already you're very sick. You'll have nothing to do but track your enemies—or just stay away from people altogether."

"Why that? Why does that follow?"

"Look at the company you've been keeping these few days," he said. "I was fine when I could fade into a swamp. I was away from people, so I was fine. Tauber stayed among the voices and chewed himself up. Our skills are only useful when we have enemies to hunt, secrets to uncover. Otherwise, life is empty, without purpose, without hope of purpose."

"I've been there already," I said. "This is better. I was locked in myself. Now I'm out." I looked at him with some gratitude. "You've liberated me."

He soaked that in and sighed. "These last couple of days have been a liberation for me, too—but an evil one. It's a horrible wonderful temptation, needing danger to feel free, to feel useful. I need evil in the world so I can do good."

"We'll beat them," I said, not understanding his point.

"I hope so," he answered. "But then what will we do?"

Eight

There are kids squirreling around the shed, maybe eight, nine years old. They might be stealing something—that would be okay. But they might not. They hide bomb material in sheds like that sometimes—they could be using the kids to get it or set the fuses. They use them like that sometimes too. We met a guy who was stationed in Najaf who said that happened to his outfit last week. Maybe there's another reason—maybe they're just playing—but we don't know. And what you don't know can hurt you. So our fingers are on triggers, everybody's fingers, waiting, tense, clenched twitching. Eventually Marshall's finger twitches and we have screaming kids with a bullet through the jaw or a broken collarbone or something. Maybe there was a reason. Maybe there wasn't.

We're convoying. We're always convoying. Low stretches of stores and houses, business signs in Arabic, French and English, laundry hanging from windows and long corridors of smooth wide highway—Saddam built great roads, gotta give him that. We pass a market and everybody in the stand waves. We wave back— this is the first couple weeks, where people are still waving. I hear a noise and look the other way for just a second—when I look back, the woman behind the stand is leveling a Kalishnikov at us. The first time it was a woman, we hesitated. Hendricks took a round in the neck that time, just above the armor. Now, nobody hesitates—she takes about twenty rounds in three seconds, the blood seeping into the sand as fast as it comes out of her and then her body seeping into the ground, swallowed up like quicksand or vanishing powder.

We drive as fast as we can go. Anything, just *anything*, could be a bomb—garbage cans, maildrops, cardboard boxes along the road. They trigger them with alarm clocks, cell phones, garage door openers, VCR remotes. Clever shit people here, dammit. The first time we take a direct hit, we start cursing a blue streak and laughing, laughing from relief. *Shit, that was big. Good baby, good baby, this Hummer is good.* What nobody says but everybody thinks is *We made it.* But sometimes, it isn't bombs—it's just bullets, stray bullets, aimed bullets, who knows? This time, the big diesel rig in front of us takes five bullets in the engine and loses power and we leave him behind with a Hummer to take on personnel. We keep moving—we've got three more trucks to get to destination. *Watch that bottle there—move that fucking VW, make him move.* It's boring and endless; beyond all the rest, the *tension* can kill you.

And two minutes later, the horizon erupts, end to end—the earth jumps up and down like it's a trampoline and the world ahead is billowing smoke. The KBR truck in front took an IED and there's a hole the size of a house in the middle of the highway. So now we've got to stop, stop completely, try to establish a perimeter and bag everything—all the pieces, shards of bone and bits of flesh, any speck that might have once been part of a person. *Is this something? Take it.* Inspecting every sliver, every fiber on the ground, carefully, thoroughly, always aware we're stopped, stopped dead, completely in the open. They'll shoot us, shoot at us. That's what they do. They do it when we're hauling sixty around the perimeter so what are they going to do now that we're hauling zero in the middle of town, on our knees picking up the pieces? They'll be shooting and soon. Ignore it. Keep looking. Miss nothing. Take everything that's human, every mote that might be, anything that might once have breathed. Don't miss one…anything. Because there's folks at home who don't want to be watching TV one night and see part of their kid being waved around, beaten on, burned up one last little bit more by some raghead geek on a bridge. Don't miss a speck.

And then I was awake—breathing hard in total darkness and, after flicking the light on, in an illuminated room that meant nothing to me, that could have been anywhere in the world— anywhere other than where I'd been a second earlier. And knowing that anywhere other than that was a better place to be.

The sheets looked almost new, unused, unwrinkled, like I'd spent the night paralyzed—but they were drenched as well. I pulled the shades open and cut my fingers on the vanes as they whipped upward. Dropping below were the cliffs, rock ledges and trees pointing toward town, the town where we'd been earlier last night, where life was.

It's the master bedroom, is what came to me slowly, the world returning to me or me to it, whatever. *Max gave me the master bedroom since he wasn't a sleeper.* A family bedroom—makeup and perfume bottles on the dresser, an analog and a digital clock atop one night table and a pile of romance novels on the other, several pairs of slippers in the corner by the closet, grandchildren photos, the progression of growing up, sweeping across the wall opposite—all the tokens of intimacy, of a long life of deep ties. It was strange, eerie, more alien to me than the landscape in my nightmares. I stared out the window again, at the tiered hillside, at the third ridge down, where Max had left the Subaru just a few yards off the road—"we don't need anybody seeing a strange car in the driveway," he'd said–just seeking landmarks, markers, boundaries. Nothing seemed familiar. It was the real world. I was an alien everywhere.

I banged my elbow on the way out of the room, stumbling into the dresser. Five steps later, I ran right into the crawlspace door. I was sure I'd closed it the night before—it was hanging open when we came in. Damn, that hurt! The whole place was out to attack me.

"L Corp was founded six years ago, right after September 11th," Max said, looking up from the computer as I hobbled into the living room. "The restaurant last night has more real information on their site than L Corp does."

"Maybe they're just from the old school," I offered.

"I don't think so," he replied. "The most interesting part is the blurb on 'security solutions'—it's buried three pages deep in the 'Products' section. 'Innovative security solutions that go far beyond intelligence gathering, threat scenarios and routine digital imaging. L Corp has a track record of identifying impending threats to both physical and information assets and responding before they can become active.'"

"Sounds impressive. What's it mean?"

"It's jargon for 'We figure out what's going to happen and stop it before it does.'"

"Mmm. Mindbenders would be good at that."

"That occurred to me," he said coolly. He stood up. "Do me a favor, would you? I'm getting a headache trying to find an address for the security headquarters. You think you can find it?"

"I'll do better after breakfast."

"There's English muffins and eggs on the table—I just finished mine." He arched an eyebrow again. "Eat quickly."

"Why?"

"We're being probed again and much closer than last night. I just sent them on a wild goose chase. So I think we have about two hours grace."

"I'll be ready in ten minutes," I told him.

"Good. But I have something to do that'll take fifteen, maybe twenty."

"What?"

"Visiting L Corp headquarters."

"Where is it?"

"I don't know. That's why I want you to get me the address."

"What if it's a thousand miles from here?" I asked. This made no sense, though that no longer threw me in Max's company. "How're you going to get there in fifteen minutes?"

"You just get me the address—actually longitude and latitude would be better. Let me worry about getting there."

"—and back."

"And back," he said, attempting to reassure me, which he wasn't much good at.

He proceeded to the center of the room, sat cross-legged on the floor and began his Ommm thing again. I wandered into the kitchen, put together my muffin and eggs and started searching the web site. Nothing came easy—eventually, I drilled down below 'Join Us' to where five security jobs hid beneath 'subcontractor tasking'. All five were based in Herndon, Virginia though I couldn't find any company telephone listing there.

"All I can get you is the town," I told him and he held a hand up for a moment, to shush me long enough for his coma to pass.

"I'll make do," he said. "Just write the coordinates on a piece of paper. I'll be gone for maybe fifteen, twenty minutes, tops. My body will be here but I won't. If the house burns down or the IRS shows up to confiscate the place, I'll be dead weight unless you wake me. If you have to kick or punch me a bit, that's okay — just make sure it's necessary, okay?"

"Whoah," I said. "Replay that one for me. The body'll be here but you won't?"

"It's called remote viewing. I'll be at L Corp, hovering and eavesdropping, just getting the lay of the land."

"Isn't it dangerous to float around without a body? Can they see you?"

"They'd have to know how and they'd have to be looking for me. They're not the KGB," he said roughly. "Contractors talk big but their own security stinks, generally. They get complacent. I don't know if they have anything we want but Fine works there so it seems like the next move."

"Without a body, can you see through walls? Read the files in the vault?" It was weird even asking the question but, following everything else I'd seen, this was just another step.

"If the VP has something interesting on his desk," he said, "I can read the top page—as long as it's not numbers. If I want to see more, I have to convince him to turn the page. Which, strangely enough, isn't so easy when my body's at a distance."

"And I'll be able to wake you up if there's trouble? You're sure?"

"I don't see why not." This didn't sound real conclusive.

"Has anyone tried it? Lately?"

"You'll be fine."

"What if they probe again? While you're away, are you still blocking me?"

"No, I can't. I won't be here. Just pretend you're someplace you were last week or last month." He glanced at the ceiling: I could see him trying to figure out how to explain this next thought. "Consciousness is time-specific," he told me.

"In English, please."

"One time the Americans had a mindbender agent locked in a dark room in Maryland. His job was to describe a site he'd never seen or heard of in California. The Agency was sending a team to the location, who also had never been there—his job was to read their minds and describe what they saw. As soon as he was given the task, he performed it, including a description of a specific routine the camp personnel performed for the team's visit."

"Wow," I said, not sure what this had to do with blocking. Or time-specific consciousness. Or anything else, for that matter.

"Oh, that's not the interesting part," Max said. "What's interesting is that the California team got held up by bad weather. They didn't arrive until three hours *after* the agent finished describing their visit."

"Huh?" I tried to wrap my head around this but 'huh?' was all I got.

"All time exists at once—Einstein predicted this. So the agent locked onto the people he was supposed to track and read their impressions of the site. It's just that they hadn't been there yet. And the things they saw—that he reported—hadn't happened yet." He laughed at the expression on my face. "Tauber could've told you all about this—they sent him back once to meet *Jesus*." At this point, he wisely gave up trying to explain. "Okay, here's what you need to know: if you put yourself in any other place *or* time— back with that girl in the car last night, or in Iraq again; something so vivid you're not just remembering but really *there*, these guys'll never be able to read you, probe you, anything. They're looking for someone who's here, now. And you won't be." He stared at me for a while, waiting.

"I'll never figure out how to do that," I said finally.

"But you already *have*, Gregor," he laughed. "That's how you spent half your time in Florida." I hated being called Gregor. He settled into his crouch again, humming to stir the rafters.

There were still eggs left in the kitchen. I threw another muffin in the toaster and wandered around. I wanted cereal. There were Corn Flakes in the cupboard but no milk in the fridge. We had a guy at Dave's who ate cereal with orange juice, but he wasn't someone I wanted to be like. We had guys who blinked uncontrollably or freaked out at loud noises or picked their skin raw. If sanity was a matter of degree, eggs and a muffin were better than cereal and orange juice, as far as I was concerned.

That's what I was thinking when I looked out the window and saw the vans coming hard up the driveway.

"Max! Come on, Max! Time to wake up Max! Now! *Now!* Max, no time for sleeping. Back to the world now! Shit! Shit shit shit shit shit!!!" He was in full trance mode, of course. I pummeled his shoulders and kicked him in the back and the butt and anyplace else I could kick him without breaking anything but he wasn't stirring. Pulling and shaking—same result. The vans were screeching to a halt now and I could hear footsteps all around the house. I left him long enough to push a kitchen cabinet up against that door—happily, it was just a few inches. I saw dark-blue jumpsuits swarming outside the windows. Happily, the windows were where the house overhung the cliff so they couldn't reach them to get in--yet. The front of the house—the part that faced the horse runs—had a hundred little cubby-hole windows but no big plate glass you could shatter and walk through—apparently, the owners liked their privacy. But this didn't buy me much time—they were already smashing against the door and it was making buckling noises. I had a choice: surrender out front or dive over the cliff—suddenly this didn't seem like such a great hideout.

And then I heard a commanding voice—deep, foreign accent, powerful, someone used to being listened to—bellowing "You said he was here! Where?"

"He *was* here! We matched his waveform from Raleigh—100%!"

A third voice: "The other one's here."

"Who cares? I want *Renn*! Open this door, damn you!"

And then, somehow, I knew what to do. I grabbed Max under the arms and dragged him across the floor—he was like lead, the son-of-a-bitch—to the crawlspace. I shoved his body inside and checked the door twice to make sure it closed. Then I ran like a maniac to the kitchen, grabbed the biggest carving knife I could find and ducked onto the balcony.

It was a sheer drop directly below but there were trees growing from the next ledge, about six or eight feet down—something like that, I'm no good at estimating. Too far to jump, I knew that. I was getting vertigo just peeking over the edge. I mounted the table on the balcony and scrambled up onto the awning, climbing toward the top. It was a rickety old green canvas thing that barely held my weight—I could hear the aluminum arms creaking under me as I went. At the top, the awning was tied to the roof, thick rope looped through metal eyes punched into the canvas. The metal arms below ended with four screws set into wood blocks—old moldy wood, cracked and covered with flecks of old paint.

As I reached the top of the awning, I heard the crash of the front door splintering open and men kicking their way into the house. I had seconds left. I drove the knife down hard, hacking at the rope in two places, hoping I'd cut through both at roughly the same time. The cable was old and brittle—the strands flew apart with every swing of the knife. The awning sagged immediately, slumping down and forward over the edge of the balcony. I grabbed hunks of canvas and held on for all I was worth. Then I stretched my legs out and pushed off hard from the wall.

I failed science in school. Several times. I was good with words because they could be manipulated, played with—I could make them do what I wanted. Facts, natural law—those things don't bend to the will quite so easily.

I'd visualized the awning ripping loose from the wall, catching the wind like a parachute and cushioning my fall to the treetops below, a relatively soft landing leaving me a head start running from the blue-jumpsuit crowd.

Of course, nothing remotely like that happened. I pushed hard enough to split the final strands of rope and carry the awning over the edge. One end did indeed rip out of the wood mounting. But the other held and the whole shrieking assembly dropped down in an arc, skittering sideways across the rock face, scraping loud as a factory, until the bottom end hit the first tree it found and stopped dead. The impact jarred me loose instantly, ripped my hands free and I fell. I had enough time in midair, the world gone slow-motion, to understand what an idiot I was even trying something this ridiculous and to blame the movies that had convinced me I had any chance of success.

And then I hit hard and the wind went completely out of me.

I'm not sure how long it was before I could think again. It couldn't have been very long but I drifted back to consciousness, fading in as from a dream or some potent anesthesia, to treetops swaying in the updraft and the sound of voices—not words but sound, a flat kind of music, John Cage wind chimes, which must have been what Cage had in mind in the first place.

As I came to and checked above me, I realized I'd succeeded—at least partly. My hasty plan was both to get away and, crucially, to draw them after me. When I'd heard the commanding voice outside calling 'Where is he!' I'd realized that, as long as Max was in his coma, they couldn't read him at all. Somehow they'd broken through his blocking, because they'd found us. But, while he was out-of-body traveling, he was in a different place, like he'd said—so he'd disappeared off their radar. Above me now, I saw ropes dropping over the side of the balcony and climbers starting to lower themselves over the edge, so the second part of my plan was succeeding.

The other part, I realized, might be a bit more complicated.

If I'd managed my soft landing in the trees, my feverish plan was to climb down and hustle over to the car, two ledges below. If I could lure the bad guys after me, Max could come to undisturbed in the crawlspace, reverse time and space and send them all packing to some other dimension for rest and recreation. Yeah, it sounds stupid now but this hope was no more outrageous than several things he'd already done and, under the circumstances, I clung to it like a raft in a hurricane.

What was—painfully—clear, though, was that the hardest part of this plan would be getting out of the tree, or maybe even just sitting up and trying to move. I was taking inventory of my body; there were parts that hurt like hell and parts I couldn't feel at all; my suspicion was that the parts that hurt were the good ones.

I managed to roll over, just enough to take a look around— and nearly fell out of the cradle of branches I'd landed in. I managed to grab on and roll back carefully, discovering a whole new group of body parts that hurt like hell. My right ankle didn't feel good and my cheek was all cut up from falling through pine needles—there's a *reason* they call them needles—at about 700 miles an hour. It was encouraging in a sick sort of way—if they weren't numb, they probably weren't broken. I wasn't a doctor, so my figuring didn't count for much but at least I could be optimistic as long as I was in pain.

The branches sagged under me way out over the edge of the cliff—I had really misjudged the direction of my fall. It was a long drop below, acres of rock leading to the inevitable Wile E. Coyote river at the base of the cliff. If I was getting out of here—and I'd better get out before sag turned to collapse—the only way was to climb down the branch, slide downhill to the next shelf and beat the climbers to our car. Oh yeah—and be somewhere else at the same time so they couldn't read my mind.

The web of branches dipped with every move and the climbers were halfway to me. It's amazing how much being in the crosshairs can motivate you. I told myself I didn't care how much I hurt, took a deep breath and pushed down the branch, arching my back so as not to take all of them full in the crotch. With multiple contusions and the wind knocked out of me, I made it to the trunk in eight seconds, with the cradle of branches creaking and cracking but holding. I put one foot onto the branch below—the branch held and, amazingly, so did the ankle. I rolled over and carefully put the right one down—it burned like a stove but held too. After that, it was a scramble for the bottom. Needles pricked, branches stabbed, I wrenched my knees twice and my back. But I made it to the ground.

Touching down and digging my toes in, I nearly swooned from the pain shooting up my legs but I didn't stop moving. I heard them shouting behind me, "There he is! There!" and I wondered how they could not know where I was—couldn't they read me in the tree? I hadn't been trying to block them.

And then I realized I had. All the time I was climbing down, I was already at the bottom. I'd seen myself all the way standing at the foot of the tree, worrying about my ankles, about getting away. Max said *shift into the future* and I'd done it. Now I ran towards the car, taking no precautions. If they could see me, let them follow, at least for the moment.

Just ahead, a bundle of trees, thick and tightly-placed, thrust up over the ridge, covering the view from above. When I reached that spot, I'd be out of their sight. If I could block them when I got there, putting my mind back in the rear seat of the car with Tess— she seemed plenty vivid at the moment—I could slide down between the trees to the next ledge and hopefully make it to the car before they caught up with me. I'd let them read me once I got close to the car. If I got away with it, they'd end up in a blue frenzy, following me away from the house.

I reached the tree cover and looked over the lip of the ridge at a bed of leaves and grass, moss and mountain flowers. I looked back—no one in sight—and launched myself over the edge.

Oh, this was *easy*—a slick incline with only a few bumps, easy on the butt and the back going down. I was going to make it—if they just missed this one move, it should be enough to give me a clear shot all the way to the car.

I felt smug for about half a second. Then I saw the man standing watching me from the ridge below—a man like none I'd ever seen before, a man I was sure hadn't been there a moment earlier. Tall and near-anorexic, with skin like a hundred-year-old saddle and white hair to his waist, he stood wrapped in some parchment-like garment from shoulders to feet. His eyes said: *Not interested. In Anything.* As I approached, he lifted his arm in my direction and sparks flickered off the end of his fingers. Ohhh that couldn't be good. I kicked at the dirt and moss in front of me, trying to stop or change direction—why I thought that would do any good, I don't know. All it did was kick a load of dirt in his face, which turned out to be a great strategy. He twitched at the dust cloud and I twisted around, not a whole lot but just enough— the lightning bolt from his finger sizzled by my ankle and slammed into the ground right beside me. The mossy earth singed smoking hot as I went by. I hit the ledge, stood and ran.

I felt no pain now. There was no sense trying to block anything, what with his footsteps right behind me, always sounding the same distance away even though I was running and he was walking. I could hear more footsteps behind and above, some of the blueshirts having reached the shelf above and others scrambling downhill behind them. Twice, I thought about jumping to the next shelf down but, each time, a lightning bolt smashed into the edge of the path and set it burning. *He's trying to run me out of energy*, I thought, *run me till I can't run anymore*. It wasn't a bad plan, except for the car being just ahead. Unless he hit me with a bolt head-on, which he didn't seem to want to do, I was going to get there first.

I dove into the driver's seat and reached under the dash for the wires—not that I knew any better how to hotwire a car today than yesterday but how many wires could there be? And then I heard that deep commanding foreign-accented voice echoing from the back seat. "Wouldn't it be easier to use the key?" it said and a hand appeared, holding out the key for me. Except I couldn't take it. I couldn't move, not at all, not any part of me.

The man with the commanding voice—not real tall, middle-aged but muscular, piercing eyes and a goatee—opened the back door and came around to the passenger seat. He looked me over searchingly. "You murdered him, didn't you? Renn—you cut him to pieces and threw him off the cliff."

What was he talking about? Had someone else done it? Found him in the crawlspace and dismembered him? And now they were going to blame it on me?

And then the man in the passenger seat smiled and I saw in his eyes that I had just told him where Max was.

Nine

"We'll wait for Marat," Goatee Man said. Marat, apparently, was Old Leatherskin the Lightning Bearer. I was quickly developing way too much familiarity with sinister nicknames. Marat appeared a moment later, though, once again, I didn't see him arrive, despite watching for him in all the mirrors. All at once, he was just there, taking the back seat.

"Can't you just levitate up to the house?" I said. I felt safe with sarcasm—if they were going to kill me, there wasn't a thing I could do about it.

"You can drive now," Goatee Man announced and—how about that!—I could. "If we all arrive together, Max—you know him as Max, don't you?—Max will be more cooperative."

"You know him?" I felt somehow that I already knew the answer.

"We were schoolmates," he said, "a long time ago."

When we reached the house, Max was standing in the driveway waiting. He was making no effort to get away and I instantly felt guilty. Goatee Man got out of the car as soon as we rolled to a stop. I could see the jumpsuits climbing back to the top of the hill. One of them held out one of those plastic ties but Goatee Man waved him off.

"You won't try to strangle me, will you, Maximka?"

"If I'd known it was you, Pietr—" Max began.

"You wouldn't have resisted so?"

"I would have run first thing this morning." They were both smiling their most horrible smiles—they must have taught bad smiling at that school of theirs. It was like a pair of grizzly bears circling a dumpster.

Max took a seat in the back of a black SUV. Goatee Man took the passenger front and someone shoved me into the back next to Max. A jumpsuit was already at the wheel.

"You didn't wake me," Max accused me.

"If you'd been alive at the time, I would have," I snapped and he shut up. The van rocked off the lawn and joined a procession down the driveway onto the road.

"That was clever—the trance," Goatee Man said. "I haven't seen that in years."

"You've been surrounded by feeble minds," Max answered. Goatee Man turned to me and offered his hand.

"I'm Jonathan Tapir," he said, smiling.

"You're *who*?" Max said.

"That's my name now," Goatee Man said.

"If I'm Max Renn," Max replied, "you're Pietr Volkov." He leaned back in his seat. "So—is this a Russian operation? Ironman Putin wants us back to work?"

"Patience," Volkov counseled. "It's far more interesting than that. But I can't deny my partner the pleasure of explaining it to you."

"Partner?" Max exclaimed but Volkov held a finger to his lips with an arch smile. We drove, following the river, listening to Bob Dylan's radio show on satellite. The highways kept getting wider and the traffic thicker through countryside and suburbs and, all that time, nobody said a word. I concentrated on being someplace else in time. I was vividly remembering Tess in the back seat of her car when I caught Volkov's bemused smile in reflection and that was the end of that. Surely, everybody in that car was furiously trying to read everyone else's thoughts—if you'd had a think-o-meter, we would have been around 14 on a 10 scale.

Finally we banked onto a cloverleaf and across a thickposted bridge and there was the Lincoln Memorial glistening in front of us, the Washington Monument and Capitol like puzzle pieces behind. We paused alongside the Memorial, letting an unruly line of people cross the street and filter down the incline to the Mall—all manner of families, dragging their kids or grandchildren, banners bobbing in the bright midday light:

Downsize the Bomb-Makers and *Who Are We Fighting?* The near end
of the mall was full of people, several thousand moving out to join
clusters at the other end, moving toward the Monument and the
White House, up there in the distance somewhere. They were
working their lungs, several competing slogans in the air at once.
Then the van turned along the Potomac and into the parking lot of
the Kennedy Center.

"You'll turn around, please?" Volkov asked politely,
holding up a pair of the hand ties. "I'm afraid it's necessary just for
the moment." Max turned around and Volkov slid them on and
pulled them tight. I followed his lead and was surprised how tight
they were. A moment later, he placed a pair of the funny goggles
on each of us.

It was a strange device. I could see through the smoked
lenses and hear despite the plug ends over my ears. All I felt was a
kind of pressure at the top of my skull and a sensation as though
all the little unheard voices in my head—the ones you don't hear
until they go away—had gone silent. Not that they really
disappeared, mind you, they just seemed muffled. I'd need a
degree in Idon'tknowwhat before I could get any more specific.

The parking lot was full at 2 in the afternoon and we drove
through, under the building, to a backstage entrance. There were
two guards at the doorway, dressed in business suits but it wasn't
hard to imagine them in blue nylon jumpsuits. When the doors
opened, Marat the assassin was there, too, appearing out of

nowhere again like usual. I looked into his eyes for a moment and then away—you wouldn't want to look any longer than that. They were dead blank.

One of the guards led us up a staircase and through a warren of backstage passageways and dressing rooms. He stopped before every opened door, every change of hallway, checking—for what? Who was going to care about *us* at the Kennedy Center? Somebody took the glasses off me when we reached the third floor, though they left Max's on.

Finally, we came out of a stairwell into the huge backstage area, risers and dollies and flats of scenery piled up all around and Volkov led us unnecessarily through the clutter toward the front. I say unnecessarily because it was immediately obvious where we were going—there was only one voice now in the whole place and we were headed straight for it.

We stopped in the wings. The auditorium was packed, a well-heeled crowd rapt, the stage lights glinting off pearls, expensive watches and cellphones, all those tiny cameras reflecting back onto the stage where, prowling like seven thousand hours of television, Jim Avery smiled.

I'd been several days in the company of people who couldn't smile to save their lives and now here was Avery, blinding bright at center stage and with the look of a man who knew—*knew*—that you couldn't take your eyes off him. And when he turned his back to the audience for just a moment and faced us, closeup, the reason was in plain view—nervous tension that couldn't quit, that percolated fulltime beneath that demanding smile—the constant awareness of mastery, of grabbing the audience and holding them, not letting go for even a second, of his determination to hold off that unruly second for as long as it took. Max was alongside me—his expression said he hadn't expected this, but that wasn't the same as saying he looked surprised.

"So," Avery emoted into the spotlights, dragging out the word to comic effect, "So-you know this-I have a standard talk I give. I start with notes and wing it-in Trieste and Bucharest. By the time I've gotten to Tokyo and Paris, I know what I mean to say and it doesn't change much after that. "

Avery took a pause, a theatrical moment of taking in the audience from one end of to the other.

"But every year, this one is different. Because this is not your average audience. When this audience gets mad, you call the Vice President at his undisclosed location—and he takes the call!"

(Laughter from the audience)

"Most people dream of hitting the jackpot. You people own the casino. Which is the only role worth having in a casino, by the way. So—if you're so powerful, so accomplished: Why spend money to watch me talk? Not even *sing*."

More laughter. This time, though, Avery's smile was harder, tougher, his eyes piercing.

"This year, we *know* why you're here. Because the world's gotten shaky for *everyone*. Even you guys. Fabled businesses have got the heaves, basic systems—water, power, investing—all look questionable. The best information money can buy is full of half-truths and gossip. Nothing's a sure thing anymore. And you guys have gotten used to the sure thing."

The gaping hall was dead silent. No polite conversation, no jokes, no competition for attention. He had them and, as close as we were to him, it was clear he knew it. Now the ease slipped out of his voice—the tone got sharper, more challenging.

"Which is the problem. You've forgotten where you come from. Chaos, turmoil—they're *opportunities*! Those are just the conditions that *made* you. I always talk about Hope but you know Hope isn't *Kumbaya, why can't we be friends*? Hope is how you get knocked down ten times and get up eleven. No hope means the best idea in history doesn't get built. Hope is what told you, years ago, that you could conquer the world.

"Hope's come easy for you guys for quite a while now," Avery said, holding his laser smile with a satisfaction that had to be the dead opposite of the way his audience felt. "Well-guess what? You're going to have to dig a little deeper for it now."

"So say it with me:" Avery called. "*I have hope*" and the audience responded in unison, once and again, a second, third and fourth time, volume rising, the words ringing through the hall. "*I have hope*. And this one: *It's MY World*. Again: *It's MY World*." They chanted every phrase he prompted, over and over, several thousand voices including mine.

How many times had I heard Avery give this speech on TV? When I couldn't sleep at night—when I was afraid to try—I'd sit in the living room of Dave's house and watch him stalk back and forth across some stage somewhere in the world talking like this. But, this close, I felt the raw power he had to lift a person's spirit. The thought that kept turning over in my head was: *I have every reason to feel good about myself.* There I was, at the edge of the stage, in plastic handcuffs, surrounded by Pietr Volkov and ten guards, feeling buoyant somehow, thrilled, transported. I felt the power of Avery's message filling me up.

"Funny how it works, isn't it?" Avery said, flashing that famous smile (*The Billion Dollar Smile*-Newsweek) as the chants died away. "They're just words and I can't pretend they're all that articulate either—yet just saying them lifts our spirits. What vision do you carry inside you today? What World are you creating right now? Tonight? Tomorrow? When hope fuels our visions, we start *making them real.*"

"We should move on," Volkov said and the guard led us to the back of the stage and opened a door-in-a-door—a normal-sized door set into a huge unload-the-tractor-trailer door. On the other side, where you would have expected scenery or at least machinery—or, since Avery worked alone on a bare stage, a wide expanse of empty space—we found a room filled with people, mostly young people in the lotus position, eyes closed and breathing deeply.

As we passed a whiteboard in the front of the room, I read:

Here. Now. Your Assigned Seats

The World Crushes the Average Person But I Am NOT Average

The Rules Don't Apply To Me—I Can Accomplish Anything

I Have Every Reason To Feel Good About Myself

We funneled through a side door to a row of dressing rooms—the guard showed us into the second. It looked like the ones I'd seen in the movies—a small table set against a mirrored wall, a love seat, several chairs and a bathroom door. I would have taken the room for a spare except for the opened basket of fruit and two trays of organic cookies, each individually wrapped in plastic with hippyish hand-lettered labels. The guards let us sit and even removed Max's goggles but not our hand ties. I certainly wasn't comfortable but nobody had waved a Glock under my nose in a while and I took that as an good sign. Improvement's where you find it.

And then, all at once, Max straightened up and looked around like a shot, startled. I looked around too in reaction, wondering what I'd missed. Max turned to Volkov and said, "It's *quiet.*" His eyes were wide as though something miraculous had happened. "No voices. I can't hear *anything.*"

"Yes," Volkov breathed. "It's peaceful, isn't it?"

"How do you do it?"

"White noise generators," Volkov explained. "Like the ones that suppress noise in headphones—whatever noise they detect, they send out the opposite waveform and nullify it. We've retuned ours to work on brainwaves. Just like the goggles we gave you on the way over. We knew you'd show up eventually, Maximka—we prepared."

So, I thought, we're disarmed. Then again, so are they, except for the guns.

And then the door opened and Jim Avery walked in. "Max!" he said, holding out his hand. When he saw the plastic ties, he glanced at Volkov and then upward—I thought immediately of the white noise machines. "Are those necessary?" he said sharply.

"Not here," Volkov shrugged.

"Then let's get them off," Avery said pleasantly, as though they'd forced us to wear clown hats or something. He held out his hand to shake, saying 'Jim Avery' as though I wouldn't know who he was. He was as tall in person as he looked on TV and shiny, like his cheeks had that wax they put on apples. But he didn't wait for my name.

"I'll eventually find a way around your machine," Max said, nodding toward the ceiling. "You won't hold me long."

"Max," Avery cooed, the TV smile appearing like a flare over a battlefield, "you seriously think we planned to hold *you* with plastic ties? And an anti-noise machine? Give us a little credit." He sat opposite us, the back of his head appearing in twenty mirrors, like salt-'n-pepper tulips. "The machines keep us from interfering with our kids in the back room. They're busy 'influencing' our guests for another few minutes while they file into the parking lot. If you're paying for a seminar on Hope, you'd better leave feeling hopeful, don't you think?"

He gestured at Max's wrists. "As to the ties, I simply knew you wouldn't come any other way. Miriam shouldn't have made such a fuss in Raleigh—I was very stern with her about that. My plan is for us to have a good talk. I'm not going to hold anything back with you—I think you'll be very impressed with what we're doing. You'll listen to what I have to say, won't you? Without trying to escape?" Max thought about it for a moment and then nodded. Avery glanced at Volkov. "We should go," he said and a moment later, we were out in the hall, surrounded by bodyguards and hustling toward the back of the building.

It occurred to me to run—I'd made no promises—but the guards were still all around us and, as soon as we stepped outside, there was Marat, Old Leatherface with his flickering fingertips. I saw Max look him up and down while we piled back into the big black SUV; it quickly rolled down the driveway past the few remaining cars and out toward the same bridge we came in over.

"I can't tell you the impression you made on me, those years ago," Avery told Max, watching his reaction like the performer he was. "I remember you lamenting there was nothing positive you could do with your gifts," he continued, pointing out the tinted windows at the last stragglers leaving his lecture. "This is just a tiny part of what we do, Max, but I think we help. People come to me in distress and anxiety. Whether their anxiety is real or imagined, it can be crippling. And they leave feeling good about themselves. They can't help it."

"You might even say they have no choice," Max replied, smiling as loosely as he knew how. I'd seen all his smiles by that point. "Where'd all this come from, Jim? You certainly weren't so chipper as the Senator's Chief of Staff." Avery's smile vanished suddenly; the words came out of his mouth clenched, struggling for air.

"I worked for Alan Hammond for eighteen years. My first job out of college was with his campaign. He promised I'd succeed him—several times, he promised. I made the same mistake with Alan that lots of people made over the years—I thought he could deliver. The instant he announced his retirement, he became the old geezer mumbling to himself in the back of the room. None of the people who made the actual decisions cared a damn what he thought or what promises he'd made."

We filtered onto a highway heading west—it might have been the same highway we drove in on, though I couldn't tell for sure—and then, after a few minutes, smaller local roads, grubby vistas of gas stations, motels, fast food joints and slow-moving traffic heading South in glum orderly columns.

"I'd been with him sixteen years when the bottom blew out. I'd shot my wad on a dead end. Do you know what that feels like?" he raged, voice rising but not really even seeking an answer, talking really to himself. "I flipped. I swore to myself that nothing like that would ever—*ever*—happen to me again. I was going to find something rock-solid to build the rest of my life on. Something I could control, some valuable resource that couldn't get voted out of office, couldn't forget its promises—something the smart money hadn't bought up already." He tried to recover, laughing out the window but going nervous about it a moment later, as though recognizing the admission in it.

"When you work for a lame duck, nobody's logging your time anymore. Nobody cared if I showed up at the office. So I got in the car and drove, drove whichever direction looked good at the crossroads." He counted the suburban streets stacked up across the hillsides. "That's where I discovered the power of *real* fear— fear for *yourself*, fear for your own life.

"See, when you're in government, you're always worrying about *out there*. Social Security needs help and the terrorists are out to get us. But those things are happening *out there*, to somebody else. Now, with Alan useless and no idea where I fit in the world, for the first time, it was *me*. All my doors opened over a cliff."

All at once, Avery's ease returned—the big smile flashed across his face again. "So I drove. And once I'd driven around a while, I discovered that gnawing fear just made me a good

American. Out in the world, eating in diners and staying in local motels and filling up where the price was good, I met people who hated their jobs but worked eighteen hours a day because they were afraid of losing them, people who were using credit cards to pay credit card bills or their groceries, people who knew their choice was to pay their kid's college or get sick but not both. This wasn't *out there* anymore—this was just normal life. Fear was what everybody lived with *all the time*.

"And the good news for me was, even though they were desperate for things to get better, people had no real hope it ever would. Because they knew what I'd just discovered—that big business and government *don't live in their world*. People like me never come in contact with that fear, don't know it exists—we've got a safety net. And since people in government and business are the ones who make the laws, how could it ever get better? The man pumping gas or selling iPods knows how the world works. We have the helicopters and bodyguards and photo ops; they have the bills and the insecurity and twenty different ways to go completely off the tracks."

We were off the main roads now, into an area of Virginia dense with trees and constantly overflown by low-hanging airliners. Avery sat straight in his seat and sized up the view through the smoked windows. "And that's when I figured it out: the really scarce natural resource is Hope. Most people are starving for it. Better yet, the winners—the imperial few—aren't used to anything going wrong anymore and they have *so much to lose*. So *nobody's* confident, not for long. Everybody falters, shudders—even if they don't, everybody *fears*. So they all need Hope—and I can provide that. That was my answer and fortunately I was able to figure out what to do about it. I'm a cartel, Max," he said, his smile going even brighter. "I'm the OPEC of Hope."

The van headed into a walled-off industrial park, passing four or five boxlike glass structures on its way to a bunkerlike building with slit windows scarring its concrete face. I recognized the place from the picture I'd torn out of the paper: L Corp headquarters.

We pulled under an awning in front. Bodyguards ringed us immediately, opening the car doors and ushering us into the lobby. Attendants in familiar jumpsuits bustled behind a brushed aluminum counter with inset computer monitors and one of those free-standing security scanners like the airports. One of the bodyguards opened the gate for Avery. A very attractive blonde met him immediately and pinned a security badge on his lapel, then handed another to Volkov, who grinned and pinned it to his own jacket.

"Sam, we need two more badges for our guests," Avery said and the blonde gave us the once-over. From her expression, we must not have looked too impressive, which wasn't real surprising, considering we'd been in the same clothes since Florida.

"What grade?" she asked.

"Full grade," Avery answered. "This is the House that Renn built—and that," he gestured, "that is Renn."

Sam the blonde gave Max another pass now, with that same awestruck look they all had who knew his name. She pulled two yellow badges from a cabinet at the back wall, pinning one to Max's collar—they seemed to be having a staring contest the whole time—and handing me mine, just to let me know how I rated. We followed Avery through a pair of electric swooshing doors like in Star Trek and down an antiseptic hallway cluttered with projectors and monitors on roll-away carts and handtrucks piled with fold-up chairs. "It's a mess," Avery conceded. "We're expanding rapidly. We'll have a new headquarters next year but until then we're overflowing."

"This is part of *Your World*?" Max asked. He had that wide-eyed look he'd had in the dressing room—apparently this place was also wired for white noise. Which didn't make me feel any more secure.

"Oh no," Avery tutted. "*Your World* is a non-profit charitable foundation, with headquarters three blocks from the White House. *Your World* supports personal growth and discovery around the world. L Corp's business is more...pragmatic, shall we say. The two have no connection, as far as anyone can tell."

"So then, how is this the house Renn built?" Max asked.

We were filing down the corridors of what seemed to be a technical university. Classrooms lined both sides of the hall, filled with young people (actually, only a little younger than me, I guess, but they hadn't had my life), expensive computer-aided whiteboards, chairs and floor mats—lotus-style seemed to be all the rage. One of the doors opened as we passed and the sucking sound said the room was airtight and soundproofed, even though there didn't seem to be much sound to muffle.

"When you burst in on Alan and me," Avery reminisced to Max, "the first time, years ago, you said you were Renn and I remember the terror I felt in that moment. I checked later and found that Alan felt it too. And what hit me just the next day, when I thought back on it, was that the fear was there before I even remembered who Renn was. You were a footnote in intelligence reports, the great missing Soviet asset and there were rumblings you'd been sighted but there were always rumblings. So you weren't the first thing on my mind yet the fear was just overpowering.

"When I sat in on your debriefing, you talked about how you did it—how anytime someone came across your name, even just on paper, you could send a shock of fear at a distance, without them knowing you were doing it, without you even knowing you were doing it."

"It can be useful," Max nodded, "to make an adversary afraid of you before you face him."

"Well, when I figured out my calling," Avery said, "I went looking for you. This was after 9/11, after you'd gone missing and no one could find you." He turned and smiled at Volkov. "But I put the word out in the right places, apparently. One day, Pietr walked up to me on the street and said, 'I know what you're looking for and why you can't find it.'"

"He wanted an army of mindbenders!" Volkov smiled. "Like we live on every block, Max—imagine!"

"Well, it's what we have now," Avery insisted and you could hear the pride in his voice.

"Feeble-minded ones," Max grumbled and Volkov shrugged.

"Feeble-minded ones are easier to use," he said. "And, the truth is, they're all we need."

We were passing another classroom door. I moved closer to the wall, where I could get a glimpse inside as we passed. The teacher was up front, monitoring the class though nobody was doing much of anything—the group of them eyes closed, palms up, humming like cats on a windowsill. The whiteboard up front read:

20 Minutes

40.02588N, 105.24102 W

Everything I've Ever Built Is In Danger; Who Will Protect Me?

The Borgen Takeover Bid Makes Good Business Sense

"This is where Jim is a genius," Volkov said and Avery smiled modestly, a man who'd won the game and was now above praise. "He realized what was needed."

Max's forehead looked like a topographical map all of a sudden. It must have been a weird experience for him, having to guess at answers. "What? Feeble minds? How can these shallow ones read *anybody* reliably?"

"The mistake," Avery said quietly, "is in the terminology: mindreader. The important skill for business isn't reading people's minds—it's the other side of the equation, *influencing* the thoughts of others. That's worth money. *Lots* of money."

We passed another classroom. The whiteboard read:

20 Minutes

53N25, 2W55

Who Can I Turn to when No One Cares?

Labour is Still Better for the Working Man

Avery led us through an open door into an empty classroom. You could see it had done its duty recently—coffee cups and notepads were scattered across tables pushed out to odd angles to leave room for squatting on floor mats. The whiteboard was partly but not completely erased. What remained was:

20 mi

3 5' 19.1" N, 122 05'   W

othing Lasts Forev

he Royal Fam   Provides Stabil

"I explained to Jim how few prime talents there were," Volkov shrugged. "But, the more we talked, the more I realized that what he wanted to do didn't require real power. Twenty or thirty drones at a time could do the job. And better maybe, since they can attack a multitude of frequencies at the same time."

"So when people walk out of my seminars feeling better, really hopeful, liberated, inspired, fearless, at a time when the world is going down the crapper," Avery added with real enthusiasm, "what's that worth? All through the seminars, we're sending them the message: *You Are Special. Others May Fail but You Won't. You Can Do It.* We clear away the roadblocks inside, which are the ones that really bite, don't you agree?

"At the same time, we've offered our more practical services for hire. That has proved to be *very* profitable."

"Influencing votes in Congress," Max murmured, without sounding very distressed.

Volkov looked almost condescending. "Your thinking is outmoded, Max," he said, shaking his head. "Government is not even a player anymore."

"Everything is *business* now," Avery interrupted. "Government, Media, Religion—it's all business, competing for attention, for mindshare. Most of our work is influencing consumer attitudes and spending, stockholder's meetings, Nielsen ratings, neutralizing or misleading competitors, cerebral placement for new products—"

"Cerebral placement?" Max said.

Avery shrugged. "It's the marketing buzzword," he said. "There's a section of the brain, the—what's it called?" He clicked his fingers a few times.

"Orbitofrontal cortex," Volkov interjected.

"—Right. If you plant a product suggestion there, you're home free. That part of the brain just bypasses all rational judgment or vetting. It's an automatic purchase. Saves an incredible amount of money in advertising and PR."

"And you're telling me that's funding this whole enterprise?" Max said and the skepticism in his voice seemed to set something off in Avery.

"I don't think you realize the scope of what we're doing. Remember five years ago, when the analysts started saying real estate had peaked, that it was a bubble about to burst? That anybody who got in after that was going to get killed? Yet people kept buying—adjustable-rate mortgages that were built to explode, right? You think that just happened?"

Avery was up and pacing around now, feeding on his own pitchman energy. "SUV's—they drive like trucks but they go off-road. Except that almost none of their drivers ever even bother. They get half the gas mileage of cars. Gas went from $1.50 to $3.50 a gallon in less than three years and sales of SUV's kept growing— at twice the profit margin of cars. You think that was an accident?" He had abandoned his composure now and was waving his arms around like a traffic cop.

"Think of the power, Max, to show a client you can move an *entire marketplace* like that! We started with a staff of five and twenty part-time drones. Now we have over five thousand in forty locations. Geneva and Shanghai open in the next two months."

"But you haven't mentioned the most creative part of your work," Max said, in a light tone that didn't sound like him. "Making nuclear plants malfunction and the Mayor of Copenhagen bark like a dog in front of witnesses."

Avery's smile didn't waver but he glanced at Volkov, who responded quickly. "A child's tricks," he said. "We used to change the instrument needles in the lab from a half mile away, Maximka, just for fun. You remember." Max nodded, though there was no nostalgia on his face. "There was no real harm done."

"I don't think we had anything to do with the Mayor of Copenhagen," Avery mused. "At least none that I know of."

"Well, let's just say you benefit from instability anywhere in the world," Max offered. "When people doubt their officials, utilities, religion, the institutions that make them feel safe, that's an opportunity for the OPEC of Hope."

"A lot of what's unfortunate in the world," Avery answered, "is fortunate for us." He shrugged. "The world is filled with misfortune. That only shows how much we're needed."

"Don't you think somebody's going to catch on eventually?" Max pressed. "Some ambitious prosecutor? Scandal-sheet reporter?"

"We're protected," Avery said.

"From *everybody*?" Max burst, looking amused and skeptical at once. At this, Avery and Volkov struggled to suppress self-satisfied grins.

"I told you he was a genius," Vokov said. "Jim knows how the game is played."

"We had our own rider," Avery confided, "in the Homeland Security Bill. Our work is national security and classified top secret—anything we do, no matter who the client or even if there is no client. We can't be prosecuted."

"Can't even be *charged*," Volkov crowed. "No congressional oversight, no subpoenas, no grand juries. Offer *that* to a client and see them light up. It's beautiful."

"What congressman proposed *that*?"

"Well, no one's name is on it," Volkov answered. "But the Majority and Minority Leader both think they put it in, so no one is going to ask questions."

"This is Pietr's territory," Avery said and there was a medal and a caution in the phrase.

Max stared at Avery for a long moment. "And you really think you can keep this quiet? Over time? With all the people who'll know? With all the people who'll be watching?"

Volkov rose instantly at this. He wasn't a tall man, not next to Avery but he pulled himself up to his full height and there was fire in his eyes. "How do you think Bush won in Ohio?" he said, his voice rasping. "All those precincts where the exit polls said Kerry won—exit polls that are dead accurate, time after time, suddenly all wrong? Those people told the pollsters who they *meant* to vote for. Once they got inside the booth, that's not the button they pushed." He glowered at the bunch of us skeptics. "Of course people were watching. There were articles in high-profile publications, preaching to the choir. They were roundly ignored." He leaned over the table and rapped on it with his forefinger. "People need to feel *secure* to challenge power. When they're frightened, they have their own problems to worry about." He paced back and forth a few more times before finally acknowledging Avery glaring at him. Then he took his seat again sullenly.

"That all might change after the next election," I said. Volkov looked at me like he hadn't considered I could speak on my own. But he answered the point, though he answered it to Max.

"We work for *both* parties. *Everyone* wants us deep and dark."

"The point," Avery concluded, "is that we're *protected*. From the top down." He jumped up to the whiteboard, eager to change the subject.

"We recruit on college campuses, smart kids who need some extra money or want to start paying off their student loans. Who complains about getting paid for meditating on different subjects a few hours a day? Most of our persuasion targets require no more than twenty minutes at a clip, so we can service fifty clients a day just out of this office. Our work is all billable hours, like lawyers and accountants. We're all over the world and, as you can see, growing fast."

Max was smiling now, not a happy smile—he didn't seem to have a happy smile—but an intrigued one. "Okay, I'll bite," he said. "It's brilliant. You've got the world on a string. What do you need *me* for?"

Volkov started rubbing the side of his nose, as though he'd suddenly developed a boil. "We have...other work," he said. "Sensitive jobs, the kind you can't give to drones. Some of which you've already figured out, some of which you know nothing. I have built a small crew I can trust. I know what they're capable of and I know they will be discreet, they will not act rashly and they will not be caught. You are the Crown Jewel of the Soviet system, Maximka. You could choose your own jobs."

"I'll get Bin Laden for you," Max said. "I could do that."

"Come on, Max," Volkov moaned. "It has to be something they'll *pay* us for."

"No one would pay you to find Bin Laden?"

"Finding him isn't an issue," Avery sighed. "He's off-limits."

"C'mon, Max, think like a grown-up," Volkov urged. "When there was that whole flap about wiretaps without court orders, we cleaned up—they farmed out all the important cases to us. Remember—no oversight."

"More to the point," Avery said, "is it so terrible to help Company A get Company B's peanut butter recipe? Or to find out how much they plan to bid for that big contract? To tip off the cameraman when and where Angelina and Brad are getting married? Or where they're arguing? You'd be amazed at the return on smalltime stuff like this."

"Or it might be a little more...gritty," Max said, his expression dark. "Yes?"

Avery wanted to settle the waters, to smooth the room but Volkov was squirming, full of energy and fight, though it wasn't at all clear who he was fighting. "Max," he said, rising as though he couldn't remain in his seat another second, "you don't have to be a miserable stunted monk running from the world, hiding in back alleys and paranoid about everyone who wants to speak to you. You could be a consultant to a major corporation, with a nice house in the suburbs and a wife and kids, a Mercedes, vacations — a normal life." I must have snickered — Volkov turned on me as though I'd pulled a gun out of my pocket. "Don't laugh unless you know what it means to never be normal, to never be *able* to be normal!" and the anger and frustration in his voice were close to the bone. "You wanted that once, Max, you wanted it badly — I haven't forgotten how badly."

"I made a mistake," Max said gravely. "I haven't forgotten either."

"Maybe you couldn't do better at the time," Volkov's voice softened. "I'm not judging. But now —" he glanced at Avery, who nodded, "—now Max, twenty jobs a year. Twenty! You choose! Some of them, you'll probably come in here or to one of our other centers, control someone for twenty minutes at a distant location or send out a suggestion and be finished. Sometimes there'll be a little travel, first-class, on us, with layovers. Three quarters of a million dollars a year plus an expense account and bonuses for jobs we particularly want your help with." Volkov tried to muster a look of sympathy, without quite putting it across. "I remember your scruples, Max — that's not a problem. Surely there are twenty jobs we could all agree on?"

The two men stood across from one another, leaning over the table like rams about to butt horns. I don't think either of them was aware of it. Max bit his lip; he was doing a slow burn and I started looking for the storm cellar. "Twenty jobs," he mulled. "And not Bin Laden."

"I told you, he's—"

"Off-limits, yes, you said that. What kind of job were you doing in Florida two days ago?"

"We had no job in Florida," Avery added.

"Yes, you did," Max continued, voice rising. "They were your guys. Same van, same guns and headsets, same feeble-minded approach."

"I don't know what you're talking about," Avery insisted. He glanced at Volkov but received no glance in reply.

"Your men killed Dave Monaghan, two days ago in Florida. If there's any chance of us working together, I need to know why."

"Who's Dave Monaghan?" Avery asked, now staring hard in Volkov's direction, still without response.

"I'm sorry," Max said, turning toward the door. "We can't do business on this basis." He looked over at me. "Time to go," he said quietly.

Volkov finally found a way to look Avery in the eye, fleetingly. "Let us talk a few minutes, Jim," Volkov said. "Privately."

"You said he—"

"We'll come to your office. Just a few minutes," Volkov was the one trying to soothe things now. Avery, glaring at Volkov, stepped deftly between Max and the door.

"We're doing great things here, Max," he said. "I want you to be part of it." He clapped him on the shoulder, reassuring and turning him away at the same time. Then he went out, closing the door behind him with a resounding *thunk*.

Volkov watched the door close and seemed to expand in the chair. He had been solicitous and respectful, second banana, with Avery around; now he was filling the empty space, the man in charge.

"So," Max sighed, "nothing changes, eh, Pietr? You don't tell Avery everything?"

"Your friend was a mistake," Volkov said impassively. "If he was important to you, I'm sorry."

"What kind of mistake?"

"I don't know—I didn't even know his name until you mentioned it to Miriam." He shrugged, a big theatrical shrug, a Russian shrug if I had any idea what that was. "Someone exceeded his authority. Someone decided he was a threat. Why? I don't know. I am sorry, truly."

"He was shot through the head and then they blew up his house, made it look like a gas explosion. The guys who did it were under suggestion. Don't tell me this was some local *apparatchik* going off on his own." His eyes narrowed. "You have some operation on the side, something Avery doesn't know about."

"Jim was in politics for sixteen years," Volkov muttered. "He's very comfortable with what he doesn't know."

Max leveled a finger at him. "It's the old game—he'll only be comfortable as long as you succeed, Petushka."

Volkov drew himself up again, as though on rails. "How can we fail?" he asked. "Who do you think will stop us? If you tell people, straight-out, what we do, they'll think you're joking or deranged. They'll laugh at you. Meanwhile, we're backing candidates—who will win—in Kenya, Estonia, South Korea and France—*this* year. We already have elected friends in high places in twenty-two countries. Who will stand against us?" He leaned over the desk again, a plaintive note in his voice. "Max, all your life, you cling to ambivalence. Nothing makes you happy. Be what you are. Use what nature has given you."

"Dave said the opposite," Max responded. "He said just because we could, didn't mean we should. He said we had too much power to give it to governments. Now you want to offer it to *corporations!*"

"Dave Monaghan was a cancer," Volkov spat. "He'd have us all bank tellers, begging for scraps."

"Ahh, you *do* remember him," Max said and I could see something in him relax. "That makes this so much easier."

I didn't see Volkov touch any buttons or trip any wires but, all at once, the door opened, four very colorful-looking guards appeared and took positions around the table. There was a tall bullet-headed guy, a very skinny black man with very cool-looking dreads and tattoos and a kind of drowned-rat in a sweatshirt and rippling muscles. Marat followed them in but Volkov waved him off, annoyed. "We're fine," he said and the white-haired assassin turned, glowering and left.

"Max," Volkov said, his voice deepening, "think about this. What is this wonderful life you have, out among the alligators, not using the skills you were bred for? Making nothing of yourself? Sincerely—I'm asking as an old friend who's concerned for you."

Max looked at him for a long time before answering. "That's done, one way or the other," he said finally. "I have nothing to go back to, whatever happens."

Volkov beamed, though it only proved again that none of them knew how to smile. "So then, there's no problem. Join us! We'll be comrades again, doing great things."

"They're not great things, Pietr."

"It's a brilliant system."

"Sure. You're a great businessman. You plant bombs with one hand and sell bomb shelters with the other. What could be better?"

Volkov's eyes were wary now. "Don't mock me, Max," he said. "We're serious here."

"I'm serious," Max said.

"You admitted you have nothing to go back to."

"I've spent too much time looking backwards," Max nodded. "But now I've finally found that positive use for my skills."

Long pause, the two of them staring each other down, no one willing to be the next to speak. Finally, Volkov said, "And that would be?"

"What you just said: Standing against you—*there's* something positive I can do." Max was actually smiling, as relaxed as I'd ever seen him. "Probably better than anyone."

"Stand against me *here*?" Volkov spat. "In my own building? With white noise generators and guards? You won't get three feet."

"We'll see."

"And how do you expect me to respond? Lock you up? Imprison you?"

"That won't work—not for long."

"Then what? Kill you?"

"Would you?"

"I could call Marat back—he'd do it without a single conscious thought. Don't make me choose." It was a plea and a threat at the same time.

"Alright—here's another idea: let me go."

Volkov coughed out a laugh, a deep laugh of real surprise. "I forget, sometimes, what a fantasist you are," he said. "This is the real world, Max. You *must* join us. You know we can't let you wander around now that we've had our talk." He waited several long seconds for Max to reply. Max just stood, waiting—for what, I didn't know. When it became clear he wouldn't be offering any reply, all the emotion drained from Volkov's face. "This will not end well," he threatened.

"That's correct," Max agreed and looked me in the eye. And gulped. His eyes were wide on me and I knew right away that it wasn't a casual move, that there was a message in it. He nodded— *c'mon, you can get this*—and gulped again. And somehow, I did—I got it. I gulped myself, gulped in a deep breath and held it. Max held out his fingers to Volkov; they crackled with electricity.

"No!" Volkov yelled to the guards. "Stop—"

That was as far as he got. Max snapped his sparking fingers, there was a flash of light and a loud crack in the room and all at once the others were gasping and gagging and staggering around like drunken sailors. The guards keeled over onto the floor almost immediately. The fire alarm was squawking, red lights flashing and sprinklers sprinkling. Volkov lunged for Max, but he gasped and slumped over halfway through the motion. Max reached out to catch him, searched his pockets for a moment and then dropped him flat on the floor. He stuck Volkov's cardkey in the door lock and we ran into the hall.

"What the hell happened?" I demanded as the hall filled with drones and guards exiting in response to the flashing alarms and sprinklers.

"Oxygen *burns*," Max said, "if you know how to ignite it."

A burly guard rushed up the hall.

"Ozone!" Max yelled, pointing through the door window. "They keeled over! I saw them! You need a mask!"

"Shit! *10-45 in R36!*" the guard shouted into his headset. "Bring masks! *Gas* masks!"

One second later, the overhead speakers began advising all personnel to *evacuate in an orderly fashion, please; move directly to the exits and do not open any closed doorways.* Not that it made anything more orderly—the hall was packed, the crowd pushing and shoving toward exits far down the end, more nervous and insistent by the second. Max pulled me out of the stream and down a narrow side corridor. "Tauber's here," he said, pointing.

"How do you know?" These rooms looked like storage closets, certainly nothing big enough for a man.

"Remember I came here? When they were chasing you around the hillside? You were jumping off the balcony and I was hovering over this place, all eyes and ears and no body."

He stopped in front of the fourth closet and slipped Volkov's keycard into the lock. Crammed inside was what was left of Mark Tauber once the pack of wolves had finished with him. His cheeks, arms and legs were bruised blue and full of cross-cuts, chunks of his hair seemed to be missing and his nose looked more crooked than I remembered.

"Feel like a ride in the country?" Max asked and Tauber started, as though expecting someone to hit him. One of his eyes was puffed closed—it was painful to look at. But he broke into a crooked smile as he realized who we were. Maybe one or two of his teeth were missing too, but they hadn't been that great to begin with so it was hard to tell.

"I could use a little fresh air," he croaked and we helped him to his feet and out into the flow of staff rushing out of the building.

When we burst into the afternoon air, Max led us around to the front parking lot, the executive section with the high-zoot machines. He pulled Volkov's keycard from his pocket— a very fancy car key hung from the ring—and pushed the red button. A BMW nearby gave an answering chirp; we jumped in. "Pietr always liked nice cars," Max said as we sped for the exit gate.

Ten

At first, I assumed we were trying to get away.

It at least made sense to try — the black vans were all around us and I could feel the thickness in the air as Max blocked all of us at once, locking us out of the collective unconscious of the neighborhood, trapping all our free-floating thoughts inside the narrow car. Or maybe all that was in my head — now that we were free, my shoulders and neck felt like they'd been released from a clamp. I ached all over from sudden relaxing.

After ten minutes of changing roads and directions, I could see we really hadn't gone very far. The airplanes were still close overhead. That got me real upset. I started sweating. We had to head back to the mountains, to the house on the cliffside. I don't know why I fixated on that place but it all came rushing back to me at once. The wall of windows and the balcony and the crazy awning, the hillside I scrambled over like a maniac, trying not to get cut in half by Marat's lightning bolts — and the town with the dance floor and Tess and Cindy. That whole memory was clear—I was in it, living in it. That was where we had to go. We'd be safe there, if only because that's where they caught us, which made it the last place they'd expect us to go.

Every few minutes, some new airliner threatened to land on the roof of our car. And then we came out of a sidestreet and Max bought a ticket and we were in the long-term parking lot at Dulles Airport. We circulated the rows until he found a Maxima he liked. It had one of those touchpad things on the door and he was able to fry it with his fingers; Tauber hot-wired the car in about seven seconds. And then we were back on the road again. But again, we weren't making any effort to get away. Max made a series of turns, as though looking for a location.

"Volkov lives 'roundabouts," Tauber said. "Miriam took me to his house when we first got up here." He'd pulled a bottle of water from the center console and was holding it up to his puffy eye. "I was an idjit for staying with her."

Max shook his head. "You knew her—you didn't know me."

"They want ya bad. They did everything to try to get your whereabouts out of me."

"Which they knew immediately you didn't have."

"They didn't trust my thoughts."

"Ha! Spies not trusting? I'm shocked." Max's look at Tauber was sympathetic and even grateful.

"Volkov thought he could turn you," Tauber continued. "Avery said you wouldn't give, that they'd have to kill you. Anyway, I'm sorry I didn't trust you. We've got to get the hell outta here—they all live nearby, the whole area's crawling with shooters."

"Shooters?"

"Yeah—they've got drones and shooters. Drones send out messages and don't remember a thing after. Shooters are Volkov's strike force. There's not many of them but they're dirty tricks mindbenders—and killers."

"That's what they wanted Stargate to move to," Max said. "That's what Dave objected to."

"A lot of us objected. Dave did it out loud, to senior officers."

"So now they've outsourced it."

"Anyway, they're deadly. We've got to get going."

"We've got a little time," Max said, "Right now, they're scouring the highway to Shenandoah National Park for us. I've told them that's where we're going."

"They're not going to buy that they've tapped into you. They know you're not that sloppy."

"They think they're tapping Greg," Max said. "I'm sending out his memories."

"Excuse me?" I said.

"Your memories are cleaner than mine—mine are always mixed up with the rest of the neighborhood. And you're more nostalgic for that place—with good reason—than I am."

"And they'll believe," Tauber said, giving me a thoughtful look, "they're intercepting your thoughts."

"Well, that's okay," I said. "Couldn't you ask before you just share my head with other people?"

"Excuse me," Max said immediately. "Would you like to live? Or shall I stop?" Theatrical pause. "That's the choice."

"Fuck you."

"You're not my type," he said. "If they know we're here, they'll be on us in minutes. And we have to stay in the neighborhood for another half hour or so. So we need your memories. Sorry."

"As long as you're sorry…"

"And *remember* this," he ordered me. "This is what it feels like to send out a message or a suggestion. I'm doing it but it's your head—so learn what it feels like. If you can recapture the feeling later, you'll be able to start doing it yourself." He pulled into a parking lot alongside a warehouse, nestled between several locked-up trucks. Looking around, I realized it was a good strategic location—we would be hard to see from the nearby streets but we had a good view out.

"Why are we hangin' around?" Tauber asked. "What's the objective?"

"Low-hanging fruit," Max said, looking across the street at an apartment complex glinting in the light of the setting sun. "Strategic information." He looked Tauber up and down. "Are you in shape to block yourself?"

"I'm okay," Tauber allowed. "Gettin' the shit beat outta me lit the ol' fuse." He croaked out a laugh. "Nostalgia'll kill ya," he added and Max smiled.

"Okay, we're going across the street as soon as the sun goes down. Our subject is not powerful but she is alert. She'll be able to read us so block yourself till we get into the apartment. You too, Greg. You know the feeling now."

"So concentrate," I said, furrowing my forehead.

"No," Max said. "*Don't* concentrate."

"Why not?"

"Concentration is a conscious mind trick," Tauber drawled. "If ye're concentrating on being powerful, you're reminding yourself that ya feel weak. The more ya concentrate on something, the more you feel the opposite."

"When you were with Tess, were you concentrating on anything?" Max asked.

"You bet."

"That's not concentrating," he said and they both laughed. "Moments like that, you're just soaking up the feeling. So just get back to that. Find the feeling in your fingertips and the tip of your tongue and the rest will come back to you."

We sat in the parking lot for about 45 minutes, while the darkness gathered and it began to drizzle. Cars came and went, a truck pulled into the lot, idled ominously for about seven minutes and then pulled out. Police cars flew by, lights flashing and sirens bleating.

I was working on getting back to the house on the hill and I thought I did okay but it was more fun to work on Tess. At one point, Max turned to me and said, "You're trying too hard. You're working memory."

"Memory is useless," Tauber sniped. "It's shorthand for the conscious mind. It's eating soup with a fork," he spat. "Don't *remember*; just *feel* it again. The feeling's still inside ya, in places the conscious mind don't rule. Feeling ain't part o'the past—it's alive right now. Get inside it, get one detail real clear, so it's alive right now and POW! You'll be back there."

"Where?"

"*There*. In the middle of it. With her again, like it's happening again *right now*."

I was probably looking at him cockeyed. "However you do it," Max said, "what matters is, you won't be *here*." He opened the car door. "It's time."

We crossed the road—it was a main drag and we were forced to rush across between tractor-trailers like elephants stampeding along the river. We were left in a thicket of trees and shrubs that seemed to have grown out of a bed of garbage—

supermarket circulars, handouts for car washes and a traveling circus, beer bottles and water jugs, several cans of motor oil and two pairs of panties in the nook of a tree trunk. Stepping carefully took us over a low fence to the service entrance of the apartment building, where suddenly everything was pristine. In through the wide truck-delivery door and up a ramp we went, to a wide-mouth elevator. Max hit the button for the sixth floor.

In my mind, I was trying to hold Tess' hand, trying to pull the feeling of it out of the air. I couldn't figure out how I was supposed to do this without remembering. As I got frantic, Tauber suddenly shot me a look, leaned over my shoulder and cackled, "Pretend you're holding her *tit*, son" and *that* I could feel right away. Which unlocked the door—once I felt her breast in my hand, other feelings...came to me.

By the time we reached the sixth floor, I really wasn't there at all—I was in the backseat of her car, feeling the sticky leather of the seats and the blast of the air conditioning turned all the way up and her scent and the way my hands and mouth were all over her and...well, that's as much as I feel like sharing. I got out of the elevator but it felt like *that* was the dream, like I was just watching it happen, like I was along for the ride but somebody else was driving.

Max rang the bell to the corner apartment, the one that overlooked the river. It took a few rings before a woman's voice answered, approaching but still a few feet inside the door. "Hello?

Who's there?" Max motioned us against the wall away from the door. Tauber pushed me over where Max wanted—I wasn't paying attention—and we heard the voice say "Hello? Hello?" and then the metal door gave a little groan as she leaned against it on the inside. As soon as she did, Max touched a finger to the surface of the door and whispered, "Open" and, an instant later, we heard the locks unbolting from the inside.

It was Sam the blonde, the aide from L Corp headquarters, the one who seemed so chummy with Avery. She seemed to be holding her eyes open wide as we filed past her across the threshold—she wasn't blinking. Apparently she was getting ready to go out—she wore a light blouse and panties but the rest of her clothes were laid out on the bed a few yards away. As we came inside, Max touched her forehead and her whole body relaxed. It was like she was standing out of habit. She followed Max's finger on her forehead into the living room like she was stuck to it. He led her to a high-backed wooden chair and she sat without being prompted.

"Hello Sam," Max said.

"Hello," she replied like reciting off a page.

"Tell me about your day," Max said in the blandest of tones.

"It was a mess," she replied. "We had to evacuate because of you and Pietr was furious. He wants to know how you did that trick with the air, because he thought he knew all your tricks but he doesn't know that one. He was ranting about it for like twenty minutes non-stop when we got back inside. Like we should have known air was a security hazard. And you stole his car which *really* pissed him off. It had Lo-Jak and the cops got it back but they didn't get you and they're trying to figure out what kind of car is missing from the long-term lot but all they have on the records is blue Nissan and the plate number but the plate number wasn't written clear on the tag so they're trying to find the guy who wrote it to see if he can read it or remember what it was but they think he's on a bender because tomorrow's his day off and that's what he does when he has tomorrow off."

"This is called a brain dump," Tauber groaned, "for obvious reasons."

"She hasn't had a chance to organize her thoughts," Max explained, pausing every few seconds to monitor whatever Sam was spouting. "By tomorrow morning, she'll have everything capsulized but all the details will be smoothed over and the details are usually the things that are useful." Sam was complaining now about the time that was spent trying to get good staff who wouldn't drink too much or smoke pot too much and and and…Max finally touched her forehead again and she stopped.

"You work for Avery—you've been having an affair with him—and you're sleeping with Pietr as well," Renn said, like they were facts.

"I thought you couldn't read anything in their headquarters," I said.

"No," Sam said. "I flirt with Jim all the time but he's never made a move. I don't know why. Do you think I'm past my prime?"

"Absolutely not," Max answered, giving her a quick appraisal, then back to me. "I didn't have to—it's how Pietr works," he replied. "He uses her to monitor Avery, to make sure Avery's not looking too deeply into what he's up to." He returned to Sam. "What about Pietr? What is he up to?"

"I can't tell you. He's locked me up so I can't tell you anything about him." There was a note of pride in her voice. "He figured you might want to talk to me and I'll tell him you did as soon as I come out of this."

"Who says I'm letting you out of this?" Renn said. And waited. It took a few seconds for this thought to penetrate and then Sam's composure visibly faltered. "I need information out of you now. After that, I don't need you."

"You—" Sam's voice wavered and then stopped. Her expression hadn't changed, neither had her anesthetized tone of voice. But there was no mistaking the alarm in her all the same. "—you wouldn't. Pietr said you didn't—"

"That was then," Renn answered and the chill in his voice made *me* tremble. "This is now. Pietr's trying to kill or capture me. He's already killed my friend. All bets are off."

"Pietr would hunt you down," she vowed. "Forever. He would never rest—"

"Pietr would forget you in five minutes," Renn answered harshly, cutting her off hard, "and you know it. He likes that girl in Asian section, the one he takes to lunch all the time. She'll be sympathetic when he remembers you later."

"Don't try that shit with me!" Sam insisted, her voice suddenly taut. "I know your tricks! Pietr told me about your problems with women!"

Max's eyes lowered at this and came up dark. "Well, it doesn't really matter," he said, "what you think of me, does it, as long as you don't give me your password?"

There was a pause then, for just a second, and the air freshened, like someone had thrown the window open in winter. I saw a look of recognition pass through Samantha's eyes to Renn's.

"*Barbie's Dream House*," he said quietly and she slumped in the chair. Tauber grinned ear to ear. I must have been giving him the eye because Max turned to me to explain. "Like I said, trying not to think about something makes you think about it. I remind her she's not supposed to think of her password so it's the next thing she thinks of. Like sticking out your arm when you're falling." He turned back to Samantha, breathing quietly and peacefully now in the chair. "*Barbie's Dream House*. What is the plan?"

"Which one?" she asked, drowsy.

"The one Pietr's keeping from Avery. Or the one Avery's using you to keep track of, the one he doesn't admit knowing about."

"Pietr doesn't talk about it much," the blonde answered, now slouching across the couch, looking very sweet in her filmy blouse and panties, "and I don't ask questions when he doesn't want to tell me. He scares me. He's made people squawk like chickens and lick the dust off the floor in front of me, just for fun. *His* fun. He's not a nice person, really. I guess I like guys who scare me." She looked at Max now and suddenly she didn't seem anesthetized at all. "You're a scary guy," she told him. "I saw that when you first came in this morning."

"What do you know about the plan?" Max persisted. She smiled hopefully and he offered a sad-eyed smile in return.

"Do you think I'm pretty?" she asked, her voice gone girlish.

His face was almost tender—as close as he let himself get. "You're very pretty. And much smarter than you let yourself be. Pietr could benefit from the advice you avoid offering." His expression faded. "*Barbie's Dream House*. What do you know about the plan?" Tauber returned from the fridge with a couple bottles of water—he kept one and handed the other to Sam, who chugged it like she'd been traipsing the Sahara for a week.

"It's soon," she said finally, after belching and smiling like a child, "and it's a big deal. He's got a group of six training for it here. They're not like the others; they're the scary guys, throwbacks like the old mindbenders, I guess—no offense. There's Marat—you know him—a Russian, an Israeli, along with two Americans. And a Jamaican guy with dreads and the best weed in the world, Jesus. He gets his own room 'cause nobody can think once he lights up."

"What's the objective?" Max asked. His voice had gotten quieter but more distinct.

"They didn't say and I didn't ask. I don't want to know."

"You know more," he persisted. "I know you do—and so do you." She continued with her blank silence for about ten seconds, like she didn't hear him.

"You live in Pietr's world," Renn said, "and Avery's. You like being in between—you like the danger. You think they don't know about each other. I assure you they do. They're both comfortable using you to watch the other. They both trust you to keep the confidences they actually want you to keep. Frankly, they both take you for granted. Their trust in you is justified by the fact that you've never used your position to play one against the other." He looked at her searchingly, which seemed kind of comical, what with the dazed look on her face. "You could, you know," he said and she nodded like a marionette.

"I could," she mumbled, half a second behind him. "I know."

"You know more. You know something you're not supposed to know, that you didn't even intend to find out." As he said this, his voice deepened again, taking on that echo chamber sound. "Share *that* with me."

Samantha sat up and motioned as though writing on a pad. Tauber grabbed a pen and paper immediately off the table and put them in Sam's hands—and she started writing strange. She started writing upside down, is how it turned out. When I looked up at her, her eyes were closed. And some of the letter forms were a bit garbled. But there she sat, writing it.

"She saw *him* write it," Max whispered, "across the desk." He waited until he was sure she was finished and then took the paper from her. Turning it around, we all read: *Sun 1230 IAD-CIA*

"'*Sun*'—It's Sunday?" Tauber said. "Day after tomorrow?"

"Yeah," she nodded her head.

"You're working with CIA?" Max asked.

Sam shook her head. "That's what he wrote but it doesn't make sense. Jim always says we can't work with the agencies because that would put us on the radar, up for investigations. I don't know who the client is." She thought about it for a moment. "Actually, I don't even know if there *is* a client. The other night, Pietr said—he's a man, you all boast in bed—he said, 'When this is done, we'll be in the driver's seat. They'll dance to our tune.'

"Who will?" Max asked. "*Who'll* dance to our tune?"

"That's all he said." Max and Tauber exchanged looks, perplexed and concerned. But they looked like they were going to stop there. I leaned forward.

"What did he mean?" I asked.

"He didn't tell her," Max hissed in my ear. "She has no facts."

"You said everybody mindreads," I told him. "She's been sleeping with him." I turned back to Sam. "What's your intuition tell you? What did he mean? Who'll *dance to our tune?*"

She stared blankly for just a moment and then, something inside her seemed to gather itself. She cleared her throat and said, "Everybody."

"What's that mean?" Max asked.

"*Everybody,*" she repeated, but now like she *knew*, certainty without proof but certainty nonetheless. "Governments, Business—Everybody."

And then it was quiet, for what felt like a long time. We waited to make sure she had nothing more to say—and to let it all sink in.

"Okay," Max said in his echoey voice, "you fell asleep while preparing to go out. You were stressed from the events of the day. Do you understand?"

"Of course. I'll tell him you were here," she said cheerily.

Max smiled. "Of course you will," he replied respectfully. "But I didn't get anything out of you because I couldn't get the password."

"You couldn't get the password," she repeated half a second behind and you could see her relief at the thought, as his suggestion faded her actual mistake away, out of memory, out of existence. "You didn't get it..." she murmured, fading away.

"I didn't get it," Max repeated softly. "Tell Pietr you did well. *You have every reason to feel good about yourself*," he ended, touching her forehead and she slouched back onto the couch, snoring like a buzzsaw. He led us out the door, down the elevator and back outside.

"What now?" I asked, pulling the car out of the parking lot. "It's Friday night. If they've got a big deal Sunday—"

"What are they doing with CIA?" he demanded, handing the piece of paper with Sam's writing to Tauber in the back seat. "Does that make any sense to you?"

"Maybe if we knew who IAD is..." Tauber muttered.

"It's the rat squad," I said and felt all eyes on me at once. "It's on all the cop shows—Internal Affairs, the cops that watch the cops."

"That's what I was supposed to do for Alan Hammond," Max said, seeming to find the memory impossibly strange now.

"So does CIA have a rat squad?" Tauber asked. "Is L Corp watchin' CIA?"

"How would that make everyone dance to their tune?" I asked.

"Maybe they've got some secret—maybe they're blackmailin' CIA."

"Do they really want to cross the Government like that?"

"It would explain why they're meetin' on a Sunday," Tauber held onto his point. "Keep it off the record."

"They've already built themselves a position where the government can't hurt them," Max shook his head. "Why open Pandora's box? Blackmail doesn't make sense."

"And it's not what she said," I added, as surprised as anyone to hear myself speaking up. "She said there was an operation, that Volkov had a group of six in training and it's Sunday. Blackmail isn't an operation."

"—ya don't need six black ops to handle it," Tauber added. "Maybe they're gonna steal something from CIA and blackmail 'em with it. Maybe that's what they're doin' Sunday."

"But what's that got to do with Dave?" I asked. "Why kill Dave?"

Silence. Several beats of silence.

"It seems," Max said, "that the only thing we know for sure is who CIA is." He shrugged. "We've got to go someplace and dope this out."

"Someplace we can *think*," Tauber added, "and this ain't it—it's a probe a minute around here. Where do we go?" Tauber asked and Max looked blank for a moment.

"Ruben Crowell," I said. "Gettysburg, Pennsylvania."

"Ruben?" Tauber exclaimed. His face got all screwed up.

"You know him?" Max asked. "Good guy?"

"One o' the best, back in the day," Tauber said. "Smart guy, kind of a rebel—part o' Dave's klatch. Now? Who knows? None of us are what we were. How about Marjorie, his wife? They were both in the program."

"Don't know her," I answered. "I just have Ruben's name."

"What about him?" Max asked again. "How would he fit into all this?"

"Let's put it this way," Tauber said. "I can imagine Ruben havin' nothing to do with *any* of us. I can imagine him makin' pizzas or analyzin' nut cases for a living. I *can't* imagine him workin' for Jim Avery."

I could see a highway overpass ahead, the truck lights running off in both directions. Max shrugged. "Okay then," he said, "North, Pancho."

Eleven

We crept up on Gettysburg like Lee's Army, coming out of the South up what is now called Confederate Avenue. The sun rose through haze on the hill by the university, dense lines of trees setting off the old town below, the long straight streets marching into the distance, columns of upright woodframe and brick houses bearing the bulletholes of the battle that made America. We'd been driving all night—East, West, Southwest, Northeast—we were on our third car since Virginia.

"Wow!" Tauber breathed out as soon as he got out of the car.

"What?" I asked.

"I don't feel any old-time mindbenders," he said, "but there's sure a whole lot o' *them*—L Corp—lotsa fuzzy, dim signals." He moved around a bit, as though the signal might improve facing a slightly different direction. "But nobody like us. Nobody like Ruben."

"I don't know," Max cautioned. "There's an odd one. Not a mindbender signal but powerful. Very deep—like an 8 Hz tone." Tauber seemed to be trying to reach for this without success.

"Can you read it?" he asked.

"Not in a way that makes any sense," Max said. "But—if he wasn't here, why would *they* be here?"

"They're waitin' fer us," Tauber said. "We'll have to be careful."

"If you can't be careful, you have to be *quick*," Max said.

He drove through town, feinting in one direction and then another. We didn't see any suspicious SUV's or jumpsuits but the two of them kept watch out the windows all the same, tense and twitchy. "The signal's very strong," Max said, "but it's not organized, if that makes any sense. It's not focused at all."

"Some kid? Practicing the remote viewing he learned on MySpace?" Tauber asked.

"No," Max said. "This isn't some lonely geek conquering the world. This is pain and confusion and... I don't know, something else ..."

"Where's it coming from?" I asked, just as it became obvious. Max turned off the road under a huge brick archway into a cemetery, a vast cemetery stretched across a rolling hillside, intersected by stone walls and rows of gravestones like an old man's ragged yellow teeth.

"This is it," Tauber said in a hushed voice.

"What?"

"They fought here. Lincoln gave the speech here." A note of awe and pain was in his voice.

"You've been here?"

"Not me," he said. "My great-grandaddy. 26th North Carolina. Died here, Cemetery Ridge. Pickett's Charge." There was pain and pride in his voice.

We drove the treed lanes. Max seemed to know where he was going without being in any hurry to get there. Apparently, I wasn't the only one who noticed.

"What's up?" Tauber asked finally.

"I'm trying to suss out what's going on here," Max answered, his voice really sober, almost mournful. "I'm trying to get a sense of what we're walking into. It isn't Ruben."

"How do you know?"

"The signal's female."

"Yep, that lets Ruben out. Marjorie?"

"Maybe." He listened a little longer. "In for a penny, in for a pound," he shrugged finally and nosed the car around some trees until we could see the little rise ahead holding ten or fifteen people communing over an open grave. I didn't see the priest but we could hear the blunt music of one voice prompting and a group responding. Max parked at the bottom of the rise, where the road ended. We started up the hill but we didn't get far.

The sudden rumble made us all turn. Two familiar black SUV's were tearing down both entry roads simultaneously. They stopped and emptied and then there were six of them to three of us, all of them wearing the LED goggles with earpieces. The leader came out last—Miriam Fine, looking even more fetching in the tight blue nylon jumpsuit than she had in her gray suit and pearls. Her eyes winked at me from inside the goggles—though I knew, when I thought about it, that I couldn't actually see in there.

"Well, this *is* convenient," she said cheerfully. "I come to wrap up one loose end and the other drops into my lap." She motioned at the open van doors. "Take a seat—we'll all go for a drive."

"Not happening," Tauber said before Max could get a word out. "I've already had yer hospitality." His eye was still half-shut and deep blue.

"Why don't we discuss it?" Max asked. The offer took Tauber by surprise and didn't seem to suit Fine any better.

"Over there?" she offered, pointing to a dense copse of trees across the road.

"I like you better with witnesses," Max answered, glancing at the burial party twenty feet up the hill. "You can't erase that many, can you? We'll talk here."

"The Russians were right about you," Fine shook her head. "You're no spy. You're negotiating? With what?" She whipped a Glock from the hip pocket of her jumpsuit and held it to my forehead. "We're wearing the glasses—send any suggestion you want; we can't hear it. But everyone knows what *I* want." Her posse—all men around my age, gazing at her adoringly—pulled their Glocks from their side pockets and leveled them at us. I was *soooo* weary of guns. Fine's cold steel tingled at my forehead and somehow I still couldn't help but stare longingly at her. She felt so good to be in bed with…or she would've if we'd ever been there.

"What you will all do now is lie on the ground, arms out."

"You gonna carry us outta here?" Tauber cracked.

"As long as you cooperate," Fine said, looking around at the gravestones dotting the hill. "If not, we'll leave you in an appropriate place."

By the time she finished the sentence, it became clear she was struggling, though it was hard to tell with what. She was fighting her own words, face grimacing and sounds spewing out of her in a rush, forced past some unseen barrier.

One of her boys—gymrat muscles and a bright red Mohawk—stepped forward and leveled his pistol at Max. "Make it stop or I'll shoot!" he screamed in his ear. Max's eyes were as wide as the rest of us. He shook his head very slowly back and forth to say *Not me.*

A moment later, Mohawk Boy's arm began to quiver like a diving board, his gun swinging up and down a tiny distance but an impossible speed. At that moment, he couldn't have pulled the trigger if he'd wanted to. He stared wide-eyed at his own body shaking itself apart.

When I thought that phrase—*shaking itself apart*—it was just an expression. A moment later, it became reality. With a crack and a shriek, I saw something bulge up under the skin around Mohawk Boy's elbow and his lower arm went limp; a moment later, something much bigger jerked upward through his shoulder blades and his whole arm fell. He cried in pain and reached over to grab his limp, useless right arm.

Fine pushed the muzzle of her gun right into my forehead. "I said *Stop!*" she yelled at Max but he just shrugged helplessly.

Mohawk Boy's arm hung limp at his side, but his gun hadn't moved—it remained suspended in mid-air, shaking itself to bits, piece after piece splitting off, spitting away as though spontaneously disassembling. A moment later, the unruly stream burst high into the sky—all eyes following—and spiraled in a disorganized stream into the open grave at the top of the rise.

There was a new expression on Fine's face—and nothing I could have expected. If the rest of us were mystified, Fine was suddenly angry with herself, guilty even, like this was something she should have foreseen.

Following her glance, I couldn't miss the reed of a girl marching downhill out of the crowd of mourners. Tall, long face full of freckles, strong nose and dark hair glinting chestnut in morning light. Her expression was fierce. And nervous. Maybe even frightened. But determined. Let's say she was hard to read. At very least, she was *confusing* to read.

Mohawk Boy was suffering pretty loudly. He made a kind of bleating noise and the girl threw a piercing glance at him; immediately there was a loud crack at his knee and he buckled to the ground. This time, the bone actually poked through the skin. The other L Corps all predictably leveled their guns at her for a moment, until they leapt out of their hands and performed a lovely ellipse, high into the air and down into the grave, following the remains of Mohawk Boy's pistol.

"*No more guns,*" the girl ordered, in a voice shaking, barely under control. "*No more fighting.*" She stopped and glanced at us and her gaze wavered uncertain for about a fifth of a second. Then she turned her attention back to the L Corp crew, whose goggles, cell phones and car keys flew into the air and joined their other toys in the now-crowded grave above. A moment later, the pile of earth next to the grave began to pour with rising force into the hole.

Mohawk Boy was writhing on the ground, crying out and trying to push his bones back where they belonged. He kept staring at Fine, pleading, but Fine ignored him—her angry frustrated gaze remained locked on the chestnut-haired girl, who coolly returned it. I saw a flash of something almost like amusement on her face for just a moment. "Take your clothes off," she ordered, in the tone of voice the librarian used to tell you *no talking* in the stacks.

"You don't—" Fine began but her jumpsuit began unzipping on its own and her shoelaces immediately unraveled and tied themselves together until she fell helplessly over onto the grassy hill. The girl gave the others a sharp glance and they proceeded without further argument to unbutton and unzip.

"When you're finished," she told them, "you can walk back to your hotel."

She turned her attention to us. "That should slow them down—I have a bag in my trunk," she said, pointing to an old Honda parked a few yards away. "We should go before they call for reinforcements, right?" We all scrambled up the hill to her car, while she collected the L Corp clothes and threw them into our trunk.

~~~~

Tauber drove—it was his turn. I rode shotgun, Max and our passenger slid into the back seat. She seemed in a daze for several minutes, just staring at the seatback in front of her. When she started to recover herself, she drew up into some kind of parody of perfect posture. All at once, she really was the sexy librarian.

"They're from something called the L Corporation," she said finally, the words arriving in spurts. "It's supposed to be some kind of consulting group but—"

"We've met," Tauber said, adjusting the rear-view mirror to get a better look at her.

"The operations head is Pietr Volkov," she added, staring at Max. "You should know him."

Max nodded. "Again, we've met—just recently, in fact."

Her eyebrow went up. "You think in English."

"I was raised to be an American," Max smiled his best smile, which was still not so hot. Another lull followed—the young woman seemed to drift away from us again. Then, all at once, she looked around startled and thrust her hand at me like an insurance agent on the make. "I'm Kate Crowell," she said. "You were with Dave Monaghan?"

"Yes." Here was another one who read your mind as deadpan as Max. By now, that was only a little shock.

"I'm sorry," she said. "When did they kill him?"

"Three days ago."

"First thing in the morning," she said, although it was a question, not a statement. I nodded. "That's when they ran my father over. Outside the supermarket. Stolen car, hit and run." Her voice cracked in the middle but she just pushed past it.

"Did they catch the driver?"

"I just did."

"The guy back at the cemetery?"

"Yes. He did it." Each word seemed to come out of her as a separate effort.

"So you broke every bone in his body," Max said, a judgment in his voice.

"I didn't," she answered, voice quivering. Every eye in the car must have gone wide at that, because she gathered herself up in protest. "I didn't do anything." She turned with a forced brightness to Tauber. "You're Mark—you knew my father."

"Yeah," Tauber said, "he was a good 'un. One of the best."

"That's not what you mean to say," she said and waited for more.

"He...he was a full dose. An adult portion." Tauber's cheeks colored as he laughed and she followed, though everything she did seemed a little vacant. The way it would be if you'd just buried your father.

"And you—I know all about you," she said, returning to Max.

"I doubt that."

"My father went down to Washington when they debriefed you. The program was over but he still had a few friends—he pulled strings just to watch. He was so excited—he was going to see Renn!"

"He just wanted to see the horns on my forehead," Max flashed his horrible smile again. "He was interested in seeing someone else like him—someone else like you."

"You're somethin', sweetie," Tauber crowed. "You're just what we've been needin'."

Kate started at that, throwing an alarmed look around the car.

"Whoa—wait a minute," she said, hands raised in protest. "Let's get something straight. I don't do this stuff. My dad's been calling me for weeks to do research for him—I'm in school in Philadelphia and he's useless on the Internet—*was* useless."

Her eyes fluttered. She tucked her chin up and plunged ahead.

"He and Dave Monaghan worked themselves up about this whole L Corp business. They went into spasms about something every couple years. Except I guess they got it right this time. So I have his research and the notes I took for him. I'll share them with you. But after that, I'm going back. To School. Where I belong."

"That's what I said the other day," Max told her. "That I wasn't getting involved."

"We need ya," Tauber drawled. "This is a big fight we're in. With what you did back there—"

"I have no *idea* what I did back there!" Kate burst and shrunk back into her seat, defiant and guilty at once. "Look, I've seen what happens to...people like you. Nobody wants you running loose. Nobody trusts you."

"People like *us*?" Tauber said. "Honey, we're people like *you*."

"I am a graduate student in Museum Planning," Kate insisted, talking right over him. "I have a life and a boyfriend. As soon as I finish my thesis, I've got six good institutions that want me."

"You are the possessor of very powerful forces and senses, more powerful than 99% of the population. If you don't—" Max paused, looking at his lapel. A funny smell filled the car.

"I spent my whole childhood getting disciplined," Kate rattled on, "for things I didn't mean to do. My parents got in the way of every good date I had, because they thought I gave boys crushes on me. I didn't even know—"

"Stop," Max said.

"What good is it anyway? The things you find out, no one even wants to know. It's like—"

"STOP!!"

Kate flinched. "Stop what?" We all seemed to notice the smoke at the same time.

"You're burning a hole in my shirt," Max said. A little plume of blue steam was rising from the corner of his breast pocket.

"I'm not," Kate whispered, pulling her head back into her shoulders.

"You may not be aware of it," Max said, "but...you are," and he tamped the smoke out with his finger.

Kate gulped hard and jerked her head sideways into the window. "Dammit! I'm not...Shit!" She clamped her arms across her chest. "I'm—*beyond* all this!" She dissolved into tears, drawing herself into the corner of the chair. Max offered a hand on her shoulder, but of course he didn't have the touch for it and she wasn't interested anyway.

We headed north through Harrisburg. The highway whittled down a few lanes due to construction and we crawled for a while. Max probably could have made everybody pull out of the way if he wanted, but it seemed like everyone needed to breathe, to regain a sense of the world around.

"Are we going somewhere?" Tauber asked finally.

"I'm not sure yet, just keep moving," Max said. "They don't know where we're going."

"Well, neither do *we*," Tauber answered, "so they're on the money." Max shot him a look.

"Where's the rest of your team?" Kate asked, ending a long silence. "Who else is working with you?"

Long pause.

"It's—it's just us," I said.

Recognition broke over her face in waves. Disbelief came first. She searched our faces, to confirm we were serious. Then she started to laugh, almost against her will. "Are you kidding?"

"No," Max sighed. That was when reality swept over me all at once. I'd been so caught up in what we were doing, in the energy and activity of it, I'd lost track of just how crazy the whole idea was. The ring in her question was reality and it wasn't pretty.

"Do you know who these guys are?" she demanded. "I mean, anything these companies say in public record is meant to mislead and L Corp *admits* to thirty billion annual revenue. They opened the doors six years ago, supposedly for political consulting but last year wasn't even an election year, at least not in this country. So it's either Defense or they're selling drugs—who else makes that kind of money that fast? They had a couple guys camped around my house the last few days—I figured, if they were trying to get inside my head, I'd get inside theirs first. They're serious, they've got big resources and big backers and some big deal happening really soon."

"Tomorrow," Tauber said.

Kate's eyebrows went up like exclamation points.

"You know that? For a fact?"

She kept looking back and forth from one to the next of us. You could feel the air leaking out of the car. She stared out the window, tapping her knuckles against it like a drummer.

"I have an apartment," she said finally, "in Philadelphia. Dad never visited me, so they couldn't have gotten the address from him. You should be safe there overnight." She made a disgruntled count of the company. "Someone's going to have to sleep in the bathtub," she announced.

~~~~

Her apartment was in what looked like a very dignified old garage. "It's a mews," her voice echoed as she opened the huge door—someone had built it some time ago to fit the ornate archway on the street. "We're tracing back the documents—I know it's at least two centuries old but that's as far as we've gotten." The neighborhood was one of those arty places where everything looks a little rundown but one neighbor stacks huge paintings in his window while the sound of a jazz band drifts out of the next.

The TV was on when she opened the front door. The two spooks, Tauber and Max, immediately went stiff and cautious, moving through the place door to door, throwing open and checking each room thoroughly before relaxing. Kate walked calmly past them into the kitchen to make coffee.

"Steve leaves the TV on all the time—when he's here, when he's gone. It's his imaginary friend."

"Steve?" I asked.

"My boyfriend."

"You live together?" Max demanded. The tone of voice said he wasn't convinced there was no threat. "He stays here even when you're gone?"

"Well—he and Morgan were here. They're away this weekend." She hesitated for a moment. "She's my roommate— Steve's with her too," she said with a little hesitation.

"So he's the *apartment* boyfriend," I remarked and Tauber shot me a look. Kate just nodded and went back to her coffee. "Do you have tea?" Max asked and she nodded and ran water into a kettle.

"They won't barge in on us?" Max asked. "The roommate and...your boyfriend?"

"They're gone till Monday," Kate answered wistfully, kindling a questioning look on Max's face.

There was an artist's easel propped against a corner, holding a book of drawing paper. Max tore off a page.

"We're going to spread out on the table," he announced, setting Kate scrambling to move a pile of academic journals onto the floor before he could upend them. Max spread the paper across the surface. Kate pulled out a speckled journal out of the side pocket of her suitcase and opened it to a page marked by a yellow stickie.

"These are my father's notes from his talks with Dave, my notes from our conversations and my research. I can't promise they're word for word but the gist should be right."

The pot started to whistle. Kate turned but Tauber held up his hand. "You stay, sweetie," he said. "I can make tea—and coffee."

"My hero," she answered. She opened her book and started reading out loud. Each major point she made, Max jotted on the sheet, lines drawn between known connections and dotted lines between suspected or hypothetical ones. It was a familiar list—L Corp, using mindbenders to bolster candidates and business clients, an army of low-level mindbenders to send out mental suggestions and the Big Scheme coming soon.

"There's not much new here," Tauber said when she'd finished. The table was a nice mess of papers and coffee mugs, doodles on art paper and lots of names with arrows pointing at other names pointing at question marks, mostly because we didn't really know a whole lot more than we did before.

"What did you do to the shooters at the cemetery?" Max asked again. When she didn't answer immediately, he explained, "You made their guns fly away. They got naked without a peep."

"Can't you do that?"

"I want to know how *you* did it. Their goggles were supposed to hold down outside influences like us."

"I don't know exactly."

"You usually make guns fly around without knowing what you're doing?"

"I don't usually deal with people with guns!" she answered, again as though fighting to get the words out. Or fighting to control herself.

"So you took their guns—and cell phones," Max said. "And goggles. And clothes. And you broke the killer's bones." Having seen her temper, I wouldn't have kept pushing this point but that didn't stop him.

"I—I didn't," Kate protested again. A long moment passed, the two staring each other down across the table. Then she added, "Not on purpose. He really did kill my father! It was in his head. He drove the car himself, so no one would botch the job. He ran over him twice to make sure he couldn't survive and then just drove off." The tears were brimming but she fought them off stubbornly, heroically. A long moment passed in silence.

"But *not on purpose* isn't the same as *I didn't do it*, is it?" Max said finally. "What did you know when you marched down that hill into the face of six people with serious guns and bad intent?"

"I knew I was sick of guns," she answered fiercely. "I knew you were coming from Dave."

"How did you know that?"

"He told my father that, if anything happened to him, you'd be coming." This was a shock to me but Max just smiled, as though it confirmed something he'd already been thinking.

"And what *else* did you know?" he said, voice softening.

"Why is it so important?"

"If you're really fooling yourself that you didn't make those things happen, I need to know it."

"You don't need to know anything about me."

"And if you broke his bones at ten feet without meaning to, I would think *you'd* better know it. People like us can't afford illusions about ourselves."

"Why? The psychiatrists are all booked up?" She was building up a slow boil again; I started looking for a soft place to land.

Max eyes flared. They seemed to draw up into his skull. I felt his voice coming at me through the floorboards.

"Our illusions have consequences. They have a way of becoming real."

Kate's face went paler, if such a thing were possible. "I don't know what you mean."

"Where is this boyfriend of yours? Where's your roommate?"

"I—I told you. They—they went camping. They made plans... a long time ago."

"You just buried your father."

"You can't expect them to feel the way I do."

"I could expect them to go to the funeral for your sake." Kate's jaw was set but her eyes were nowhere near as confident.

"Does Morgan share Steve with you when she's around? Or are you the only one sharing?"

Max was inches from her now. His voice was so soft, I couldn't believe I really heard it. I saw his lips moving but the words seemed to come from inside my head.

"Your feelings run very deep; they frighten you. Millions of people with the depth of a coat of varnish are frightened by their feelings. And you carry oceans—so I understand your caution." He stared into Kate's eyes like he was pulling her inside-out through them. "But instead of learning to deal with the power of them, you've gone into hiding. You've taken partners who don't touch anything in you and given them free reign. It's safe—you know they're only using you for sex and company—you're in no danger of feeling anything that could get out of hand. Your career keeps you at an academic distance from all of human history. You've got the illusion of a life but no nourishment. The longer you bottle those feelings up, the more powerfully they'll spill out in the end."

His eyes were hard on her and for a moment she looked stung, almost shamed. But then her face turned defiant. She took him on and stared him down.

"Funny-from what I'm reading, you've spent the last twenty years hiding—from *everything*."

Max didn't bend. "I said I understood—I didn't say I was different."

The place was quiet for a long moment before Kate gave out a long sigh.

"Okay," she admitted, "when I came down the hill, I knew I wasn't going to let them kill anyone else. And I knew I could *do* something about it."

She was confiding now instead of confronting. But her voice gained strength as she went.

Tauber came out of the kitchen with a fresh pot of coffee and refilled the cups.

"Well now, that's the thing, ain't it? Knowin' you can *do* somethin' 'bout it. There's somethin' big comin' down in the next day or two and we seem to be the only ones in the world who can *do* somethin' 'bout it." He clicked his cup into hers. "Yer daddy'd be with us if he was around."

She was wavering, still conflicted. "They're defense contractors. Let the government squeeze the purse strings—they can stop them."

"They don't need the government's money."

"They've got Jim Avery!" I burst.

"*Your World*? On TV?"

"He's the bankroll," Tauber said.

"Hmph!" Kate puffed. "That's some bankroll."

"They've got all the connections in the world," Max said, looking intently at her again. "No one will ever investigate your father's death—or Dave's. They'll be papered over. No justice for them if we don't make it ourselves."

You could see this pound its way into her. She'd been holding herself in ever since the funeral and now every feeling in her simmered just an inch beneath the surface. Max sat up and his voice was straightforward, unemotional.

"I've spent twenty years," he said, "hiding from what I am. Sounds like you've done the same. And we see the results: I've lost my best friend; you've lost your father."

Kate was struggling now. "There's got to be an answer," she whispered. "There's got to be hope."

"Ya want Hope? Avery'll sell it to ya, sixty bucks a barrel," Tauber said with satire in his voice. "He's the OPEC o' Hope."

Kate wheeled around so fast, we all jumped in place. "I've *heard* that!" she hissed. "Where did I—? From the man in the car! When I got home from... identifying Dad's...body, I went into the kitchen to make coffee and I got this weird headache, like the back of my skull was hot. A probe. Dad used to probe me in high school, to make sure I hadn't gone over some boy's house." Her voice wavered again and now she kept talking despite tears rolling down her cheeks. "It was the guy in the van parked across the street."

"You can handle probes?" Max asked.

"I was a good girl," Kate answered, lifting her chin. "When my parents made me promise never ever to do something, I only tried it a couple times." She flashed a sly smile, almost despite herself. "Besides, I had to learn so I *could* go over the boy's house, didn't I?" Her smile faded fast. "So I followed the probe back to the guy across the street and started riding his thoughts, letting them carry me, for hours at a time."

She saw Max's eyes on her and she reddened.

"I had a hard time making friends, okay? I was the eerie girl in middle school who talked to herself and commented on *what people were thinking* instead of what they'd said out loud. Eventually, you make use of your advantages. I started getting into boy's heads. It got me a better class of dates." She laughed and placed her cup in the sink. "Anyway, when I got inside the guy across the street, I found out about the big operation—he's doing security for the flight."

"There's a flight?" Tauber asked.

"Definitely," Kate answered. "More than one—he's in charge of his and two others. And there's more besides."

"Then they're not goin' to Langley," Tauber concluded.

"Langley? That's CIA, right?" Kate said. "It's always in the movies."

Max nodded. "This whole thing's tied up with the CIA somehow. But nobody's flying from Herndon to Langley—it's ten miles."

"What was weird was, he was doing security and they didn't give him the details. All he knew was, it's soon—"

"Tomorrow—"

"—they told him to bring his passport and warm weather clothes for a week. And they told him, *This is the big shot. We won't get another chance like this for years.*"

"A chance for what? Did they tell him that?"

"To kill hope. That's what they said, to kill hope everywhere."

"That doesn't make a lot of sense," Tauber said. "If they kill hope, what's Avery got to offer 'em?"

The room went silent for awhile. Then I heard myself speaking. "What he's offering is a *fix*," I said. They all turned to look at me and damned if I had any idea what I wanted to say but that didn't stop the words from coming.

"My outfit had a local guy, a translator, in Najaf. He was real useful when we first got there and everybody was friendly. Six months later, everybody—Sunnis, Shiites—started targeting his family because he was helping the Americans. We had to smuggle them all to Jordan. He applied for a visa to the States and our CO promised to help him get it.

"And then word filtered down that they—whoever 'they' were—weren't processing visas, not fast, and then not ever. Which didn't stop him from showing up in my quarters every couple days, bugging *me* about it. 'Are they helping me? We getting a visa?' What was I supposed to say? 'It's America,' I told him.

'They'll do the right thing.' After the fourth or fifth time, no way either of us believed it.

"But it ate at me. Why didn't he go to the CO? Why me? The answer is, because I'm not tough—never been. He came to me because I'd tell him what he wanted to hear. I gave him his fix, his hope for the week. I felt like a pusher, too. Who made *me* a spokesman for America?"

I could feel the memory burning inside, like it had just happened, like it was happening right *now*. My fists and teeth were clenched tight. "That's what Avery's doing—offering everybody their fix."

We filtered around for a while, aimless, each of us wandering around the room, uncertain of the next step.

"It makes sense," Max finally said. "It's what Avery told us—supply *and* demand. If they kill hope, he's got this huge organization designed to offer it—for a price."

"And it's so much safer sellin' measured portions to them that can afford it," Tauber said. "Real hope's messy. Unruly. Bad business."

"But what does the CIA have to do with it?" Kate asked.

"Five minutes talkin' to them'll kill any hope ya got left," Tauber cracked and we all smiled. But the joke didn't get us any closer to an answer.

The TV was in front of me; I wasn't thinking of escape or boredom. I wasn't interested in what was on. If there's a TV in front of me, I pick up the remote and turn up the sound. Thirty seconds later, I change the channel. It's what I do. It's the way I survived Iraq and a year in the middle of a swamp and probably my childhood. So now I did it again, just out of habit.

"Preparations continued for tomorrow's G8 Summit in Rome," the announcer droned, trying to sound important if not exciting. "Demonstrations were held on four continents today in support of Indian Premier Aryana Singh's proposal for worldwide nuclear disarmament. Rome police are out in force, covering the major squares and thoroughfares to keep the demonstrations from spiraling into unruliness."

"There, ya see?" Tauber cracked. "Unruliness! Them bastards have *hope!*"

"Tomorrow's arrivals of foreign dignitaries have been moved to Rome's Ciampino Airport, a rigidly-secured military facility. Authorities have assured foreign governments that..."

My eyes must have gone huge. Kate saw it from across the room. "What?" she demanded.

"We've got it all wrong," I said and Max slapped his forehead across the room, reading me.

"Got *what* wrong?"

"Everything. CIA!"

"They're behind it?" Tauber barked. "Against it?"

"Neither. It's not *the* CIA. It's just CIA—the *airport* is CIA!" I ran to Kate's computer and punched up Google. "I flew into

Ciampino once on leave. The airport code—the three letter ID on your luggage?" I waited a second for the information to display. "Ciampino is CIA."

"And IAD?"

I scanned down the list. "Dulles."

"They're flying to Rome tomorrow," Tauber said. "From Dulles to the G8."

"To *kill hope*," Kate murmured, staring at the TV, where Singh was addressing a raucous crowd from a balcony in New Delhi.

"We seek a new world," her voice echoed across the square. "In our lifetime, we have seen walls dissolve between East and West. Now it is time to continue that work, to push down the walls of fear between us, to keep pushing until no more walls are left. This is a long road but, as the philosopher says, every journey must begin with a first step."

The crowd cheered.

"Them bastards have *hope*," Max repeated quietly. "We're going to need passports."

Twelve

We left for New York around two in the morning. Kate had locked herself in her room for a couple of hours, the sound of her crying surfacing every once in a while, whenever she lifted her face out of the pillow. Max went out in the afternoon, saying he was 'going hunting,' whatever that meant—he returned twenty minutes later, talked to Tauber a minute and went right out again. When Kate finally emerged, eyes bloodshot and suspended between collapse and explosion, Tauber quietly said, "If we're boardin' an international flight with no suitcases, they'll have us in the interrogation room in about half a second." When Kate looked up, he waved a stack of fifties in her face—apparently Max had done another bank run.

She dragged us out shopping and spent the evening expertly packing suitcases in the living room, refusing to let any of us help. But when Max finally returned at 11 with Chinese and said we'd soon be ready to go, she boiled over.

"I'm totally unreliable. I'll be a danger to you all. I don't know what I'm doing till I've done it. And I won't be any good in a fight. There are things I'm not willing to do, even to my enemies."

"Breaking every bone in their bodies should get us through most situations," Max answered drily and Kate surprised herself by breaking into laughter.

"That's very reassuring," she said.

Tauber returned from down the block with a very lived-in hearse.

"This won't attract attention?"

"They'll notice ya but nobody's gonna stop ya," he smirked.

"Here's your passports," Max announced, handing each of us a packet of several. "Use the American ones for now."

"Keep no more'n one on ya at a time," Tauber cautioned. "The rest go in yer suitcase. Invent a good backstory for yourself, a history. Nothin' fancy, just simple so we can all remember."

The little blue books looked very realistic—mine had several pages of dog-eared destination stamps.

"Are these for real?" Kate asked.

"The guy who made them is the CIA's guy in Philadelphia," Max explained. "He has the real machines."

"So they're real."

"No. The serial numbers come from dead people whose passports haven't expired and a couple of variations in the holograms make them forgeries. So they're just wrong enough that the government can deny us." He smiled. "Does that make me a patriot?"

"Will he remember making them once the suggestion runs out?"

"No suggestion," Max said. "It would have worn off before the G8 ends, so not a good idea." He held up the chain with the ID card and BMW key fob. "I told him it was L Corp business. They're the fair-haired boys these days, so he'll make sure he forgets."

Halfway up the Jersey Turnpike, everybody had settled in. Tauber and Max were lights-out in the back seat, Tauber with his arms crossed over his chest like a mummy, Max rousing with tremors every few minutes, taking a drowsy look around and settling back to sleep.

Kate rocked slightly in the passenger seat, humming to herself but staring at me every once in a while. "What does he want?"

"Who?"

"Renn." She was rolling around in the seat, giving me the girly eye. I'd taken a few peeks at her too, though the memory of her breaking the guy's bones at the graveyard (and knowing she could read my thoughts) kept me respectful. She was pretty in a distracted tomboy sort of way, the girl who didn't pay attention to her own looks. Which, in the real world, meant she was pretty enough not to have to—and knew it.

"I don't know. It's a big question," I asked.

She ran her finger up the side window of the car—it had started to rain again; we'd been moving through showers the whole way. "Well, that's the hard part, isn't it? To know what you want."

She reminded me of Tess all of a sudden, which didn't make sense; they didn't look at all alike. Maybe it was just the way we were talking, softly, the rain patting on the roof, like lovers after bed.

"I've seen how you pay attention—to everything," she observed. "You're a watcher. You have to know *something* about him."

I was a little annoyed she wasn't more interested in *me*. "I know who he is," I said firmly and she sat up. "He's a superhero who wants to be a person, but he's not really cut out for either one." She didn't seem impressed, though I thought I was reasonably brilliant.

The overhead lights rolled across the windshield like the drum lights on a copy machine. The rain came in bursts and other cars hovered in ragged clusters every couple miles.

"What do you remember?" she asked after ten minutes of silence.

"What?"

"That's your problem, isn't it? Remembering?"

"It's one of my problems."

"So what do you remember?"

I wanted her to be interested in me but then I went all suspicious when she was. That's what I got for the kind of company I was keeping. But the look on her face drew me in. She had power and she was the first one in this whole crew to ask me the slightest thing about myself. She cared—I could see it, just looking at her. Max kept telling me not to worry about how I knew things anyway, right? Just *know what you know*—I could hear him voice pounding that line into my head. I felt like I knew Kate—and I trusted her. She could probably find out more about me in three seconds than I knew myself—if she wanted to.

"What do I remember? Lots and nothing. I remember being a kid—riding a bike, stacking hay in a field and binding it. I remember the porch and the steps and the dark green screens over the window but I can't remember where we lived, not even what state. I remember sitting in the kitchen with my mother, singing Doobie Brothers songs along with the radio. I remember she'd cut her hair short and I remember her dress—some bright orange thing with a big swirly pattern on it—but I can't see her face. How can I not remember my mother's face?" The images were there always, fragments, bits and pieces that didn't add up to anything bigger, any sort of whole. They were always there behind my eyes, behind every conscious thought. "I remember women—dates, my arm around some girl at a movie, parked in the high weeds in my car. I remember the dashboard light and the feel of some girl's blouse, her perfume and the taste of her neck. And the crickets, *so* loud. But it's flashes and feelings, nothing...complete. What do you remember?"

"Of my life?" she asked, confused.

"Of *my* life," I said. "You're the mindreader, right? You see any more than I do?"

"I'm not much of a mindreader," she answered, "But—can I touch your forehead?"

I pulled away. "I don't like anybody touching me," I insisted though it wasn't true. I was just instinctively afraid of her opening me up like Pandora's Box. Of course, as soon as I thought it, she read it.

"I'm nothing to be scared of," she said. "I backed into this thing."

She smiled and it was a blushing, half-shy, real smile, not that gargoyle smile of Max's. "I'll look inside if you want—it'll be as much of an adventure for me as for you." Then she stopped and I could see her play back what she'd just said; she cackled a moment later. "I guess that *does* sound a bit scary," she admitted but I was already over it.

In the highway light, she was unbearably lovely. Her green eyes just seemed to soak me up. She'd been waiting, waiting for someone—why couldn't it be me?

"I want to help you," she breathed in an impossibly soft voice, "but you have to let me touch you."

If she'd told me to shoot myself in that tone of voice, I couldn't have said no.

She put her fingers to my temples and I got an instant erection. A long blast screeched from a truck horn right alongside and I swerved back into our lane. "Sorry," she said, reddening. "I—I didn't...I never know when I'm going to do that to a guy."

"You mean ...that happens a lot?"

"Not always...but...with some guys, yeah, every time."

"You must be very popular," I said and she giggled. She reached for my temples again; ohh did I not want to resist but I had to pull away.

"I can help you," she murmured. "I can *feel* it."

"I believe it," I said and I sure did. "But maybe while I'm driving isn't the best time."

She settled back into her seat and—just like that—the whole thing fell apart. She was still Kate, real pretty and interested in me but...normal pretty and interested, in a normal way. The magic was gone. I was back in the real world. Tess must have felt that way when Renn released her, though she wouldn't have known what was happening. But Max hadn't anything to do with this—he was still dozing in the back.

This was all Kate, feeding me what I wanted, locating my desire and offering it back. That would be part of a mindbender's arsenal, wouldn't it? Part of a woman's, too. I waited for her to read that I'd caught on, waited a long moment but she just kept staring out the window and then flashed me her cute smile when she caught me watching. I was left wondering if she knew what she was doing at all.

Crossing the Verrazano Bridge, Max roused and Kate immediately asked, "Why mindbenders? If they want to assassinate her, mindbenders are a nuclear reactor for boiling water. All they need is a marksman with a telescopic sight."

"All they need," Max replied, "is a marksman with *access*. This is the G8. Rome will be totally locked down. Even before all this disarmament craziness, you would have had 100,000 protesters. Now? You'll need DNA scans to get past the first barrier."

She sat mulling a moment. "You don't mean disarmament is crazy."

"What's it matter what I think?"

"You're *serious*."

"It's not practical," he said. "For smaller countries, nukes are their chance to play on the big stage. If the G8 agree to disarm, the small countries will just see it as a plot to keep them down."

"It's not worth trying?"

"It's actually dangerous," he continued. "At the moment, you have nation-states hiring and paying—paying well—the best nuke-making talent in the world. They build quality-controlled arsenals with oversight and checks and balances, if only because the Presidents don't trust the Generals and vice versa.

"Nation-states have trade on the world market. Their politicians like going to the UN, getting their picture taken smiling with the President or insulting him. All these pressures tip nation-states toward some sort of moderation.

"Take them out of the nuke business, what's left? An international class of brilliant bomb-makers with no paycheck or, if you pay them to do nothing, a pack of creative lunatics bored to death. And who comes calling on them next? Guys who are *way* scarier than the ones they work for now."

Kate took this in and shook her head. She didn't have an answer but she didn't like his either. Max shrugged. I drove on as the sun came up over Brooklyn.

~~~~

When we reached JFK, Tauber almost fell flat on his face getting out of the car. He threw an arm out to keep himself from capsizing completely, staggered upright and nearly swooned a second time.

I grabbed him by the shoulders. He was quivering like someone had put him in a deepfreeze. "Are you okay?"

"Mostly," he lied, watching his feet like they might start jumping around on their own. "They denied me liquid companionship at L Corp and we haven't had a lot of...time...since then..."

"Is this a good time to go cold turkey?" Max asked him.

"The question I keep askin's if I'm more use to ya drunk or sober." He frowned and rubbed his forehead—his hands were trembling. "Guess we'll find out pretty quick."

The garage elevator was right across from the terminal. Max and Kate came to a sudden stop as soon as the doors opened.

"Jesus," Kate whistled. Nothing seemed wrong that I could see. Then Max whispered, "They're all over the place."

"Where?"

"Look for the lapel pins," Tauber said and everybody turned on him like he'd lit a spotlight. A series of tremors passed through his shoulders—he shrugged, sheepish. "I'm sorry—didn't think of it before. Special Duty, male or female, all have lapel pins."

"To make it easy for us to pick them out?" Max asked.

"There's six pins in a set," Tauber answered. "each one stands fer a frequency. It's a security double-check. If ya have L Corp ID but no pin—or ye're ridin' the wrong frequency for your pin—they've got ya." He smiled. "Volkov's paranoid about his shooters goin' off on their own. Us bein' able to spot 'em easy— that's a bonus."

"They told you this?" I asked.

"They didn't tell me shit. But," he pointed to the black-and-blue bulge, "I know how to keep my eye open—"

"That's good work," Max said and Tauber cracked a smile between tremors. "We'll be as inconspicuous as we can, get our passes, check the luggage and disappear until boarding. Okay?"

We hustled through ticketing and dropping luggage at the bomb-detector. Then we found ourselves on a mezzanine looking down on the food court. It was a sea of lapel pins, men and women in dark-suited clusters killing time, buying magazines and beers and duty-free IPods, arguing sports and reality shows but sticking to their little groups and eyeing their watches.

"They're not here for us," Tauber said. "They're not even watchful."

"Are they *all* flying to Rome?" I asked Max.

"Don't know," he said. "They're blocking."

"Can't you break it?"

"Of course," he sniffed like I'd insulted him.

I'm impatient—I know that. Maybe it's my addled state—if I don't find something out right away, I forget I wanted to know it. "So probe," I suggested.

"That's what I'm *not* doing. They're are all on headset. One probe'll set off alarm bells all over the place." Max's look swept from one end of the floor to the other. "Hang out here," he said. "I'll do a survey and be right back."

He went down the steps and through the crowd, staggering slightly like he'd just left Happy Hour. He threaded a route that allowed him to bump into at least one member of each lapel-pin cluster, hitting them from angles that prevented their getting much of a look at him. Then he wandered up the stairs at the far end and returned to us.

"You're right," he told Tauber. "They're not here for us. And you're right too," aimed at me, "they're all going to Rome. There's *thirty* of them on several flights—not ours, thankfully— and that's just New York. The Washington crowd is going through Dulles and more are coming from North Carolina—Miriam Fine's pupils—and Boston. They got the call two days ago; no plans, no details. Just show up with a suitcase for purposes unknown." He looked down and shook his head. "The weakest minds in the bunch."

"They're plenty effective when they work together," Tauber shivered. "They made me...feel things...at the headquarters. Like I was going to die, like I was suffocating." He cleared his throat loudly. "And worse than that. They're a weapon. If they're sending that many, there's a plan."

"There's a staircase at the other end of the mezzanine," Max said, "We go to the bottom and keep our distance until they call our flight." He turned to Kate. "Don't focus on anybody as we pass, okay?"

"Meaning what?" She sounded offended. "You don't want me to probe them?"

"I don't want you to set them on *fire*, okay?" He set off smirking—she smacked him on the shoulder as he passed.

The stairwell dropped two stories into a hallway to nowhere. Surely there was a way out from here but it wasn't apparent. Tauber walked away from us immediately—you could see the tremors taking him. We all watched, concerned, while he fought it off. Max was next to him when he turned to face us again. He handed Tauber some money.

"Here—take this."

"For what?"

"Maybe it would be smarter if you went home."

"Which home is that, exactly?" Tauber said. "We kinda put paid to my apartment."

"I'm just trying to be sensible. It's your safety."

"And yours. I get it. I can't hack it."

"I didn't say that."

"Then don't. I'm an old gnarly son-of-a-bitch. I'm an alcoholic walkin' disaster. But I'm one thing none o' you is."

"What's that?"

"A spy. A spy who knows how it's done. A spy who can get what he needs without gettin' himself killed."

"We could all die here," Max said, pressing the money at him but Tauber pushed it back.

"Nothin' wrong with dyin'," he said firmly. "Livin' without a reason, *that's* the bad thing. Put your money away—I'm goin'. You'll need me yet."

They exchanged heavy stares for a couple long seconds—Tauber won. Max turned back to us with a kind of fake cheer on his face. "We've got a few hours," he said. "Let's work on defense."

"Such as?"

Max held his hands a few inches apart for several seconds, letting them waver in and out a few inches at a time, as though measuring some invisible distance only he could judge.

"Okay," he said finally, "touch the space between my hands."

"Touch what?" Kate said.

"Between my hands. Touch it."

Kate looked like she'd just swallowed a lemon drop and you couldn't blame her. There was nothing there. But she held her finger out and pushed and the finger buckled.

"Whoa!" she exclaimed, eyes wide. She poked again, having the range now, and her finger stopped at the same spot. That was all it took—her face lit up and she started running her hands over the invisible object, her palms defining the top and sides and pressing a bit at the edges, her eyes bright and smile growing. As she measured, I was able to make out a faint shimmer in the air, a bending of the light filling that space.

"What is it?" she said.

Tauber stuck his hand forward much harder than Kate had and seemed almost to bounce off. "That's not mindbending," he gaped.

Max shrugged. "It's what I did in Novosibirsk when I was supposed to be studying."

He moved towards her, his hands extended in front of him and the empty space somehow pushed her backward. After several shoves, Kate returned the favor, pushing back hard and Max fell backwards onto the floor.

"It's ionized air," he laughed, getting up and brushing himself off. "Molecules with an electrical charge. They pull together like a gas, a connected mass instead of individual particles, but with a strength like a solid object. I generate enough electricity to charge the air around me. And I've learned how to manipulate it."

He turned to Kate. "Hold your hands apart, open to each other. Do you feel a pull—a magnetism—between them?" I tried with mine but didn't feel a thing. Kate looked doubtful too. "It's not going to jump out and kiss you on the lips," Max told her firmly. "You have to know what you know. Either you feel something or you don't."

"I feel *something*," she said uncertainly. "But I don't generate electricity—do I?"

"Enough, I'll bet," he answered. "They're subatomic particles so it doesn't take much. Just follow the hum between your hands, follow it like the thoughts of the guy in the van across the street. The longer you hold the feeling, the more fluid you'll get with it."

She worked her hands back and forth for a long moment, the fascination on her face competing with embarrassment—this was a typical combination when you were dealing with Max. All at once, he flicked his index finger out close to hers—a spark jumped, bright and sharp, from his fingertip to hers.

"You've got juice," he smiled, an uncoiled smile for a change. She returned the smile and I immediately felt a bit queasy, like I was intruding or something.

"Opposites attract—you've heard that, of course."

Her eyes widened, her breath quickened. "I've heard," she answered. This was pretty juvenile banter as far as I was concerned but no one was asking my opinion.

"Positive attracts negative," he said and if he'd held out his finger at that moment, they might have electrocuted each other. "Particles that have to join together to accomplish anything."

"How do I know which I am?" she asked.

He laughed. "You're both, depending on the moment. You don't have to worry about it—you'll automatically attract the opposite. There's always power around you, once you know what to do with it." Kate had her hands wide apart as she eagerly worked up a field, a charge, whatever the hell it was.

"It takes a while," Max advised, close behind her shoulder, "to build and then all at once—you'll feel it—it takes on a shape and consistency of its own, a wholeness. You've got to keep track of that; it's the one tricky bit. When it actually takes shape, you have to hold your breath—the rest of us, too if we're close by—because it sucks all the oxygen out of the air for about five seconds and all that's left is ozone, which is poisonous. So stay sharp."

He bent over and swept his hand out in front of him. You could see a kind of dusty glimmer forming ahead of him. "It works horizontally, too," he said, reaching into his pocket for a handful of coins and tossing them out. The pile scattered, clinking and bouncing, two inches *over* the floor. Max grabbed Kate's hand and she stepped up, eyes wide, onto the surface of the thing. He steadied her as she wobbled around, slipping back and forth like it was wet marble, grinning like a five-year-old on an ice rink. And then the glimmer vanished, the shell disappeared and Kate landed awkwardly, both feet firmly on the floor.

"Okay, it's loads o'fun," Tauber griped. "What *good* is it?" He was tightly-wrapped, like forty minutes before Happy Hour.

"Ever want to hit me?" Max asked.

"Right now, I'd box Jesus."

"Go ahead." He swiped the air between them. "Not too hard, okay?"

"I won't hurt ya," Tauber snarled, throwing a punch at Max's midsection. It snapped through the air and stopped dead, muffled by a thick curtain about three inches deep. Tauber paused for just a second and slapped out another blow, this time at Max's shoulder. The fist stopped fast this time and he almost fell from the deceleration.

"It's an illusion," Tauber protested. "You've put me under."

"Try my knees—but lightly," Max said. Tauber slid his own knee forward and hit Max's—the two of them teetered away from each other. "I didn't charge the air down there."

"Okay, it stops girls and old men," Tauber said. "Will it stop bullets?"

"It'll deflect some and absorb others."

"You control it?"

"No—it responds to the vibrations of the bullet. This is the stuff that drove the commisars crazy. The people that study this stuff will tell you that electrons are electrons. The electrons in me could just as easily be in a desk, a cloud, a peanut or a nuclear warhead. And—I know this for a fact but I'm not sure it's exactly official science—the electrons in the desk *become* part of the peanuts and then the floor and then the cloud overhead. Matter is fluid—there's a continual exchange process. Meanwhile, all that matter reacts to input. To put it simply, our environment— everything around us—reacts to everything else around us. And to us. So the field got thicker and grew when Kate approached it enthusiastically, and toughened up, got denser, when you decided to beat the shit out of it."

"Ye're saying everything's alive?"

"That's over my pay grade," Max said. "But I can't wait until scientists announce that grass has feelings."

"Will it stop lightning bolts?" I asked.

"What?" All eyes on me. I *hate* that.

"Volkov's guy—Marat—he can shoot lightning bolts from his fingers. He was shooting at me when I was trying to get down the hillside."

"How far could he shoot? What kinda' distance?"

"At least a couple yards."

Max, who never really stood still, was still now. "I—I don't know," he said. "That's a new one to me."

"That's no good," Tauber said, staring at Max like he'd been betrayed. "I thought you were the big cheese."

"I don't know Marat—I don't know where he got his training." Max looked thrown. "Anyway, I bet the shield would stop it."

"What do you mean, *bet*?" Tauber growled. "We're four people against an army. They've got training, equipment, systems and backup. The cops and government are with *them*. I don't wanna hear *should*." He was livid. "We need offense. *Hard* offense, something that'll scare 'em back to their cribs. We have to even the odds a little bit here."

"We're trying to prevent an assassination," Max said. "We're not trying to start a war."

"We're trying to stay *alive*." Tauber pulled a cigarette butt out of his pocket and held it to his mouth. "Light it!" he ordered.

Max stared at him uncertainly—he held out a finger and produced a couple of sparks until the cigarette lit.

Tauber pulled a couple of times, took a decent drag and exhaled a long plume of smoke.

"Okay," he said, "now figure out how to do that to a *man*. At thirty feet."

~~~~

The plane wasn't full. They seated us in one center row but we ended up sprawled across several. Max sat shielding Tauber from the attendants and their little booze bottles until the old guy sputtered to sleep. Kate stretched out across the row behind me, covered by four little airline blankets, but I could hear her toss and turn, showing no signs of really being sleepy. I drifted in and out myself, blessedly without bad dreams but also without sustaining any sort of rest. In the middle of the night, I came to, groggy and with voices over my shoulder, whispers out of a dream. The music of the voices came first and for a long interval before the meaning of the words began to kindle.

Kate's voice first: "...but what *kind* of life? Where do you live?"

Max: "I have places to go."

"Are they home? Nobody waiting for you someplace?"

"I'm difficult to get along with."

Her laughter. "If that was the criteria, no man would ever get a date."

Renn laughed(!). And then got over it. "Our gifts make normal ties difficult."

"Shouldn't it be the opposite? If you know what the other person wants—?"

"The other person's not the problem. We have an overwhelming ability to delude others—and ourselves. It's not a wonderful gift."

"We can't see through it?"

A psychiatrist is someone who's trained and gifted at recognizing *other* people's neuroses. We're all blind to our own."

Pause.

"It's not stopping you from flying to Rome," Kate answered. "The dangers aren't stopping you."

"This has been a very scary week for me," Renn whispered. "Scary and terrible and seductive. Pietr is trying to kill me. Anything—*anything*—I do in return is justified; self-defense! I have no limits. I can indulge anything in my power. I can be, as he says, everything I am. Which makes me terribly dangerous. To you,

Greg and Mark. To people who believe in Aryana Singh and nuclear disarmament. If I get lost in self-importance or simply make a mistake, a real-world problem gets much worse than it already is. That's why I've been so tough on you.

"Fear is a reasonable response to this world. Are you shocked when a friend is unhappy or in pain? Of course not, it's common. A friend who's ecstatic--or even truly content? You'd have to know their secret or start measuring them for a rubber suit. Yet, given the choice, we have to choose hope, don't we? Avery wants to commercialize it, turn it into a commodity he can sell like everything else. He may be right, hope may just be an illusion, but that choice—which direction each person tilts, hope or fear—matters. Which is why we've got to keep our heads about us—we can't let that that difference get lost. The lines get blurred so easily, you see?"

Long pause. I almost fell asleep again before Kate said, "Wouldn't that be what real friends are for? To keep us from going off the tracks?"

"I've never been lonely. I'm always surrounded by other people's thoughts."

"What could be lonelier than that? There was a boy I wanted…a few years ago. I was mooning after him across the classroom like girls do and suddenly I was inside his head. I knew everything he thought and felt. I stayed inside him a whole day and night."

"That must have been eye-opening."

"The truth? What surprised me, when he wasn't being a sick pig, was how romantic he was—men don't talk about that, do they?"

"It—it may not be our strong suit."

"I realized how easy it would be, to be just what he wanted. He was playing out all the scenes in his head. So I ambushed him before the next class, dressed like the girl in his dreams, came on just like her. He couldn't get away fast enough! As a fantasy, it was fine. In real life...scared him to death." (laughs)

"Fantasies are frightening because we feel we don't *deserve* them." Max's voice, very soft. "We all feel our lover is too good for us, don't we? We rediscover the world through them, *everything* changes shape because of them. Whereas, we know that power isn't inside *us*; we know what *un*-magical creatures we are."

Kate was still giggling. "It's like, every boy I ever dated, once they found out what I could do, they'd get all intimidated, because I *knew what they were thinking*. Like women don't know that anyway."

Her musical laughter stopped abruptly. I don't know if she read something in him or saw something on his face but I could feel the air chill as he started speaking.

"When I was 17, there was a girl I wanted terribly. She was the daughter of one of the keepers, one of the scientists in the program. Elena...a luminous spirit. I knew she was too good to even look at me. My ineptitude with women was famous in the program, a source of great satisfaction to my peers. But somehow this time, I conquered my own fears. I went after her and—amazingly—she responded. More amazingly, we were wonderful together. Instinctive, natural, all the things my life had never been. We saw the possibilities in each other and were somehow oblivious to the weaknesses. Her father opposed me with good reason—I'd recently killed a man who tried to 'discipline' me—but the program leaned on him. They wanted me to 'develop'; she surely would have bad dates with someone—it might as well be me."

At this point, I wasn't sure I *wanted* to listen but I couldn't help it, like waking up and hearing your parents talking downstairs at night when you're a kid. The moon glistened through the porthole like a snowball.

"We were together for five months. I was...I don't know how to describe it. (laughs) Happy, I suppose. Light. Free. I didn't think too much. I knew what I wanted. I was *content*." Dark bitter laugh. "And then I discovered I'd forced her, coerced her. I'd made her come to me. I hadn't meant to, I'd done nothing consciously. I just wanted her so badly I made it happen. *I made my longing real*. As soon as I understood what I'd done, I released her and she felt...violated." Long pause. "I think she did love me at one point. I am certain there was something real between us...but how real can any feeling be if it's been compelled at first? We were very young and…sheltered. She was in pain and I was terribly guilty…" His voice trailed off.

"So what happened? How did you resolve it?"

"Resolve it? She killed herself is how we resolved it."

"Omigod."

"Yeah. Omigod."

Silence. Engine noise, baby crying on the other end of the plane, headphone whoosh on the other side of me.

Max, taking deep breath: "So when I worry about us deceiving ourselves, there's a reason. I failed my apprenticeship as a spy. I've spent twenty years running from anyone who would use my skills. I've never been put to the test. I have no reason to trust my own judgment."

"Well, you figured out what was happening with…Elena. You did something bad but you didn't deceive yourself about it."

"Ah! No, I can't take credit for that." Pause. "Someone else figured that out."

"What? How?"

"He was right. There was no doubt. I knew it as soon as I was told."

"But how did he know?" A short pause and then a different tone of voice, a more matter-of-fact tone. "Another mindbender."

"Yes. He knew her better than me, I suppose. Her lover before me. I took her from him, I suppose, not that I ever thought of it that way. I wasn't thinking of…I just wasn't thinking."

"A friend?"

"A rival. Pietr Volkov, actually. He saw what I couldn't see. He told me off and rightly, not that it did anyone any good." Many sighs now, hard exhales. I was wide-awake. "It's...it's all history," Max stammered. "It's got nothing to do with now. There's more at stake here."

"Mmm," Kate murmured. "But the lines *do* get blurry, don't they?"

Thirteen

Rome.

As the plane skimmed down through the clouds, the squat red and tan hills came into sight and I started smiling. The Umbrian hills are umber—the culture is so old, they named the color of the *land* after themselves. I found myself misting up. Not only was it a lovely scene, it was one I actually remembered, a little piece of my life come back to me. Just a hint of a remembered past was enough to fill me with a strange gratitude.

We were on a low-budget carrier connecting from Dublin, the long route that, presumably, Volkov wouldn't be watching. The low-budget airline did without the telescoping offramp the big boys use; we descended a shiny metal staircase like the Beatles at Idlewild and boarded a shuttle bus to the terminal. Guards ringed the perimeter of the building, rifles at the ready. Nonetheless, this was Rome—even the low-rent terminal was clad in mottled dark marble gleaming in the sharp sunlight.

The line for Customs was ridiculous. "We should have used EU passports," Max said. There were two lines for EU citizens versus one (much longer) line for the rest of the world—and our scrutiny was far more exacting. "Could've told you," Tauber grumbled without explaining why he didn't.

I guess I heard the voice behind me say "Greg?" but I didn't even think to look. After all the months I'd spent unable to remember a single soul, a single memory, the thought of someone remembering *me* was from Mars. But Max was staring so I turned and there was Bill Szymzck towering over me and if I could remember how to spell his name, how could I not be sure who he was? He threw his arms around me and I melted—my brain didn't register but my arms knew this overgrown bear of a man. It was miraculous to know someone, even if all I knew was that I knew him.

"Great to see you!" he shouted like he really meant it. He was huffing like he'd been running laps. Alongside him, a photographer in full battle gear—three cameras round his neck, flak jacket stuffed with lenses, batteries and memory cards—waited impatiently, legs twitching. "Are you covering this show?" Bill demanded. "Back in the game?"

"Yeah—sure," I stammered and Billy thrust a card into my hand.

"My number's there," he said. "Call me—have to run." He waved a finger at the photographer and they both took off, part of an army of ink-stained wretches pouring down the tunnel in the opposite direction.

I stuck the card in my pocket and shrugged at Max and the others. "I—I know him," I smirked though it was all still a blank.

As soon as we stepped outside, the crowd noise swallowed us. The courtyard was packed, crowds swarming against barricades manned by lines of carabinieri in their silly black hats. A few buses and scooters puttered through the middle of the crowd like coffee through a spout. Signs bobbed in the thick air, French, German, English and some Cyrillic lettering joining the Italian. As we squeezed into the crowd, heads began to swivel upward, tracking an Air India jet making its approach. Murmurs and applause filtered in from all angles, until they filled the square.

"Singh," Max said and his face went dark. He swept the crowd and then retraced the scan. "This way!" he said and the urgency in his voice was obvious. We pushed through the crowd, clearing people roughly out of our way, pushing hard for the center of the square. Max's head was swiveling, searching, tracking something ahead of us. And then I saw him start, as though a shock had passed through him.

A moment later, a face appeared in the sky—no, in my head, it was in my head, but the way it looked was like it was floating translucent in the air above the courtyard. I could see through it or past it, but when I looked right at it, it had texture and shadows and substance. A youngish man, moving through the crowd, moving swiftly, purposefully, away from us. I knew this without knowing how I knew it. A moment later, I realized it had to be Max's vision—the thought came to me before the image had ceased to be startling.

Next, in a progression I could barely understand, everything amplified and deepened. I jumped, all at once, *inside* the young man—feeling what *he* was feeling; rapid heartbeat and shallow rabbit's breath, desperation and fear, fear of failure and fear of success. I could feel him now, somewhere just across the traffic island, moving through the crush, arms folded in front of his chest, sheltering the package there, the wires and plastic leading off the detonator on his chest. Suddenly I was pushing hard at the crowd, clearing them away rudely, sharply, yelling louder and moving faster. Kate and Tauber branched out behind me, apparently reacting to the same vision.

Max was ahead of us, moving fast—of course, people just got out of his way. He plunged into traffic, tipping his hand at a black-suited officer, who waved him on. The same cop jumped to stop us when we arrived three seconds later. "Max!" I shouted. I saw him turn, just a glance over his shoulder; the officer straightened like a ramrod and got the hell out of the way.

"Over there!" Max yelled, pointing toward the terminal exits. "Spread out!" The bomber was moving across the grain of the crowd and I kept riding his feelings. It was like a late-night drive, trying to hold onto a staticky distant radio broadcast that kept fading in and out—you held onto the fragments that made sense and tried to assemble the rest from context and guesswork.

He wasn't aware of us, the bomber wasn't. He kept repeating the same frantic thoughts in succession. *Get there. Not too soon. Get there. Not too soon.*

I kept waiting for something about the mission—the bomb, Singh, *something*—the kind of compulsion that could drive a person to suicide. But the connection ebbed instantly when I did, so I cleared my mind and returned to simply receiving what he was sending and following it. Necklaces and rings in the air rotated through his head in rotation with *Get there. Not too soon.*

A second later, I glimpsed a close-cropped haircut jerking through the crowd ahead and knew immediately this was him, this was the bomber, in plain sight, moving across the edges of the crowd where it was thinner and he could move faster.

Tauber crossed over, moving to an angle where he could cut him off. I changed my angle to catch up behind them and threw myself through the crush. I could feel the boy's desperation mounting, the sweat pouring down his face and chest, his hands twitching. *Too soon, too soon. She'll be here soon.*

His desperation matched my own. We'd come all this way and barely made it in time—*if* we were in time. Minutes to go—seconds? He still wasn't aware of us—he wasn't aware of anything now but her, the imminence of her. The plane had surely taxied in by now—she'd be at the gate anytime.

Tauber burst out of the crowd right behind the bomber, lifted his arms to grab him and—crack!—he was on the ground, writhing and quivering. I was there a second later—I reached for him but somehow managed to pull my hands back at the last second. The electricity made a crackling noise as it pulsed through his body. His skin was bluish and shimmering; the smell and sizzling noise were the same as in the back of Dave's store in Florida.

Max rushed up, touched Tauber's shoulder and the blue light drained off. "He'll be okay," he said. "Get after *him!*" The bomber had reached the edge of the traffic island—I could feel his satisfaction, a sense of finality, of relief. He'd made it. I anticipated his next step, jumping across traffic and making that last dash—a good run, but the last one—to the exit gate. To his target. But somehow, he stopped instead, lolling like he was right where he meant to be.

There was no one between us now. I ran, sprinting headlong, abandoning any concern about frightening or upsetting the crowd. But, with a couple yards to go, Max grabbed me by the shoulder and pulled me to the curb to watch. We had a front-row seat for the scuffle that made the news—the camera crew, in fact, stood right in front of us.

Five or six guys came from nowhere, swarming the bomber, wrestling and throwing him to the ground, pinning his arms behind him to eliminate any chance of tripping wires or throwing triggers. His shirt came open and the squares of plastic explosive on his chest, the wires and battery taped there, were suddenly visible to all.

The crowd started to shriek and scatter in every direction. The panic spread like an infection through the crowd, starting close-by and gushing out in all directions, becoming more desperate with distance, blindness always worse than the most terrible sight.

Max pulled me the short distance back to Tauber—Kate was helping him regain his footing. His hair was sticking out in all directions and he was hissing like a dry cleaner.

"Are you alright?" Max asked.

"Fuck no, I'm not alright! What the hell happened?"

"You took a lightning bolt. I guess Marat can temper them enough to knock you over without killing you."

"Ain't that *genteel* of 'im!" Tauber growled. He kept trying to lean against the lamppost but sparks kept flickering from his fingers when they got close together.

"I think the air shield would have protected you, if we'd known" Max offered, not that he sounded real confident.

"*Frying* him first would protect me!" Tauber yelled. "Torching him down to his shoes would protect me!" They were arguing in the midst of a riot, understand—people rushing by, screaming, others rooted, paralyzed, watching the guards struggling with the bomber. He was still flailing and kicking, the whole group staggering back and forth until they finally tied his hands and clamped their own arms solidly around his neck and waist. Then the team lifted the bomber entirely off the ground, a van pulled up with perfect timing and they dragged him inside, shouting and protesting.

As the van made its way out of the square, the crowd seemed to get the message. Applause rippled through the courtyard and followed the van, lights flashing and siren whooping, as it pulled out of sight. We stood, deflated, in the midst of the cheering crowd, staring at each other blankly.

"So?" Kate said. "Are we done? Is that what we came for?"

People were filtering back into the square now that the drama had ended. We wandered to the corner where the guards had overpowered the bomber. Bits of wire and one brand-new Nike sneaker remained at the curb.

"Expensive shoe," I said, "for an anarchist."

"Too far away," Tauber growled, gauging the distance to the gate. "Couldn'a done much damage from here if he wanted to."

"He wanted to," Kate said. "He *had* to. He was panicked, running late, frantic to make up time, I could feel it. Though, once he got here, he was totally confused, like he didn't know the next step."

"That's not what *I* got," I said and suddenly they were all staring at me.

"What did *you* get?" Max asked.

"What you sent! Wait—you mean you *weren't* sending out his thoughts? For us to pick up?" Max shook his head immediately. "Then what *was* I getting?"

"What did you read?" he repeated and the sound of his voice reverberated inside my head.

"*Get there. Too soon.* He was panicked about being *early*— and, once he got here, to this corner, he was satisfied. He'd done it—reached his goal. He knew it—it was very clear to me." Kate shook her head, listening and all I could do was shrug. "I'm probably wrong, I don't have the power like you guys. In my head, he kept thinking about *jewelry*." Every eyebrow went up. "Big red stones."

"I didn't get anything about jewelry," Kate offered.

"Ruby Red," Tauber said but it was a question and I nodded. He turned to Max immediately. "It's a control—rubies. Like the lapel pins."

Max stared, mulling for another moment—then he wheeled on Kate. "Could you see his face?"

"What do you mean?"

"The image you got from him. Was the camera on him—or was he the camera?"

"Oh, he was the camera, for sure. I saw what *he* was seeing, the street in front of him."

"And you?" he turned on me next, fierce and rushed. "What did you see?"

"I saw his face, sometimes," I answered. "Sometimes closer, sometimes further. Sometimes from the side, sometimes from behind." I panicked a little, replaying it all in my head. "I must have got it wrong. How could he see the back of his own—?"

I didn't get the chance to finish the sentence.

"Come on!" Max cried, jumping against the flow of the crowd, leading us at a tear away from the terminal.

We rushed headlong toward the outer edge of the square. As we went, Ciampino's exit gate opened and the first motorcycle came through, siren wobbling. A solid row of caribineri took up positions alongside the gate and another motorcycle followed. That was when the chant started, voices rising from every part of the courtyard. "Pace" and "Friede," "Paix," "Paz" "Peace" and other variations, one chanted after the next, call and response like gospel church.

This was not the roaring crowd demagogues (and most politicians) hope for—this was a strong, individual voicing, quiet, respectful, gaining strength with every repetition, with the power of the same idea in fifty languages in close proximity. Scanning the faces as we ran past, I couldn't say that these were really hopeful faces. Mournful seemed more accurate. Maybe they just hoped to be hopeful, hoped for the chance someday to feel hopeful again.

And then the gate opened and the motorcade came through, four Mercedes limos followed by two more rows of motorcycles. One flipped its siren, a momentary honk and the crowd hushed for a second but the chant continued immediately, almost a whisper. And, a moment later, a hand extended from the rear window and waved a thumbs up.

"This way!" Max said. He led us across a blinding marble courtyard and through the echoing lobby of an office building onto the street beyond. He hailed a cab and gave the driver an address and some directions. We hurtled off as soon as the doors closed behind us.

"Where are we going?"

"To the bomber's apartment," Max whispered.

"How do you know where he lives?" I asked. He just shot me a look like *Have you been paying attention the last week?* and I moved on. "Why are we going there?"

"Because of what you saw."

"I probably saw it wrong."

"Maybe," he said. "Let's find out."

It took us fifteen minutes in traffic to get where we were going. Rome is a beehive—the traffic moves slowly but comes from everywhere, cars feeding in from sidestreets, alleys, driveways and thoroughfares built on twenty separate levels, buses and cars crowding through insanely small openings and motor scooters like mosquitoes buzzing around everything else at random. Traffic lights were obeyed as much by coincidence as duty. Blocks of buff-colored sixteenth-century apartments nestled between sleek glass office towers curving around an arch built in the year 2 (II) to honor the Roman Conquest of the Week.

At one point, the wide shopping thoroughfare we were on, lined with cypress trees in neat rows, sidewalk cafes and leather and haute couture boutiques, changed without warning or transition to a one-lane brick shelf descending three stories across the face of an ancient stone wall, dropping to a narrow cobblestoned roadway twisting through the middle of a pruned, manicured park—all in the space of a quarter mile—before dumping us in the midst of a working-class neighborhood filled with grimy apartment houses, *trattorias* and a spectacular domed temple built before Christ to a God I'd never heard of and restored later by a Pope I'd never heard of in commemoration of an apostle I'd never heard of.

All this to reach a pretty ordinary-looking block of apartments built above a Laundromat, an electronics store and a local flea market offering sheets, plumbing supplies and live ducks and pigs for on-the-spot slaughter.

"We've got a problem," Max said as the cab stopped. A pair of carabinieri stood all puffed-up outside the front door. We loitered, stymied, wandering into the stores to keep from being too obvious.

"We've got to find a way in," Max said as we lingered among the IPods and laptop computers, electric pasta makers (in Italy?) and the latest digital cameras. "The caretaker's in the basement. He's already trying to figure out how to turn this unfortunate boarder into cash." He pulled a couple of hundred-Euro notes out of his pocket. "But we need an excuse to get in there without alarming the cops. You know, normal everyday graft."

"You couldn't just suggest they leave us alone?"

"Suggestions are short-term; when they remember, they get very pissed. Not good pissing off cops, especially if you need them later."

I'd been admiring a really nice digital video camera behind the counter, sizing up the detachable microphone and the very nice zoom lens. That's when I had one of those cartoon moments, the thought balloon with the exclamation point going off right over my head. "It's a *story!*"

"What is?"

"The apartment—the bomber. Billy asked me if I was covering the summit. I'm a reporter, remember? At least I was. We got this guy's address from a source and we're checking it out."

"If you're the reporter," Kate demanded, "who are *we?*"

It took a two-second glance at this group to answer the question. "*You're* the reporter," I told her. "I'm your producer, Max is cameraman and Mark is audio." I pulled Max's bogus credit card out of my back pocket, gesturing at the counterwoman and the video camera.

Five minutes later, we tramped around the back of the apartment house, skirting the edges of a deep pit covered by heavy planks and rubber sheeting. The pit filled the space between the rear walls of several adjoining houses. Kate threw a curious look at the spades and brushes stacked against the outer wall as we went by.

"Keep the lens on wide-angle," I told Max. "It'll keep the picture from shaking too much. Get as close as you can to your subject. If you want a wider shot, back up but remember, it's TV — closeups still read better across the room." I knocked on the door several times before a slightly feral face appeared, bearing that universal hungry look. That hunger was a great reassurance.

"GNN," I told him in English, assuming like an arrogant American that he could speak it. "We want pictures. Video. TV." I held out my bogus passport without actually giving him time to read it. That's all the look he'd have gotten if I'd had real ID. We tried to dance past him through the door but he stepped over to block it. He wasn't big but he was built like an oak tree.

"Polizia is coming," he said in accented but reasonable English.

"We want pictures," I said. "*Before* the polizia come."

"Polizia *statale*," he clarified. "Especiale. They want everything very clean. Nobody sees nothing."

His words said good citizen, his eyes read *hungry*. I pulled out 200 Euro and kept adding 50 Euro increments (slower and slower each time) until we reached 450 and he grabbed for the money. I pulled it back. "Fifteen minutes," I told him.

"Fifteen," he repeated with a look that said *450 Euro*.

"We don't have fifteen minutes," Max said as we went up the stairs. "Marat got into a cab just ahead of us —"

"You saw him?!" Tauber nearly lifted out of his shoes. "And you let the son-of-a-bitch get away?"

"It was more important to get here first," Max answered. "Besides, I got this address when he gave it to his cab driver."

"How'd we beat him here?"

"That unfortunate cab driver is temporarily seeing left as right and right as left. So Marat is now on the wrong side of town and getting into a new cab. He's not stupid — he'll call in reinforcements. We have approximately seven to ten minutes."

"Give me the camera," I told Max and he handed it over gratefully. "Nobody's going to let us carry evidence out of here. We've got to document as much as we can."

The room was a classic student clutter, a hovel, clothes piled on the ripped second-hand couch, Godard and Che on the wall, books and pamphlets in piles on the floor and bomb-making equipment spread across the table.

Tauber pulled a pair of latex gloves from a box and handed each of us a pair. "Put them on *now*. Nobody touches anything nekkid." Then he set to work examining wires and diagrams.

Max wandered to the desk by the side window, and picked up a battered leatherette slipcase that was lying open. "The bomb maker was doing his bills," he said.

"What?"

"He was writing checks—my Italian's not perfect but it looks like the gas company, electric, telephone…" I jumped to the desk and got pictures of the ledger.

"Putting his affairs in order?" Kate offered.

"He's a nihilist—he's going out in a few minutes with a bomb strapped to his chest. He's paying the phone bill?"

"This is even better," Tauber said and we grouped around him. A pad of longwise European paper displayed bomb-making preparations, a diagram of the bomb, a scrawled map of the airport and scribbled notes around the edges. "He marked down his destination," Tauber said. "Look *where*," holding up the pad and angling it so I could get video. "He wasn't even *trying* to reach the gate; his goal was the corner. Across the street. Several lanes of traffic between him and the target."

"Too far away—you said so yourself," Kate said.

"Only," Tauber twinkled, "if ya actually intend to blow somebody up."

"Look! The rubies!" Scribbles of the gems were all over the edges of the page, obsessively drawn and colored in with marker or something. I shot close-ups.

"Yeah," Tauber nodded like this was no surprise. "Gems are a good control. Almost everybody sees rubies as the same shade — even if you're color-blind, it's a consistent, vivid shade o'gray."

"And color," Max cut in, "is a frequency, just like sound. So if you want to maintain control over somebody at a distance, you program them to replay the image in their heads over and over. It keeps them around the right frequency, so they keep receiving your suggestions." He kept picking through the wire and clutter on the table, examining each bit and holding it out to the camera, moving rapidly. "This was a fall guy. They monitored him—"

"Who did?"

"That, we'll see—I think we all know the prime candidate— they controlled and moved him around like a dog on a leash. Kate heard his panic—he had to reach the right spot on time but, when he did, he had no idea what to do, no further goal. It was all fed to him and now the feed dropped off."

"So I *was* wrong." I wasn't surprised but a little disappointed. It sure felt like I'd been tapped into somebody.

"No—you were right too," Max said and I was totally confused. "You, I'm certain, tuned into the *suggestion*—the signal from his minder, his runner. The guy whose job was to lead him to the wrong spot and abandon him there."

This, strangely, was confounding. I had a much harder time accepting I'd succeeded than a few moments earlier accepting that I'd failed. "So I did it? I'm a mindreader?" I'd hardly *spoken* more than a few words a day the week before.

"Don't get cocky," Max said, rummaging through cabinets and drawers, pulling out papers and holding them under my camera for recording. "You picked up a specific mind intentionally beaming out a message. You've been around Tauber and me, you had to fight off Volkov and Marat and now we've got Kate and a bunch of drones trying to probe us. That's a lot of activity all at once, so you're getting stimulated. You probably live on the minder's frequency anyway." He looked me square in the eye. "But you paid attention," he said. "Give yourself credit for that. And fix those rubies in the back of your mind—you may find them handy later on."

"But what was the point?" Kate asked. "Why send out a bomber intentionally to get captured?"

"Good question," Max said.

"Think of the damage he could've done if nobody'd stopped him," she mused.

"He wouldn't'a done shit," Tauber said, holding up the bomb blueprints for us. I focused the camera on the drawings in the center, where he was pointing. "See?" he challenged Max, who stared at it blankly. "Didn't they teach you *anything* in that program?"

"I told you, I resisted."

"Shee—it!" The blueprints quivered in his hands but not as bad as they had the day before. "It was no bomb to begin with! Damn thing *couldn't* go off the way they had it wired. No way, no how. Wiring's all wrong."

"Jesus," Kate moaned. "What a sitting duck."

"Time's up!" Max yelled suddenly, throwing another few documents under my lens for preservation. "We've got company."

A moment later, we heard shouts and a crackle of electricity in the street below. Tauber started badly at the electrical sound; he had the door open before Max yelled "Go!"

"Head for the staircase at the end of the hall!" Renn ordered but there was a stairwell just in front of us. Tauber and I both made for it, Tauber arriving just in time for a bolt of electricity to rip past his ear and blow a hole in the ceiling above. Leonardo light poured gloriously down through the billowing plaster. Tauber turned two shades paler than he already was and we scrambled backward.

Shouts and footsteps echoed up the stairwell, but Max came tearing around the corner, his arms swinging over his head and down the stairwell. He looked crazy at first but, then you could see the energy ball arcing through the smoky lightshaft and plunging down the metal staircase. The banisters buckled and bent, the steel latticework groaned and screeched and several steps collapsed, crushed like someone had dropped a steam roller. We heard the cries of shooters scrambling away as the ball bounced down into the lobby below, taking the rest of the staircase behind it.

Tauber gaped but Max simply pointed at the far end of the hall like this happened to him all the time. *"That* staircase, dammit!" Kate was already ahead of us, hitting the landing and disappearing down the shaft.

We bounded down two flights before the crunch hit. Kate went first, slipping-jumping as many steps as she could without falling, the rest of us a few rungs behind. We had just about made the lobby when a lightning bolt hit the staircase just above us, slicing it away from the wall. I looked up just long enough to catch Marat's white hair and the arm of his dark robe flapping over the railing. The staircase groaned and began to list at a nasty angle. We stumbled on, the lobby just ahead.

That's when I saw something that wasn't there. Just like at the airport, that distant radio station began drifting in and out of my head again. This time, I knew what was happening, so I focused—*rubies, rubies.* I held that color, that frequency, vivid in my head and locked into the signal right away. And I found myself staring at the staircase—the staircase we were descending, except I was seeing it from the lobby just below.

The lobby where Marat and five L Corp guys with stun guns and anti-noise headsets waited to take us the moment we appeared. Marat and five others, including the guy whose head I'd just gotten inside of again.

Kate was inches from the last step. I threw myself into the air and grabbed her just above the last step, our momentum carrying us hard into the far wall. We flew through the doorway in two seconds—the third second, the place opened up, bullets and lightning bolts everywhere. We lay flattened on the floor, scrunched tight together as the place erupted.

In the fifth second, dead silence, except for the tinkling of glass hitting the floor. We were cramped into the corner behind the doorframe, staring across at Max and Tauber still clinging to the precarious staircase.

At the same time, I still saw the other angle as well, the same doorway but now from down the hall, through the eyes of my L Corp contact, as his crowd waited for us to show, for a clear shot at us.

"You wrecked the other staircase," said a dry voice from down the hall. Through the L Corp side of my head, I could see the head blueshirt—a bullethead with a full red beard—talking and Marat slinking up behind him. How'd *he* get back downstairs if there was no other staircase? "So there's no place else for you to go."

"Like hell," Max muttered. He and Tauber were hanging onto the monkey-bar staircase, their weight threatening to pull it down altogether at any moment.

"That's all you got?" Max answered loudly, moving hand-over-hand very deliberately toward the landing. "Volkov offered three-quarters mill and a country house."

"Offer?" Redbeard answered, sounding almost amused. "You're taking *offers*?"

"We need an escape route before I run out of bullshit," Max whispered. "Anyone has suggestions, now's the time."

The staircase shrieked and sagged sickeningly toward the outside wall of the building. If I'd ever heard that sound onboard a ship, I'd be looking for life rafts. The whole apparatus now hung entirely over the wide-open stairwell, Max and Tauber literally clinging to the handrails.

"The Italian police just want accomplices; you're better off with us," came Redbeard's voice again.

I don't know if Kate had risen to her feet or if I'd just lost track of her, but suddenly she was at the back of the stairwell, sheltered behind the doorframe, out of the line of fire, peering down into the dim landing.

"I think I can get a better offer," Max yelled. In seconds, he and Tauber were either going to have to swing over onto the landing—in full view of our attackers—or plummet two stories down into the stairwell.

"I think you're misinformed," Redbeard answered drily, clearly close to the end of his patience.

"It's a plumb-bob!" Kate mumbled, talking to herself, gazing into the stairwell with an idiotic level of excitement. *It's a cannon*, I'd have understood. A *plumb-bob*?

"Are we outside the walls of Rome?" she demanded.

"*What* walls?" Tauber rasped. His fingers were slipping; he was in no mood.

"The ancient city had walls!" she burst, like this was absurdly obvious. And, looking over the railing, I saw the plumb-bob, conical, pointed, ridiculous, string looped over the doorknob two flights down. "We *have* to be outside the ancient city," she muttered to herself.

"Time's up, Renn! Come out or we come in!"

"What's the *point*, Kate?"

She was smiling now, which was insane. "We go," she said softly.

"Go? Where?"

"*Down*," she answered. She was already working her hands back and forth, in and out. A moment later, she leaned into the doorway and threw an air ball down the corridor. I had to grab the doorframe to keep from being sucked out after it. Marat's team scattered in twenty directions as it flew between them, ripping pictures off the walls and pulling potted trees, newspapers, doormats, pairs of shoes and every bit of dirt and lint and paper in the hall into a crazy, swirling, rolling tide.

"Go!" Kate yelled, jumping brazenly across the landing into the stairwell. Max and Tauber swung and landed hard on the steps. We scrambled down two flights, breakneck, to the basement door. Max threw it open and then melted the lock, sitzing and sparking, behind us.

A rickety wood staircase plunged two *more* stories in seconds through a rough-cut chamber that looked carved out of the earth instead of built. An ancient narrow stone archway blocked the view below. I heard the others gasp as they reached it—when my turn came, I couldn't help but do the same.

Stretched out below, under floodlights, lay the open-air courtyard of the Emperor Nero's summer house. Two huge fountains framed an archway like the Lincoln Memorial but fancier; behind that stretched an open-roofed courtyard with a wading pool and a mosaic floor hand-painted by a cast of thousands.

"What's the point of a museum education?" Kate whooped. "I know excavating equipment when I see it, *that's* what." Behind us, I could hear fists pounding at the melted doorway.

We ran a central corridor, between rooms painted with flat pre-perspective murals—mountain and garden landscapes, well-dressed Roman citizens dancing, drinking, bathing and some other stuff. Some of it looked pretty dirty, actually. I wouldn't have minded spending a little more time there, under better circumstances. The lights cast dramatic shadows behind the pillars and the timber skeleton bracing the cavern ceiling.

"What the hell *is* this?"

"Rome is built on *top* of ancient Rome," Kate yelled back. "They just buried the old neighborhoods and used the old buildings for foundations."

She dashed to the last chamber, the largest, deepest room, where picks and trowels and paint brushes lay among wheelbarrows and two-by-fours in a disorderly pile.

"Lecture later!" Tauber yelled. "We need *outta* here, dammit!"

Kate lit a torch from the pile and threw it at me. Everyone grabbed one and she ran to the farthest corner, kicking over a construction pile with a clattering roar. She poked her torch into the corner, close to the ground, where a small oblong hole appeared just above the base of the wall.

It wasn't a place you'd think of going on your own. It looked like the floor had given way. If you *were* going, you'd at least want a wetsuit.

"*That's* the way out," Kate said. "But I'm not going first."

Just at that moment, we heard a groan above us as the door to the apartment building began to give way.

I dropped my torch into the gap. It landed on a nearby floor with a muffled clatter. The walls within shown with an eerie glow.

I took a breath as though diving underwater, swung into the hole and let go.

I fell further than expected and landed in a kind of silt that cushioned the impact. But it didn't feel right from the first second—I got shivers just trying to get my footing. The torch was above me and only a few feet away but the floor was unstable— every time I reached for it, the ground underneath would shift under me.

"You okay?" Tauber called but I kept my mouth shut—I didn't like it.

When I finally got the torch over my head, I saw...bones. The whole floor was bones, bones in layers, bones several layers deep, bones that turned to dust as soon as I touched them. All I wanted was to jump and run, get the hell away from this place as fast as I could. But with every movement, the ground kept dissolving under my feet.

I probably would have lost it right there except for hearing the door above give way with a crash. That was it—panic was something we couldn't afford. I remembered what they said in the movies about quicksand—instead of struggling, I slowed down, moving slow and deliberate and suddenly, I was making headway. A solid stone ledge lined the room; I climbed up onto it and took a quick survey. The room was vast, the walls lined with small chambers covered with painted images.

"C'mon down. Just move slow," I called and the others started dropping through the hole.

Several passages ran into the black distance. I ventured in that direction, torch in hand, and came face to face with Jesus, an ancient flat-perspective version painted three times life-size, rough-featured, stark, a whole lot edgier than the greeting-card Jesus I grew up with. This guy looked like a carpenter. I could see him losing his temper, tossing the money-lenders bodily out of the Temple. A working-man's savior, with a wand(!) in hand.

"Catacombs," Kate said, scrambling up the ledge. "Common people couldn't bury in the Holy City, so outside the walls, it's all catacombs, miles and miles of them." She leaned her torch into the passages, the light dancing into the distance.

"We should split up," Max said.

"Bad idea," Kate answered sharply. "These bones aren't all ancient. People go into catacombs and don't come out." She ran down the center passage and we followed, bunched into the narrow space.

The passage quickly got so tight, we could barely scrape through. Rough-hewn walls ran to several-story-high ceilings, miles of stone wall, every few steps bringing another row of chambers floor-to-ceiling, some wide-open displaying loose bones or skeletons, others marked by stone blocks with handwritten legends in Greek.

Everything was painted chalky white, set off with bright borders, flat-perspective trees, real and mythical animals, charioteers and soldiers, muscular heroes and some rather shapely goddesses. With our torches held high, we still couldn't see the end.

Behind us, Marat and gang dropped through the gap in the wall and made the same noises we had climbing out of the bone pile.

"How are we getting *out* of here?" Max asked.

Kate shrugged. "I'm depending on *you* for that."

In minutes, we heard them on our heels. They had split up and were moving down the narrow corridors faster than we could. With us lighting the way, they'd be on us in minutes.

A lightning bolt smashed the wall to our left; it collapsed in a deafening cloud of smoke. Another bolt overhead scattered a chunk of stone into the passage in front of us. We peeled off to the last clear corridor, but with them now right behind.

And then, a minute later, we hit a dead end. A hole halfway up the white-painted wall showed where the ancients had wriggled through to the next chamber, but we had no wriggling time.

The two groups faced off in close quarters. There was a sudden lull, like maybe they'd caught up with us faster than they expected and nobody was quite certain what to do. Each breath sounded lurid, echoing against the high walls full of painted witnesses. A rumbling groan warned that the ruptured corridor nearby was breaking down and not slowly.

Max's hand swiped the air in front of us and I could feel the shell forming. We held our breath but not for long—it got tight in the corridor all of a sudden, like a belt worn a notch too close. The shooters were eyeing us in no particular hurry. Marat held out several headpieces like an offering.

I felt the rock wall behind me creep upward a quarter-inch and then drop back into place. Even Max couldn't maintain a shield and rearrange several hundred tons of rock at the same time.

"Come along," Redbeard said. "Put on the headsets and we're good. When this is over, you can tell anyone you want about us. Levitate cars on YouTube for all I care. We know your tricks, pal. Nobody's getting close enough for you to do anything. Take the glasses or we take you down—your choice."

I felt Max reach behind me, reach for Kate. "This isn't the time," she muttered but he pulled her close and whispered, "Remember what you did... at home? To amuse your boyfriends?" He nodded at the chalky walls, the gallery of Orthodox crosses and pagan gods. "Do it now... with all *this*."

Kate's eyes opened wide. And, right away, things began to change.

She leaned against us and I heard the rumble inside me like a generator, pulsing through my shoulders and trunk. I got a raging erection—it would be a problem if we had to run real soon. The shooters heads swiveled and I realized they could hear it too. But clearly they had no idea where it was coming from.

A moment later, the deep blackness turned to mist, chalky paint sifting off the walls into the boneyard air. The shooters, being he-man types, tried not to react but it was a real effort—their shoulders rose half a foot pretending nothing was happening.

This was good for about five seconds.

Then the ancient paintings began to dance off the stone walls and out over our heads. Painted chariots began racing up and down the shaft, the drivers lashing each other and the flailing shooters when they wouldn't or couldn't get out of the way.

Soldiers marched tight rows in thin air two feet above us and then broke ranks, laying bets on the chariot race, drinking from giant jugs and trying to make time with the shapely goddesses. Centaurs and unicorns dueled just below the ceiling, peacocks drank from fountains guarded by teasing nymphs and huge bushes flowered in every empty space.

None of this was even slightly realistic; these were the piecework no-dimensional paintings that came with your entry-level Roman funeral. But you could feel the air kick up when the chariots roared past and a drizzle hit your hair from the fountains. The fact that it was all totally unconvincing only made the whole thing eerier. All around us, paintings grew, changed shape, mingled, argued, fought and fornicated. Well, I'm not 100% certain about the fornicating but it got difficult to keep track once the shooting started.

The shooting was kind of inevitable, once a couple hundred bones flew out of their burial chambers, arced into the air like somebody was chucking them and tore straight for the blueshirts. They were shooters, after all, so, when attacked in a very narrow space by pagan gods most of them had never heard of, they responded about the way you'd expect. Redbeard kept screaming at them to stop, as each discharge brought more and more of the ceiling down on us.

Crazily, in the midst of the insanity, I detached. I found myself focused on a sandy-haired shooter ducking under a chariot wheel because I saw the wheel close-up, inches from my face, just as it brushed by his.

This is the guy, I thought, *the guy from the apartment and the airport, the guy I can read.* Jesus, he was panicked! Not that you could blame him, attacked by Mars, Hercules, St. Peter and their really hot girlfriends all at the same time. *It's a trick*, he kept repeating with mounting fervor. In his panic, he never noticed our connection—but I knew I'd remember him.

Max yelled, "Push!" We jumped forward, smacking the air shield into the wall. There was a spongy reaction and we bounced backward. He shouted 'Again!" and this time, I heard his voice in my head saying *Scream after you push*. We pushed together and the wall teetered, wobbled and finally collapsed, locking Redbeard's crew on the other side.

I was screaming the whole time but exactly nothing came out. Just as the wall came down, I heard all our voices at once— and then snuffed out just as abruptly. The screams came mixed into the sound of several other sections of wall giving way. Max emerged out of the dust with a finger to his lips and pointed in the other direction—we squeezed around a pile of rubble.

Kate still had her torch—she re-lit it and the dust in the air scrambled the light like a Seurat. You couldn't see three inches in front of you. I could feel myself coughing but somehow didn't make a sound doing it.

We were in some kind of huge high-ceilinged room. When we finally reached the staircase at the far end, Kate turned to Max and he held his arms out to her. She punched him hard in the shoulder.

"Ow! That's the thanks I get."

"For what? Almost getting us killed?"

"Hopefully for *getting* us killed—as far as they're concerned. They had us cornered but we were crushed under a wall trying to escape."

"They'll buy that?" Tauber, ever the skeptic.

"Marat knows better—he's probing and I'm blocking. But, for some reason, he's not the boss—they don't trust him. The leader, the guy with the beard, knows they'll all be heroes—as long as they stick to their story. The other choice is to spend the next week digging through every corridor and passageway around here on the off-chance we escaped. So we're dead. By the time they get back to headquarters, they'll probably have decided there were fifty of us and we fell into a volcano." He turned back to Kate. "Which gives us one more chance to surprise them when the time comes. Okay?"

"You could have told me," she griped.

"If I'd thought of it a second earlier, I would have. Really. I'm just making this up as I go." It was a pretty good Harrison Ford imitation, actually. She nodded grudgingly.

The mist finally began to dissipate. It turned out we were in a wine cellar and a beautiful one at that: floor-to-ceiling darkwood shelving, bottles organized by brand and years, the rows all aligned toward a grand modern staircase.

Tauber crept up and back in seconds. "Where are we?" Max asked.

"Guessing through the door slit, a fuckin' palace."

"Are we company?"

"After that bang? If they're not down here already, six'll get you ten we've got the run of the place."

"Let's have a look."

Fourteen

The villa was a place out of time, one that had long since abandoned history and found its own solitary track. Frescoes danced on the ceilings, twenty-foot glass double doors opened onto deep iron-railed balconies, every piece of furniture in the place seemed to come off the millennium version of Antiques Roadshow. Max and Tauber fell to prowling out of habit, throwing doors open and fretting over security, but after twenty yawning-huge unoccupied drawing rooms, the whole idea got comical.

We stepped into an open central courtyard wrapped in three stories of block-shaped stucco, locust trees towering over a garden gone natural (one step short of gone to seed). White flowers crawled up the walls and the light poured through vines and bushes that probably dated to Garibaldi. After drifting through four more ornate rooms—one holding a grand piano and a bronze harp taller than any of us—we found the renovation project, a stainless-steel kitchen with the inevitable granite-topped center island (Iron Chef, season two).

"No cameras," Tauber announced, returning from his sweep of the place. "No security wiring either. There's an Alfa parked out back—doors unlocked."

"Light magnetic field," Max said—apparently this was agreement. "I feel the fridge and the air conditioners—there's a home theatre with big speakers on the second floor. But nobody home and no signs of a hasty retreat."

Kate returned from the office, which boasted a spectacular view of the fountain (if you have a villa, you've gotta have a fountain) and a birdhouse the size of a Mini-Cooper, carrying a day planner scrawled with notes.

"Sardinia," she said. "They're in Sardinia for the week."

"Why hassle that nasty G8 traffic?" Tauber smirked.

"Especially when you can be in Sardinia," Kate sighed. "Why come home? Ever?"

Tauber, all at once, was full of energy, a DT's second wind. Surviving the catacombs seemed to have galvanized him and he insisted on leading a security tour.

"The front gate's got a proper lock; the back's just a padlock on a chain. So if they're comin', they'll clip the chain; keep yer ears tuned that way. It's about a minute's run, gate to house and up the stairs. We all sleep here, the east corner. See that gazebo below? Locked gates on both sides; I just jammed 'em. So we keep ropes or sheets on the balcony; things get tight, we drop off and have a shot at the river before they nail us."

"What are our odds?" I asked and saw from Tauber's scowl that this wasn't a proper question.

"If they're good, we won't have time to go anywhere," Max answered. "But Mark's is a good plan if they're incompetent."

"Which is a 50/50 shot," Tauber added. "That's the worst of it. Otherwise, ya got neighbors at a distance, no breaks in the fence. Better'n most."

"Okay," Max said, "this is base of operations."

There was a stock of really high-priced food in the fridge. Five minutes later, the place was stuffed with burbling pots and pans, every new discovery from the pantry (anchovies, peppers for roasting, really expensive veal slices and Saturday's fresh mozzarella) added to the mix, dishes being carried out to the closest dining room as fast as they were done.

"Do we have time for this?" Tauber asked, not that he seemed to care. For a skinny dude, nothing got past him without damage being done.

"Gotta eat," I insisted and Kate nodded, pressing garlic into slices of veal and eggplant. I threw her contents over penne in garlic, oil and lemon juice. A speck of the mix dropped onto the counter in front of me and I tossed it at her. She tossed back and, three seconds later, the whole bunch of us were chucking around everything loose. Still alive, as well as hungry.

"It really stuck in my craw when I saw that bastard at the airport and figgered we were too late," Tauber said across the forty-foot darkwood table in Dining Room #1. "And we coulda been." The man was a coiled spring but he brought us down to earth pretty quick.

"That was a fake-out," Max said, carrying in a chopped salad, chopped a little too thoroughly if you weren't planning to eat with a spoon. "If that was it, they wouldn't have been flying people in today. This was giving a false sense of security. They'll let everyone relax before they move again."

"But why send a bomber out to get caught?" Kate asked. "Won't that just *tighten* security?"

"Damn straight," Tauber said.

Full as a python in mid-cow, I dropped into the informal living room, the one with the TV. I'm comfortable anywhere with a working television. Two seconds later, I had Kate's answer.

"*Here's* why," I said, loud enough to gather them all in. On the TV, pixeling away in front of me, stood Pietr Volkov and two other L Corp types I recognized from the airport. The police chief of Rome and the G8 security head were reading a joint statement, subtitled onscreen.

"Wanna guess whose people took out the bomber?" I asked.

"The people who programmed him to stand on a street corner like a sitting duck," Max answered.

"You win."

A man identified as an L Corp VP rambled on about "proprietary multi-point body-language analysis software that screens crowd scenes and identifies anti-social behavior before it actually occurs."

"You're saying," came a reporter's voice, "that you can predict crimes before they happen?"

"We're saying we can identify individuals with bad intent," the VP answered. "The software is still experimental and by no means foolproof. It requires a good deal of support and fine tuning. But—"

"Let me guess…" Max said drily.

"—we have agreed to a trial here, to provide additional security for this conference. Anyone who wants to crash this party will have us to reckon with."

"…unless they're already wearin' an L Corp badge," Tauber said. "Fan-tastic."

"Why set up the bomber to fail? To get yourself *access*," Max answered, smiling hideously. "It's actually very clever in a perverted sort of way."

"They'll be with her every step," Tauber said. "No need fer a sniper if ye're a foot away."

"Worse yet," Max added, "they've set her up as a martyr. Someone's tried to kill her. Everyone's focus now will be her safety—so when she dies, hope will feel even more futile."

"*If*," Kate said. "*If* she dies." Max nodded stiffly.

We ruined the last couple of dishes, overcooking perfectly good food because, all at once, nobody was paying attention. We'd kept away from the half-wrecked cellar, feeling funny about drinking in front of Tauber until he came back upstairs with some really expensive booze.

"It ain't Prohibition," he said. "I'll see somebody drinking soon—might as well be y'all."

We ended up sprawled across forty-year-old overstuffed couches on one of the balconies. Kate and I both dove for the same couch—we'd had a gang of wine and she ended up nuzzling up against me, having her usual effect on my anatomy. Things got real warm there, notwithstanding the breeze. We were all giggly and exhausted and dopey.

"Where did them ghosts come from?" Tauber drawled lazily. "Chariots and peacocks and Hercules with a golden hammer? What the hell was *that*?"

"Hercules didn't have a golden hammer. That was Thor."

"What's Thor doing in Rome?"

"Not what I meant. I meant—"

"And where'd Jesus get a wand? What was *that* about?"

"It's Kate's power, how she's developed her skills." Max nodded to her. "You don't have to talk about it if you don't want to." He seemed to be trying to make amends for the way he'd pushed her in Philadelphia. Which made sense, once you knew what she could do if you pissed her off.

"No, it's okay," she said, rousing herself. "We're a team. You need to know what you can expect of me—which is that I don't know what to expect of myself.

"My dolls had their own lives, that's how it started. At first, I just talked to them the way little girls do. But eventually, they talked back, stole each other's clothes and the horses from my brother's cavalry set to ride around the house."

"You have a brother?"

"He died ten years ago. He decided he could levitate off a tenth-story balcony. We don't last long, the Crowell's. As I got older, the dolls told me things I couldn't have known—"

"You did," Max said flatly. "You knew things you weren't supposed to know, maybe, so you projected them on the dolls."

"They...knew my mother was dying," Kate stammered, "before the doctors. When the doctors were still saying she'd be fine.

"In college, I...got lonely. I guess everyone creates their own world, but mine was more...elaborate than most. I replayed my bad dates, saying all the lines I wished I had, y'know? Except I started hearing answers from the boys I didn't expect. What they really thought, what they really wanted."

"Things you read in them," Max said conclusively. "You just didn't want to admit what you knew." He kept trying to reel her in, to persuade her she'd maintained some kind of control but clearly Kate wasn't buying.

"We went to Morocco once. We strolled through the marketplace, ate dates overlooking the ocean, I got sunburnt, we made love in a rocky cove. We never left Philadelphia. It was all in my head. Those memories are more real to me still than anything that really happened."

"Everyone does that," I tried to console her—you could see her getting more frantic as she went along. "We all get carried by imagination."

She shook her head. "This wasn't just me. My boyfriend insisted on showing everyone our pictures from the trip. We took cameras wherever we went. Of course, no pictures. We never left the apartment."

"Wow," Tauber said.

"So understand—I learned to do this by fooling myself. And that's scary."

"You need practice," Max said, "enough practice to catch yourself before you go off the rails."

"We don't have time for practice," she said, wandering to the edge of the balcony.

The sun was going down. Sunset in Rome—like any other time in Rome—is spiritual overload. The clouds billowed like they were being conducted. The warm light burnished church domes and swaying trees, the god's head fountain across the street and the Fiat 500 that kept circling the block, buzzing like a bee on steroids. In this light, the whole world seemed precious and Kate, blocking the sun, hair aflame, seemed miraculous. The sadness in her eyes would have pierced a dead man's heart. I wandered to the rail and had my hands on her shoulders before I realized I'd stood up.

"You don't have to know everything," I said. It wasn't good but it was what came out.

"But I have to know *enough*, don't I? This is *it*. Whatever we came to do, it's soon. I want to do good. But this is opening things inside that scare me to death."

She was in my arms and I was swooning a bit just from proximity. Balancing against that was the fact that she could read my mind; that threw a monkey wrench into every way I knew to be with women. There was no point offering false comfort—like Max, she would know it instantly for what it was. I struggled to find something both true and encouraging to say and found I didn't have much experience with that combination.

"What's good about you," I said finally, "is that you're so twisted up trying to do what's right. When the time comes, you'll know the right answer."

She flickered a smile—like she was trying to encourage *me*—settled against my arm and, as long as no one disturbed us, I wouldn't have needed anything else for the rest of the day.

But those moments don't last. Max seemed to have wandered away but Tauber was stalking the rooms like an alien energy force was chewing on him, singing some classic rock song in a terrible off-key voice. Probably Neil Young—off-key seemed to suit the song. We were all drowning in jet lag while he was getting wired.

"So?" he demanded on his next pass through. "How do we protect Singh if L Corps' got access?"

"What's *our* problem?" Kate asked lazily, lolling on the railing. "Why does everyone have access but us?" and it was like streamers going off in my skull.

I leapt to the bureau to check our video camera really held the images we'd taken in the bomber's apartment, that I hadn't imagined or erased them. Then I grabbed the phone, pulling the business card from the airport out of my pocket.

"Billy Symczck, please. Billy? Greg! Listen, my crew and I need credentials—yeah, for the G8. Same to you, buddy. I'll *tell* you why. You have any friends in G8 security? Good—call and tell them their bomb is wired wrong. No chance of it going off. See what they have to say and call me back."

I slouched into a chair, crossing my legs over another ornate table.

"We gon' get *access!*"

~~~~

"It's called Tiber Island," Kate said. Not that you could miss the place—a stone wall and concrete deck breaching the water like the prow of a ship, a collection of Renaissance buildings rising through thickets of palm and locust trees, awash in spotlights, the island curved into the elbow bend of the Tiber, Vatican domes in distant silhouette and two ancient bridges like a belt propping it up.

Getting there, though, was like trying to push a ham through a sieve. Soldiers clustered behind concrete roadblocks at every corner starting a half-mile away, in visible body armor, over-the-ear helmets and automatic weapons at the ready. Each stop required ID, a body check and interrogation (*Purpose of your visit? Press Credentials? So Late? We're disorganized.* No one in Italy seems shocked by this answer).

"The bridge dates to 62 BC," Kate narrated, reading the museum tour off her cell. "One story says the Romans killed a dictator, threw his body in the river and the silt collected around it to create the island. It looked like a ship so they added the prow and stern." She was chattering, nerves on edge—I could feel it as well as hear it. Or maybe it was my own nerves I was feeling.

The air had that stuffy, close feeling like when Max blocked us—I wondered if he was keeping tabs now. He'd run through several techniques with me as we prepared, step by step. When I said, 'You think I can handle this?' he answered, 'Think how far you've come in a few days. You're not the same man' and I knew it was true.

So now I worked the system, like a new driver obsessively checking the mirrors before pulling out of the driveway. *Ruby. Emerald. Sapphire. Turquoise. Don't look for anything in particular; don't anticipate. Listen for words or rhythms of speaking in your head that aren't your own. Just follow those and see where they take you.*

It didn't take long. I started feeling paranoid and defensive and realized it was coming in waves; it only took a beat after that to realize it wasn't my own paranoia but theirs, whoever they were. I relaxed into the vibration and suddenly it was coming from everywhere. Lingering in doorways and street cafes, watchful eyes from cars on strategic corners, waiters and newspaper sellers, students and telephone lineworkers, everywhere we went, the vibrations and those tiny green-tipped lapel pins. If I wasn't successfully blocking myself, we'd find out pretty quick.

Billy said he'd meet me at the bridge but two blocks early, a car pulled up alongside us and he jumped out the open door. "In!" he demanded, grabbing me and throwing me into the seat. He slammed the door in Kate's face, crying, "One ride per customer."

And then we were off, weaving through a maze of alleyways onto a wide avenue past the Coliseum and Circus Maximus.

"Your friends think they're spies," he said, rechecking the rear-view mirror. "Are they?"

In the vanity mirror I made out an Alfa Romeo following at a respectable distance but I didn't know the driver. I never would've noticed on my own.

"Not mine," I shook my head.

Billy shrugged, "No matter." A sharp right bounced us across a sidewalk and into an archaeological site marked 'No Admittance' in three languages. We detoured past a 2200-year-old arch and between 40-foot-high marble slabs fallen from a temple, then sped the wrong way down a one-way street onto a service road under a viaduct and into a warehouse district. There was nobody in sight. "If they *are* spies," Billy remarked, "they're overpaid."

He screeched to a stop in front of a shuttered plant, all graffiti'd walls and glass skylight roof panels. The whole district was shut tight, not a car or moving body in sight on a Sunday in the capitol of Roman Catholicism. Billy jumped out, punched a couple of keys on a touchpad and the front gate rattled upward. It closed automatically when he pulled inside.

"Come on," he said, politely, considering he was already dragging me by the collar. Up a metal staircase to a row of locked offices, dragging me like he didn't care if I got hurt—or maybe preferred that I did.

I don't know what happened to me, but somehow I was taking this pretty calmly. Billy was taller and broader than me but that was a nice way of saying he was a pudgy media grunt, more used to bullying a word processor than a man. He was already puffing from climbing the stairs. A year out of the Army, I could probably take him. 'Probably' was a big word but it relaxed me a bit. *Let him drag me around a little more, wear himself out. Let things develop a bit. Then we'll see.* The place was deserted; it wasn't like he had three guys waiting to jump me. He counted the offices as we went and I noticed there weren't any numbers on the doors. He dragged me to 'Six' and pulled me roughly against the wall.

"You listen to me," he gasped, jingling through a mass of keys on a White Sox keyring. "I don't know how stupid you think I am but I don't take this shit lightly. I made your fucking phone call. I know a guy at *Intervento Speciale*—the Italian counter-terrorists? I told him what you said; he dropped the fucking phone! I hear him scrambling around trying to pick it up, I take it as a sign from God. Duck down the back steps and by the time I hit the corner, there's six military police cars outside my door. I haven't stopped in one place for two minutes since." He found the key and fumbled it into the lock. "They told me you lost it a year ago but I had no clue. This is fucking Italy! I'll be locked up for weeks before anybody gets to talk to me! I could end up in fucking Baku getting waterboarded! So I don't give a rat's ass about your goddamn credentials—you're going to tell me what, how and where or *you* can send me a postcard from Baku whenever you get a chance."

He was totally panicked and panic does scary things, even to sensible people. That's what was going through my head when he threw the door open and flicked on the light and I stopped worrying.

Max was lounging behind Billy's desk; Kate was next to him in a straight-back wooden chair, sitting quietly, waiting. Tauber stepped from the darkened far side of the room, closed the door behind Billy and conducted him politely but firmly into another wood chair directly opposite the desk. When that was done, he took up a position leaning alertly next to the now-closed door.

"Locking him up won't help you," Max said calmly. "And it isn't necessary. We'll tell you what you want to know. We just need credentials."

Billy's eyes bulged. He kept staring from one unexpected visitor to the next, eyes like billiard balls. "How—how'd you get in here?" When no one answered, he gulped hard and said, "I had to tell them who told me. They won't give you credentials no matter what."

"You didn't get the chance to tell them—you were ducking down the back steps, remember?" Max said with that assurance that so impressed strangers. "It's not an issue. You get us the meeting with the right people—I'll take care of the rest."

Billy was still flustered, still mulling the *previous* question. "You—how'd you find this place? You didn't follow us, I was watching."

"We got here first," Max nodded. "So no, we didn't follow you."

"So how'd you know…we were coming here?"

"If your network will get us in, you can tell them later that I forced you. They'll believe you, I promise."

"Why would they?"

"Because that's what I do," Max said darkly. "I make people do things they don't want to do." He was using the quiet voice, which only brought out the menace in him. Billy sank into a chair next to the desk. Then he stared, alarmed, at the desk itself. Max slid away and held his hands up to show they were empty.

"I haven't opened anything. Your weed's still in the top drawer and your revolver still in the leg. The emails from your publisher's wife—"

"That's enough!" Billy yelled. "You had no right; this is a private—"

"Check the locks," Max said, stepping away and motioning. Billy showed no sign of moving from his chair. "I didn't have to look. I knew you would tell me what's there." This struck me odd and I saw Tauber and Kate also staring at Max now. Where was he going with this?

"You've been troubled recently by memories of a woman named Christina. You haven't seen her in years but she's in your dreams and waking thoughts. You've been trying to think of a way to ask your ex for her address but—"

Billy was trembling now; it took a lot of visible effort before he was actually able to speak. "In the time you've spent monitoring me," he burst, "you could've got the credentials yourself."

"How could I monitor something you haven't said aloud? To anyone?" Max asked, as low-key as a hospital shrink. "I'm reading your mind, Billy." It was shocking to hear him say it out loud. We just needed credentials—why give away the farm?

"Bullshit," Billy answered. I remembered saying the same thing...two days ago? Was that possible?

Max stared him down for about ten seconds. "Twenty-five," he replied coolly, responding to an unspoken question. "4672 Rogers Court, Medina Illinois. Dwight Eisenhower High School. There was a small mole on her left breast—left from your point of view, not hers."

"Fuck you!" Billy jumped from his seat and lurched toward the door. He never made it. He stopped dead, frozen in air for twenty seconds, hand outstretched for the knob but going nowhere. Slowly, tortuously, the hand turned, moving mere inches from his eyes, fingers outstretched and pointing. Billy was shaking, sweating, trying with all his might to control his own body, without success. I remembered how frightening that felt. After a long moment, the fingers folded up, one by one, until he was giving himself the bird at close range.

Billy groaned and I cracked up but Max stayed focused behind the desk. "Like I said—I make people do things they don't want to do. Why don't you have a seat and we'll talk." No reply. "I'm not going to let you do anything else, so you might as well." Billy finally, stiffly, returned to his chair.

"If you can do this, what do you need *me* for?" he asked.

"Our enemies are watching for us. We won't get credentials without them noticing. On the other hand, a big network adding a crew at the last minute, even at the G8, is nothing special. But there's more to it than that."

He glanced at me. "I've had time to think about this since you called Billy. The more time we spend in Rome, the more obvious it is—you felt it along the river just now. They're *everywhere,* the drones. I don't know why—all they need is one guy a few feet from her—but look at how many they brought. Even if we manage to stop them here, this won't be over. And the chances of us getting out alive aren't great." I shivered, simply because there was no drama in him, in what he'd just said. He'd sized up our situation, assessed the odds and they weren't good. He was being Max, following his blessed facts. "So someone has to put out this story, has to let ordinary citizens know what's happening. The fight will have to get bigger. It can't be just us."

"You see, Billy, you don't look on the bright side. You're worrying about what I might do *to* you. You're missing what I can do *for* you."

Billy, hair heavy with sweat, shirt soaked through, didn't appear encouraged. "Such as?"

"I don't know—what would make you happy? A Peabody? How about a *Pulitzer*?"

It took a minute for Billy to get his breathing under control but suddenly he was making the effort.

"How's this for a story? Assassination. Governments toppled. Trillions in play. The fate of the World at stake. Mindreaders running wild, tipping the balance of power. Top of the News Hour and you tell our side of the story. Exclusive. "

Billy slumped. "Jaysus! Conspiracies, Psychic Phenomena. UFO's killed Kennedy. Not worth shit."

"What if we can prove it? Pull back the curtain in public? In front of witnesses?" Billy's face was cautious, but his eyes were ravenous.

"But here's the rest," Max warned. "You can't tell this story until everything's over. You'll win awards but you probably won't be able to accept them—you might not survive the trip. You'll have to protect yourself against threats from people like me— threats inside your own head. So there's a pricetag—and it won't be fun."

"I *guess*," Billy laughed—a coarse, harsh cynical laugh. "Why would I want something like that?"

Max smiled his sad smile. "We all want to matter. Most of us don't ever get the chance to really affect things. It's an evil world and the worst threats come from inside, the places we're not watching. You haven't been a journalist all these years for the money, Billy," he said and Billy laughed again. "You love the truth, even if it doesn't always love you back. We'll feed you the facts, new stuff on a regular basis. And you'll post the stories Gregg writes too."

"Me?"

"You've been keeping a journal," Max told me, fervent. "Tell people what it's like *inside* our little team. We'll need to get our side out. Eventually, we'll need accomplices."

Billy was wearing the reporter's gaze now. "What are you talking about? Worldwide revolution?"

"Not against governments," Max shrugged. "They won't take sides, not openly at least. This will be a rebellion by people who've had everything taken away from them—their dignity, control over their own lives. It'll be their way to matter. You're an old Commie, Billy—you should *like* that."

Billy pulled a notepad off the desk. "What's it all about?"

Fifteen

We sat on the balcony staring at the night sky, full of dinner and tipsy from the villa's good wine, going over the G8 agenda. Billy arranged a five-minute preliminary meeting with the head of credentials; Max walked out with full access to all events and the run of the island for the four of us. Billy handed me $100 on the spot. "Don't bet against Max," I told him. Now we were going over the details.

"They won't wait long," Tauber said.

"What do you mean?"

"Think about it. They wanta kill hope. She's only hope till she's made her pitch. After that, either they're all in it together or more'n likely they knock it down and she's over. So if they're gonna kill hope, they've gotta take her out early."

"In public," I added.

"What's not public now?" Kate asked. She was as tipsy as the rest but she was on the same couch as me, with her head on my shoulder. "There's a hundred events this week and you need one cell camera to record it forever. So almost anything qualifies." She stabbed at the agenda without looking. "'Pediatrics for Africa, twenty-minute event, ten children who've survived traditionally-fatal diseases. With Heads of State, entourage and Media Pool.' There's twenty more like that tomorrow and that many more every day to the end."

"Shit!" Tauber groaned. "This is no good. We can't sit around guessin'."

"I can't start probing," Max said. "The one advantage we have is if they think we're dead. I can't blow that without a reason."

"Why's it always *probing*?" Tauber spat. "*Kidnap* somebody, knock 'em on the head and sodium pentothal 'em, do *something*! *Drag* some information outta somebody!" Kate took a step back, involuntarily. "I'm sorry but it's time ta get our hands dirty or admit we're fakin' it. You're not stoppin' these guys politely— they'll walk right over ya."

"I don't think—" Kate started and fizzled out.

"So who do we kidnap?" Max asked. "Pietr Volkov? Marat? Surely they know the plan but I don't want to try taking them. The drones don't know anything. I could feel it when we were filing out of L Corp headquarters; they send out a message, they don't know what they're sending and it vanishes as soon as they're finished."

"*Somebody's* gotta know," Tauber snarled. "They've got a system—they don't have all those people beamin' out all those messages without somebody riding herd on 'em."

"Well, there's the question," Kate said. "Their own men are with security, right at her hip. If they're going to shoot her, why beam anything out at all? I can feel the humming all night long. They've got crowds of drones on it right *now*! What are they beaming out? To *who*?"

"We've got to narrow the possibilities," Max said, "and be ready to defend her at a moment's notice." He blinked at Kate. "You've got to work on making shields."

"*Now?*" She was blinking too. We were all fried, braindead. It had been three days since that morning.

"We're not getting a second chance." He turned to me. "You've got to work on blocking yourself and reading danger when it's near. You could be an early warning."

"I don't know what I'm doing; I've got no power."

"But you're not preoccupied with twenty other things. Concentrate on that." He turned to Tauber. "And you can—"

"I can get zapped in the head or run over or otherwise beat the shit out of because *we don't have a plan*," Tauber said. He was boiling over finally, after simmering for days. "Because we're too pure to start a fight."

"We're here to *prevent* damage," Kate said. "*First do no harm.*"

"I'm not a fuckin' doctor, sweetie. I'm a spy. Nice people put the garbage in the can; my job's takin' out what nobody wants. If it stinks, it's mine. And if I *don't* take it, ain't no molelike son-of-a-bitch comin' up behind me to do it." He headed for the door.

"Where are you going?" Max demanded.

"Out!" Tauber replied, slamming the door behind him.

We stared at the door like the answer was written in the wood. The air was thick now—nothing felt right.

"Okay, let's get to work," Max told Kate. "Make a shield."

Kate sunk into the chair. "I don't think I can make *coffee* right now," she replied, head in her hands. "What if they attack and we're so worn out we can't respond? Does that help anyone?"

Max sighed. "Let's try these things once or twice— just get the feel of them—then sleep if you need to."

Kate constructed an energy shield. Max tested it with his hands—it gave and pushed back. Then he held up his fingers, sitzing and sparking. He tried to throw a lightning bolt but the spark only went a couple inches before fading out. He zapped the shield and Kate flinched.

"Once you've made it, let it go," he instructed. "It grows from energy but then it has its own life. If you try to retain control, you only make it weaker."

"So Tauber was right—it's alive?" she asked.

"The Universe is alive. Children, birds, mosquitoes, those are reactive forms of matter; rocks, not so much." Renn's voice was firm. "I'm only comfortable with a philosophy that develops out of what I know—which is not necessarily what I can prove. What I know is, the same little things make all the big things. Electrons are electrons—everything is one thing."

"You're working on lightning bolts," Kate murmured—it was a reproach, though a polite one.

Max shrugged. "I don't have a plan, so I have to prepare for *everything*. Mark is right—at the moment, *they're* running the table."

~~~~

When I woke, Kate's face was inches from me. Which would have made me very happy, except for the look on her face, which was alarming.

"You were crying out in your sleep."

Her hand was on my chest. When she took it away, I could feel the absence like a memory. The sky was still black outside the window—the clock on the night table read 4 in the morning. And then Max was in the doorway behind her and the way he looked at us on the bed together cut my heart out. Jealousy didn't become him but I knew the feeling myself.

"Do you remember anything?" Kate asked. She'd glanced over at Max and had to have seen what I did, but she didn't budge. "Do you remember the dream?"

"Touch me again," I said. That took her by surprise so I added, "It's how I felt when I woke up. Maybe I can use it to get back there." She laid her hand down—it fit right where it had been. I closed my eyes and, in two seconds, I was in a room, a tiny room. In the toilet. Literally. I had locked myself in the toilet, avoiding the knock at the door and the voice calling, "Are you alright?" My mother. My mother? It was supposed to be my mother but I couldn't see her face or pinpoint her voice. I knew what she was saying and how I was expected to answer but I was overcome by her memory being so close and the fact that I still couldn't see her face. And then I was in the living room in uniform, ready to ship out, and here was an older face straining to be younger—but this mother's face didn't go with the voice in the bathroom. This face came accompanied by another voice, more musical and familiar. And then I was back in a living room decked with party hats, a huge cake and kids waiting for a party—waiting for me. Waiting while I hid in the bathroom, refusing to come out. Not wanting them or the party.

I opened my eyes and blushed because I could see, looking at Kate, that she'd seen everything I had. And Max as well. But what did it mean? I'd been in combat—I'd killed men and seen my friends killed. What was the trauma about a birthday party?

"How did you feel?" Kate asked.

"Confused."

"That's it? You were panicked when I woke you."

"Maybe the problem is, it's not his memory," Max said. "It's mine."

Kate swiveled on the bed like someone had kicked her.

"You're a receptor," Max told me quietly. "You're picking up bits and pieces of memories and thoughts around you."

"I didn't at Dave's," I protested. I wasn't sure why I was against this idea; it seemed obvious as soon as he said it.

"Dave was against all this," Max said. "He stopped emanating a long time ago. If he'd kept it up, maybe he'd still be alive. Since Florida, everyone around you's been getting into your head, making connections. You're responding. Just not always as expected."

"So it was *your* birthday party?"

He nodded. "Remember, my parents were never together—nor my grandparents, for that matter. They mated for the state and disappeared, expunged so I shouldn't go looking for them. I grew up in a collective of teachers and parents. When I got to be 3 or 4, the program became concerned I should have American memories of childhood. So I suddenly acquired a split-level house and a room with a television and a father and mother from the film academy in Moscow. I'm not sure they loved performing for an audience of one in Novosibirsk but they were patriots and did their duty. To no good end. I saw through them in days—it was my first out-of-laboratory invasion of someone else's mind. Not that mindreading was really called for in this case. I longed for family enough to know this wasn't it. I could sense what was missing even though I'd never had it."

He stared at the floor now, embarrassed. I'd seen Max do things that would embarrass most people but I'd never seen him embarrassed before.

"Russians don't have cake, pizza and ice cream at birthdays. In the Soviet, you had a sit-down dinner, very formal. After the meal, the adults started drinking and the kids lay waste. That morning, the dining room—which was odd to me anyway, since we'd just moved in—was surreal, paper party hats, balloons, banners and cupcakes. I was a Taliban prisoner hauled into Disneyland. It was the moment of separation—the moment when, even that young, I understood my life wasn't real, that I was a fiction."

"So you locked yourself in the bathroom?"

"I locked myself in the bathroom. And listened to the kids pretend to be American in the next room. Not my most effective rebellion—but my first, and the first anything is always memorable."

"It still bothers you?" Kate asked.

"It comes back to me in times of stress. I have no anchor. I resent it. Greg is the lucky one."

"Me?"

"Of all of us, you're the most concentrated self. You've lost your memory, your habits, your training. You've forgotten all the messy entanglements. What's left is the essence of your self. You're getting the chance to rebuild from scratch. I envy you that."

"I don't know what you're envying."

Kate stared at Max like she'd never seen him before. "You listen to people your whole life without knowing a thing about them," she said. "We find ourselves in others, in those messy entanglements. Our family, our lovers, they force the doors open. That's what you need, maybe-somebody who can read you like you read everyone else. Someone you don't have to fear you're controlling."

"That's...a good answer," Max smiled, and this was a different smile, a smile of admiration for such a thought. He smiled at the floor for a moment and then raised his head to look her straight in the eye. Kate flushed red. I felt embarrassed watching, like I was intruding. *You're the entanglement I need*, is what the look on his face said. Kate was as strong in her way as he was. He wouldn't have to worry about forcing her. Whatever she felt for him, it would be for real. She might be his only chance at real, ever.

I realized now why he'd looked so torn up, seeing the two of us on the bed together.

And I realized, in that same rush, that I hadn't just divined this information out of thin air. I hadn't miraculously gained the ability to crack the mindbender of mindbenders, the man who could block the universe. If I'd received this message, it was because Max had sent it. He'd made himself vulnerable, but, as always, with a purpose, an end in mind. Maybe his tragedy was that he didn't know any other way to be with people.

I understood. I even felt a little sorry for him. But, looking at Kate, whose hand was still on my chest, I knew there were limits to my loyalty. I had hopes of my own.

That was the moment I consciously began to block the two of them.

And then the phone rang and we all flinched—who was calling at 4 in the morning? The answer was obvious by the time I picked up the phone.

"I should be pissed ye're not all running around searchin' for me already," Tauber said. "Meet me at the Stefano Rotunda."

"What've you got?"

"Nuthin' much. Just a guy who knows what they're plannin'."

The Rotunda sat on one of the Roman hills. Round and squat, with columns arrayed in overlapping arcs, the Rotunda would have been a showstopper anywhere else; in Rome, it was just another church. But it made the Top Ten spy-friendly locations list; Tauber stepped out from behind a pillar, taking us all by surprise, when we were already right on top of him.

He led us to the far side of the building, which looked down on a complex of low office buildings, six narrow rows running off a central courtyard but only two of them lit at 4:30 in the morning.

"Once I knocked the vinegar out of myself," Tauber said, grinning, "I realized *this* was prime time. If ye're gonna send a message—and they didn't bring the drones for nothin'—yer best worktime—"

"—is when your subject is asleep," Max completed the thought.

"So I went over to the Island and waited for the eager salarymen with the lapel pins. I followed a group of 'em back here. They've been hummin' away all night." He was really pleased by his own accomplishment. "I figgered I was better off up here, seein' as how I'm not as dead as I'm s'posed to be."

"Good thinking," Max muttered and they both smiled. This was their common ground—any tension between them dissolved as soon as there was *action*.

"There's two offices down there with twenty drones apiece; they took a break three hours ago so they should be close to the end of the shift. I can't read the stream but I can feel it. Things are coming back to me. They're working 'Emerald'—and I found another stream too, a different head, like a 10 Hz vibration. You feel it?"

Max listened for a few seconds. "Yeah," he said. "Is that your man?"

"He's got to be the leader. The others are locked in, focused on the message—"

"—and he's focused on them, making sure they're sending together, no disruptions, beaming to the right location. Supervising."

"He puts 'em under suggestion so he *has* to know the message." Since we'd first met him, he'd been a cranky, nasty old guy, someone who always found the mold in the yogurt. Now he was twinkling like a three-year-old boy bouncing on his parent's bed.

Max nodded. "You're right. That's got to be right." He clapped Tauber on the shoulder and almost knocked him over. "That's good shit, Mark."

"I'll be useful to ya yet," Tauber murmured to no one in particular.

"Does that mean they're attacking her now?" Kate asked.

"They're not trying to *assassinate* her now. But feel the stream coming out of there! They're working *somebody* pretty hard."

"Can you read it?"

"I guarantee that'd raise the roof. But Mark's plan is, we wait till they shut down and then pull it out of the supervisor. Am I right?"

Tauber nodded, grinning wide.

"*Pull* it out?" Kate said. "I don't like the sound of that."

"You'll have a chance to test your scruples," Max told her. "I want *you* to do the pulling."

~~~~

Jerry Lowery was mulling the velocity of boredom. From his table at the front of the classroom, he had a good view up the skirt of the brunette in the front row and apparently she didn't mind. She kept crossing and uncrossing her legs and squirming in her seat, offering a varied but ever-more-enticing view of the pumpkin orange thong underneath. After a year at L Corp, Lowery had developed his skills to the point that he was certain the brunette knew exactly what she was showing at each moment, even under suggestion. Which only made his boredom in the face of this display more infuriating.

When he'd signed up, three weeks before graduation, choosing L Corp over the CIA, DIA and Livermore Labs, he'd told himself he was making the brash move, taking the unconventional, daring route. L Corp might not be as recognizable on his resume but surely he wouldn't be bored.

Wrong. Sitting in Rome in the middle of the night, keeping watch on the girl with the pumpkin thong and a room full of less-gaudy colleagues, he was bored to the teeth. Bored bored bored

bored bored. The rumors said this was the big one, the operation that would put the company over, make their stock options gold. Of course, if they told you how, they'd have to kill you, haha. He'd told himself the job was undercover work, duties he'd never be able to confide, changing history (in a small way, of course — Lowery was not a boastful man), betrayal and intrigue. Just like Wall Street but legit. And now here he was, making sure the vectoring was right, checking it against the instrument readings every five minutes (or so — Jerry wasn't the most exacting of souls), making sure the stream of suggestion maintained its consistency, that the message was reaching the target coordinates at full strength. The truth is, a teenager could learn to implant a suggestion and, after that, you might as well be giving an algebra quiz. The brunette kept moving her leg in and out now, popping the skirt up and down as though waving it at him. Ho Hum. In the end, she wouldn't take him home; she probably wouldn't even remember the tease.

Life was a tease. Hang in there, Jerry, it's not challenging work but, if you do your bit, if this is the Big Hit, there'll be promotions and raises and bonuses. That was the tease. In the end, he'd still be at a desk in front of a group of post-grads doing invisible work with invisible consequences. He'd get more out of tasking the brunette with a few suggestions of his own. Even if they caught you, the first time was just two weeks lecturing from HR.

The watch he'd laid across the desk in front of him began to beep. "Alright, that's it for tonight," he announced and the group began to sit up straight, rub their eyes, filter back in stages to the real world. "Straight to your apartments and to sleep. *Sleep*. We need you back here, *rested*, 7pm sharp. No wandering around , no parties—we'll be monitoring everyone, so don't get cute." He threw a sad-eyed glance at the brunette, mourning the loss of possibility. The girl didn't seem to notice the gesture.

As they wandered out, Jerry scrubbed the whiteboard. Spies, teachers, brokers or Mafiosi—all jobs were routine. Consistency, do the job reasonably well, reasonably the same, time after time. No wonder he was bored. He checked in with the cathedral by cell—they were closing up as well. Managers meeting 530p. Stay sharp tomorrow.

He flipped off the lights and walked out into the warm night. Was there someplace to eat? He was hungry. There was a waitress at a place near the Pantheon who'd flirted with him the night before but she couldn't still be working at this hour. And he refused to eat based on sex that might possibly maybe happen someday if he got ridiculously lucky. Not.

He headed in that direction anyway. There were lots of restaurants and he wasn't ready for sleep, no matter the company line. L Corp wouldn't be monitoring *managers*. At least, not him specifically. At least, he didn't think so.

The Coliseum shown through the dark streets like the world's grandest jack O'lantern. Lowery cut through a grove of trees across the street and under brick arches extending from one of several hundred local churches. From God's power to man's — that was the progression of the human race.

When Rome was the center of the European world, it built three churches a block to God's glory—now the cathedral on Tiber Island was decommissioned, a conference center for businessmen and politicians to hold polite dinners and divvy up their worldly scraps—financial aid, military assistance, the strings-attached charity of the World Bank. The early Christians had received communion in church; so had his mother, probably last week. Lowery, a man with no active God, had gone to the center several times in the past few days to receive his suggestion, the mental image that he passed on to his charges in the viewing room. An image was all it took, in the Information Age, to conquer the World—an image and the power of the mind.

As he crossed the next street and worked his way around the remains of Palatine Stadium, he didn't feel much like a conqueror. Rome was a big city; wandering dark places alone at night wasn't particularly brilliant—but then, what mugger would be looking for a muggee at 5 in the morning?

The ruins had weathered smooth like skulls, the clay red like everything else in this furnace of a city. In June, Rome remained hot all night. The arches of Domitian's Palace towered in deep shadow, the lights at the Forum nearby placing everything else in silhouette. Jerry wanted a beer. A couple of beers. And maybe a cognac. Tomorrow was the day.

Jerry had walked this way at least twenty times, day and night, since arriving in Rome but somehow, this time, the sightlines looked different, the landmarks springing from the ground at odd angles and odder locations. Where he expected to break out of the Emperor's overhanging confines, instead he found himself more deeply withdrawn, walled-in. Rows of bone-white pillars stood against the red clay wreckage, pointing skyward like missiles. When he looked up for stars, clouds were gathering, swirling, too quickly and very specifically too close to him. The wind kicked up, gusting through the cavernous gaps between pillars and arches and ruins, whipping his jacket from his hands. He ran after the stupid thing, ending up even deeper in the labyrinth of ancient passageways. Ripples of lightning pulsed through the clouds—this felt just about obligatory, with all else that was happening—next had to be ghosts of Emperors long dead, Lowery both joking with himself and admitting real fear simultaneously. The atmosphere had gone deathly way too fast for real life.

And then there was Pietr Volkov, advancing on him like a general across a battlefield, lit up like he'd swallowed a neon tube and marching right *through* the bars of the fence surrounding the ruins. What the hell did *he* want? Lowery had only met the man once, which was plenty. He'd heard the rumors—or the rumors about the rumors—that surrounded Volkov. Lowery thought back—had he missed a cue somewhere? Nobody had missed session tonight or last night. He'd checked them all in. He hadn't checked the clarity of the transmission as often as the regs demanded, but *nobody* did, except Vlada, the toadie—every time he'd checked, everything had been to spec.

Volkov should have reached him by now but he was still marching and Lowery's panic kept rising. What about check-out? Making sure none of the drones carried any of the suggestion out of the room after they were done? Had he checked *everyone*? Oh Jesus—the girl with the pumpkin thong! She'd seemed so disinterested, even disdainful—maybe he hadn't...Shit! Shit! Now...?

"Is it possible," Volkov bellowed, still a few yards away, "that our enemies *know our plans*?" The last words exploded inside Lowery's skull like someone was pounding with a hammer.

"Not from me!" Lowery cried immediately, trying halfway through to drag his voice down and exert some kind of control. Volkov was right on top of him, the two of them alone in the center of the center of the Ancient World.

"Alright, not from you! Maybe from one you were responsible for!" Volkov drilled at Lowery. "Maybe from this girl you have the stupid infatuation with. *Is it possible?*"

"How *can* they?" Lowery blubbered, desperately trying not to think of the pumpkin-colored line between the girl's legs, even though—especially because—Volkov clearly knew about it already. "That's the whole idea, isn't it? We each had our portion. I only had Emerald. If they don't have them all—?"

"Don't *quibble* with me!" Volkov bellowed into Lowery's face. He was backing him into one of Domition's ancient walls. Behind Volkov, an ancient alcove rose skull-like five stories above them, flashing blue now in the sudden lightning. "You got your instruction at the same time as the others, yes?"

"Y—yes!" Lowery admitted, not sure what infraction he could have committed there.

"So you had Emerald. Who sat next to you?"

"Ruby."

"How would you know that unless you paid attention to *that* portion as well?" Volkov thundered. All Lowery had seen was the identifying logo on the screen as they started feeding the images to them—that was *all*. He was *sure*. He clung to that denial, repeating it over and over like a mantra. If Volkov was going to read his mind, let him read that, please.

Maybe he did. Instead of ripping his skull off, Volkov held back now a moment, still only half a foot away but regarding him with at least a little detachment. Maybe this was how they looked at you just before they turned you to dust, Lowery thought. It wasn't like there was any point resisting. An odd thought occurred to him as lightning struck the skull arch behind Volkov and the light seemed to gleam *through* him.

"Are you here?" Lowery asked, unable to think of a more elegant way to ask the question.

"No, I'm not here, you idiot," Volkov swiped. "I can't administer every lazy mid-level in person."

So he was a projection—Lowery had heard of *that*, too. The old mindbenders were full of tricks. This Volkov didn't blink— yes, he did. Now he did, that is, though Lowery swore he hadn't until just then. He wondered if the projections only blinked once you noticed they weren't blinking. "That won't keep me from disciplining you in any method that strikes me as appropriate. *Do you understand?*"

A second later, the tree in front of them erupted with a lightning hit. Lowery felt the charge in the air and went deaf for a few seconds after the crack. A tree branch the size of a Fiat came down a foot away and Volkov was in his face again.

"Yes, yessir, I understand," Jerry stammered, trying with difficulty to make eye contact.

"Charge me with tonight's suggestion," Volkov ordered.

"What?"

"PLAY IT BACK. NOW! I want to see what you gave your charges tonight, what they sent out. Or shall I just extract it from your frontal lobe?"

"No, no, that—" It was not the easiest time to put himself into a meditative state but at least the lightning seemed to pause while he closed his eyes. Maybe Volkov was just gathering a big bolt to smite him if he didn't like what he saw. Jerry tried to concentrate. When he opened his eyes momentarily, Volkov was standing, tapping his feet in exasperation.

Finally, Lowery was able to put himself back in the tasking room in the convention center, the place where they all received the images for their shifts. He felt himself in the chair and saw the ruby logo on the screen. He could see the flash of ruby on the next screen but only for a second, *see, it's just peripheral vision and my eyes go right back to my own screen and that's it!*

And then, in the air around him, filling the space between him and Volkov, here was his image, his message—the grainy, jagged, useless image he'd given his team to send out. Flashes of close movement, the grunting noises of a struggle and cries for help, jerky shards of picture skimming across the air between them, the desperate movement in the pictures heightened by the frenzied shrieking of the orchestra in the background. And rain— he hadn't noticed the rain when he learned the transmission but now it was everywhere and he realized it had come off the video image.

Everything was just as he'd been given it, he was sure. All the control bytes showed in proper order, the color bars were correct, the control tone was accurate. He'd remembered it objectively, without coloring it with any of his own input. It was an successful tasking, he was sure of it.

Several seconds had passed since the image ended. He was still there. Volkov hadn't said anything. Lowery convinced himself it was alright to open his eyes—at very least, his transmission couldn't be held against him. When he did, Volkov had stepped a little further away. He seemed to be concentrating elsewhere.

When he saw Lowery's eyes were open, Volkov said, "Go about your business. Say nothing of this to anyone. We still have a leak. It wouldn't do for them to know we're looking for them, would it?" He took a few steps, then turned back just for a moment. *"You don't know who to trust,"* Volkov warned. Then he stepped into the swirling wind embracing the arches and was gone, disappeared, vanished.

Lowery touched his coat—it wasn't even damp. No rain. He took off toward a street, anyplace with cars and other people. Anyplace he could find several—no, many—cognacs with breakfast.

Sixteen

"That was terrific," Max told Kate as we watched Lowery sprint downhill away from the Palatine. "Except you dropped a plate."

"Huh?"

"Volkov didn't blink. He caught on it was an image. No harm done this time but, when you're making an illusion, you've got to keep *all* the plates in the air."

"You could do better?"

"Not a chance, but not the point."

"Forget about next time, dammit!" Tauber burst. "*That* was the message?"

"I know—not much, is it? It's what was in his head—it's the message they were sending out. We got it without probing and he won't tell anyone. But I'm not sure what it's worth." We started back toward the villa. "Let's get home and play it back," Max said.

"Play it back?"

They had a very nice home theatre system on the second floor. Max went in behind the digital recorder, pulled out the input cables and placed his fingers over the inputs.

"It's a hard drive," he said. "Magnetic impulses on a platter. The same process, actually, as skewing instrument readings in the nuclear plant two or three miles away."

He pushed 'Record' and stood over the inputs, eyes closed, humming a kind of odd, unmusical tone for a couple of minutes. I don't know what possessed me to do it, but I came real close to the machine—it was humming the same tone. When he finally pushed 'Play,' the scene Lowery had shown us appeared on the screen, tumult and frenzied movement but fuzzy images and indecipherable.

"Is it the assassination of her father?" Kate asked.

"Sounds kinda like it."

"This *can't* be right. How can they influence her when ya can't tell what the picture is?"

Max replayed the thing to the end, where the control bits showed—color bars, audio tone and a slate. Emerald, 3 of 4.

"They're a couple steps ahead of us. They've split up the signal. Emerald, Sapphire, Ruby, Diamond—four teams, each sending out separate parts of an image. The recipient gets all four—"

"—we get static," Kate said and Max nodded. "This is less than useless."

"How come the music comes through while the rest is all broken up?" I asked and he shrugged.

The sun was coming up over the hills of Rome. Cars and trucks rumbled just outside, the beginnings of Sunday's traffic. Church bells rang from every direction. Max was at the window, pulling a twenty-foot door open and shut, open and shut, all nervous energy.

"Today's the day," he said. "It's going to happen today." There was no excitement in his voice, only dread.

"We need another team leader," Tauber said. "We need at least one more part o' the puzzle."

"That's insane—finding the first guy took you hours."

"It's what we need, 'less you got a better idea."

Kate and I were dispatched to Tiber Island. "They've definitely got pictures of Mark and me," Max said. "If anybody looks sideways at you—even once—cut your losses and get out." It was pretty clear from the way he was talking that he didn't expect much from the attempt.

Tauber looked even more wiped out—he really thought he'd found the missing link the night before; it tore into him to come up empty.

Getting onto the Island was insanity—five security checkpoints, passports and credentials and interrogation from scratch at each one. First day of the conference, everybody on full alert. With all that, I didn't notice what was missing until we actually reached the conference center.

"Do you feel it?" I asked as soon as we crossed the threshold.

"What?"

"*Nothing*. The air's clear—no probing, no blocking, no nothing."

The place was a dead zone, despite media geeks running around interviewing each other, security guards bulky at every entrance, world leaders behind closed doors, entourage busy looking important, caterers, drivers, runners, lots of pretty girls with clipboards and earpieces—but, once we got past the checkpoints, no L Corp.

We hustled the corridors of the conference center, the old cathedral, getting bolder with every minute, until we found their conference rooms—they were nervy enough to put decals on the door. Ornate, huge rooms—thirty-foot ceilings, fifteen-foot stained-glass windows, statues of long-forgotten saints, angels with wings folded standing across from angels with wings outstretched. Glorious rooms—glorious and empty, seats neatly stacked, whiteboards blank. We were actually giddy for a moment, triumphant at being inside their rooms, unchallenged—for just a moment. Then we realized how wrong it was, how bad it was for us.

"Nothing," we had to report when we returned. "Not a sticky note. Dead empty."

Tauber banged his hand on the kitchen table hard enough I thought he was going to break something. Max just sighed.

"Are they done?" he asked, not expecting an answer. "Are they attacking any minute and they're clearing everyone out in advance?"

"No," Tauber said immediately. "If they were attackin' now, they'd've cleared out at the end o' last night. Why keep 'em in town *this* long?"

"Then what? Where'd they go?" Max's hands were in the air, grasping for anything, for any scrap of an idea. We were all dry.

"What's on the schedule?" Kate asked and we tore to the dining room to check the itinerary again.

"Twenty things." The 4000th session of Aid to the Third World, the 2500th session about Climate Change (formerly the 2500th session about Global Warming), address by Al Gore, meet and greet with Bono, briefing by former victims of sex trafficking ('bet that 'un's well-attended' — Tauber), starvation as a growing threat to stability and currency fluctuation as economic policy. All sessions behind closed doors, but with photo ops before or after (no open microphones, media please note). Evening dinner, 7 courses, festival of Italian regional dishes ('no threat to stability there'-Tauber) and the evening concert, Holst and Benjamin/Wyndham-Lewis.

We stood staring at the paper spread out across the table.

"It's there," Max said grimly. "The answer's right there in front of us."

"Then why are they all gone?"

We were staring at each other like somebody was hiding the secret on purpose. We'd all gone stupid from tension. I slumped onto the couch. There was no answer, that was the answer, but what good was an answer like that?

I don't know how I fell asleep. I was wired as a cat from exhaustion. I closed my eyes and dropped right out, maybe twenty seconds, maybe two minutes. It wasn't long, but somehow it was long enough.

When I opened my eyes, everything looked different.

"It's the music!"

"What?"

"The music last night—in Lowery's suggestion! It's Holst!"

"The concert!" Kate ran for the agenda. "Holst—the Planets!"

"'Mars' was playing in the background. They're not feeding her a memory—they're telling her what's *coming*."

"That doesn't make sense," Max said. "They dragged a huge crew here to *warn* her?"

"Maybe they want to beat her down, make her accept it when it comes?" I offered but it sounded stupid coming out of my mouth.

A long pause now but everyone rapt, feeling how close we were to the answer.

"We're *assuming* the message is for her," Kate said finally. "What if it's for one of the guards— to force one of the guards to kill her?"

"So L Corp doesn't get the blame. So they can keep their lucrative security trade afterward."

"Doesn't work," Billy said when I got him on the phone. "The concert is the only part of the day that *can't* work. It's Heads of State only in a Plexiglas bubble overlooking the orchestra. Security, L Corp, everybody else locked outside. If the plan is to kill her, that would be the *toughest* time to do it."

We each found a different corner of the room now, resentful, disturbed, isolated even from each other. After running so hard to get this far, silence was terrifying. Not having something to do—not *knowing* what to do—was chewing us up.

I didn't like my thoughts and I didn't like being uncomfortable with my thoughts either. I grappled with them for several minutes of silence before opening my mouth.

"There's no chance we're fooling ourselves, is there?"

"About which part?" Max asked.

"*All* of it," I answered. "What if—what if you got tired of sitting around the Everglades playing with the electrons in the desk? What if you wanted to do something important? To *be* important? What if—?"

"What if I made it *all* up. Volkov, Avery, the bomber in the square—all the people in the square. What if the whole thing is an illusion? Is that what you mean?" He'd read me—I couldn't deny it.

"Well—you said you made your girlfriend fall in love with you. Kate went to Morocco without leaving the apartment."

"So I just bought into his fantasy?" Kate snarled. I hated raising that look on her face. "I was so unhappy with my life that I got sucked into—?" She was all wound up but Max cut her off.

"We could all get killed here. We could rot in jail for the rest of our natural lives, whether we stop them or not. And it's not like you and I *couldn't* have made all this up—and convincingly. If anyone's got doubts, now's the time to raise them." He stared out the window for a long moment. "I've got doubts myself."

"Where's Avery?" Kate sat up like a mannequin on a stand. "If they're doing a major operation, he should be here, right?"

We ran into the other room and switched on the set. Naturally, they had *Your World* TV in Italy too. All the big sports stadiums look the same so we weren't sure for a moment what we were seeing but then the camera tilted back and upward for a moment and we saw the Sydney Opera House in the background.

I head a hissing noise and realized a moment later I was making it. It was the sound of the air coming out of the room.

"Did we get it all wrong?" Kate asked, looking sharply at Max. But his eyes were on Avery, striding the massive stage in Sydney.

"People say to me, 'Jim, you're a dreamer. Hope by itself won't fix what's broken in the world. Don't you see the dark clouds on the horizon? Hope's not an answer.

"And, you see, all that proves is, they don't understand *Your World*. This isn't about me giving you the answers. This is about what we can build *together*." Avery stepped toward the camera, eyeing it like the prettiest girl at the dance. "Hope isn't The Answer—Hope is our belief that, together, we can *find* answers. When you join Your World, you become a member of a worldwide community who refuse to be categorized, refuse to be led, people who band together to make their own towns and cities into better places to live. Not to build the world I want for them or what Government wants. What *they* want."

"What a crock," I said but Max shushed me right away.

"Quiet," he said. "He's talking to *us*."

Avery stood heroic, right above the camera, a spotlight winking out behind him as he gestured. "So if the dark clouds are coming, I say let them come. They always have, all through history. But we have a way to fight back!"

Max switched it off. He turned to us, galvanized. "It's real," he said. "We're not wrong."

"So the whole thing's a recruiting drive for *Your World?*" Kate asked, not convinced and I wasn't sure either.

"Why not? He's positioning, marketing his corporation. Tonight, he sounds optimistic: *I'm not worried about the dark clouds.* Tomorrow, they'll look back at how brilliant, prescient—"

"Almost like he knew what was comin'—"

"Eerie, isn't it?"

"But what does it get him? What's he do when they're all members?"

"Every time Avery speaks of Hope, underneath, he's festering anger, resentment. I sensed it in the car going to L Corp— in him, they're the two sides of the same coin. He's telling his followers, 'Bring us your anger and we'll *do* something about it'. I don't have to know every detail to know how bad that is."

Kate bit her lip until it bled. "I'm not asking for details. I just want to know we're not fooling ourselves. How do we *know*? For sure?"

Tauber stepped up between the three of us and rolled up his sleeve.

"Bruise," he announced, pointing. He rolled up the other sleeve. "*Big* bruise." Shirt collar pulled to the side. "Big dark *nasty* bruise. Souvenirs from my stay at the L Corp Holiday Hotel. If I'm real, *they're* real. And if I'm not real, why've I got the DT's and arthritis in my knee?"

"What about Dave?" Max asked me. "What about your father?" he said to Kate. And suddenly I was back in the house in the swamp. The musky smell was up my nostrils, I could see his tongue out and his eyes open and dull. I felt my finger as it touched his eye, the damp squishy feel of it. I remembered the way I felt; the way I thought, the way my brain worked back those few days ago.

And then I had the answer.

"It's the concert," I said.

"You don't know that," Max said.

"We don't know anything. At this point, we're going to have to go with what we can *guess*." I took them in with a glance. "It explains why they're not out there now. Their plans are set, close-to-deadline. They're sleeping, recouping, getting ready for their big night. Tonight."

"It still doesn't explain the music on the video," Kate said. "The sound is all mangled except the orchestra—that's clear like it's off a disc."

"It's a music cue," Tauber said, like it had just come to him.

"What'?"

"The earliest form of mind control," Max said, as though he too was just seeing it for the first time. "Pavlov's dogs—they hear the bell, they think of food. The message says: Act when you hear this sound, this measure, this part of the music."

"They got most o' the sound from the original video, so it's split up," Tauber added. "The orchestra track's on all four streams so it don't get lost."

" 'Mars', two-thirds of the way through. It's the concert," I said and this time no dissent.

I called Billy again, to inform him we were his crew for the concert tonight.

"I don't *have* a crew," he said. "Nobody does. The concert is being broadcast on RAI. We're all taking their feed."

"Tell the security office you're doing an end-of-day wrapup on the lawn with the orchestra in the background. We're your crew. We'll get there about fifteen minutes early—there are too many pictures of Max's face out there; we can't hang around."

"Okay," Max stood as soon as I hung up, energized, "we all need sleep. Four hours will get us one sleep cycle—that'll have to do. After that, Kate, you work on making shields and fast—you've got to protect yourself tonight, I won't be able to. Greg, work with her—no, actually, I'll do it."

"I can work with her." I didn't like him taking this away from me. If it was my last day on Earth, I could think of worse company.

"No, I have to work on lightning bolts, she has to work on shields." He shrugged to Kate.

"Don't be so damn apologetic about it!" Tauber said. "Either we're fighting or not."

"We're here to prevent—" Kate started.

"You don't win on defense," Tauber drilled.

"*Stop!!*" Max said, loud enough that the room went silent. "This isn't a game. I'm going to prepare every possible weapon." He turned to Tauber, who was smirking. "I've killed before, but never on purpose. I know what it does to me. It's the last choice."

"Those are expensive scruples," Tauber grumbled.

"Everything is part of everything," Max replied. "What I kill, kills a bit of me. Greg, work on your blocking and detecting— we'll send out messages, you call out who's sending and when."

"Anything you want me to do?" Tauber asked; his expression said he didn't expect much.

"You're a crafty son-of-a-bitch—and a spy," Max said and Tauber lit up. "They've got a plan—and we're going to have to figure it out on the fly. You're my fresh pair of eyes." He turned to the group. "Okay? Any comments? Concerns?"

"I toss and turn; it takes me a while to fall asleep," Kate said.

"Toss quickly," Max replied.

~~~~

I awoke with a start—there was someone in the room, whispering to me. Not a familiar voice but a lover's tone, one that asked for intimacy. I fumbled for the light and then, somehow, moved myself, in that half-awake state, back to Tess, to the back seat of her car again. And woke the others immediately.

"I just got probed bigtime." Kate nodded like she knew— Tauber, who'd been standing watch, didn't even turn around. What was up? Then I saw Max on the floor, eyes closed and limp.

"What happened?"

"They're probin' for him all over the place. They didn't buy the crushed-by-a-rock-wall act; they've got us narrowed to a couple houses 'round here. You have yer stuff?"

"All I've got is what I'm wearing."

"As soon as he stops breathin', we'll take him down to the car. If he's out like this, hopefully they won't catch on till it's too late."

"They know about this trick," I warned.

"Knowin' it ain't solvin' it," he answered. "Hopefully."

And, once the coma took effect, we carried the body out to the Alfa Romeo parked alongside the house.

Billy was waiting with a satellite truck five blocks from the first checkpoint. "The roof saucer by itself should get you halfway through," he said, staring as we carried Max's body into the back.

The guards at the second checkpoint took their time—they made an effort at a thorough search—but Billy kept ranting against

Berlusconi and how unfair the TV business was to anyone over 40 until they just slammed the door in his face.

It wasn't like they didn't have anything else to keep themselves busy. We were surrounded the whole way by crowds heading for the concert. The floodlights glinted off the Plexiglas viewing box set up for the leaders at the end of the island and the bleachers on both banks, filling rapidly with jostling guests contending for choice locations with their wine bottles and cellphone cameras.

Finally, we were at the final checkpoint and over the bridge, assigned a spot amidst the other satellite trucks. As soon as we settled, I gave Max a good kick—I wasn't taking chances. This time, he came to with a start.

"They're sending out suggestions, really concentrated—do you feel it?" he asked, shaking himself awake. "You and Kate know where their conference rooms are—shut them down. Disrupt them, knock over the furniture, get in their faces, break their concentration. Interrupt the message. Two minutes is enough. Then *get off the island* as fast as you can. It's going to get hairy."

He turned to Tauber. "We're heading for the orchestra— you're my eyes and ears..." As he pushed the doors open, we all heard the thrums of the strings starting to beat in the night air. "That's *it*! Mars! We've got five minutes! Go!"

The guards at the conference center grew half a foot taller just from us running at them.

"Halt or show ident—"

Kate swiped her hand at them and they flew backwards into the stone wall. She had that look on her face now, the one I'd seen in the cemetery. I pitied anyone who got in her way.

We ran headlong toward the two rooms we'd visited that morning. "Get in, mess them up and get out!" she yelled. "We've got to get back to the concert as soon as we're done."

"But Max said—" I started and cut myself short—I had no more intention of skipping out than she did. "Never mind," I said and saw the light glinting in her eyes.

Two more guards waited outside the L Corps doors—Kate concentrated real hard this time; one hit the ceiling, the other flew straight backward through the door. By the time we burst in behind him, rows of meditating drones were already jumping up out of their yoga poses and scattering.

I grabbed a monitor from the front of the room and smashed it to the floor. A studly guy in a Dallas Cowboys jersey jumped me—I grabbed the whiteboard and smacked him in the face with it. The whole group was yelling and scattering, the way anyone would, attacked by crazy people for no reason—I realized they really *didn't* know what they were doing there.

Lowery's familiar figure rushed for cover under an ornate arch, finger to his ear, talking hard into his headpiece. There'd be guards coming on the run, I realized. After the first rush of fear, I recognized this as a *good* thing — it would clear the other end of the island for Max. But it was still trouble for us.

And sooner than I thought. The partition to the next conference room slid open and several burly shooters barged through. The drones were scattering behind them, so we had officially accomplished our mission.

More guards pounded through the door behind us and I spied reinforcements coming hard across the courtyard outside. Drones scattered, we suddenly had a new goal: getting out alive.

I shot Kate a look, feeling like a bulls-eye on a stand. Her eyes were closed and her lips pursed, the prissy girl throwing a fit in school because somebody stole her notebook. She was humming up a storm. I relaxed the way you do when your only choice is to go over the oncoming waterfall.

A moment later, the angel statue with the folded wings unfolded them and took to the air; the one who'd started out unfolded was already flapping hard around the suite, scattering papers and loose jackets and scaring the shit out of everybody. Saints floated out of the stained-glass windows and the fountains round the edge of the room shot straight into the air, showering the whole scattering bunch.

I flunked science but there's a limit. I reached out my hand, groping for the spot where the statues had stood a few moments earlier. My hand touched marble and, all at once, without drama or fanfare, the statues were there again. Or there *still*, I guess. I removed my hand and they disappeared. Kate had a smirk on her face.

"This way!" she said, pointing at a granite staircase under another of the arches. I started after her and then stopped dead in my tracks. She whirled, questioning but it was too late. With all the craziness, I couldn't move.

One drone remained stubbornly in place, brow furrowed under his sandy hair, furiously sending out his message. All I had to do was knock over his chair, kick his ass and get the hell out.

But, five feet away from him, it hit me, full-strength, full-on: the screaming, the shots going off, the tumult of bodies in every direction, trying to get the gun away from—? And the music, the Holst, but not the Holst outside, the same piece but a minute advanced, a hundred bars ahead.

I staggered like a sailor in a squall as the complete suggestion hit me, all four channels feverishly relayed by the man seated in front of me, the man who hadn't faltered, the mindshare buddy I'd channeled in the hallway outside the bomber's apartment and at the airport. The man whose wavelength I shared.

"We've got to get to Max!" I yelled. "I know the plan!"

We dove down the stairwell and rushed headlong across the corridor below, past a succession of storage rooms and offices. We could hear shouting and footsteps behind us but we weren't waiting for company.

At the far end, Kate threw open a door and then another and we were outside in the lovely oppressive night air. She put her fingers to the lock and waited. Nothing. She grimaced, shook them in the air and finally rubbed enough to get a spark. She fused the lock shut just as the guards reached it. We ran the high concrete skirt of the island, tearing reckless toward the prow and the sound of the raging orchestra.

And then it was pouring, just like in Lowery's image, the rain coming down in buckets. As we neared the prow, the whole scene opened up like a pageant in front of us—spotlights glaring on the dome where the leaders sat like mannequins, facing the open-sided tent covering the orchestra. The Holst was pounding away, strings bowing furiously and horns blaring, a huge wall of sound. I knew the piece—we had a minute, maybe less, before the cue.

Three guards rushed us in formation. Kate threw two into the river with a flick of the wrist. The third pulled a gun, then howled and dropped it. The weapon glowed hitting the ground, setting the grass all round to burning.

Singh sat in the middle of the dome, everyone's primary safety concern but not really a proper member of the G8. I'd seen enough on TV to know her usual self-possession; the conflict on her face now was chilling. She was fighting herself—fighting what her mind was telling her to do. She didn't look like she'd be able to fight much longer.

Max and Tauber stood next to the tent; I veered wildly toward them—several heads swiveled in percussion as I ran past.

A lightning bolt crackled past my ear. I turned to face it and it exploded—against an invisible shield. Kate ran up next to me. "Keep going," she yelled, deflecting another blast with a swipe of her hand. On the far side of the island, Pietr Volkov stood close alongside the viewing box while Marat headed straight for us.

Less than thirty seconds to the cue. Volkov, near the dome, began to mutter and Singh rose like a marionette out of her chair. The French President turned to check on her but no one, characteristically, left their positions.

"Max!" I yelled. I was right on top of him now. He was frozen, his face full of fear. Considering the things I'd seen him do, that sent a chill up my back. He was fixated on Volkov, staring hard but clearly getting no voices, no answers, no clear idea of what was happening.

"Not now!" he yelled.

"We got it wrong!" I grabbed him by the shoulders. "She's not the victim—she's the *assassin!*"

My skull went hot and, in a moment, he knew what I knew, what I'd read from the sandy-haired drone: the plan wasn't to kill the messenger of hope—that wouldn't be enough, there could always be another. It was to discredit the *idea* of hope, to show up the Emissary of Hope as a loon, a crackpot, someone who went crazy just on the verge of success.

Singh had carried her own gun into the enclosure—nobody was searching World Leaders on their way to a concert. She would kill as many in the dome as she could, until the guards brought her down or she killed herself, all in full view of the television cameras, the ambassador of peace become the instrument of violence, betrayer of all she'd stood for and all the hope she'd inspired. Her eyes grew large now, recognizing the swelling of the music cue.

I felt Max suck all this out of me. He wheeled toward the dome and the few seconds left before it was too late. Lightning bolts burst inches away against another Kate shield. She advanced on Marat now, throwing shields at him, blowing his own blasts back in his face, forcing him to retreat.

Volkov remained focused on Singh. If the drones were down, he could accomplish the mission on his own—at this range, she couldn't resist. He repeated instructions and made tiny gestures and she moved in lockstep, pulling her bag open, grasping for the revolver inside.

Max seemed fixated, just taking in the scene, for far too long. But then, all at once, he began to speak, in a language I'd never heard—and Singh flinched again and withdrew her hand from the bag. Volkov saw this and upped his tempo. The two voices echoed and clashed inside my head, each growing louder, more insistent, with repetition, like each hoped somehow to drown the other out.

Seconds to the climax, the music cue, the moment for killing. The tempo was pounding, the music rising to crescendo.

Singh was taut, quivering back and forth, fighting to reconcile the competing orders in her head. Volkov grimaced, his face grim and determined. I could hear his voice ordering her with ferocious energy: *Take the gun out, Fire away.*

Max's voice, on the other hand, actually faded now. I looked over with alarm and saw his face struggling, suffering, full of confusion. He was muttering to himself, his voice repeating his indecipherable phrases like a mantra but also babbling and arguing back and forth. At first, I thought we were lost, until I realized I wasn't hearing Max's voice at all—his lips were moving but what I heard in my head, in that unknown language, was *Singh's* voice speaking. Her face and Max's were synchronized, the same emotions, the same convulsions and confusion passing back and forth, from one to the other.

Volkov was ordering her around; Max had gotten *inside* her, taking over the load and helping her fight back. And now I saw his determination begin to creep onto her face.

A moment later, Volkov realized what was going on—did he read it from *me?*—and his stare went murderous. His attention narrowed to Max and Max responded, the two locked together, throwing every ounce of energy into competing suggestions and opposing methods, into beating the other, all the imperatives of a lifetime come together.

All at once Max threw his hands in front of him, defensively, like he was being pushed. His face was confused and desperate and I thought, Volkov's hit him with something he can't counter. But Volkov's shoulder was up, pushing back at some unseen force, legs pumping hard just to keep him upright. He was every bit as shaken and off-kilter as Max. Whatever was happening, it was new territory for the two of them.

Until that moment, the five of us fighting were the only ones who knew what was going on. A moment later, the audience on both banks of the river gasped aloud, loud enough to be heard over the shrieking orchestra as the whole affair went public, as all assembled saw what no one could later explain, the sight replayed on video two million times after it was all over.

Two lines of energy were converging on Singh—one from Volkov, the other from Max, each hell-bent on overwhelming the other. Now, all at once, that force went visible.

A seam opened in the air, like a thick snake writhing in the night sky, throwing off the raindrops, slipping back and forth as the two men battled for control. It slithered above the orchestra tent and suddenly the music warped Doppler, like the sound of an ambulance passing in traffic, pitch wavering and flexing.

The musicians were throwing nervous looks around and above, trying to figure out what was happening. The leaders in the dome were up, staring at the seam and the men at the two ends of it. Max and Volkov were as shocked as everyone else, their mouths open, lost in their own power gone beserk.

And then the leaders were scrambling for the exit door, their bodyguards struggling to open the lock but even at a distance it was clear they'd be way too late to affect the outcome. Singh was frozen, hand still inside her bag—the confusion on her face was suffocating.

The seam bubbled and squirmed in the middle now, like a pig squeezed through the belly of the snake, the bubble rumbling back and forth as the two men poured it on. And then the seam flicked sideways, in an eyeblink, and nicked the rim of the dome itself and the Plexiglas buckled and exploded, a million tiny shards of plastic hurled in every direction.

The leaders hit the floor with the guards piled on top of them. Shouts and screams from both sides of the river, a panicked crush fleeing the bleachers.

I was running too, sprinting up the riverbank. Kate was in front of me, pushing Marat back. The harder he tried, the harder she pushed him back and I could see him really getting hot.

I went straight for Volkov. He was still grappling with the seam, puffing like a general on an obstacle course. But as the guards began hustling the leaders to shelter, he saw the situation was hopeless. He released the bubble with a wave of his hand—it vanished as he focused a murderous look on Singh.

He threw his hand out but I threw myself at him first and we went head over heels, tumbling down the side of the island. I hit a tree squarely and that stopped me but good. Volkov continued straight into the river. When I looked up, Singh was gone—when I turned back to the river, so was Volkov.

I stood the best I could, vowing to keep clear of trees the rest of my life. Tauber ran toward us, somehow supporting Max, who was wheezing as bad as Volkov. The musicians, disciplined as soldiers, were finishing their piece but looking around wildly while playing.

Kate had pushed Marat to the bank of the river, both of them grim-faced and determined. All at once, Marat stopped firing. He turned from Kate and fired at Max, who managed to block the blast with a high swipe of his hand. As he reached upward, Marat lowered his aim and fired another blast directly into Tauber.

The old man turned blue and glowed like one of those bars you break open to light your campsite. He twitched and shook, making growling noises like an animal in a trap. And then a look of recognition moved across his face—almost a smile but not quite —and he collapsed like a bag of bones.

Marat lowered his arms now, satisfaction on his face. Max and Kate turned a black look on him simultaneously. At the moment their looks converged, Marat vaporized—imploded into the night air, sucked into particles that glowed for an instant and flickered out.

And then the music was over and all was chaos, the cries of the crowd and the sound of a hundred musicians abandoning their instruments, running across the sodden lawn for cover.

Kate and I bent over Tauber but there was nobody there. He was just a shell in the grass. I flashed back all of a sudden to Dave, to the way I'd gone vacant and distant a moment after Dave was killed. There was nothing distant here—this *hurt*.

"We've got to go," Max was saying but we weren't listening.

"We've can't just leave him behind," Kate answered. "We—" but she didn't know how to finish.

"We have to," Max repeated, gesturing behind us. Turning, I saw security pouring around the front of the island, seeking culprits for the morning papers.

Kate wasn't budging. "He—we've got to do something for him. Something for...respect."

"He's got that," Max said, closing Tauber's eyes and laying his head back on the grass. Kate glared at him—she wasn't going without him. Max nodded at me and I knew what he wanted, because of course he put the idea into my head. The idea did nothing for me—I wanted what Kate wanted, to do something for the old warrior instead of leaving him on the battlefield. We'd said in Iraq, *don't miss a speck.* But now I did what Max told me to, because I knew it was necessary or because he made me, I can't tell you which. I can tell you I hated him for it. I grabbed Kate under the arm, Max took her from the other side and we dragged her as fast as we could to the river, the guards coming fast behind us.

Max threw out his hand, drawing a line over the roiling surface. That's how we ended up on a million web videos, appearing to run across the surface of the Tiber, Kate kicking and screaming between us, while our pursuers dropped into the water seconds later trying to follow.

Now

So now we're on the run, the best-known fugitives in the world, other than Bin Laden. TV shows regularly cite us right behind him on their 'most dangerous terrorists' lists. I never realized how many shows there were like that until we started showing up on them.

The video of the fight has been seen on the web over a million times. Whichever angle you watch—there were certainly enough cellphone cameras present that night—nothing's ever clear. Which provides enough ambiguity to fuel fifteen discussion groups, connecting us to sightings of Jesus, Elvis, aliens and 9/11 conspiracy theories. Actually, the one I liked the best was the one that suggested we were fallen angels. Unless they meant we were followers of Lucifer. I may rethink my affection for that one.

It's hard to argue that we accomplished a whole lot, once the G8 rejected Singh's proposal and she was deposed by her own party two weeks after the conference. I can't really argue that this world is a whole lot better than the one that might have been, although you have to hope.

Which is why I'm writing this. Max says just write it the best you can and give people the chance to see the truth in it. Which is interesting coming from him, considering he's spent his whole life making people see things that weren't there. But I think there's a bit of a dreamer in him that comes out in moments like this. I find it funny, to tell the truth.

~~~~

Author's Note

I have my trusted readers, who tell me when I've confused or put them to sleep. Significant contributions to this book were made by Marsha Garelick, David Leaf, Tom Monteleone, F. Paul Wilson, Maureen Gallagher, Elena Kushnerova, Steve Cosgrove and Margie Nicholson, Billy Papaleo and Dianna Dennis. Many thanks to all of them. Special thanks to the members of Stargate, Grill Flame and the other real American mindbender programs who wrote about it—their reminiscences are wilder than anything I've put in these pages.

Previews of
Other Ted Krever books:

Mindbenders 2: The Fiery Sky
On sale now

~~~~

reunion 1
december 2008

Darwin, Australia

The man tied to the slab means nothing to me.

He's about my age, muscled, dark hair and eyes—and they're cutting him open right in front of me, two L Corp flunkies, a big blonde lumberjack one and a smaller oily one with an Asian tattoo at the base of his neck. Tat Man is holding him down while Blondie slits into him with a razor.

The poor jerk keeps looking from one to the other, screaming "What do you want? I'll tell you! What do you want?" They don't answer, don't seem to want anything—unless it's just to get at me. And, since L Corp is the McDonalds of mindbenders, I suspect that's just the thought they intend me to have.

If I could look away, close my eyes, hum real loud and drown out the screams, maybe I could just not care. I don't know this fucker from a doorknob. It should be easier watching someone else get tortured—there but for the grace, etc. But I know better. Because of Iraq, I know better.

All those guys on the far side of the gun sight, we didn't like their attitude or their wardrobe, we called them rude names in loud voices. It shouldn't have been an issue forgetting them since we never knew them in the first place. But they came back to us, took vengeance on us, later, in our dreams. Some of them have lingered a thousand times longer and more vividly in my memory than they ever did in my life.

And now, here's this guy right in front of me crying for mercy in English— clearly, I'll never get rid of him unless I do something.

Which is a challenge, what with me being tied to a chair.

"Tell me where Renn is!" Straw Hat, who seems to be the L Corp crewboss, yells at me. "Then we can avoid all this." He's a natty little fuck—neat handlebar mustache, baby face, straw hat with a feather in the brim, jacket and pants tailored and fitted a size too small. Everybody else in the requisite blue L Corp jumpsuits and he's out of *LA Style*, hipster edition. "Tell me and we'll patch him up before he's useless to everyone."

When they dig the razor into the prisoner's leg, I *feel* it. It's like his cries are coming from inside my head. It's so vivid—realer than real. Why aren't they slicing *me* open? Wouldn't that work better? It makes me wonder if *any* of this is real.

There has to be at least one mindbender in the bunch. I'm confident that I'm blocking them—that they can't read my thoughts—but that didn't stop them from pulling me off the flying boat from the islands and dragging me out to these warehouses on the edge of the city, jetliners whooshing overhead every thirty seconds.

"Duuude, make it easy, for Christ's sake!" Straw Hat says, like I'm upsetting his plans for a pleasant afternoon. "Next, we'll have to start cutting things *off*!"

The razor digs in and I flinch at the screams. I'm not going to be able to do this for long.

"Why do I need to *tell* you anything?" I demand. "Why don't you just read my mind?"

Tat Man smacks me upside the head. But I see it coming just far enough ahead to go with the blow—it glances off without really biting.

"Shut up and answer!" he bellows. A moment later, I feel the closed-air heaviness of a mind probe. Somebody wants inside my head. But who? Who's the boss? Who's the mindbender? I toss a bone and wait for a reaction.

"Max Renn's dead!" I blurt. "He died in Nepal three days ago."

Blondie and Tat Man immediately look at Straw Hat. Okay, *he's* the mindbender.

Ted Krever   Mindbenders

"You don't know that," he says but the probe instantly gets thicker, more powerful. Which tells me a) my blocking is working and b) he's no surer where Max was three days ago than I am.

When they're probing, Max told me, they're searching for your mind in the here and now. So don't be here and now. Get inside a memory that takes you out of yourself, out of the moment. For me, that means back to Fallujah. Back to the tinbox popping of automatic weapons, the shrieking of twisted metal, the smell of smoke and haze, burning rubber and gasoline. I can make the switch in my sleep - I do, in fact, all too often. That fucking memory is more real to me than anything happening in my life is, ever—and so, once I learned how to drop into it while wide-awake, nobody could ever force their way into my head. At least, no one has so far.

"Okay," I yell, like he's dragged it out of me, "I'm not sure. I haven't seen him in six months!"

"Since Rome. Since the G8."

"Right."

"But you're here to meet him—right?"

Straw Hat is pressing, making me think in the here and now, feeling for a way to squeeze inside my head. He's powerful and relentless - it's like someone wrapping a blanket tight around your face. Either I break this probe quick or he'll have me. I can't risk a lie while he's probing. *Stay as close to the truth as possible,* I tell myself, *and see how far along you can string him.*

"Maybe."

Tat Man smacks me again, on the temple this time, but he's over-eager and catches me at an angle instead of square to the cheek. The guy is hopeless— I let out a cry just to encourage him. If you're going to get tortured, this is the guy to ask for.

"What's 'maybe' mean?"

"It means when Max Renn gives you directions, you never know if you're following them right. He told me *Follow the Sounds.*"

"Follow the—?"

"Follow the Sounds. Travel 'til sunrise. I'll meet you there."

"Meet you where?"

"Wherever I ended up, I guess."

"That's stupid."

"Tell me about it."

Straw Hat looks positively amused. "How did he tell you this?"

The truth, as much as possible. "In a note."

"Where'd you get the note?"

"He gave it to me."

"So you *did* see him!"

"He gave it to me six months ago."

"The note that told you to come here today…"

"Well, it didn't say that when he gave it to me."

"You expect us to believe that?"

"If Max Renn ever gave you directions, you'd believe it. *All* his directions are like that."

"Enough!" Straw Hat yells. "Show him what we do!"

Blondie pins the guy to the table; immediately, he starts writhing and shrieking. The sound of a grown man screaming and crying for his life is a pathetic and terrible sound. When Tat Man raises the razor to his eye, it's too much for me and I just fade away.

night of the G8
june 30, 2008
six months earlier

Trastevere, Rome

It was the walking on water that broke the spell for me.

We ran uphill through thick panicking crowds, away from Tiber Island and the wreckage of the G8 Concert, away from the sirens that said L Corp and G8 Security were right on our tail — and all I could think about was the sight of Max Renn kneading the air, changing its molecular structure (or maybe the magnetic field; I'm a soldier, not a geek) so it thickened into a shield he set hovering over the river.

We clattered across that spongy shield, from the tip of Tiber Island onto the south bank and the G8 guards fell into the water seconds later when the shield dissolved under their feet as they tried to follow.

After all the crazy shit that had already happened, *that* somehow put me over the edge.

A lone *caribiniere* appeared around the corner of an ancient church (it's Rome, they're everywhere). Kate Crowell, sprinting to my left, flicked a shield that smacked him hard across the forehead and flattened him against the wall, unconscious. She'd done the same thing a hundred times in the last hour, fending off a platoon of L Corp guards and the white-haired assassin Marat, who shot lightning bolts from his fingers.

How did I let *that* detail go by without crying 'Foul'?

The sirens howled real close for a moment—I went twitchy, looking over my shoulder—and then, all at once, turned eastward and waned in a hurry.

"Max has a whole neighborhood calling the emergency line," Kate chuckled. "'Who are those people running through my garden?'"

And, as soon as she said it, I could see blocks of people jumping up from the kitchen table or out of bed, complaining of phantoms in the backyard, intruders who were actually half a mile away and headed in the other direction. I wondered if the images were my imagination at work or the real thing, Max channeling the vision of people he was influencing and sharing it with us. I'd been with him long enough to know it could be either.

We walked out of Trastavere six minutes after we'd entered it, past three *carabinieri* and a BND German intelligence officer, all of whom looked sharp and on-guard and all of whom totally ignored us going by. Ignored us like we were invisible.

By the time we clomped onboard the *Cerberus*, a fishing boat heading out before dawn, scrounging for anchovies and sea lobster, the strangeness of it all was finally clear to me.

The crew wanted nothing to do with passengers until Kate went to work and they suddenly decided it was their sacred duty to smuggle us away from the Nazis.

"None of these guys was born the last time there were Nazis here," I told her. "And wasn't Italy their ally?"

"They watch a lot of movies," she replied.

The waters near Fiumicino were salted with police boats but our crew knew the cops by name—they bantered about *futbol* and fussed with the nets while we puttered slowly away. By afternoon, we were south of Sicily and safe to go on-deck.

"When do we land?" I asked.

"Tomorrow night—in Tunisia," Max said.

"That's a long time in the open, isn't it? Isn't there a faster way?"

"That's the point—they're watching all the fast ways out of town. By the time we surface again, they'll have decided they lost us."

I was leaned half over the rail but it wasn't the choppy water, it was the memories flooding over me. Three tours in Iraq, a year in VA hospitals and then Dave Monaghan's PTSD halfway house in the Everglades. Until Dave got shot dead in the bathtub and his friend Max showed up looking for information Dave had hidden, only to find—when I started spouting the names and addresses of people I'd never heard of—that Dave had hidden it all inside my head.

After that, we were riding the wave and I just got swept up in the moment. We picked up Mark Tauber, the American mindbender in Savannah, almost got captured by his old teammate(?)(!), Miriam Fine, in Durham, actually got captured by Marat and Pietr Volkov, the L Corp head and Max's old comrade from Mindbender High School in Novosibirsk, Siberia.

Oh yeah—by that time, Max had explained to me not only that he was a mind control agent, but also *not* one of ours. Bred to be a Soviet spy but still in training when the country collapsed, now out of early retirement because he was as determined as I was to find out who killed Dave.

Volkov did, was the short answer—at least, he ordered the shooting, the same way he sent agents to run over Kate's father, one of the only other remaining American mindbenders. After we escaped by way of Max setting the air on fire, we found out that L Corp was going after Aryana Singh, the Indian Prime Minister, champion of nonviolence and nuclear disarmament. Because that's what L Corp does, using mind control to get people to buy SUV's even though they never go off-road and vote for politicians who work totally against their interests.

Still hung out over the rail, watching the cruise ships and our fishing net picking up a couple strays, I ticked off the list of weird shit that had happened to us and marveled that I'd gone along without demanding a rubber room and one of those suits with the arms that tie.

But I hadn't. I made it all the way to Rome, to the Concert on the opening night of the G8, where Max held off Volkov long enough to save Singh, where Marat killed Tauber with a lightning blast and where Max and Kate turned on Marat simultaneously and...

Kate was staring at me with an expression I wanted to bottle. Every time she brushed against me, I got an erection—she insisted this was coincidence. "What did you do to Marat?" I demanded.

Her face went a shade of green. "How do I know? What did you see?"

"He killed Tauber and you and Max just gave him a stare like—like death..."

"And he disappeared!"

"Well, he burst into all those nice twirly spirals in the air," I said."At least he died pretty." It wasn't funny but I wasn't really feeling funny. Tauber was my Max-translator when we first started rolling together. He kept my feet on the ground and now he was gone. We'd stopped L Corp, which was payback for them killing Dave but it still didn't feel like victory.

On the North African coast, we were met by a couple of very shy individuals who didn't seem to know how they'd gotten there. Max said a few words and they handed over a bunch of really-convincing passports, credit cards and stacks of currency— Euros, dollars and yen. Max distributed them among us at Tunis

Airport, by which time we'd acquired suitcases and a couple changes of clothes, lack of baggage being a dead giveaway. He told us to stick the money inside our clothes, suitcase sidewalls and socks.

"The money's good?" Kate asked, grinning.

"It might not always be real," Max said, "but it's from the finest local forgers. They've funded wars, Presidents and even peace between nations. I'd use up the dollars first, all the same." He led us to the middle of the international terminal.

"They're looking for three of us," he said, "so the smart thing to do is split up for a while." He handed us each a hand-written note, folded in half. "Don't open them until you're on the plane," he said, "then follow the instructions to the letter." And just like that, he was gone at a sprint, heading for his gate.

Kate and I turned to each other, awkward as ever.

"I—I—" I've always fumbled for words with girls but it was a million times worse when she knew *everything* you were thinking.

"I feel like we barely know each other...for a thousand years," she said and, just like that, nailed the thing. We embraced and I checked my tickets as she walked away. Dubai and Singapore!

I breathed an involuntary sigh. Singapore felt right, a long way from everything.

I'll slip away, I remember thinking, *find some peace and quiet, figure out what 'normal' means.*

And, for a few hours, that almost seemed possible.

~~~~

Preview of 'Swindler & Son,'
On Sale December 2018

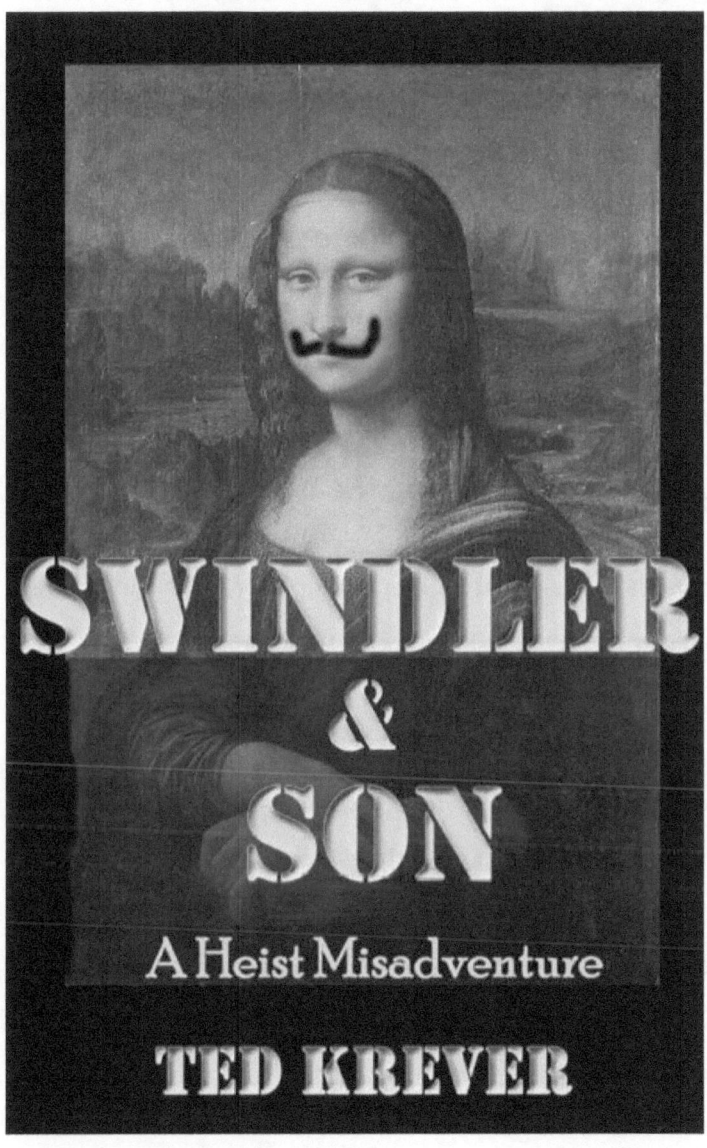

THE START

-So how does it start?

It starts with the sound of my own name spoken aloud.

Call me Nicholas, I'm fine. Nick or Nicky, even better.

But 'Nicholas Marsh' enunciated, first and last, all the way through—when I hear it *that* way, I know I've done something I'm about to pay for.

Hearing it in French, every syllable twisted and slurred and leaking from the earpiece of a Parisian counter-terrorism officer in a Kevlar vest, his back to me and his binoculars trained on my kitchen window—*that's* rock-bottom.

That's how it starts, in the snowy garden of the *Hopital Saint-Louis* in the Tenth Arrondissement, just past sundown on Christmas day, at what I fervently hoped was the end of one of the worst days of my life.

Well, actually, no...

Actually, it started about fifteen minutes earlier, on the other side of the canal, where I was mugged by some twenty-five year-old junkie in a purple-tinted mohawk and a leather jacket. And several nice tats on his neck that distracted my attention when I should have been focusing on his oncoming fist. He took my wallet and phone and left me aching and dizzy, which is why I wandered groggy several blocks out of my way and approached home through the garden.

I love that garden but none of the official exits land anywhere near my apartment. A few years ago, I found a back door, through the *Musee des Moulages* on the hospital grounds, that let me out near a construction gate right across the street from my building.

I'm just opening that back door when I hear my name and see GIGN, French Special Forces, two officers, huddled like Martians in flak suits, gas masks and sniper rifles, peeking through the construction gate at the wide corner, the entrance to my building and, eight floors above, at the dead coleus drooping from my night table.

Frozen in place, I scan the rooftops and find a squad of dark gray uniforms—and, in case I harbor any last doubts, hear my name one more time from the headset hanging from the blonde officer's right ear. I back instinctively into the doorway, sweating and making twenty-five different plans at the same time.

The bus! They won't be checking the bus on the Boulevard de la Villette, that's an answer. Having any sort of answer helps calms the quiver in my legs, brings them back into something like working order.

This is a mistake—it's got to be. If I'd done something to deserve counter-terrorism, I'd remember it, wouldn't I? More importantly, why in hell didn't somebody tip me off? Who do I know at GIGN?

Out through the door and the museum, retracing my steps, back out the far end of the compound, past the *Chapelle* to the *Rue de la Grange aux Belles*. Up toward the roundabout at a regular clip, walking briskly like a Parisian.

Am I thinking of escape? Hell no, I'm just getting pissed. Why hasn't somebody warned me? Why haven't they given me a chance to buy my way out of this?

Oh sure, GIGN makes it look serious but that just raises the price. I know somebody in every department of government and what they cost. Serious things have been undone before.

By the time the bus makes three stops, I know who to talk to—Beltoise, the second man at the *Surete*. He was at our Christmas party just last night.

I *own* him! At least, I should. If I had a middle-class clientele, if I dealt pot or owned a brothel, I could expect a phone call 24 hours in advance of a raid. It's common courtesy!

He'll be at *D'Azur*, of course, charging his dinner to us as usual.

When I arrive, he's tucked into a dim corner. He rises before I can reach him.

"Why is GIGN all around my apartment? You don't warn me?"

His eyes bulge like marbles. "Where's your phone?"

"Phone? Stolen. I got mugged."

He looks *relieved*. "That's why they're not here yet," he mutters and pulls me into the private room in back.

"Nicky, our past history—and the fact that I like you—is why I'll give you a minute's grace before I call you in." He's serious! His face goes cold—not like he doesn't know me, like he's never *seen* me before. "Normal corruption is one thing—but this?"

Normal corruption? Normal corruption is my *specialty*! He's reducing ten thousand years of civilized give-and-take to a catchphrase. Not to mention, it's fed him quite nicely, thank you, over the years.

I look at his face, at the disappointment and condescension there, and realize what a farce it all is. You treat them like princes but the first time you actually need them to put out...they might as well be in insurance.

Faced with this ingratitude, something inside me just gives up.

"Okay," I tell him. "I surrender."

"What?"

"I'll confess, right now. It's the jet ramps, isn't it?"

He looks confused.

"We have this client, a dictator...you know the old joke about, you're not really a country unless you have your own stamps, your own airline and your own beer? Well, he's got commemorative stamps, a brewery, a Mercedes stretch limo and a portrait of himself as Julius Caesar. But he gets embarrassed when his guests have to descend a staircase off the plane.

"There's a staircase on Air Force One' I tell him and he says, 'They could have a ramp if they wanted one.' So when Kumbatta collapsed, we flew a cargo plane in and liberated a couple of jetramps. The guy was so happy, he painted two Cessna's and proclaimed them the national airline. I don't think we *hurt* anybody."

Beltoise settles into the nearest chair, not saying a word.

"That's not it?"

Silence.

"Okay, Napoleon's penis—that was a good deed, I swear."

"*Excusez moi?*"

"It's your Minister of Defence's fault! Not the present Minister, the old one. He had this...thing about Napoleon's penis, that it should be back in France where it belongs."

"It is in France! Napoleon's body is at Les Invalides!"

"The body, sure, but his penis was removed during the autopsy and it's floated around ever since from collector to collector. It's now owned by a urologist, naturally, in Philadelphia."

"Don't be funny."

"It's true. The BBC measured it a few years ago and found it a bit small. Naturally, that outraged the Minister, who insisted the English don't know how to measure. The urologist's price was just *outrageous* so we found a…more generously-sized one around the same age, for a price the Minister could afford. It made him *happy*."

"You found him another penis?"

"Another *old* penis! You think that was easy? How many three-hundred-year-old penises you think are floating around?"

Beltoise stares at me with—I can't tell if it's respect or concern. The odd thing is, to me, this is actually beginning to feel pretty *righteous*. Confession really *is* good for the soul. "Okay, not the answer. Give me a chance. The eighteen identical one-of-a-kind Moroccan emeralds—"

"No."

"The Van Gogh with the wrong ear missing?"

Beltoise rolls his eyes. "We've never met," he warns, "except for a few state dinners with hundreds of other people I've never met either—but my advice is, you find a quick way out of France now. And don't bother replacing your phone—they'll find you as soon as you do. You understand?"

This is terrifying—Beltoise is a glorified flatfoot with a fancy office. I'm *begging* to be arrested and he's not biting. It's *unnatural*.

"Throw me a bone here," I say. "I don't understand what's happened."

He grimaces. "You know damn well it's the bomb."

"The *BOMB*?"

Of course, I know all about the bomb. I'd arrived back in Paris the day before, just in time for the funerals. Twelve dead, 37 injured, a miracle it wasn't more. A mountain of flowers in plastic sleeves heaped on the rubble, candles arrayed like soldiers in front of the dress shop left somehow intact on the corner.

And a march from the *Place De la Republique* to the *Place de la Nacion*, thousands, orderly and dogged, middle-class families and university students, *Le President* and his rivals, butchers, bakers, artists and computer technicians shuffling through neighborhood streets between broad public squares, solemn and chattering, sombre but fashionable—Paris, formal but somehow intimate. Great buildings and beautiful women dressed in black. Paris is a grand dame, maybe a bit past her prime, but she still knows how to put on a funeral.

'It's an escalation,' they say, the voices that multiply in crowds. Just a few years ago, 'they' were content to shoot up a restaurant or concert hall. Now, somehow, they bring in a bomb the size of a safe to bring down half a block of five-story apartment buildings.

The size of the explosion makes people nervous. Nobody builds a bomb that size to bring down the Rue Breguet. We all sense a grander plan that went awry and the fact that no one claimed responsibility only seems to heighten the tension. You don't even have the consolation of knowing who to be afraid of.

Beltoise, however, has made up his mind.

"It's your shipping certificate!" he yells, no longer caring who hears. "Your company's letterhead! Your *signature* on the bloody thing! You think I will cover for *that*, you're insane!"

I stand frozen for an endless moment, until words I never thought I'd hear myself say come tumbling out of my mouth.

"I didn't do *that*! I'm *innocent*!"

And then, I run.

RUNNING

-You ran?

It's an expression. I know better than to run. I walk at my usual quick pace but not fast enough to attract attention. Okay?

I lose myself in the tangle of back streets, staying off the boulevards, sticking to shorter blocks and parks where I can change direction at will. I stop short in front of angled store windows several times, switch direction several more, take a cab for a short distance and then another to double-back on myself. I'm overdoing it, in truth—if GIGN were really on my tail, they'd just throw on the sirens and take me. Once I'm sure I'm not being followed, I find a thrift shop that's just closing in a church, buy a pair of slacks and a short dark hoodie and wear them out of the store.

-This is tradecraft. Where did you acquire your technique?

Like you don't know. I had a very brief career in—what do you tell strangers at parties? About what you do for a living?

-I don't speak of such things.

We used to call it 'compliance.' I was recruited out of college. They trained me to take in a room or a street, to be invisible when that was useful. Trust no one, calculate the odds, tote up the angles and assume everyone follows their own self-interest.

But they couldn't teach me to be shrewd. I got myself involved in an 'extracurricular' scheme supporting freedom fighters—that is, it became extracurricular once it led to screaming headlines. Next thing I know, I'm getting chewed out in front of a Congressional committee for the exact same things they'd urged us to do in private.

We were thrown out like Big Mac wrappers, three fall guys, small potatoes. A generous severance package—under the table, of course—just go quietly into the night, thank you.

That training comes back to me, now that I'm on the run. Focus! *The bomb! What have I got to do with the fucking bomb?*

I need real information. Somewhere in our files, says Beltoise, is a shipping certificate for a bomb with my signature on it. I can't go home so I almost certainly can't go back to the office. But maybe Harry's apartment is clear.

If this had happened any other time—last week, even!—I could have counted on Harry's counsel, his expertise, his instincts. For fifteen years, he's been there when I needed him.

But that's a huge part of what made this feel like the worst day of my life, even before GIGN's visit. I've no idea if I can count on Harry anymore.

> -Explain this please. Who is this Harry and
> why can't you count on him?

Harry is the majordomo, the ringmaster of our circus, the senior partner in Sandler & Son, affectionately known to staff and select members of the governing elite as Swindler & Son. Everything that isn't about Sara in this story is about Harry.

-And Harry's got problems?

Oh hell no, Harry's got no problems. Harry *is* the problem. Everybody *loves* Harry, *that's* the problem.

And why shouldn't they? Harry makes life a party, a twenty-four-hour Remy Martin and shellfish from the little inlet over *there* and put away your business cards, this isn't some vulgar networking grind, we're here to have *fun*! Remember fun? Harry does.

If you liked the Remy, you must try this cognac—it's Venetian, Dante mentioned it (disparagingly, but he mentioned it) in the *Divine Comedy* and let me introduce you to the Ambassador's wife, she has all the good gossip about the orgies at that other embassy—maybe it was the Czechs but we're not saying. Meanwhile, other groups are discussing 70's film and sex robots and if there's anything else you want to know, the person to speak to is over *there*. The band plays good acoustic jazz, the Argentine tango couple are giving lessons one-on-one on the terrace and the star of the national football club is kicking balls around with enchanted kids and dazzled grownups on the south lawn.

In Paris, of course. That's our home base. It's one of God's jokes—Harry hated the French so, once we'd been thrown out of every other country in Europe, the only place left to go was Paris. Which, of course, he now loves because how can you not love Paris? It's *Paris*, for God's sake.

And the French love Harry. Big gnarly elegant gay Englishman, what's not to love? He ignores their culture, conducts himself like tenth-generation nobility fallen to trade or maybe a good Savile Row tailor, speaks only enough French to be fed and catered to but laughs and charms so naturally, they can't help themselves. Seduction is the French national pastime; they recognize a Master at work.

I was in Mumbai two years ago, picking up a load of Indian cotton. There was a rash of suicides among cotton farmers in Vidarbha and I was able to pick up several farms' entire crop just by paying off the bank loans. I told myself it was a good deed and a good deal. So I'm in the hotel bar at the end of the day chatting up some girl when a man behind me says, "Oh, you work with Harry Sandler? I was in a steeplechase syndicate with him in Ireland once. Took me for £65,000 quid. Most wonderful time I ever had." He bought us both a drink.

Everybody loves Harry; that's what nearly killed us all. As I watched the Iranian commandos lining up on the deck of the ship three hours ago, in their black stocking caps and their

Kalashnikovs aimed at our temples, all I could think was, *Everybody loves Harry*.

Fucking goddamn Harry.

Author Biography

Ted Krever watched the Beatles on Ed Sullivan, went to
Woodstock (the good one), and graduated Sarah Lawrence College
with a useless degree in creative writing.
He spent several decades creating programs for ABC News, CBS,
CNN, A&E, Court TV, MTV News, Discovery People and CBS/48
Hours, and as VP/Production of a short-lived dotcom.
He has driven a 16-wheeler across the Rockies, shot overnight
news in NY City, managed a revival-house movie theater and
married twice, in a triumph of optimism.
He was once accused of attempting to blow up Ethel Kennedy
with a Super-8 projector.
Read more at www.tedkrever.com